George Alfred Townsend

**Mrs. Reynolds and Hamilton**

A romance by George Alfred Townsend

George Alfred Townsend

**Mrs. Reynolds and Hamilton**
*A romance by George Alfred Townsend*

ISBN/EAN: 9783743382084

Manufactured in Europe, USA, Canada, Australia, Japa

Cover: Foto ©Andreas Hilbeck / pixelio.de

Manufactured and distributed by brebook publishing software (www.brebook.com)

George Alfred Townsend

**Mrs. Reynolds and Hamilton**

# MRS. REYNOLDS

AND

# HAMILTON

*A ROMANCE*

BY

## GEORGE ALFRED TOWNSEND
*"GATH"*

AUTHOR OF "THE ENTAILED HAT," "KATY OF CATOCTIN,"
"TALES OF THE CHESAPEAKE," "BOHEMIAN DAYS."

ETC.

NEW YORK
E. F. BONAVENTURE
31ST STREET AND BROADWAY
1890

Press of J. J. Little & Co.,
Astor Place, New York.

To John G. Moore

OF NEW YORK.

Friend Indeed.

# CONTENTS.

6     •     CONTENTS.

# MRS. REYNOLDS AND HAMILTON.

## CHAPTER I.

### THE PRIESTLEYS.

At sixty years of age Doctor Priestley bade his married daughter adieu—his first-born child.

Sarah played with her father's changing ringlets and nursed his head upon her shoulder, the tears coming out as her eyes tried to smile.

"Harry," she said to her brother, "be very kind to father, and study to be a preacher like him. You will be sure to come back, because you are so young ; but he —oh, cruel, cruel, to take this old, soft head away !—I may never see him again ! "

"Daughter, there is a bridge above our heads that spans the ocean—heaven. We shall walk across it into the fast piers of each other's arms, if we persevere."

"Oh ! I shall hear your voice until I die ; but, taken from me before death, all gentle and breathing as I see you, with every brother going also, it seems as if the righteous are forsaken and the scoffer's boast is true."

"Sarah, we are to go to a land where there can be no more controversy," said Mrs. Priestley ; "what profit is there in it all ? I hoped your father would minister to his own fold, keep his own heart pure, and let all his metaphysics be natural philosophy. Now I see him rejected by Britain, while Lavoisier is safe in blood-stained France."

"Do not upbraid father," pleaded Sarah.

"Never has she upbraided," said Priestley, "but suf-

fered for me.  Of her—poor lodger in so many broken
homes—it can be said :

> " ' Many a weary mile she beat
> With her brood about her feet—
> Lodging in another's nest.
> Lord ! at last thy parsonage door
> Open to her, evermore ;
> Take her cross, and give her rest.' "

All felt the pathos of these simple lines, and their sobs
were broken by Priestley's quavering voice, saying :

"I think I see rest in America, and the end of political
dispute ; that shall be my desire.  But whether we meet
again, my daughter, in this world or not, there is a resurrection, and it must be in these bodies we rejoiced and
suffered in.  Though worms destroy me, yet in my flesh
I shall see God.  There is the blissful hope of everlasting meeting."

The vessel took all their household effects, library and
apparatus, and sailed from the Thames to New York in
fifty-eight days.

As the Priestleys' vessel dropped anchor, Mr. Thomas
Cooper met them, and soon said :

"Lavoisier is dead."

"Dead !" exclaimed Doctor Priestley.  "He was alive
when I sailed."

"He died while you were upon the ocean, and by the
guillotine—aged fifty-one."

"Oh," sighed Doctor Priestley, "could a head like that,
which a thousand years can rarely grow, be severed in
one moment ? "

Before they started from New York Mr. Cooper had
some publications made to exploit Doctor Priestley as a
firm friend of America and a public abjurer of England.

This anonymous praise, however well intended, brought
immediate enmity upon the learned exile.

Priestley opened the small, party-fanged journals when
he arrived in Philadelphia, and saw himself made the
subject of political controversy.

"Oh, Joseph," exclaimed his wife, "who has misrepre-
sented you like this?  Will we never find peace this side
of heaven ? "

"It is all false," answered the doctor ; "I do not rejoice in the defeats of my countrymen, and I shall never

be else than an Englishman—never be naturalized in this or any other land. I will reply to this reporter."

"Oh, let it alone, husband ; it may be forgotten. Let us travel as fast as we can to the peaceful vale of the Susquehanna, beyond the strife of cities and of states."

While waiting to send their extensive effects overland to the new town of Northumberland, the discoverer of Oxygen preached a sermon at the small chapel of the Universalists, and amongst his auditors were Vice-President Adams and Thomas Jefferson.

Mr. Adams went to lodgings with Priestley, and took dinner with the exile's family. They were surprised by Senator Aaron Burr, who, dressed in new widower's habiliments, dropped in to pay his respects.

A queenly-looking young woman, a Mrs. Reynolds, had made the acquaintance of the strangers, being a fellow-lodger with them; and this American brunette, with languid address and easy and engaging ways, was the first study of a female of the country Mary Priestley and her daughter-in-law had made.

Joe Priestley, the doctor's oldest son, had come out with his wife, late Lizzie Ryland—whose family's property the Tory mob had destroyed at Birmingham—a young mother of hardly twenty, and the bride of but two years ; one whose comforts and condition in England gave the greatest solicitude to the Priestleys as to her being happy with their son in this new world, whither she had unreluctantly come. They feared that, her curiosity being satisfied, her strong social nature would have a reaction, and take her husband home to England.

"You must like America, ladies," said the Vice-President, a chubby, bald man of very blue eyes and a Jewish nose, wearing hair powder and shaking it off when excited. "If you were in Boston, now, I could guarantee you. Why, I had to carry Independence in this city single-handed and alone ! Jefferson did a little writing on the subject—he was no speaker—but *he* put the cart before the horse in accusing the king instead of parliament and ministry. Indeed, I rather like George III. He told me, when in response to his insinuation that I liked the English better than the French, and I said, ' No, your majesty ; I have no attachment but to my own country,'—what do you think he said, now ? He said,

looking right at me : 'An honest man will never have
any other !' I tell you, Doctor, I felt *that* compliment."

The Vice-President crossed his buff stockings, shook
his hair powder upon his knee-buckles, and went on to
compliment the sermon.

But Priestley felt that this man might have spared him,
in delicacy of feeling, the reflection the king's remark
was upon his own exile.

Colonel Burr felt for Priestley, apparently, for he said,
as Mr. Adams retired :

"How egotism shrivels up real merits ! It does not
become me, ladies "—looking at the younger Mrs. Priestley and at Mrs. Reynolds—"to compliment New York ;
but as that city is gathering into its symposium all that is
rare and beautiful, why did you not tarry with us, who
have the imperial gateway of the West and beautiful
women—but nothing like Mrs. Priestley and these ?"

He waved his head and hand toward each of the three
women.

Mrs. Priestley looked up, and paid a new attention to
Colonel Burr ; a smile of pleasure stayed on Mrs. Reynolds' face ; Lizzie Priestley said :

"Colonel Burr, what sort of person is your New York
minister, Hamilton ? My father and our English mercantile class all admire Colonel Hamilton, and I would
like to write home some account of him."

" Dear me ! " remarked Colonel Burr ; " is little Ham.
known over there, too ? Well, he always was enter-
prising in his advertisements. Every time the contribu-
tion-box was passed around for him in the West Indies
—he being a sort of charity scholar in America—he took
part of the money to publish some pamphlet or other.
Something over twenty years ago I saw a new boy at
the Elizabethtown Grammar School, burnt almost black,
upon a fair, girlish skin. That was my home, and the
stranger was Secretary Hamilton, then probably fifteen
years of age. He had come to see my uncle Edwards,
to make some religious inquiries with a view to the Presbyterian ministry. A little midget, as he seemed, he
already wanted to lay himself alongside of the fame of
my grandfather, Rev. Jonathan Edwards. There you
have Hamilton, my friends ! He never hears of anything
celebrated but he compares himself with it at once ; and

when he meets you, Doctor, he will be crammed full of chemistry for the occasion."

"I can see no evil in early maturity of purpose," said Doctor Priestley, "except the commonplace enemies it makes. Often puny and undersized men mature fast, being no match for the athletes of the playground, and by that amount of time are set forward in acquirements. I preached while a boy, and was sneered at by the same people who, after I obtained some reputation, crowded the chapel to hear me ; but I was as sincere in the first case as in the last."

"And so is Colonel Hamilton," mildly remarked Mrs. Reynolds. "For seventeen years, or since I was a child, his name has been connected with everything of importance in America, and he is now hardly thirty-seven. Yet he is deeply disliked. What is the reason of it?"

"For one thing," said Joe Priestley, the younger, "because he separates justice from bias and resentment. He opposed further confiscations, and demanded that British debts stand as good as other honest obligations. I think well of him. There seems to be an element in the United States subsisting upon the hostilities of the last war, and I don't believe they were the best soldiers, either."

Mrs. Reynolds barely raised her eyes to observe Colonel Burr, who had taken Mrs. Joe Priestley's smelling-bottle to make it the basis of a light compliment.

Harry Priestley, a fine, slender boy of sixteen, was looking at Mrs. Reynolds with frank respect.

"You loike men to be ambitious-loike," he said, with Yorkshire diphthongs on his tongue.

"No, Harry ; young as this country and government are, I have seen enough of public intrigue. I wish I could go, like you all, to the Susquehanna, and never see Philadelphia again."

"Would farm-life suit thee?" asked Harry.

"A farm? It is what I have always desired, Hal."

"I feel confirmed," said Mrs. Priestley, "in every prejudice I ever formed against sincere men taking up public life. For every talent they offer, a host of hate starts up ; yet there seem a multitude of men who can think of nothing else—and what is disinterested about it all? Think of Burke spurning the friendly hand of Fox

because they could not think alike about the French!
Here are we, made homeless for the same subject, and
met on this side of the Atlantic, not as victims, but as
parts of a foreign and nearly universal contention."

" I like America very well," said Lizzie Priestley, " from
what I have seen of it. Men must be patriotic, and,
therefore, politicians. I like to see young senators, like
Colonel Burr, and financial philosophers, like his com-
petitor, Hamilton, start up like the bees in Samson's
dead lion. Not even women can run away from the
dangers of nature and of institutions—such as marriage,
for example. Who knows how a husband will turn out ?
Who knows what temptations will come to one's self ?
The joy of children is nearly related to the perils of death.
Yet we marry, and so men become politicians. Father
Priestley has merely incurred some of the distresses of
defeat, and is set ashore safe and sound, with rest and
competence before him ; but here is President Washington, the noblest man in the world, who might ere this have
been executed for high treason ; politics brought him
from provincial rust to the light of——"

" Oxygen," finished Colonel Burr, playfully.

" Phlogiston, I'll thank you to say, Senator," cried
Thomas Cooper, coming in. " We will have no new-
fangled nitrogens, nor oxygens neither. The point of
my coming is that here are the names of both Hamilton
and Jefferson, and they may make an awkward arrival."

" I cannot be supposed to know," said Doctor Priestley,
" all the involutions of American personal life ; and so
let them come, as to a sanctuary, together."

" Will you stay, Colonel Burr ? " asked Mrs. Reynolds,
archly.

" How could I leave these charms ? " replied Senator
Burr. " Hamilton is a little sore because I got his pa-in-
law's seat in the Senate ; but, in spite of my raillery of
his youth, he is full of imagination."

As Mr. Cooper brought the two distinguished men in,
separately, he looked like some hereditary and privileged
lacquey of an old British household, with bodily signs of
having been descended from a king's jester.

As Hamilton entered and observed the other two, he
betrayed no feeling at all ; but greeting Doctor Priestley, whose person he readily identified, he welcomed Mrs.

Priestley also to the new republic, and waited to be
presented to the other ladies.

When Mrs. Reynolds was introduced, last, she called
him "Hamilton ; " and Aaron Burr saw that they were
former acquaintances.

Colonel Hamilton addressed Mr. Jefferson cordially as
" Governor," and bowed to Colonel Burr with no less
promptness ; while to Joseph Priestley, Jr., and wife, he
paid the marked attention due to people who had
chosen America for long to come.

" No man has come to us, Doctor," said Hamilton,
" more impartially desired. No one, I am sure, will find
the ground so new and to his own making. As there are
no Pennsylvanians here, I desire to put in the first word
for the city of New York, where I have assisted to plan
an infant University. There, to all appearances, will be
the western London, and we need your name and knowledge to head our faculty."

" Pardon me, Colonel Hamilton," said Jefferson. " I
confess you the victor in the government, for I am out.
But that very thing of a state University is under consideration now in Virginia, and I beseech you, let Priestley
come to us."

" With all my heart," spoke Hamilton. " So Doctor
Priestley be employed in the material sciences somewhere, there can be no objection to this or that spot. I
only desire to save him, for the sacred purposes of physical discovery, from the wretched political dialectics he
may be tempted to listen to. Since Doctor Franklin's
death we have no other men of science than a few phy-
sicians, and I apprehend that chemistry will overwhelm
such physic as we have, which is bleeding to death the
most valuable and venerable lives in the land."

" Princeton College, the scene of my father's martyrdom, has been the only institution to invite Doctor Priestley to preach," said Senator Burr, "though its theology
and his differ as the two poles. There is the true place
for him to apply his science, central to all these states."

" I do not desire the Doctor to enter any institution,"
said Mrs. Priestley. " He has declined already to teach
in the College of Philadelphia. Nearly every useful discovery or philosophical instrument which he has made
came from his private studies, aided by the stimulation of

his private friends.   He is falling behind and others are
pushing on.   Lavoisier has left a rounded fame ; Count
Rumford, an American, has taken Franklin's place.  Look
at that lamp of M. Argand upon the mantel : it will light
learning a hundred years, and yet it was Franklin's
*caveat*, whom politics drew away before he could perfect it.
Gentlemen, Doctor Priestley and I are old, and both politics and theology are speculative sciences."

" Oxygen must take a back seat," insisted Thomas
Cooper, perseveringly.   " Doctor Priestley will hunt
Lavoisier to his hole."

Doctor Priestley's agreeable anticipations of Jefferson
were not disappointed by his warm support of the exile's
fading theory of phlogiston, but Hamilton held his
peace.

" I have heard, Colonel Hamilton, of your rapid ac-
quisition of knowledge," said Doctor Priestley's married
son.  " Where did you study chemistry ?"

" Oh ! in these provinces we have always had alert
ears for the sounds beyond the deep.   I found men in
New York, like Doctor Mitchell, not unequal to a debate
with your father, Mr. Joseph, to instruct me ; and being
both Scotch and French, mechanics and natural philosophy
came ardently to my tastes.   If I could see this land settled to its honest obligations, and the law would deliver
me to a respectable independence, such as my wife's station entitles her to, I would ask you, Doctor Priestley, to
take me into your sylvan laboratory and educate me
for the great applications of natural philosophy to the
revenues of America.  We must have manufactures to
nurse the arts and create another England.  My mother's ancestry were driven from France, to start the looms
of Britain, by Louis XIV.  May I also see, before I
die, the rude hand of George III. compel in these states
every manual craft with pneumatic power to multiply our
hands !"

Senator Burr, this while, had been paying compliments
to all the ladies, without qualification ; but Lizzie Priestley was too much engaged with the scene before her to
give much regard to that cool, presuming little man.

She recognized the interesting representatives of the
last-born race and nation in its three public men—perfectly different from the English, whose language they

spoke, but nearer woman's taste in men, she thought, than any men she had ever seen.

At home, in England, men's topics were seldom discussed before women.   Here the successive speakers looked at the women as earnestly as at the men, paying them not merely the compliment of common-sense talk, but the reality of confidence in their judgment and perception.

To that real compliment Lizzie Priestley's nature sprang ; she liked men more than ever, and Hamilton seemed to her the Adonis of politicians—young, sincere, pleasing, vitalized and gallant, with habits testified by his radiant skin, and something like royalty in his gracious reserve.

He was small, but every joint and muscle had been trained by exercise and war till he seemed the Dauphin of the State, held back from his full honors only by the regency of another till his time should be ripe.

A little of young William Pitt was in Hamilton's high, steepling forehead.

Here was a man who had made his way to Washington's side from orphanage and exile, and he seemed a bright omen of her husband's promotion in America.

She marked the perfect neatness of this Secretary of the Treasury ; his powdered hair flowing into its queue-like woman's braids ; no powder dust was on his blue, gilt-buttoned coat, which rose to the seam of his high-collared waistcoat of white silk, delineating there almost feminine shoulders ; his head was held erect and was the flower of the firm, military spine, its every inclination emphasizing strength and grace.   His eyes were regular and clear, holding a smile distilled in reason, and were becoming to the rose and lily in his cheeks and temples. Hamilton's nose was the warrior's, Roman to the bridge, creole to the nostrils ; the mouth was kissable, all women thought, and explained no more ; for in that face were lines, toward the mouth, of the enjoyments of the roving sons of God.

" What a gentleman ! " thought Lizzie Priestley, as she noted the swan-formed breast of Hamilton beneath his spotless shirt ruffles, and saw the turn of his silken hose crossed upon his knee.   His black small-clothes were drawn to the delicacy of his hips, and his white ruffles at

the wrists were tinted by the azure veins there, which fed
the fingers that wrote like majesty.

.All good women sometimes pine for a man refined toward their own delicacy of body and mind, and that
feeling drew young Joseph Priestley's wife toward Hamilton.

Colonel Burr was also small, symmetrical and pleasing,
but suggestions in him led toward the commonplace.

His nose turned up, after a straight, abiding course,
and ended in something between the Puritan and the
snub ; he was one of the small talkers, too, whom most
women like, but a few women will not abide.   A worldly
smartness in Burr replaced what seemed a disciplined
imagination in Hamilton, and the Secretary was now
being flattered by Colonel Burr, to which he listened
with a quiet austerity which at length resulted in
silence.

Mr. Jefferson was rather a negative guest in the presence of Hamilton—a pleasing figure and face, however
—tall, red, also woman-like, but it was the womanhood
of middle age ; he was now fifty-one, and the Priestleys
had a past knowledge of him when he was in England, as
the French Minister, upon his travels.

He seemed a little shy, quite observant, and was in a
large mould—slightly hollow in the chest, as if he had
grown too fast at school; and he assented to most of what
Hamilton had to say, sometimes was mildly analytical,
but paid to the Secretary the deference of a man out of
office to one in nearly complete power.

" Doctor Priestley," said Jefferson, as the afternoon
sun sank low, " I called to take you to see the relics and
grave of Doctor Franklin, who spoke of you so often as
his ward-in-science and friend in adversity.   Perhaps
Colonel Hamilton and the rest of these friends will.go
with us."

All expressed a desire to go, and while the ladies
were retiring for their bonnets the men went toward the
street to take the air.

Mrs. Reynolds, lingering behind, called the name of
" Hamilton " in a hurried, hardly voluntary whisper, as
the last of these had turned his back.

The Minister of the Treasury heard it, and hesitated
and returned.

" Madame, did you call my name?" he asked, respectfully, and a little constrained.

"Oh, Colonel Hamilton! why do you treat me so?"

The parlor, empty of all but these, she started to
make more private by touching the open door.

" No," said Hamilton, with kind but positive decision;
" no privacy ; I can afford no more.   You know, madame,
where my duty lies.   Are you in need?"

The tall, rich-tinted woman dropped her blue eyes,
trembled, raised her handkerchief to her face and sank
into a chair.

" *Madame!*" she faltered, with her mouth wavering
upon the long, low wail of an intercepted sob ; " I am
no more ' Maria.'"

"Yes," said Hamilton, "you are ' Maria ' where your
duty, too, bids you expect that familiar name.   As I
recall my fellow-man, in contrition, think you, my friend,
upon your fellow-woman ; as you are a wife, I have
one."

Mrs. Reynolds recoiled, yet instantly raised her eyes,
and with a fluttering, finally wilful impulse, she rose to
her full length and extended her arms.

" Hamilton," she whispered, loud and eloquently, " I
love you ; you taught me to do so.   How cruel to forbid me now !"

" All are ready, friends," pealed the voice of Senator
Burr at the open door, where the strange pair in their
strange colloquy saw him smoothing his craped widower's
hat with his mourning gloves.   " Come, my charming
Mrs. Reynolds."

" Colonel Burr," replied the lady, her composure seized
rather than secured, " I will not go to-day.   I have
been making a request of Colonel Hamilton on behalf
of a friend."

" He must grant it," said Burr ; " no gallant man ever
refused a lady with such graces.   Go get your hat, Mrs.
Reynolds ; I'll wait for you.'

2

## CHAPTER II.

### HAMILTON.

As Hamilton turned away from Franklin's house and passed with his guests through the alley to High Street, Mrs. Lizzie Priestley remarked :

" I cannot get over the feeling that something has happened in this city unlike the spirit of itself ; it reminds me of a family run down in habits. The American lady, Mrs. Reynolds, represents what I mean—she is interesting till you come to examine her."

"You are not wrong as to Philadelphia," said Hamilton, with heightened color ; "the yellow fever of last year had the same effect on this place as the plague upon London or the Reign of Terror upon Paris. In three months it buried five thousand inhabitants, and reduced the population one-half. Familiarity with horror, sudden destitution, and the fatal relations of change and recklessness, broke the habits of both the city and the government. I felt the alteration in my own nature."

He looked ill at ease till Mrs. Priestley, the elder, said:

" And Paris was never so gay and frivolous as in that Reign of Terror, which still is carrying off its forty victims a day."

" I hope you have been entertained," remarked Colonel Hamilton to the Priestley family, as they were about to part. " I am to all things American so wrapt up that this afternoon has seemed a visit to my native isle."

" This is my most lovely day in America," exclaimed Lizzie Priestley. " Joe, I know you feel so, too ! I shall write it down, to let my child know that Hamilton gave us almost half of one of his precious days."

" But marriage is a jealous wall," added Hamilton, " and women cavil at friendship across it. I suppose we shall part just as we begin to know each other."

" I am sure you will find no wall in me," cried Joe Priestley, " if you like my wife. She is too necessary to me to have her separated from strong and bright men in this country, where I want her to appreciate the social freedom of a new land. See ! she is blushing ; and I know she likes you, Mr. Secretary."

" If I blush," said Joe Priestley's bride, " it is to see
how true gentlemen rise above smallness when they see
that a woman appreciates them both.    I am as proud of
my husband as of——"

She stopped and blushed again.

" Say ' of your friend,' " interpolated Joe Priestley,
bluntly.    " Say *my* friend, too.    He is welcome to call
on my wife whenever he likes."

" And no need of hurrying away now," added Joe's
mother ; " for I confess I always liked the men.    My husband took me to a boarding-school at our marriage, and
I was thrown among his fellow tutors, and for years we
had young men boarders in our parsonage for whom I
sewed and kept their secrets.    Lord Shelburne's son was
like my own.    We are not afraid of State folks ; so come
up and be one of my boys, Colonel Hamilton."

They went to Doctor Priestley's lodgings, and there
was some commotion on the stairs.    Mrs. Reynolds was
standing there by a strange, sullen man, and the landlady
of the house, behind them both, glared angry and interrupted.

" There he is—there is Colonel Hamilton," said the
sullen man ; " speak to him for yourself ! "

Seeing tears in Mrs. Reynolds' eyes, the Priestley
women stopped inquiringly, but Joe Priestley motioned
them on, and only Hamilton remained.

" You mentioned my name, madame," the Minister of
Finance observed, with sobered countenance.    " Be as-
sured I shall always answer to it."

His glance was fixed rather upon the man than the
woman.

" The long and short of it is," muttered the man, " that
Maria's things have been seized by the landlady : she
can't pay her board.    They are going to put her out.
You'll lend her the currency, Colonel Hamilton ; you
manufacture plenty of it."

A sneer was on his lip, and an evil, lurking eye attended his words.

Hamilton drew out his purse and slipped its rings to
show its emptiness.

" The cry of suffering I never pass," said he.    " Old
comrades of the war keep me poor with helping of them.
I have not here a shilling to my name."

"I suppose you can borrow," muttered the man; "you are a great person in the State. I *demand* it of you!"

He came forward with a face flushed by drink and insolence—a genteel form, a complexion naturally good —and made an awkward and menacing motion, like a highway robber's.

Mrs. Reynolds looked an instant at the two men, and came between them, brushing the tears of shame from her eyes.

"You shall not, James Reynolds!" she said; "he tells the truth. Money forced from him to feed your family in want, you have gambled and drank with, and you shall not rob this gentleman again, although I must be made to blush before these English friends and walk the streets this Sunday evening, to parade the name of such a man as I have married!"

She towered nearly to the height of the man she addressed, as if she would crush his frame in her long and muscular arms. He sank down a stair or two, and with muttering stalked away.

Hamilton, too, left the place where his dignity was being so compromised, and entered the Priestleys' parlor.

As the landlady renewed her importunities, Colonel Aaron Burr appeared before Mrs. Reynolds with young Harry Priestly at his side.

"Here, my lovely debtor, is the sum you need," whispered Colonel Burr, proffering bank-notes.

"I know the price, Colonel Burr," Mrs. Reynolds answered, with decision, "that your assistance implies, and I cannot pay it."

He smiled without noticing the woman's contempt of him, and softly observed:

"Why, I got it easily enough; I borrowed it from Master Priestley here."

"And for you, my dearest lady," said young Hal, with fervor, "I would pawn my shoes and jacket; for I know that you are good and basely persecuted-like. Take it, and be thee welcome."

The tall, stately woman wrapped the young lad in her arms and kissed him like a brother.

"Thank God!" said she, in suppressed eloquence, "that there is one pure heart to see good in me yet and feel for my injuries—whose greatest crime has been this fatal gift of beauty."

"Thou hast it," spoke the youngest son of Priestley; "thy beauty has pierced me! It is my first passion, but I have it altogaither, and would yon evil man, that can call thee woife by law, was parted from thee, that I might take thee to the woods thou didst speak of with love, and be my lady to serve and care for!"

The boy stood trembling with the depth and transport of his confession. Mrs. Reynolds looked at him in wonder and sympathy, and sighed:

"You would not marry me, poor Hal?"

"Yes," said the boy: "whenever the law can do thee right, Maria, and give me room. I never can forget thee!"

"I see a chance," intervened Colonel Burr, "to help both of you. There is no more disparity in your ages than between mine and the wife I mourn, who was ten years my senior, and my guiding star. A widow, too, with boys well grown. Let me divorce you, my charming Reynolds, from the husband who no longer supports you; this scene to-day is evidence enough of his desertion, and I am lawyer enough to get you free before young Hal is ready for your arms."

He addressed them both with kindness on his tongue, and easy, worldly sincerity.

"Indeed," remarked the landlady, as she took the proffered money from Mrs. Reynolds and retired, "there is but one way with those worthless 'hangers-on' of husbands: set them adrift by law! I've had to do it myself."

Mrs. Reynolds looked at her young deliverer with real affection and gratitude.

"Oh, to think," she said, "that you must disclose my necessities, my lovely boy, to your mother and your brother's wife; it will kill my pride forever."

"I never will betray you," Hal Priestley whispered; "I'll honor and marry thee, if thou wilt."

"God grant it!" said the woman, as she was drawn to his chaste and maiden breast.

When, after long delay, Harry Priestley entered the sitting-room of his family again, he regarded Colonel Hamilton, entertained with honor there, as if he were no longer welcome.

"I hear that you came from some other land," remarked Lizzie Priestley to Hamilton. "Pray, what was it like?"

"Like a graceful volcano, all wooded and planted from the sea, which circles it, to the serene, unclouded sky. Columbus named it, from its whitish cap, Nieves, or The Snows; the commoner people there call it Mevis, but the planters name it Nevis, from its resembling the highest mountain in Scotland, whence my father came, like many Hamiltons before him; and he settled in Saint Christopher's Island, only two miles from Nevis, across a narrow strait. There my mother removed, and found my father; and there he still lives, a poor, old, lonely man."

"And you so high in this rising government?" spoke the British bride, warmly. "Why can't you bring him here?"

"Alas!" replied Hamilton, "I am often twitted myself with being 'sheltered' here. If I should bring my poor father it would be said that I supported him on this government."

"Have you not plenty of patronage, and a gentleman's salary?"

"Oh, yes; there may be a hundred appointments under the Treasury Department, and I get a salary of seven hundred pounds; my Assistant Secretary gets three hundred."

"What!" exclaimed Lizzie Priestley, rising to her feet and looking at her husband. "Joe, this is not an honest nation!"

"No house to live in?" asked Joe—adding, when Hamilton had shaken his head, "Great King! why, father got as much as that from Lord Shelburne, and a house free besides; and he was in the light of a servant."

"Oh!" cried Hamilton, gayly, "I shall go back to law some time, and make a good living."

"Your mother lives?" asked Mrs. Priestley. "And was she Scotch, too?"

"She died in my childhood," Hamilton answered, with feeling, "and took away all heaven with her until God gave me my wife. No, Mrs. Priestley; my mother was French, and I am like the Queen of Scots, of a French mother and a Scottish father. About those Windward

Islands of the remoter West Indies I made my living as a shipping-clerk till I was fifteen, when my poor mother's kin discovered me."

" How was that ?" young Harry asked, his interest dissipating his prejudice.

" Why, my boy, I'm glad you have asked me, because your situation was my own. A tornado struck the Windward Islands, as a tornado has struck your father's fortunes ; I saw the tornado when much younger than you are now, and after it was over I wrote its description, which I published in a newspaper. A little imagination among plain and limited people brings friends and foes. The reason I did not enter Franklin's residence with you to-day was because its mistress is one of those West Indian foes : a lady, the wife of the philosopher's grandson ; she comes from St. Kitt's, and knows my father."

" But your friends ?" Joseph Priestley broke in.

" Why, they thought I ought to have an education— the good old Presbyterian clergyman told them so—and they sent me to North America, where I am still poor and still a writer."

" Poor compensation, Alexander," said mother Priestley, with motherly plainness ; " but thy youthful face shows thou hast congenial tasks."

" And what is nobler," Lizzie Priestley spoke, " than to plant in this great, fertile western world the roots of a permanent state, to shelter the fleeing millions of the just and the lowly ? King David's temple was no more to this than father Priestley's burnt meeting-house in Birmingham."

Hamilton's eyes shone with admiration and thankful gratitude for this kindred joy in his achievements by one he already felt to have his confidence.

" My wife met me in the camp," said he ; " she felt for my ambition as you do, madame ; I was nothing but a captain, but she loved me ; and often as we worked together at midnight, man and wife, we could hear the breathing of General Washington, where he slept in the adjoining room, and stopped to listen as if it was the breath of God. To be his friend and companion and to serve him to the end is the wealth I would leave my children and my country."

He rose to go.

"Stop, Alexander," spoke Mrs. Priestley, plainly. "Father is not here, and we hear him read at this time of the Sabbath evening something from the Scripture. Will thee take his place?"

Hamilton took the book and opened it. He started as if to read, and checked himself.

"I am not worthy to read this book to-night," he explained. "At another time I may feel that I can do so. Your daughter will read it for me, I know."

He handed the Bible to Lizzie Priestley.

When she had read the lesson they heard a sob, and saw Hamilton's eyes filled with tears.

He gave them his hand without taking leave by words, and left them wondering at his sweetness and unexplained sensibility.

---

## CHAPTER III.

### BURR.

As Hamilton reached his own door a voice at the step called him, and he turned and confronted Colonel Burr.

"I have been waiting for you, Mr. Hamilton," said the junior Senator from New York; "the opportunity we had at Doctor Priestley's suggested many things of mutual advantage."

Hamilton had a dislike of this man, not unmixed with superstition, and yet was too prudent, as his constituent, to show offence.

"Come in, Colonel Burr; I have a very sick child here, and can show you but scant hospitality."

He repaired to another chamber, and when he returned was all disarmed for subtle controversy.

"I feel for you, Hamilton," said Burr, with deference, seeing the Minister's grief; "all which unites me to the past is my only child. How many coincidences should bind you and me together! We were both orphans, both on the commanding general's staff, both married in Albany; you are not one year younger than I; we were the leaders of the bar in the city of New York, and here we are, some years under forty, both high in this government."

"We have frequently conducted causes together," said Hamilton, "and without antagonizing."

"Not outwardly; but there has been a reserve—I may say a distrust, and it has not been on my part. I know too well the transcendent talents I confront to suppose it ever necessary for them to deceive me or to fear me."

"Omit the language of flattery," sighed Hamilton, "because I am humbled and in sorrow. We probably know each other, and may be frank."

"Colonel, it will do for these timid civilians, like Jefferson and Randolph, to do battle with whispering and chicane and women's arts; but *we* are of the school of war, and our disputes, if made chronic by time, mean danger, especially as we inhabit the same city and have the mettlesome following of our old soldiery. My errand to-night is not to accuse you, but to forgive you, Hamilton."

"Sir?"

"Is it not to you that I owe the rejection of my name for the French mission—rejected not once, but twice, after it had been offered to my party and they had unanimously presented my name?"

"No. It was not necessary for me to interfere, even if I had been hostile to you."

"Then it was Washington alone?".

"You forget, Colonel Burr, that I am his confidential Minister."

Aaron Burr quietly crossed his black stockings.

"Your denial is ample," said he, recovering equanimity; "the President, however, does himself no credit sending that goose Monroe to the most gallant capital in Europe at a time when *finesse* would give America the great advantage of a century. You well know, Colonel Hamilton, that I am better qualified for such work than the *ci-devant* Lieutenant Monroe."

"I did not approve of the appointment; it was forced upon the President by the ungenerous action of his political opponents, to whom he desired to make a concession and allow them to be represented in the country they pretended to favor."

"Hamilton, I did not expect that appointment. My name was pressed by Jefferson, who inspired Madison and Monroe from Virginia to demand it for me. No

man can follow Jefferson's tracks, which lead everywhere.
He must have known that Washington disliked me, and
so shook us in each other's face."

Hamilton's eyes looked a deepened intelligence, but
he seemed also dispirited.

"I will not ask you," said Burr, almost playfully, "if
it was really Washington who forbade me to consult the
State Department files when Jefferson was his State Minister. That was so pointed a discourtesy that I would
have challenged any other man than Washington for it.
Mr. Jefferson had invited me there; in the name of
Washington he ordered me out. Was *that* not Jefferson,
also, who procured the order?"

"If I knew, Colonel Burr, it would be a privileged
secret. I do not know."

"I only ask because Mr. Jefferson has often expressed
himself to Giles, Mason, and others, since his retirement,
as deeply affected to have been the instrument of that
order, and they have apologized to me. Yet how could
the President have known who visited the State Department without Jefferson's information?"

He glanced at Hamilton with his large, liquid black
eyes, as if more amused than exasperated; but there was
something very still and deadly in the smile, while his
white teeth stood ajar.

"Colonel Hamilton," he resumed, "why should we,
representing a fresh, o'erwhelming empire like New York
State, be ruled by these Virginians and their deft tongues
and shallow acquirements? Here is the stupid and illit-
erate Monroe shoving out your friend, Gouverneur Morris, at France. They have prepared to crucify Chief-
Justice Jay, no matter what form of English treaty he
makes. My sympathies extend to you, my opponent,
in the pitfalls they dig for you every night, and the
slander they placard upon you every morning; for they
mean to pull you out from under Washington. and let
him fall by his own——"

"Don't finish that• sentence," spoke Hamilton, quietly, raising his finger. "I have not invited your confidence, and you must spare him whose confidence is my
honor."

"It is no matter," resumed Burr, checking himself
firmly. "The death of my wife has set me adrift for

new combinations. I have a hold in South Carolina, and intend to strengthen it ; if we could agree, I can also hold the State of New York ; for I am a politician like Jefferson, and make no pretence to economics and finance, where you are supreme. My bailiwick is the city of New York, where I am the first organizing politician under the Federal Constitution, and it will soon determine the whole State. Let us join ; I will be your politician, you shall be my statesman."

" How is that possible ? " asked Hamilton, slowly.

Colonel Burr drew his chair nearer Colonel Hamilton ; they were nearly evenly sized, both of military shoulders and erect carriage, both of delicate frame and limbs, both sinewy, both intellectual.

Burr was the more beautiful, with the rich tints of the black serpent, that a child would covet to take up, as a man would not.

As he unfolded his plans it seemed to Hamilton like the unfolding of glittering coils, and the Minister of Washington watched Burr's dark splendor with blue eyes.

" It is not easy for one of my confidence and descent," resumed Aaron Burr, with heightened energy but even a quieter tone, " to make the concession I have made to you—that you are my master in political science. It should be otherwise, for my mother's father had the greatest head since Calvin. Permit me to recoup myself with the conceit that I am your master in the manipulation of the multitude."

" There you are Pericles himself, Colonel Burr."

Colonel Burr inclined his head and grew more considerate, almost fond.

" Not that you do not possess a sweeping ken of the springs of human motive, Hamilton, and can incline the exalted and considerate to your purpose. Who else went to Washington a boy, and now guides him like a man ? "

" All this I disclaim," insisted Hamilton, " and cannot accept your candid opinion. If I had any ore of genius, the contact of that pure essence, like Mercury's, seized and refined it."

Aaron Burr looked at Hamilton with a directness and penetration he never repeated but once again in this world; it was his last suspicion of Hamilton's entire candor.

"Well," said he, finally, "I suppose it is like love, and can see no defects. But *we* are to outlive all these people and descend to the middle of the coming century. Our combinations must be made with long foresight. New York is ruled by great families, that will have neither Burr nor Hamilton. The Livingstons and Clintons hate you, both as a stranger and a Schuyler; they put me in the Senate to put your father-in-law out. At this moment the Clintons are using me to break the Livingstons in the city, but they will turn upon me also, by and by. What do the Van Cortlandts and Jays care for you, after you have put their enemies under their feet? These aristocratic families would hang us both, as they hanged Leisler and Milborne, for presuming to govern them. They have got little Ned Livingston and young De Witt Clinton all ready to challenge us to run their Dutch-Indian gauntlet to our stake."

"You must not assume that I assent by following you, Colonel Burr. How could we ever work together to any mutual or disinterested end?"

"By separating all interests of jealousy. I will make you President of the United States; you can give me the Army, or send me abroad upon a mission, or I will be your Governor of New York."

"But you forget that you are not a Federalist, and that I am."

"Pshaw! do you suppose these silly Virginia abstractions put me into the opposition? No; I went with Washington's opponents because I would have been given no career by his friends."

The Secretary of the Treasury rose and put his hands beneath his quilted coat-skirts, and his long Scottish head was slightly bent downward as he walked to the open window of his narrow library and breathed the tainted summer air, laden with the heavy inland night.

Aaron Burr followed him with his dark eyes and ferret nose and upturned chin, sanguine that he had made an impression.

Hamilton turned in a moment, and walked back and lighted two candles with a fusee. He sat down again and leaned back, and spoke with careful considerateness:

"You have already remarked," observed Hamilton, "that General Washington is obdurate as to taking you into the public employment. What is the reason?"

"I was awhile on his staff; I was rebellious and impatient, I suppose, and lost his confidence. He never gave me another chance."

"That is strange," said Hamilton, still looking respectfully at his visitor. "I joined his staff soon after you left it, and remained there four years, and then parted from Washington in anger; but he gave me the forlorn hope at Yorktown, and called me to his Cabinet."

Colonel Burr raised his eyelids, and looked at Hamilton with penetration wreathed in a smile.

"He didn't detect you in any amour, did he?"

"Certainly not," answered Hamilton.

"Well, he did me. That finished the matter."

"I never heard Washington mention it. I do recollect something of the kind talked about on the staff."

As they were still looking at each other, and as the junior of the two had left his sentence like a query, Mr. Burr, with gayety, broke out:

"I am afraid, Hamilton, you are Yankeeing me, as we Connecticut men say; but you shall have my confession all the same."

He stroked his silken gloves and recrossed his silken hose upon his knee, and went on:

"I was only twenty, voluptuous and famished for beauty, after leaving Arnold in Canada, when, returning to New York, I found the society all demoralized by the armies of Howe and Washington confronting each other, the former on Staten Island, the latter on Manhattan Island and the opposite mainlands. Now, that was my camping ground, and to everything that was young and wanton I found my way; for I had been reared in Elizabethtown as the prince of Presbyterian orphans, and doubly a preacher's son."

"Yes, you were the wonder of us lads at the boarding-school there, with your learned descent and your fine property in trust. The girls were taught not to slight you, Senator."

"There was one—a Miss Margaret Moncrieffe—in dear old Elizabethtown. Her father was a British major, just in sight where the blue Staten Island hills

stand, only two miles away; yet she did not go to
him.  Do you know why?"

"Was it because she loved Aaron Burr?"

"She said so.  At my intimation she wrote to General Putnam in New York, asking him to befriend her.
He was a poor penman, but a hospitable old fellow,
and I answered the letter, being at the time in his military family."

"Now I remember; you told her to come?"

"What else?  She came, and was my prize.  Do you
wonder that ever since I have put pleasure before ambition, when I was at the time but twenty and my conquest
not yet fourteen?"

"Pitiful heaven!"

The indignant flash from Hamilton's eyes Mr. Burr
interpreted to be the ardor of envy, and he lost his own
self-control in the reminiscence of pleasure.

"I have had a full regiment of intrigues since," said
he, "but none that I managed as well as that.  The
campaign for woman is swifter than Cæsar's conquests
and more subtle than the fine arts; every movement is
sensitive in both the charmer and the bird.  I had wooed
and won this not unwilling maid.  Ha! ha! Hamilton, I
used Washington himself to prolong the romance and
then relieve me of her."

"Used Washington in such a cause?"

"I may as well tell you, for he knows it now, and it
is probably the secret of his hostility to me.  The girl
was growing burdensome to me, and I wanted her father
to receive her back; so I made Washington believe that
she was a precocious spy, taking the number and disposition of his troops, and expressing them in the 'language
of flowers,' when she was painting a bouquet for her alien
father."

Colonel Hamilton sat still as horror would have him,
and while he feared to speak lest he might forget the
propriety of his place, a wail from his sick child pierced
his heart.

"Oh, end this tale!" he spoke.  "Nature cries out for
me—*Senator!*"

"It is ended already.  What did ignorant old Putnam
or Surveyor Washington know of the language of flowers?  They trusted to me, child of Jonathan Edwards

and of the Reverend Burr! I had my prize sent back
to King's Bridge, where Mifflin commanded—the Governor of Pennsylvania now—and in the safe seclusion of
the woods and bowers love put out of my head the
duties of a staff secretary till the battles were done and
the enemy held the city. I lost the commander's confidence, and worse than that——"

"*Worse* than that?" echoed Hamilton.

"Yes; my British red-bird told Mifflin's young Quaker
wife that I was insured to be a father, and Mifflin's
wife told Madame Washington. I hastened to send the
interesting traitor in Washington's barge to her father on
Staten Island, lest she might confirm the insinuation to
my face, before the commander."

"But you cannot deny it now?"

"Of course not, for she has run a great London career
with royal dukes, and told her tale upon the Town in
print—never upbraiding me, speaking of me tenderly;
saying, indeed, that had I been faithful she would have
been eternally pure."

"And do you wonder that Washington would not
send you to France as his Minister?"

"I do. A reputation for gallantry like that would have
been my decoration there. The race of women admire
a fine man for such misdeeds as mine, and never have I
been injured by one of that obliging, venal sex."

"Surely you except your mother, Colonel Burr?"

"My mother! I never saw her. Therefore I am not to
be set in a corner by that hackneyed sentiment. My
father never courted her, but sent for her as for some
biblical handmaiden, and married her at the inn, half-
way; and ere my eyes were well opened both parents
died; so I come, like Minerva, from the brain and not
from the breast. I know your mettle too well, Hamilton, to see it sublimate this social, joyous *vanitas de
vanitatum!*"

"What act of mine," asked Hamilton, rising, "do
you consider to resemble the case of betrayal of a child
you have seen fit to confess to me? I tell you, sir, that
if President Washington knows and believes what you
say of yourself, he would not have the hardihood to
relate it to me; we should blush before each other to
share such a confidence!"

As Hamilton rose, flushed and severe, Colonel Burr, who had already stood up, in the confidentiality of his narrative, backed a step before his host and took his own cocked hat up from the writing-table, and put it on his head.

"By the way you look at me," said Burr, " I think we must have been exchanged in our childhoods at Elizabethtown, for you seem to be the pastor's son, ready to sermonize me, and I the hot West Indian, relating pleasure with the freedom of the tropics ! "

A cry, repeated and repeated, came from the sick child's chamber.

"I won't detain you, my dear fellow," cordially concluded Hamilton's guest ; "the sigh of a child always touches my heart.   Only let me say, before I go, that I know you better than you think.   I am the attorney for Maria Reynolds, plaintiff against James Reynolds in an action for divorce—Alexander Hamilton summoned by both plaintiff and defendant as a witness.   As I said before, I shall give you time, for we must be friends."

Hamilton had already settled into a chair and dropped his brow into his palm.

Colonel Burr stole away without tramp or echo.

Hamilton sat thus, with his high brain working under the reënforcement of blood from his heart, till he felt a hand upon his neck.

"Almighty God ! " he sighed, "has my act of folly dragged me to the depth of shame like *that*, and made me low enough for that friendship ! "

A woman's lips kissed him, unnoting what he spoke, and he heard his wife's voice say :

"Husband, little Phil is sleeping now.   Washington has been here to see him.   His fever is broken."

---

## CHAPTER IV.

### THE WASHINGTONS.

PRIESTLEY was taken by Edmund Randolph and the President's secretary, Tobias Lear, to call upon Washington.

They came to a large, double mansion of two full
stories and two dormitory stories besides, with garden
walls and large carriage gate, and with shade trees and
stabling back.

"Here is the President's," said Mr. Lear ; " it was
the house of Robert Morris, and before that of the Penn
family."

As he unlocked the door, Doctor Priestley took in at
a glance, and upon highly elated senses, the old black
bricks and stately door lamps, the pedimented lower
windows and portal not in the middle, and large elm-trees
behind the flanking walls.

He saw, down the middle of the wide High Street, in
one direction the distant market-sheds defined against
·the floody Delaware, and in the other the lines of pop-
lar trees cease at the vacant country lots beyond the
Central Commons and leave the Schuylkill hills in the
vista.

The impending presence of General Washington gave
Priestley a quickness of the breath ; for every great
reputation in Europe the Revolution had already de-
throned, and left this magistrate the solitary sanctity in
an age of overthrow.

Mr. Lear ushered them into a hall ornamented with
a bust of the late Louis XVI. of France ; as they disposed of their hats and canes, he said :

"Genet came in here with me, and seeing that bust,
remarked that it was an insult to France for Washington to maintain it."

The parlor door, to the right of the entrance, was
thrown open, and Priestley was ushered in.   At the
same time the sound of singing and a piano came
forth.

As the three persons entered, the same white servant
who had ushered them in lighted candelabra, and there
emerged from the darkness a little family, the centre of
which was a long-limbed man contending with a small
boy who would not get off his foot.

A pretty miss, who had been singing, with a female
companion, at the harpsichord, drew the boy off, as he
cried " Harkaway ! "

" Mr. President," spoke Edmund Randolph, his grand
manner and his halting speech being resumed together,

3

"Doctor — ah — Doctor Joseph — ah — yes — Joseph Priestley, desired to be—uhm—presented. Presented, as he passed through the city to the—achew ! achew ! — to the — yes — Susquehanna. The Susquehanna ! Mr. Lear and myself — ah — took the — uhm — the liberty."

His voice rolled so nobly through the saloon that his hesitation was forgiven.

The long-limbed man had risen—a military figure in black summer clothing, with hose, ruffles and powdered hair all equally white, and as he reached out a large, warm hand to clasp the doctor's, his face looked down at the latter, in kindness and penetration together, through the bluest eyes Priestley had ever seen, while the strong jaws of Washington and large nose somewhat altered the mild and amicable expression of his orbits.

Doctor Priestley, nearly of Washington's own age, endeavored to estimate and contain the great personage before him, with the literary greed of so rare an interview ; but after it was over he retained such an impression of Washington as of his own half-identified oxygen—something which exhilarated and brightened while it lasted, but was by his own groping analysis made a mystery.

Without speaking, mastering his guest by consideration and silence, President Washington resumed his chair after the doctor had been seated by Mrs. Washington, who said :

"Doctor, we heard that you were in the city, and your coming to America has been known to none more than General Washington. I shall take advantage of his diffidence and tell you that long before he left Mount Vernon and private life he set my son lessons from your book on Perspective."

Washington smiled, barely unclosing his somewhat mastiff mouth, and Priestley saw that in that barbarous age of dentistry some mechanic had spoiled his teeth. The poor doctor's, too, were nearly useless at sixty-one.

A little mischief was in Washington's twinkle as he regarded his wife. His warm skin was now warmed to something like a young man's blush.

" Help me out, Doctor Priestley, if I have made a
mistake," spoke up Mrs. Washington.   " I see the President laughing at something ; was it not ' Perspective ' ? "

" Yes," put in the delightful spirit of grace and youth
which had been playing the piano ; " for Theodosia and I
are drawing from it now.   Are we not, Theo ? "        •

" Indeed we are," answered Miss Theodosia Burr, who
soon became known to Priestley as Senator Burr's daughter.   " Mr. Lear taught it to Nelly, and my father said I
must learn it, too, because the weak side of the female
intellect—so papa said—was the mathematics."

" I feel gratified," observed Priestley, with a happy
flutter of self-appreciation, " to have had General Washington among my scholars, and I think, madame, that I
can account for his quizzing you on the ground that your
excellent memory was a proof of your early affection."

The President's benevolent eyes were turned upon his
wife with the same cordial glow of feeling.

" He would have made a great school-teacher," said
Mrs. Washington, whose profile was not unlike the President's own, as she enlivened with her confidence her
husband's passive influence.  " I think I never was as
happy as when my husband directed my children's tasks.
The country called him away, and I lost them all.   And
now he is having my son's orphan children educated
under his own eye."

She called them forward—Eleanor and Washington.
The girl courtesied and glided to her grandfather's side;
the boy hung his head, and suddenly raised it and cried
at Priestley :

" I know you ; you make soda-water.   Make some
now ! "        .

He ran away, sharing in the loud laughter his sally had
caused ; but Doctor Priestley drew him back and exhib-
ited his skill with children by telling the story of making
mineral waters by art.

The President and all listened pleasurably, and now
Washington asked a question :

" I will inquire of you if the mathematics have received
any new impetus—like the invention of logarithms, for
instance ? "

Doctor Priestley proceeded to unroll himself, so to
speak, upon an occasion of so great contact, and re-

lieved his memory of the long issue between Newton and Liebnitz as to which had discovered calculus and flux-ions, and this the doctor illustrated by his own grievance against Lavoisier.

General Washington alone listened to the end, while the young misses were joined by the general's two nephews—sons of his sister, Mrs. Lewis ; and Tobias Lear went over to them and became as a child in their inter-course.

The same servant as before brought in tea, cold tongue and toast upon waiters, so that the good doctor was not disturbed in his discourse.

He lamented, at the end, that instead of using his eyes and ears to draw Washington out, he had consumed the most valuable time of his life in an argument.

" I stopped at logarithms," said General Washington, neither tired nor greatly interested.  " The mathematics were just opening to me as the true language of the imagination when I was called to domestic and public life."

He remarked, to another inquiry:

" The most we can expect in the present administra-tion is to settle the groundwork of our government, es-tablish the true methods of business in the departments, set up the law of mutual obligation ; and if party spirit shall finally prevail, we hope to leave the executive divi-sion solid as a fortress, requiring no correction of its angles and lines, but defensible by any patriotic garri-son."

A mild gleam of his blue eyes fell upon his Chief of Cabinet.

"Was I not fortunate, Doctor Priestley," the President said, after a pause, "to draw into my first Cabinet three qualified men of my old military staff ?  Mr. Jefferson was the only one not a soldier.  Hamilton and General Knox were artillerists, somewhat mathematically trained. Mr. Randolph did not stay with me long, but he gained a better scholarship in the law by retiring from the camp. Military discipline in the field of war helps the moral as well as the mental nature.  There was but one intrigue in all the Revolution in our army, and only one case of treason : General Arnold probably plotted his villany in this house.  Here he lived in debt and extravagant habits. The same causes are at the foundation of the unnecessary party spirit in our country."

As the young people were preparing to sing, at Mrs. Washington's command, there were ushered into the salon (the ladies bonneted) Vice-President and Mrs. Adams, Mr. Jefferson and his lovely married daughter, and Congressman Madison and his Philadelphia bride.

The appearance of the latter, fresh from Virginia, whither she had gone to be married, was Doctor Priestley's opportunity to see how little formality existed in the President's household.

Mrs. Washington ran to Mrs. Madison, and throwing both arms around her neck, kissed her.

General Washington, with less impetuosity, but no more reserve, repeated the greeting upon the bride's lips, and taking Madison's two hands, called him "James," and drawing him to his breast, said :

"Tardy lover, it was almost too late. But God bless you both !"

The salutation was repeated with Martha Jefferson by both the President and wife, while those shook hands with Mr. Jefferson unreservedly.

He and Madison were both cold, undemonstrative men, the latter smallish and impersonal, as if merely brought along accessory-like, and folding his hands upon his little stomach, he seemed, under Jefferson's straight figure, to be the curate of some Highland chieftain.

"Yes," cried Mrs. Madison, a lady very well in advance of girlhood, but with a vivacity like beads, that seemed to flash all over her, in dark eyes and ringletted hair, high color, teeth and hat, hands and parasol, all moving and ducking and darting at once—"yes ; I have made him a Benedict ! He didn't want to come, but—ha ! ha ! ha !—I thought he was too kind to be a bachelor. Dear President, dear cousin Martha, dear, darling Nelly and Theodosia ! And Larry Lewis here, too ? and his dear brother Bobby ? Come, all, and kiss your dear cousin Dolly !"

The tones of Mr. Adams were heard in the midst of this female and family gratulation, snappishly :

"Well, I thought I was somebody in Massachusetts. I can't expect to be anybody in Philadelphia ! Abigail, I told you this Vice-Presidency was a mere shadow—a neutrality, at that! I suppose I can speak to Doctor Priestley, and not be observed?" ·

"Mr. Adams, don't be jealous at your time of life," chirped up the Vice-President's wife. "A woman can be married but once; very prismatic women, as dazzling as Mrs. Madison, may be married twice. I'll let you kiss her, so will Madison."

Mr. Adams, drably dressed like a Quaker, his short clothes making his bald head and round stomach—the one a larger reproduction of the other—seem shorter still, heard his wife, and opened his mouth, and seemed yet madder, till, as everybody broke out into a laugh, he began to laugh, too, and rushed upon the bride like a boy taking a forfeit in a picnic game, and the demure bridegroom pulled him off.

"I am evidence that John Adams is not forgotten," spoke up Doctor Priestley; "for this very day I wrote a dedication of my Lectures to him, as my most encouraging American friend since Doctor Franklin died."

"There, Mr. Adams," said his wife; "I told you something great would happen to you if you would be a little more volatile. You always wanted to get into a book."

"Dear me! I am in luck!" exclaimed the giddy, abbreviated Vice-President, hastening to thank Priestley. "Jefferson said he wouldn't come here without me, and he broke up my regular Sabbath-reading of the Apocalypse. I always read it in times of epidemics, for I think 'the time' ought to be 'at hand,' the world is getting to be so fearfully perverse."

"Mr. Adams," remarked his wife, composedly laying off her lace and loosening her leghorn hat-strings, "pray don't be so volatile. Let me hear some Seventh Day wisdom from Doctor Priestley."

"I am real glad we came into the city," interjected the tidy, substantial, observant Mrs. Washington. "You know we are spending the summer at Germantown, but the President had to meet his Cabinet to-night, so we all ventured to ride in with him."

Colonel Hamilton now entered with the Attorney-General and Knox, the War Minister.

Hamilton looked pale and weary.

The President and wife and their little family pressed

upon Hamilton to ask for "Phil," his boy. When Washington took Hamilton's hand, it was with something of that glowing look he had given his wife early in the evening.

Jefferson affected not to see this, but talked of agriculture to Mrs. Adams, who said :

"I had the care of a farm during the whole Revolution, and society comes as gratefully to me as it will to you again, Mr. Jefferson, I question not, when you are over this hobby."

But John Adams was again growing uneasy at the lisping words of Washington : "Take your boy into the country, my dear friend. Had I children like you, they would be the world to me."

As Washington remained standing, Doctor Priestley felt that it was time to go, for he foresaw a Cabinet Council.

"Stay, Doctor," interposed Mrs. Washington ; "the children have a request to make. In the days of better understanding than now, when our government was a little family and there had been no contentions in it, we used to meet like a family and have some music. Nelly remembers it and wants Mr. Jefferson to take the violin again, and Colonel Hamilton to sit at the harpsichord."

Mr. Jefferson protested, but was persuaded. Hamilton assented at once. While they were getting ready, Miss Theodosia Burr was led forward by Tobias Lear and recited Mrs. Barbauld's "Inventory of the Furniture of Doctor Priestley," commencing :

> " A map of every country known,
> With not a foot of land his own.
> A list of folks that kicked the dust
> On this poor globe, from Ptol. the First. . . . .
> A group of all the British kings—
> Fair emblem—on a packthread swings. . . . .
> A shelf of bottles, jar, and phial,
> By which the rogues he can defy all—
> All filled with lightning, keen and genuine. . . . .
> A rare thermometer, by which
> He settles to the nicest pitch
> The just degrees of heat to raise
> Sermons, or politics, or praise. . . . .
> New books, like new-born infants, stand
> Waiting the printer's clothing hand. . . . .

And all, like controversial writing,
Were born with teeth and sprang up fighting.

" But what is this, I hear you say,
Which saucily provokes my eye ?
A thing unknown—without a name—
Born of the air and doomed to flame ! "

As Priestley heard these old, familiar sounds, written by his wife's dear friend and descriptive of his perished treasures the mob had burned, he sat among them melted to tears of precious recompense that he was not unknown in this centre of America's society.

" My dear, brilliant child," he spoke, rising to kiss the little miss who had recited them, " how did you ever think to learn those lines and say them to me ? "

" Hush ! " answered Theodosia, whispering in his ear. " I sat up nearly all night to commit them. Don't tell on me. My father wants me to be very ambitious, and he said you were coming, and that I must surprise you."

The child was almost convulsively affected as she spoke, clinging to Priestley's fatherly face.

" Tell father," he whispered, " not to push his child too hard ; that which she wants is love—perhaps *his* love."

The stronger tears that flowed down Priestley's face when she had disengaged it were not, as others thought, the tears of alien reminiscence ; for Priestley's heart had been pierced by the most anguished, most stifled sigh he had ever heard from a child.

" What is this Colonel Burr," he wondered, " who gives learning to his offspring when it sighs so hard for love ? "

But now the harpsichord was ready, and Hamilton had tried the keys and Jefferson had twanged his bow. Those who could sing in the choral part of the song—children and women—gathered round, and there ascended, in a treble, youthful, hymnal kind of mixture, the nervous energies and purposes of this new America, of which so much was wilderness to be subdued :

### WORKERS' HYMN.

#### I.

Hark to the cocks ! list to the birds !
Chirping of pleasure too liquid for words ;
Stilled are the beetles, the night-hawk has fled,
Pale stand the stars, and the East it is red.

### CHORUS.

Sluggard, in slumber why dost thou lurk?
While it is day get thee out and to work !
Light, it is short ; and why dost thou irk?
For the Night cometh, when no man can work.
  No man can work,
  No man can work ;
When the Night cometh, no man can work.

## II.

Soft call the bells to thy repasts:
Eat, and thy beasts eat, while the noon lasts.
Look where the sun droops : do not delay—
Seed-time is ending ; be up and away !

### CHORUS.

Husbandman, see how the clouds gather murk ;
Call to thy oxen and speed to thy work !
Leave not the furrow for quibble or quirk—
For the Night cometh, when no man can work.
  No man can work,
  No man can work, etc.

## III.

Eve falleth near ; every grain maketh ears.
Precious the day as the light disappears.
Plant ! lest the mildew come like the crow,
Black as the midnight—when, no one can know.

### CHORUS.

Night is the time for the foeman to lurk ;
Day is the prime for the good man to work.
Leave to the bat and reptile the murk—
If the Night cometh, no man can work.
  No man can work,
  No man can work, etc.

## IV.

Work thou the works of the Master that sent ;
Work in the light of the bright firmament.
Sleep in the dark when the foe goeth past,
Sowing the tares to be burnt in the blast.

### CHORUS.

Night is the time when the demons hold kirk ;
Keep thee within when the moon-witches work !
Let not the sun on thy slumbering perk—
For the Night cometh, when no man can work.
  No man can work,
  No man can work, etc.

### V.

Fight for the day, like Jacob, aglow,
Wrestling the angel—and would not let go ;
*Light* was the ladder that Jacob was given,
Lengthening Day to the threshold of heaven.

#### CHORUS.

Hands that are idle are serpents that lurk ;
Life's only friend is the spirit in work.
Sons of the morning ! toil never shirk—
For the Night cometh, when no man can work.
        No man can work,
        No man can work ;
When the Night cometh, no man can work.

It was late that Sunday night when the President went to bed and covered the wood fire on the chamber hearth with ashes that it might not all die out.

"Puss," spoke he, softly, "are you asleep ? "

"No ; I never sleep, George, till you come to bed and kiss me."

The old general leaned over his wife and kissed her twice.

"Oh, you politician !" he whispered. "To pretend that you pay no attention to such things, and yet have that long word 'perspective' ready for Doctor Priestley, and a compliment ! "

"Now, you know better, George ! That was the word you used in your first letter to me, when you said you saw me at the end of the *perspective*, looking in at Mr. Chamberlayne's colonnade, and that you fell in love with me. But listen : Nelly and Lawrence are in love—they have already quarrelled and made up ! It is something that man Jefferson had to do with. Wherever he goes there is something underneath."

"Stop, my dear," said Washington ; "it is not fair that any public man or citizen should have against him the heavy odds of the President's wife."

He lay down at her side, and for some time could not fall asleep. She heard him say to himself, finally : " Hamilton was great to-night."

In a few minutes he breathed drowsily, and his last, unconscious words were :

"Yes, sir ! I shall march with my army."

# CHAPTER V.

## CHILD AND CLIENT.

" So Madame Washington received you like one of the family, Theo ? "

" Just the same, papa. Oh, they are lovely people— Nelly and little Wash, the Lewis boys and Mr. Lear. *He* is such a funny man ! "

Colonel Burr took up a Latin book and turned its leaves.

" Did anybody at the President's ask for me ? "

" Not one, papa.. Oh, yes ! Robby Lewis spoke of you."

" What did he say ? "

Colonel Burr's daughter blushed and hesitated.

" Come here, Theo ! Do you see this Latin grammar ? Well, I am looking right into your mind, and if you do not say that off to me without mistake, you shall read this grammar till you can recite twelve pages of it without one error ! "

The girl trembled before her father's unfeeling eyes, which charmed her like a snake. She would have avoided her confession, but those eyes seemed to overflow from their dark pupils and run into her nature and suffocate it. As she gasped, he gave her the military order :

" Attention ! "

Down went her hands to her side; her shoulders straightened.

" Eyes front ! "

Her eyes fluttered and rested on her father's smooth, stoic face, in fear and love.

" Recite ! " finished Senator Burr.

" Robby Lewis," began the girl, perfunctorily, " is going home to Virginia unless—unless——"

" *Mark time !* " commanded Colonel Burr, fixing his eyes upon his child as upon some raw, common soldier out of drill.

The girl's left foot kept military time, while a tear ran down her cheek that she dared not lift her hand to wipe away.

" Theo," said her father, his face relaxing, " our understanding is—perfect confidence ; not a shadow of your nature must be concealed from me. To me you are not a child, nor a woman neither : you are a man and myself, all that I have left and all that I shall ever love. I mean to make you the greatest woman of this age ; but to do so your nature must be as unreservedly put before me as before your mirror. Come, now, and kiss me ! "

He saw the welcome light of ambition spring, like the lunar rainbow, upon a spray of her tears ; and in a moment an old, unnatural look of calculation came to her face that was delightful to Colonel Burr.

" There, it is my brave subaltern now," the father ex-claimed, kissing her, as he would forgive the hunting-dog he had disciplined. " How can I cure my darling if she will not tell me her pains? Do you love some one, Theo ? "

"Yes," spoke the girl, passionately. " I love you— nothing else."

" We will love no others," responded the father, in intellectual fondness that was like the radiance of the ruined moon. "Your beauty is my crown jewel, and nothing less than a crown can ever become it. All things here are fresh, plastic, ready for some daring hand like that of Aaron Burr. But the new world is worthless to me without my daughter, to give it to her when I have won it. Be true to me and to yourself, and tell me everything."

Theodosia arose, touched her face with water, and said :

" Do not correct me, and I will tell you all that was said, and what I felt besides—even my affections, that I must learn not to indulge, papa. Perhaps if I tell them to you, they will seem unworthy to myself now."

She began, and gave her father all the scene and cir-cumstance at the President's, in excellent mimicry of the principal personages there.

She told of her recitation, and of Priestley's tender-ness, and of the love passage with General Washing-ton's nephew. Giving way to her feelings, she wept and smiled again, and rose from agony to caricature and laughter.

Her father, impressive, insinuating, dexterous, and at times indelicate, listened to her sorrows with admiration, enjoying them like her wit, and noting the depth of that womanhood 'he would preserve as auxiliary power for the master strokes of diplomacy when artifice might fail.

Back in the paternal origin of Aaron Burr was a German strain which labored for cold, scientific method, and he threw everything into a philosophic scheme which had for its beginning the obliteration of the natural impulses. His ambition, even his propensities, were to be pursued without involving the heart, and his dream of supreme existence was to have his daughter love him entirely, and have her heartless to all besides.

"Father," finished Theodosia, " I have told you my first love touch, and have not spared my tears—for young people, I suppose, would naturally love each other if they were not corrected. Alston has been with old people; his talk is of the paddock, the race-track, his stakes on games and his herds of negroes. Bobby Lewis talks of his mother, and her goodness, and I felt his tones in my heart. Oh, did you love my mother? Did not something stronger than wealth or position break down your ambition when you married that widow with no estate but children? Is there not something of that imprudence, father, in my better nature? Can I be happy if I do not love, and only marry where you tell me ? "

"Your happiness will be in your children, Theo. Love and marriage are mere incidentals. It was the cultivation and elegance of your mother which drew me into an inconsiderate marriage. I was only twenty-six, and her oldest boy was then eleven. But I came of a race of teachers of children, and upon you, child, I bestow all their art. Master Alston has power in the last Federalistic Southern State. You will be in your prime, little queen, six years from this time, when the change of dynasty comes, and may help your father more than you know."

Thus, with childhood hardly in its prime, Theodosia had been manufactured into nearly a political woman.

As she rattled along in fresh confidences, induced by his petting, Colonel Burr examined a pistol and put fresh priming in it, and hid it in his small-clothes. Then setting Theodosia a task, to draw the map of South Carolina and learn the names of its districts and streams, he kissed her *au revoir*.

At the little State Department on Third Street, Colonel

Burr saw a crowd reading the President's fresh proclamation against the Western insurrectionists.

"Little Hamilton is a nervy fellow," thought Burr, as
he passed Hamilton's house a block below, at Walnut
Street. "Mifflin has refused to put the insurrection
down, and the United States is going to do it. Twelve
thousand men, too, called out. Hamilton is not afraid
of money ; the army will cost a million, and the Opposition will get Pennsylvania."

The streets a little way beyond began to show dilap-
idation, and many substantial houses, deserted during
the epidemic, were filled by squatters or given up to ten-
ants at will. Toward the river was a short street of
once noble brick mansions in medallioned cornices, now
flaunting from their upper windows clothes-lines and
clothes, and the loiterers of both sexes at marble steps or
open casements suggested some Hanseatic seaport purlieu rather than the Quaker metropolis of a new world.
Sailors of all nations, emigrants of all degrees came and
went, and Colonel Burr felt relieved when a sailors' fight
at the foot of the street, between English and French,
emptied every doorway and gave him unobserved admission to a broad hall which ended in a back yard filled
with old junk of every description—iron, ship tackle,
copper, and several hogsheads of what seemed to be
private papers and letters.

Colonel Burr stopped by these and drew out a letter or
two curiously, and glanced at their contents.

The yard of the next house back was open from this
purlieu yard, so that one could pass or escape from the
secluded to the public block. Going straight through,
Colonel Burr saw in the second hallway a small sign :

"*Jacob Clingman: Money Lent, Goods Bought.*"

"This is the place," said Colonel Burr, and ascended
naked stairs to the highest story and knocked upon a door.

After some whispering and shuffling of feet, the door
was opened by a particularly large man with a menacing
pair of eyes which were yet exceedingly black and bright,
and his cheeks, which had high bones and the German
contour, were of a rosy, attractive color. He had preserved this Rubens-tinted face at the sacrifice of his

shapeliness ; for he was as fat as a Pennsylvania tavern-keeper, and broad as a giant, and his large feet and hands suggested the person who might have peddled in the heavy junk in the back yard below.

For a moment this satyr with Cupid's countenance gazed at the respectable, bland figure in his door, as if to throw it down-stairs. The next minute his eyes shone acutely and his neck became creased with almost blushing dimples, and waves of fat rolled up from some vast breadth of respiration in his sailor-folded collar.

" Colonel and Senator Burr ? Now I know that this call is not upon Jake Clingman, but upon something suited to the high taste and accomplishments of his'n truly, ' A. B.' "

"Clingman, I called on Mrs. Maria Reynolds, at her request."

" Come in ! Come in ! All in the quartermaster's camp is your'n. Mari ! Mari ! Come nigh, come nigh. This call is not on his'n, but on her—from your'n truly, A. Burr. "

At this impromptu poetry Jacob Clingman squeezed his cheek bones down and raised his cheek dimples up, and so produced a hundred folds and creases, from the midst of which his dark eyes shone with humor, and also with a metallic, devil-may-care courage.

Colonel Burr heartily laughed, yet retained his self-poise while laughing.

" Clingman," said he, "you are the same old Virginia Dutchman; why don't you give a public entertainment ?"

" Simply, Mr. Burr, because Clingman his'n has been at least once in prison. Therefore does he deal in shackles, ship chains, government warrants and accommodation paper, and lies dark till he can sit down on them enemies of his'n—and mash 'em."

Saying this, with a voice like iron, firm and high-inflected, and his countenance full of a certain rude, coarse power, Jacob Clingman again gave a comic leer as he dropped into a great cane-seated chair, and made it crack and groan beneath his weight.

Colonel Burr saw that somebody had been playing cards where Clingman sat, and drinking ale as well; for there were two " hands " upon the table and a little silver mug on one side, and a stone jug by the host, who unceremoniously now put the jug to his lips, without apology, and drained it.

"By the great green spectacles of Lord Fairfax!" exclaimed the cherubic glutton. "Yes, by the guinea pigs of Greenaway Court! that ale was good, if it *was* brewed in spite of the excise. Now I say, Colonel Burr, what's to prevent truly his'n, J. Clingman, from getting a sutlership with this expedition to put down the Western ensurraction?"

"Nothing, Clingman, but what you have mentioned—your having been in prison on a felonious charge."

"And I suppose that would lay agin me?"

'"It would not with me, necessarily; it would with Washington—and Hamilton, who will control the expedition."

The giant's face lost its bright color and became of the pallor of jail walls, that is said never to permanently leave the convict's skin. He rolled from lungs like a blacksmith's bellows, oaths that had the power of his animal temperament.

"What did I do to be black-listed forever? The government had a pension list; of course it owed the money to its Revolutionary pensioners. A few of 'em died, but they didn't keep account of them. Wasn't the money due to the State of Virginia? Wasn't I tryin' to keep it thar by drawing of it out of the Treasury? They called my signing for some dead pensioners 'forgery,' but they couldn't make it out, because I held a power of attorney. Then they tried to make it conspiracy with one Jeems Reynolds, and said I had bribed him to give me the pension list. They had to let me go, but they put my name up in every department of the government, and made it dismissal to recognize his'n and your'n truly, J. Clingman."

"Yes, Jacob, it was I who beat the indictments and got you off; but, my athletic friend, I have forgotten some of the particulars of your origin. Let me see—what was it?"

"Republican," said Jacob Clingman; "you kin gamble on that. My father was a Dutchman from somewhere in Europe—he didn't bring his coat-of-arms—who settled in York County, Pennsylvany, and hired hisself and his wagon team out to General Braddock, and lost everything but his life, and never was remunerated by the State. He stopped in the valley of Virginia and enlisted a soldier in the Revolution. All he got for that was a cut over the head and the scurvy. At the close of the war the only shelter he could find was to be a hostler in a tavern in the Piedmont country. When he was found dead in the hay-loft one morning, his old colonel, Parson Muhlenberg, took me as a soldier's brat and sent me to an Old Field school. It wasn't long before your'n truly found he had a genius for a swap and a knack with the dice. So I got four horses and a coach and made the grand tour with a sweat-cloth, a slave nigger, and a sideboard ; now flush, now broke—now sparking a planter's daughter, and now a spell in a debtor's jail. From horse and nigger trading I took to politics and contracting, and when they made the naytional government and put Freddy Muhlenberg in the speaker's chair of the fust Congress at New York, I considered that if they was going to fund the State debts, maybe the old Braddock's team and my daddy's dues might come in. So I have followed every Congress from New York to Philamaclink, and buy claims, lend on watches and collateral, and am preparing for the next war, when we shall have to build a navy—and I have got a part of a ship in the back yard."

" Jacob, you have an imperial eye. You are right; politics must be the great business of a land with fifteen legislatures already, and fifty more to come, every one of them a polytechnic school for admission into the Federal lobby. Why can't you come over to New York and take one of my city wards, Jacob ? "

"Thank you, Colonel. At present the Muhlenberg and Heister influence in this State keeps me out of jail, and your'n truly is better adapted for these Middle States than to measure wit with the New York Yankees. There are fat things at Albany, no doubt. When I was there the governor's ring sold some millions of the finest land in the world for eightpence an acre—long credit and no interest—but I couldn't git in. Pennsylvany will do for a patriot like your'n truly, J. C."

" But, Jake, I suppose your grievance here is the same as Falstaff's—that you cannot 'rob the exchequer the first thing.' "

Clingman rose with fury and pallor contending on his face like thunder in bonny-clabber.

"Damn Hamilton!" he roared. "Why don't somebody kill him?"

"For shame, brother Jacob! To speak of such a gentleman as Colonel Hamilton so harshly!" came a voice from the interior apartment, followed by the imposing figure of Mrs. Reynolds.

She was dressed somewhat like Marie Antoinette in the Temple, with a white lace head-dress and black crape band over the crown, a white illusion tippet or cape translucent over her throat and shoulders, short sleeves exposing hand and forearm—not fine but cleanly muscled—and a gown of dark mourning material. She looked like a recent widow, rested into a delicate interest in life again.

"Oh, Mari! Mari!" sighed, with a rumbling growl of delight, the voice of Jacob Clingman, leaning his powerful palms upon his mighty thighs and thrusting out his hungry, carnivorous jaws to inhale the picture. "The Cumberland Vallee isn't a tech to that beauty of your'n! If you could only take pity, Mari, on your adorer and stop these groans of his'n, he would be forever your'n obediently, J. C."

Roguery, animal interest and pleasure had succeeded Mr. Clingman's late burst of impotent rage, but in his regard was something of the horse trader valuing his mare.

"There, *there!*" Jacob Clingman roared, bringing the remaining sentence down to a rhetorical whisper. "You see the shears that clipped your Samson in the Treasury —Hamilton!"

Mrs. Reynolds had thrown her arm upon the back of Mr. Clingman's chair and crossed it with her naked hand, holding her gloves. An abstracted, reminiscent look added to her widow-like appearance.

Her face was a true oval, yet broad at the chin, which, in spite of heaviness, had a sweet and attractive mouth, the most desirous of her features, though her brunette skin and light eyes accommodated an easy mantle of tranquillity and dreaminess over all, giving to the beholder the idea of a large, rich nature, which at the slightest endearment might go to sleep.

Her hair grew out of her skin so luxuriantly, that skin was so unblemished, her eyebrows and lashes were so clear and regular, like the seal's, that the word "lady" applied to her involuntarily; but Colonel Burr, who was one of the few educated men without any awe of women, mentally reflected that Mrs. Reynolds had too many charms to keep her off the pavement.

"Publicity," he thought to himself, as he studied her wandering and unbrilliant eyes, "is Mrs. Maria's temptation; for she has too much stature not to be attractive to a large crowd, and to like its admiration. Everything about her dress and toilette is studied for the street. Yes, her life is external to herself, and education seems stupid to those who exist for show and praise."

"Colonel Burr," sighed Maria, without coming forward to take his hand, but patting the rich, black ringlets of Jacob Clingman, "here is my only faithful friend. I have a husband. I have Hamilton—that is, he loved me once. But all have cruelly abandoned me, except this old, hard diamond. That is why you see me here. I wanted his advice before consulting with you upon——"

Mrs. Reynolds' throat trembled with a slight convulsion. She silently covered her face with her handkerchief, and her bosom heaved under the widow's cape.

"Oh, Mari! Mari! you'll bust my sensibilities, pore gal!" cried Jacob Clingman, leaning his head so far back to look into her eyes that it seemed his huge waist might be drawn out through his sailor's collar.

A knock came upon the door; it was a cabin-boy with a captain's chronometer to pawn.

Mr. Clingman gave the boy a silver dollar without opening his mouth or allowing a word, and then pushed the boy down the first short flight of steps.

"Stole by his'n truly, Unknown," exclaimed the portly spirit of trade. "There'll be a reward offered for it, and accepted by your'n truly, J. C."

"The divorce with James Reynolds—that is my business here," advanced Colonel Burr. "Let us not mix it with any sentiment. To begin at the foundation: who were you, madame, and where did you first see your husband?"

"Speak up, Mari! It was at the Inaugeration, wasn't it?"

"Alas! yes," answered Mrs. Reynolds, after many preparations; "I was of the large Livingston connection, and we had an excursion packet from Poughkeepsie to the city of New York; and there, amidst the festivities, I saw James Reynolds, who fell madly in love with me, entered into correspondence with me, and as I was weary of the country I listened to his implorations for a runaway marriage. He claimed to have large property in Virginia, and so he had, but it was all in wilderness land; he possessed nothing but a clerkship, which was obtained through intercession with Secretary Hamilton, as my husband was an officer's son. Upon the scanty salary of six hundred dollars a year two extravagant persons were to be maintained; we upbraided each other and lived in the shadow of perpetual debt, until his moral courage was all destroyed and he was tortured with jealousy of my consideration. We moved with the government to Philadelphia, and here, but for Jacob Clingman, my husband would have deserted me, as he had exhausted the last borrowing resource and was threatened with the jail for debtors. In this extremity I called on Colonel Hamilton. He loved me, and I discovered, upon the avowal, that I loved him better than my husband. Since then, Mr. Reynolds has browbeaten and dogged the Secretary until the culmination came at our boarding-house yesterday, when I had nearly been exposed to Dr. Priestley's family. Unexpectedly——"

"I know," interrupted Colonel Burr. "You made your mark upon the heart of Master Harry, and he went to the bottom of his purse for you. But would you marry him?"

Maria hid her face in her handkerchief, though her eyes, peeping over at Mr. Clingman, had the light of enjoyment.

"Mari never loved but one," muttered that person, "and that, of course, was his'n truly, A. Hamilton; wasn't it, Mari?"

The lady covered her eyes also, and swelled her broad bust with palpitations.

"Why shouldn't she marry the young feller?" inquired Mr. Clingman, with his somewhat snorting, high-stepping rhetoric, in which his nostrils and his outlaw's eyes rose to the nature of his great organ of voice. "Old fellers grab the young gals in their teens—Turn and turn about ! Let Mari take a shine to the colt of the chimical doctor, for it's my experience that the widows—nateral widows or grass ones—make their centre-shots on greenhorns below the age of eighteen."

"Yes, Colonel Burr, I wish a divorce," added Mrs. Reynolds; "cannot it be obtained or certified without publicity? I know of no person who could do me any injury with the Priestleys in their far inland solitude, un-less Hamilton should expose me. I do want to be free and commence another life."

She dropped some tears, and turned her face to the white wall.

"As for Hamilton," spoke Jacob Clingman, standing up with the zest of a mastiff at meal-time, his face full of predatory power, " why, by the great Connewingo jingo ! I'll bring him to book and bell if he cuts any tricks with your'n and her'n truly, Mari Reynolds and J. C. ! Yer's a pack of his letters to Mari. Yer's her'n to his'n. Where's the pride of the Schuylers now ? Where's the nice equypize and knowingness of President Washing-ton ? If these letters was to go into Washington's hand, the name of Alexander Hamilton would stand on the black list of every Federal department beside the name of your'n truly, J. Clingman, and it would be dismissal from the public service to communicate with him."

Colonel Burr softly reached out his hands to take the letters.

Jacob Clingman put them behind his back.

"Do you suppose I would give you this power over that high-bred gal?" Clingman interrogated. " Don't I know the reputation of Aaron Burr, even as counsel ? "

Colonel Burr said the letters were not of the least consequence, except as curiosities ; but where had Mr. Clingman been able to find both Maria's letters and Hamilton's ?

"Ha! ha! Well, now, I'll tell you. As a junk dealer I buy considerable paper stock. As a claim dealer I buy mercantile information. Having learned that Hamilton deposited his correspondence with Willing & Bingham, I made arrangements to take all their refuse, which is

the perquisite of the porter. I sorted over them two
hogsheads of papers you see in the yard, and out came
Hamilton's letters."

"Jake," mused Senator Burr, "I suspect you had them
dropped in that refuse."

"No, Mr. Burr," Maria spoke, in her drowsy, nasal
tone; "Mr. Clingman is a plain, shrewd man, and after
Colonel Hamilton coaxed· his own letters back from me
and I was without any proof of my wrongs against his
powerful name, I came to my old friend, whom I had
known in New York, and asked him what to do."

"And your'n truly," Mr. Clingman took up the tale,
"reflected that Hamilton wouldn't keep sech letters in
the house near his wife. He wouldn't trust 'em to a
friend. He would lay 'em up with his banker. So I
went into the junk business after my indictment was
quashed and bought barrels of old letters—and Maria
read 'em. Hamilton thinks his case is safe at Bingham's,
but it's *here;* for it isn't often that a sucker of that
magnitude is landed in the net of his'n truly, J. C."

The spirit of loot, the gambler's avarice, shone metallic in the rich eyes and under the merciless brows of the
government parasite.

"Jake, you'll be a hard man for him to settle with, I
fear," smiled Colonel Burr, looking thoughtfully toward
the letters.

"He'll pay tribute according to his rank. That's the
law of the Barbary coast. He'll add to the tribute more
injury done than he knows to his'n truly, Jacob Clingman, citizen."

Steps were heard upon the stairs, and Mr. Clingman,
peeping over the baluster, whispered back :

"Mari, it looks like Hamilton !"

"The letters! the letters!" muttered Colonel Burr.
"He probably has a search-warrant for them."

The suggestion decided the momentary hesitation of
Mr. Clingman, and Colonel Burr, with the correspondence,
slipped into the inner room, where Mrs. Reynolds was
also retiring, and the door closed upon them both.

## CHAPTER VI.

### THE ADVENTURESS.

THE apartments of Jacob Clingman were really the garret story, but spacious and plastered and finished as well as the lower parts of such Philadelphia dwellings, with large clothes-presses and closets to do the storage of a whole family.

Closed and locked within, Colonel Burr felt relieved of the coarse animal society of the man, and at last in the very boudoir of the woman he admired and respected, and who had hitherto repulsed him.

"Silence," whispered Colonel Burr; "your power over Hamilton depends upon his not discovering you. Not one sound—my dear Maria!"

The outer door had been closed by Clingman, who quickly gathered his wits together and met the knock with a hoarse

"Enter!"

The door opened upon the youth who had threatened Hamilton only the day before. He was shaved and neat, but a little nervous from his excess of yesterday.

"Ha, Jim!" exclaimed Mr. Clingman, slightly mystified. "Who's that with you, Jim? It looks like the great Colonel Hamilton—it do, now."

"I have seen you before," spoke Hamilton, coming forward with almost a playful smile. "I believe you do not come to my department as often as formerly?"

"No, Mr. Secretary; I been a-waiting for you to take that interdict off. I know you'll do it when you find what a friend and admirer you have always had in your'n truly, J. C."

He looked at Reynolds vacantly, as if to explain the connection, and meeting there an uneasy look of haughtiness and in Hamilton's face only well-bred equanimity, Clingman ventured another remembrance.

"Colonel Hamilton, I am the son of an old soldier of the line. I reckon you didn't know him, because he spoke so little English. His old colonel—now congressman—John Peter Gabriel Muhlenberg, brother of the

Speaker, was particular kind to a son of his'n under whose tent you do me this honor."

"You mean that you are that soldier's son ? I am sorry for it: A soldier's son ought not to defraud the Treasury of his country. That is unfilial—unsoldierly, my friend."

Hamilton had taken the chair just vacated by Colonel Burr, and composedly crossed his black stockings and looked at Clingman with the expression of a grown man at a Punch show, barely amused, not at all absorbed. His high French and Scotch color brought out the sallow tints of abuse and the uncertain moral hold in the young man at his side, who was taller than Hamilton by nearly a head.

"Jim, thar, knows how hard a world this is to get along in," rolled Clingman's bold tones. "It's so hard a world that anybody that can succeed in it has the admiration of your'n and his'n truly, J. C."

Hamilton barely smiled. "Whose'n ?" said he.

"You don't like my Lindley Murray ?" called Clingman, irascibly. "You use it too elegantly sometimes—addressing ladies, for instance."

"There it should be used in its perfection, friend ; and when ladies reply in their own language, they generally acquit themselves better than when supervised by a man. Every woman, one would think, knew how to spell her own name."

Seeing both visitors now quizzing him with equal interest, the host looked angry, till suddenly the perspiration began to show upon his face and he turned uneasily in his seat.

"Let me correct you on another point," said Hamilton, not altering his tone or playful countenance, "and that is the point of worldly success. It does not depend upon a legacy, nor love of money, nor anything more than health—except character. I had not your size and strength, Mr. Clingman, though I became a soldier. My education was supplied on the basis of my character. My wife and Washington took me for my responsibility alone. But this is indeed a hard world to succeed in without character and by nothing but conspicuous villany."

The tone had the sound of the prosecuting lawyer making his first impressive point.

"Colonel Hamilton, you have done the worst with me. I adopted the business of public contractor and agent, and you broke me up.   I am now in the junk business, and that's pretty low.   You drink the wine out of the bottle, and I make my living out of buying the empty bottle. Your horse flings a shoe, and I deal in that shoe.   Yet I have got the spirit of a merchant and deserve another chance.   Won't you help, sir, to start fair?"

Hamilton looked at the not unpleasing, anxious face painted upon the bowsprit of that tub-like human galleon, and for a little while was silent.

"To start fair?" he replied at last, barely serious. "That would be an unfair concession to a man of your record.   It means that all you have done to place you in the rear of fair men is to be forgiven without repentance—I may add without mercy—and you be advanced to the line of honest persons and started with possibly greater credit than they ; for I suppose you want some kind of semi-official situation or public recommendation?"

"I want to be a post-trader, or camp-sutler with the army that is to be raised to put down the ensurraction."

"That is as I supposed—starting with an advantage unfair to honest merchants.   The place to take and make another character for yourself is that which this erring young gentleman is about to take.   Tell him, Mr. Reynolds."

"Colonel Hamilton has become my adviser—I hope my friend," the young man stammered, till he felt the hand of the Secretary of the Treasury upon his arm as Reynolds stood at Hamilton's knee.   "Yes, I am going to enlist as a soldier to put down the sedition."

"Food for powder!" exclaimed Clingman, contemptuously.   "None of that for your'n truly, J. Clingman."

"No," Hamilton remarked, not maliciously.   "You will always trust to some other talent than subordination and discipline.   But this young man, atoning for the past, offering his life to his country as expiation for the past, may live to know the meaning of what we Nationalists say, that 'all true greatness comes through right limitation, all true freedom through obedience.'"

He dropped his hand to that of Reynolds, and with bright seriousness continued :

" Mr. Clingman, your wishes can be met, not by the government but by its critics. I have heard you, with considerable rude eloquence, abuse the administration of Washington in public tirades. You have only to continue that industry, and Governor Mifflin, who is our opponent, may make you the camp-trader of one of the Pennsylvania regiments, as he has hastened to befriend many of our enemies. You have claims indeed. I do not speak of those you caused this discharged clerk to give you, by copying from the public records the names of deceased soldiers of the Virginia line. But you will possess to all future times the certificate of having been the first huckster in the lobbies of American Republican Government, seeking the public agents to corrupt, the public ministers to control, through their sensibility of shame, and the public treasury, poor and scanty as it is, to pillage ! "

"By God ! " exclaimed Jacob Clingman, starting up with dangerous spirit.

" Wear the honor awhile," continued Hamilton, calm as the public prosecutor glancing toward the criminal on trial. " Thousands are to follow you in the same trade. The people are to be flattered till they will resent the idea that they cannot plunder the Treasury and will overpower the officer who resists them. You merely live before your time, and it will be the business of the historian to do you justice."

Clingman lost restraint in the fury of this bear-baiting, and strode toward Hamilton and flung his young associate aside.

" Am I, in my own lodgings, to be made a schoolboy of and be ferruled by a master hypocrite like his'n truly, A. Hamilton ? " exclaimed the insensate giant.

" Take care, Colonel Hamilton ! " warned Reynolds. " He is afraid of nothing."

"I have merely answered your questions, Mr. Clingman," the Secretary mildly answered, " and now I will tell you what brought us here."

" Yes, your business—and be quick."

" I am counsel for James Reynolds in a suit against Maria Reynolds for divorce, and the husband has traced his wife to this apartment. Last night I learned from Senator Burr, of New York, that he had been retained for Mrs. Reynolds. This was kind of her—to retain my most unscrupulous enemy. The information bade me lose no time and so I am Mr. Reynolds' lawyer. Where is the wife?"

At the name the bolt slipped on the inner chamber door and Mrs. Reynolds appeared.

Maria Reynolds was now a different creature from the respectable and striking figure in weeds which had so lately vanished.

Her loosened hair now fell upon neck and shoulders rich and white, and one long, mature, elegant arm dropped bare from only a cord at the shoulder to her knee. Her dress was that of the chaste Lucrece upon the stage, all white and in one piece. Her complexion was supernaturally white, and her lately faded eyes now flashed both brilliant and hollow, like lamps in caverns.

"Great God!" she exclaimed. "Hamilton here—with my husband?" and she fainted.

Reynolds stirred, hesitated, and half moved toward her in sympathy.

"No, my client!" commanded Hamilton, shaking his head.

The young man dropped into the chair vacated by Clingman, and turned his eyes from the scene.

"Mari! Mari!" the stalwart host voiced loud. "Is there no protector of her'n to go to her help? Jeems Reynolds, shame on you! to inlist for a soldiering and desert this angel! And you!" turning to Hamilton, "who separates man from wife and innercence from comfort, will you let your victim lie thar and never feel for her?"

Hamilton waved his hand politely for Mr. Clingman to do the honors of hospitality.

As Clingman raised the fair, strong mould of the lady, his shoulder, where her head fell to rest, and his dyed stockings and blue knee-breeches were sprinkled with powder from her face.

She opened her eyes once, made dazzling by the freshly applied belladonna, and seeing Hamilton again, uttered a loud scream and flung up her naked arm so violently that the other was also released from its sleeve, and her weight pressing upon Jacob Clingman brought him to his knee.

Across great Clingman's upright knee she lay, a wealth of bloom and bough, like a great overturned basket of fruit.

"Mari! Mari!" exclaimed Clingman, lifting up a horse whinny to express dumb grief.

Young Reynolds also left his chair and looked to Hamilton appealingly.

"No, my young friend," the youthful Secretary spoke. "She is in the proper hands at present. You have no rights there. *She is leaning upon* HER HUSBAND!"

These words were spoken with amiable, uninflected distinctness, but they produced another female scream, not of the theatrical irrelevancy of the first; it was now a very little scream, followed by a profound hush on the part of both the lady and her satyr.

"The variety of shapes which this woman can assume is endless, Mr. Reynolds," the public man quietly continued. "If I were not experienced in her arts they might deceive me still and make me melt at the scene she has enacted here.

"For a brief period," added Hamilton, "I sincerely accused myself of having injured a creature of nobler body than wit or mind, one elementary, simple and unsophisticated. I considered *you*, sir, the villain who had perverted her modesty and reduced her to want, and that you were living upon the blackmail extorted from me.

"Mr. James Reynolds," continued Hamilton, impressively, "I owe you some apology. The many letters in execrable spelling and greedy spirit sent to me in your name I suspect to have been written by yonder outlaw, in full collusion with this woman—*who is his Wife.*"

He did not rise nor even point to Clingman.

"*Not Clingman's* wife?" Reynolds uttered, incredulously.

"Yes, Reynolds. You require no divorce. If she is also married to you, she is guilty of bigamy and ripe for its punishment. You were her maiden victim; I was her highest game. She chose the hour and the minute well, for she was guided by a shameless and adroit felon —one of that class which seems to have been here earlier than laws or institutions or civilization, and which estimates liberty only for its corruptibility."

He had now turned to Clingman direct, and looked magisterially into his perspiring face.

"Get up, Mari !" Clingman ejaculated, "and hear the charge of the court.  Oh, what a hypocrite !"

He tried to look at Hamilton with this charge, but mind was conquering matter.

Rising, still beautiful—the more beautiful, indeed, because frightened and natural at last, the woman retreated, hid her face, and suddenly rushed to Hamilton's feet and stretched herself there upon her face.

"Mercy !" she moaned.  "This will break my mother's heart !"

"What of the heart of a gentleman's wife?" exclaimed Hamilton, not insensible to the cry.  "That is the only injury you can do me—to bring pain to one also a mother and the dependent of my love and hands.  Her table has gone scanty and she has heard the dun of tradesmen to whom I was in debt, because you, and this man you obey, had plundered me of my lean official salary."

His words outmatched his voice, which continued to be calm and almost persuasive.

Hamilton arose and stooped to Mrs. Reynolds' cold palms.

"You are woman," he spoke kindly.  "I know the wilful spirit in the blood of human nature.  It is not my purpose to harm you, but to warn you, that you may know your strength and your weakness.  Get up, fellow, and give your wife the chair !"

Jacob Clingman had dropped, in wondering helplessness, into the only unoccupied seat, and he obeyed Hamilton's contemptuous order like a servant.

"Your'n truly, J. C. !" he ejaculated, steadying himself afterward at the window-sill.

Maria covered her charms with the *General Advertiser* newspaper, put her head in her hands, and sobbed at intervals.

"Listen, Mr. Reynolds, and you shall determine what the local law is to do with these people," proceeded Hamilton.  "That overlooking Providence which guides the affairs of men has extricated you and me mysteriously from false situations, and made me more of a predestinarian than ever.

"My religious teachers, since I came to this country,

have been the father and the son of the same name, stout Scotch Presbyterians, the Reverends John Mason.

"The younger of these was my youthful companion, and after he took his father's pastorate I made him my confessor. I told him of my fault, and how adventurers had used it to empty my purse and threaten my reputation.

- "He heard me with sorrow and mighty pity ; for I was his idol of public men, and he loved me like Jonathan and Samuel in one.

"He could not sleep nor study after he had heard of my failure and my peril. He could only pray, and pray, and pray ! "

To this point the affable, hardly disturbed voice of the Secretary had reached without a break ; but now something choked it up and the narrative stopped.

The recollection of pious friendship touched the ducts where sensibility must go athirst and overflow those precious fountains. The tears were running down his cheeks, though he kept his silence.

The frail woman saw him crying, and she burst into tears.

"All cannot be evil there," at length said Hamilton, humbly. "If you are weeping for the friend I had disappointed so, and who loved me as a sinner, there are many years for you to recover your better nature in. I recommend you to go also *there*, where pity and religion do their noble offices. But I must be harsh, to cut short your pain."

"Hain't cried so much," rumbled Clingman, with a hard imitation of sympathy, "sence I went to Dunker love feast and eat lamb soup and seen 'em wash feet."

"Mr. Reynolds, it occurred to my young pastor to inquire the names of these parties who were making my conscience and my public duties so grievous. I gave him the names, and it came to him, like the answer of his prayers, to search the marriage registers ; and first he turned to his father's record of couples united by that old man, who had been my friend since I landed in America."

Clingman looked straight at Hamilton ; the female associate looked down. Both waited for what they knew was to follow.

"And there," continued Hamilton, in a lower voice, as

if he would not give evidence, "were the names of Jacob Clingman and Maria Livingston ! Witness, parentage, nativity : all were spread before the son, in the aged handwriting of the parent.

"Do you, who are recorded there, dispute that testimony?" He glanced to the guilty pair.

"No," Jacob Clingman replied, hastily; "we are glad you have come to the pint at last, to the great relief of your'n and her'n truly, J. C. and Mari, his wife."

"Was this before she married me?" young Reynolds faltered.

"It was," said Hamilton; "and in token of her sincerity to make amends I call on Mrs. Clingman to set you free, James Reynolds!"

"Oh, viper with so white a body and so pure a face!" the young man gasped, "what courses have you set me on—what shame have you made me feel! My father's curse, a soldier's ghost, follow you, false harlot, forever!"

"The next thing that will happen to you, Jeems, if you interfere here between lawyers," said Mr. Clingman, "I will drop you down into the aree and reduce to mush our'n no longer, J. R., the softest bilk around the government."

"Oh, peace, peace!" Mrs. Reynolds interposed. "There is one here so much a gentleman that our language, our manners, our very souls, degrade him to be of our company. I shall tell the truth, and let him go forever."

She glanced around as if for something needful. Hamilton read her, and knew it was her mirror.

"The truth!" he prompted. "Throw arts away, madame, and let us be gone."

Thus recalled to the knowledge that she could no longer dupe lawyer or client, Mrs. Reynolds arose and gracefully sank into her husband's late seat, and modulated her voice to a low, musical, almost friendly tone, and told her story :

"For my errors I can plead girlhood and country inexperience down to the moment I was so deeply affected by a great condescension, and then ambition made me unscrupulous."

She inclined her head and eyes down toward Hamilton's feet.

"The formation of the government in the vicinity of my home, the aristocratic province of New York, produced a general restlessness there, and among none more than the good families which the long war had made unthrifty. Our family was mixed Dutch and Connecticut strains, and I had been so spoiled by flattery that I determined to go to the inauguration of Washington, and see what matrimonial prize my beauty would fetch among the statesmen and officials.

"With barely enough money to take me to the city and back and board me upon the packet, I found my entertainment so agreeable that I let my party go home without me ; and my detainer was *that* man."

She raised her eyes submissively to Clingman.

"As our sins have been mutual, I will not charge upon him the whole of my ruin ; for I was idle, fond of men and suppers, of late hours and mid-day rising. He was a doorkeeper at the Federal Hall, where the government assembled—a bold, artful, unsparing, voluptuous man. And so it happened that I had no place to hide my folly, at last, but beneath his name.

"My disappointment was greater than my shame. The hopes I had raised of an influential marriage and the admiration of the noblest circles of the government were wrecked forever.

"He shrewdly followed the current of my thoughts, and offered me liberty and to find a husband for me."

"Vile pander !" exclaimed Reynolds, while Clingman merely glanced at him quizzically, returning to a look of keen admiration at his wife.

"Mr. Reynolds, supposing me single, had long pursued me with his intemperate passion, and when he received a clerkship in the department, through the interposition of his deceased father's fellow officers, Mr. Clingman recommended me to marry him, saying that the moment we moved with the government from New York to another State a divorce would apply.

"I fell again, from a mercenary husband to a tippling one. Mr. Reynolds was unable to support me, and Mr. Clingman gave Reynolds money to assist him in a job against the Treasury, and lost my husband his clerkship.

"You had him discharged, sir," she raised her eyes to Hamilton, "and then I waited upon you, and found in

Hamilton the first man I considered to be my equal who had become a captive to my appearance.

" How could one so much the sport of fortune refuse and resist you, Colonel Hamilton ? "

The chief fiscal officer of the government at last arose and concluded the interview.

" My visit has gained my client his divorce and saved us all publicity, madame. Mr. Reynolds, you observe in your ill-treatment the necessity of our government to give honor and security even to the marriage tie. At provincial boundary lines matrimonial responsibility, the security of debts, the integrity of currency appear to cease in spite of Union and Constitution. They call us Federalists because we are Christians, countrymen and *Americans.*"

" For that false woman, who never loved me," Reynolds spoke, " I have forfeited place, respect, and peace of mind. Oh ! when does the army need me, Colonel Hamilton ? "

" Anon, anon, young friend ; you are getting along very well. I have taken the yoke of evil communication and fraudulent marriage already from your neck. Can you not see—you and this lady also—the artifice of Mr. Clingman ? He has complete control of her, for she has committed the felony called bigamy, and *he* has not. His have been the letters she has copied and sent to me, for the ignorant fellow would not even permit her to correct his spelling—she is *Mari* upon his lips, and *Mari* in that tender correspondence which I have placed in safe hands.

" Before I go," spoke Hamilton with a fuller energy, " let me say that if it ever becomes necessary to avow my folly with the wife of that procurer, in order to cover my official name, I will take the step. I will live under no disguises and be used for no base ends. Not even the confidence of one dearer to me than all but my country and my public name, shall stand between me and confession, if the time ever comes of which I speak. And here I must tell you, James Reynolds, that my pity will not allow me to recommend you to a situation except in the ranks, where all are welcome."

" That is all I ask, Colonel," the young man answered ; " an obscure death and forgetfulness—of her."

5

Hamilton bowed and raised his hat upon his hand, and pointed Reynolds toward the door.

The young man stepped forward like a recruit, and his tread upon the stairs had a soldier's decision.

For a moment the two baffled people of the place stood irresolutely, hearing the descending steps, till Senator Burr glided from the inner chamber and touched Mrs. Clingman.

"Contemptible wretch !" she shouted, flying from his touch. "The fatherless orphan, the persecuted wife your selfish hand never will respect like that gentleman!"

She indicated Colonel Burr's retiring rival, and called upon her husband for protection.

"Come ! come !" roared Clingman. "Hand over the walleble letters now to your'n truly——"

"Oh, no !" replied Aaron Burr with coolness. "They belong to my client there. I intend to keep them."

"Give them up, or I will tear them from you."

As Clingman sprang upon Aaron Burr, the latter stepped back and drew the pistol he had concealed.

"Calmness ! calmness !" sighed Aaron Burr, and crossed the threshold backward, bearing the letters away.

---

## CHAPTER VII.

### THE POLITICAL MOLE.

A WEIGHT had fallen from Hamilton's mind, and he repaired to his house to kiss his wife.

"What bright color you have to-day, my love," Mrs. Hamilton remarked, returning his embrace and resting her head upon his breast. "I know it is your happiness for our dear Phil's recovery. After he was pronounced over the crisis, I slept—but such broken dreams ! There was one, love, I ought not to tell you, but it may turn aside some danger for you."

"Tell me, Eliza, and then you will forget it."

"I dreamed that I had left our first-born hardly a moment when I heard a shot, like a gun or pistol, and I went to him, saying: 'What ails you, Phil?' He was lying beside his cot and he answered me: 'Mamma, pa will have a shot at him.' Then I saw that Phil was bleeding, and it came to me that he was going to die. I called your name : 'Alexander!' and you did not reply. I started in horror from my boy to run and seek you. I thought I saw you and overtook you, and you would not stop. 'My darling,' I cried, 'Phil, our son, is shot all to pieces.' Then you turned—and instead of your face, it was the face of Colonel Burr."

As Hamilton tenderly fondled her he said : " Dreams, dearest, are love's pledges, showing that we are never out of mind, if lost to sight. I have had dreams of you, too —that you forgot me ; that I was a castaway and had shattered my own image in your heart. It was a daydream, love."

" I love you so ! " she repeated in the candor of childhood. " I know you could never forget what is due me and yourself, my father and Washington. We have been married fourteen years ; does it seem so long ? Father regards you as honor's own original, husband. Not all his children have met his expectations, but we have answered his prayers, he says. There, my darling, go talk to him awhile."

With the kiss of raptured faith, the wife turned to her child and the husband to her father, who sat in another room before his own foot, of prodigious size, which rested upon a cushion. He was a tall, slender, swarthy man of sixty, with piercing dark eyes and a voice ringing as a sword.

" General, how is the gout to-day ? "

" The gout ? Don't mind it, sir. Sit down ! I want you to resign from the Cabinet as soon as you have confounded the public enemy, and let you and I build an Erie Canal."

Repairing to his office on the next block, Hamilton saw his hundred clerks at work, glanced at the business on his desk, and felt a passion for holiday.

" That dream of Aaron Burr tallies with my own superstitions," he suddenly thought. " Jefferson is in the city, and I will go find him and see if there are not chords in his nature which will respond to candor and to patriotism. We may be friends."

The streets were full of shoppers, and Hamilton remembered that the Binghams were to give the last party

of the season in a few nights, so he called in to invite
Mr. and Mrs. Joe Priestley to go.

There sat Aaron Burr, serene as one who had been on
the premises all night, pouring compliments into the ears
of both the ladies, and Joe Priestley had gone to Northumberland and the doctor had gone to the Philosophical
Society with Mr. Jefferson.

So Hamilton went to the Philosophical Society building, in the rear of the Supreme Court wing of the State
House, and found a little circle of city savants surrounding the discoverer of Oxygen.

Jefferson went into the Philadelphia Library with
Hamilton, engaged his confidence, and made him the
subject of an *ana*.   Then calling upon Monroe, who was
packing his trunks to go upon the French mission, Jefferson was greeted by his former law student :

" Here is a batch of Hamilton's letters, brought here
by Aaron Burr.   You will see that Hamilton has paid
somebody—a clerk in his department, Burr says—the
amount of eleven hundred dollars, or thereabout, without
equivalent that is mentioned."

Mr. Jefferson's color turned from a flushed purple to
the paleness of one astonished.

He glanced at the receipts for this mysterious money.

" It is his full quarter's salary, and Hamilton is a poor
man," muttered Jefferson.

" Aaron Burr came in here to-day," said Monroe, " and
began to compliment me in almost every way.   He said
that myself and he were soldiers, and that civil politicians
—I think he used the word ' poltroons '—like you and
Madison, hated us.   He wanted to give me a proof of
his confidence.   ' Here,' said he, ' are letters involving
Hamilton's honor, and which he dare not explain.   They
put him between Scylla and Charybdis.   He is my
enemy, but the time is not come to fight him, and in the
mean time I want these letters out of the reach of both
my daughter and the parties affected by them.   Put
them in your trunk and take them to France.' The fellow
supposes that a minister's trunks can carry a library !   I
confide the letters to you, Governor."

Jefferson professed a sense of delicacy, but there was a
look upon the face of the grim Monroe he did not like.

Mr. Jefferson that night opened the packet of letters.

He soon began to stare, then to perspire. He read till evening darkened and candles were brought. When he finished the perusal his spotted hazel eyes were both weary and wanton.

"And this is Alexander the Great, son of Philip Schuyler of Macedon!" breathed Jefferson, tremblingly. "Will the morality of New England sustain him now?"

Jefferson took up his stylus and finished the record in his secret memoranda:

"*Ana.*—Think of planting the carnation cherry at Monticello. *Query*—Do lentils and savoys thrive west of Greenwich, 77°? Quaker cresses and pepper-grass might do well on the Rivanna. The *Brassica Campestris*, or Hamiltonian rape-seed, has just come to market."

At the earliest dawn Mr. Jefferson was posting for Virginia, and as he went along the drums were beating in the Pennsylvania and Maryland villages for recruits to put down the sedition.

## CHAPTER VIII.

### TO THE SUSQUEHANNA.

DOCTOR PRIESTLEY and his son Harry took the mail stage at last for the town of Reading, and with them were Mr. Cooper and wife and a full list of passengers. They preferred this route by the picturesque Schuylkill, rather than the famed new turnpike to Lancaster.

Priestley and Cooper were up with the driver to enjoy the country; Hal, who was growing too fast and suffering from his heart, sat next to the rear seat, which, having a back, was resigned to females.

Upon that seat was a veiled figure of superior attire and reserve to the other women, and Mrs. Cooper especially observed her, as almost too stately for the common stage. There was something mysterious about the stranger, too, like bereavement or grief, expressed by nervousness, and once or twice, when the stage violently struck a hole or a big stone, her sigh was like a sob.

Harry Priestley must needs sit with his back to this

lady, but the image of her dispossessed the scenery from his heart, though he had seen her but an instant.

Grace, stature, possible beauty, make the human scene in a young man's heart more alluring than tillages or large, woody hills, or mirrory vales of falling rivers, and so the Schuylkill Falls and mills Hal hardly saw, or the gorge of Wissahickon with its twenty-five mills.

Higher and higher climbed the stage, through rye and maize, orchards and lime-kilns, by Conestago wagons bowed like the crescent moon, all travelling to or from the unknown, the illusive West ; and still the young man felt the magnetism of that woman only, for he was at the susceptible age when all the fancies run to love and tender sentiment.

This young man was come to the West with natural patriotism, feeling America to be his land.

He revelled in the assurance of hard work to do in it, to fell the trees, to gather the stones, to out-wear by heroism the slow-decaying stumps, to make seed grow and rear a home ; and where did all these visions receive their incentive and point for fulfilment but to a woman, a wife, an everlasting companion down the eternity of youth's horoscope of domestic future.

To him the revealment of America involved a woman, as Eve was predestined in Paradise.

The face and form of Mrs. Reynolds, his interest in her, her injuries and needs, and the rapid burst of love and entreaty made to her in the instant of relieving her, filled Harry Priestley's mind with mist like blowing seed-dust. He sat on clouds, and his ankles and temples seemed to sprout pinions like Euphorian. Who was this other creature of that sex which was to be loved, so close behind him ?

They dismounted at Norris's, a little town of three inns and the county courts, to dine. The mysterious lady untied her veil, and Hal beheld the lady of his passion, Maria Reynolds.

" Ha ! " cried Hal, " what brings thee, madame, from yonder city so far ? "

" Misfortune, dear friend, and, if you will keep my secret, *you*, Harry ! "

" I ? The hope is too good, Mistress Maria. But thou'rt here, and I am happy. Indeed, I felt as I came

westward through the waves that something to love was
waiting for me on the coast. But not great beauty like
to this ! "

" Hush, poor boy ! People are watching us, and only
this I can tell you now, Harry: that, pending proceedings
at law to make me a free woman again, my counsel bade
me withdraw from Philadelphia to the interior of the
State. Entirely unfamiliar with Pennsylvania, I could
think of only one spot and that your destination—Northumberland."

" 'Twas for me—say not nay—thou didst recollect
Northumberland ! In that same spirit thou hast ne'er
been from my mind one hour. Fate draws us together.
I shall feel thy spirit in my axe, and the falling trees will
shout thy name. What care we for any other world, if
love be there ? And here, as my oath of new allegiance,
I swear to love thy land for thee, and thee forever ! "

Mrs. Cooper came by and whispered to the pair the
assuring word :

" Sweethearts."

Priestley and Cooper regarded the lady's journey as a
mere incident of the country, and were glad of company.
But the young man saw everything to be beautiful and
animated now.

His first passion was reciprocated and in the manner
of old romance, with beauty and sadness descending from
high station to need him and to bless him.

A sense of sudden growth and responsibility came to
Harry Priestley, and he consciously grew old ; how long
would it be before these meridian charms should be his
own, and no man besides dare demand reckoning of her
—the deceived, the glorious one, whom he, like Perseus,
should unbind and bear away?

Maria Livingston felt correspondingly relieved and
child-like as she discerned the complete passion of this
boy.

Her sense of preserved charms and mental serenity
was flattered ; her intellect was not profound enough to
accuse her conscience, and in the zephyr breath of the
tender present she dismissed the past without a care and
floated above the realities of to-morrow.

The elevated scenery swelled her bosom, that she had
already ordained to rest the young man's head when

evening should throw its shades around their journey, and she felt the power of woman and experience upon the boy's soul, and rejoiced in their exercise and conquest without evil or designing.

Maria was one of those women who, being socially disappointed, have too much self-admiration to be cast down.

Bad treatment had taught her management and slightly inclined her toward dangerous acting ; but she was too indolent to act much or be very deep, yet felt a presentiment that under Clingman's encouragement she might become incapable of good motives, and therefore had fled from him.

At present she was indulging with all her amiable languor the fragrant girlhood of a boy's maiden passion. She heard his whisper with compassion :

"Why are all the lasses here so sweet-voiced? Is it from the clear, gray air that makes one see so far? They are so gentle, too—not distant, like the lofty dames in *old* England. Thou art the first, the posy of them all. Some are but half-bloomed, some are bloomed away ; but thou art the same, and shall be always the same to me, Flower of the Americans ! "

Thoroughly frightened by Hamilton's authoritative presentment of her duplicity and bigamy, Maria had for the moment dropped an ambitious hope she once entertained of controlling him through his warm Scotch nature ; for, in spite of any continuity of purpose, Maria believed that she had only to want anything to make it come to her.

Harshly deceived in Hamilton's case, uneasy in the city, and made in other directions the sport of fortune, she had fled, under the terror of yesterday's occurrences, with the dream rather than the design of pursuing her light romance with Harry Priestley; and now the spirit of financial honesty caused her to establish, without any sinister meaning, her full character in the Priestley family.

. They had come to a German village at the roadside, and rested in sight of the limpid Schuylkill and its strong creeks, when, walking by the waters in the low afternoon light, Maria placed in Harry's hand a pocket-book.

"There, Hal, the wallet contains your initials, worked by me, and all the money you discharged my debt with."

She colored a little at the extent of the sacrifice, for she had been reckless in her honesty.

"Generous girl!" cried Harry. "I felt that I had trusted well. This will make mother glad, for I told mother, who has been my sweetheart till now."

"And keep her so, dear friend! Oh! what affection is like mother's, that revolts at no error and believes we shall all see God with her——"

The detached member of the mother sex here gave way to memory and tears.

The dropping out of passengers left the rear seat to Harry Priestley and his lady, and the sympathetic Mrs. Cooper, who followed her opinionated husband in all his crotchets.

The youth felt the shadows of the increasing hills and heard the rush of waters with the sense of blessedness.

Her head was upon his shoulder, and to him it seemed the head of modesty in the halo of mighty sorrows. From his inexperience, as the youngest son and mother's pet, he appreciated the informality of her condescension to be gratitude, and the buffeting of a wicked world.

Whatever the moral or social difference in the thoughts of the youth and the woman, that gliding antetype of the death which levels and lodges us all at last—innocent sleep—came down upon the lovers and bathed them in the music of woods and the light of stars.

Next day they were passing through the South Mountain into the great eastern valley between the Alleghanies and the plains, and the town of Reading, with its 2,500 German people, faced up to them like a red plate on a green table-cloth.

It was now eighty miles farther to Northumberland, the place selected for Doctor Priestley's American home, and the road was to be across wild mountains, with none of the conveniences of civilization; so Priestley inclined to take the Bethlehem stage, which passed twice a week, to Lancaster, and then to ascend the valley of the Susquehanna to his future abode.

The doctor found that his son was disposed to go to Northumberland direct, across the North or Blue Mountain, and, making allowance for the pleasures of female society, concealed his disappointment that for the first

time his last-born could find better company than his
father's.

The infinitely repeated *duetto* of love, therefore, had
with Harry and his lady two days and nights to mingle
with the general Orchestra of nature—nature that did
not care whether Oxygen was known to man or not, so
men did not die out while Oxygen could make them
love.

For sixty miles they were upon wild mountains or in
their rugged interstices, seeing little but new clearings
and log taverns and mills and log houses ; yet to Harry,
at least, the rough journey was too short, and woman
can take the roughest journey well in tender passion or
in compassion.

At last there opened in the mountains a wide aisle of
silver light, reflecting gray-blue ridges with manes of
olive-hued woods, and a sound burst from the young
man's lips of—

" Susquehanna !  We are almost Home."

They saw a little town on the river's bank, in a great
meadow between waves of ridge :

" Sunbury ! " said the driver.  " The place just beyant,
where the big river forks, like sugar-tongs, is Narthum-
berland."

" There, my darling," the young pilgrim whispered—
" there is the end of my journey ; there we shall live and
die."

" O Hal ! my poor, artless lover," the lady answered ;
" I may live there, but I fear I cannot die there."

Doctor Priestley also gratefully pursued his journey
to the banks of the broad river, which parted the new
world from the wilderness.

He went along its shores through the North Mountain and the Mahanoy Ridge, marvelling how exten-
sively the hand of God had ranged upon this illimitable
land.

He saw at Sunbury where late had stood the Iroquois
post, whence New York governed all the aboriginals of
Pennsylvania from the sources of the Susquehanna.

Now a rude little town of logs had commenced to take
life and association, and govern in a single shire, or
county, one-third of the Pennsylvania State.  And the
name of that mighty county was the name of his home

between the silver shafts of the great river's antlers—
Northumberland !

There Priestley sat down to build his home and feed
the divine light with the oil of love.

Near by, his son Hal was clearing a farm, animated
by the light of that human love which was to people the
wilderness.

———

## CHAPTER IX.

### BINGHAM'S SUMMER PARTY.

WHEN Bingham's great party was given, Colonel Burr
attended Mrs. Lizzie Priestley to the Bingham mansion.

It was only a square from Hamilton's residence, on
Third Street, and presented the first great city house of
the era of the Republic.

The proprietor had brought plans, furniture, and, to
some extent, social-ideas from Europe ; his house was
the extended model of a London duke's and the centre
of foreign and financiering society in America.

Mrs. Priestley, of plain wool-spinners' and dissenters'
society, felt the impending riches of America in this,
their first thorough realization, as she surveyed the great
square Bingham mansion with its stone panels and belt
courses, architectural wings and conservatories, wooded
lawn of several acres, and carriage *parterre* with double
gates, flaming lamps, and imported valets in silk stockings, and saw the moving coaches and the lighted apartments, and heard the blare of music.

"Is all this great square one family's ? " she asked of
Senator Burr.

" Not one household, but one connection.  The Pow-
ells and Byrds, to whom Mrs. Bingham is niece, adjoin,
and her father, Mr. Willing, lives next door.  They built
together, and constitute a family Belgravia."

The mansion was upon the English-basement plan,
low to the ground ; and stepping within, an expanse of
tesselated marble threw up the graceful wave of an
Italian-marble stairway, which leaned upon the air ; par-
lors were at the left, full of gay society ; on the right
were an elegant study and a library, separated by a hall,

and at the end cloak-rooms, from which Lizzie Priestley emerged to hear the cry sounded up the stairway and repeated there :

"Colonel Burr and Mrs. Joseph Priestley ! "

Burr was almost the only actor there in public life, and the original American tuft-hunter, quickest to lay hold of strangers of distinction and be gazetted with them. As he went up to the drawing-room with Lizzie Priestley, his small figure was expanded and his suavity chilled into a military consciousness.

The hosts and their assistants heard the name of Joseph Priestley with curiosity, and supposed it to be the philosopher's wife.

They saw, instead, a fair, girlish creature, with silken curls and large gray eyes, and a manner sweet, observing, and wholly unaffected by this social greatness, upon which she appeared as a looker and not an aspirant.

"I am sure you are welcome to the United States," said Mrs. Bingham after Lizzie was presented. "But why do you go so far from us to dwell ? "

The speaker was the most beautiful woman Lizzie had ever seen or dreamed of—above the size and height of most other attractive women, with arms and hands of faultless mould, flexibility and ease being governed by deliberation ; and every movement of her body or eyes was the graceful fruit of a thought.

Her hair was powdered and pushed away in skeins from a skin as white as perfect health could allow ; her breast and forearms were bare and beautiful. She wore no jewelry but a bracelet of pearls, and her dress seemed also of pearl and to flow like the waves.

In her countenance were the archness of nature and the composure of breeding. If there was something worldly in this exquisite face, it was the worldliness of a queen.

"We consult papa's taste," answered Lizzie Priestley; "where he can be happy we shall be, too."

"Oh ! that is the spirit which makes all lands glad," said Mrs. Bingham. "You are Doctor Priestley's daughter, then ? You love your husband, and he loves his father. That is all we need anywhere. Let me make you known to my father, Mr. Willing, and to Mr. Morris, his partner."

The husband of this fine lady had the lines of a Quaker, yet the wine color of a high liver. Her father was a solid, unattractive man, also wigged and powdered, but otherwise a true son of the Penns.

Senator Robert Morris, his partner, was a likeness of Doctor Franklin electrified—more English than American, with somewhat baldish head, florid square face, large throat, and of the over-fattened eagle type, where sedentary merchant habits inclosed a mind that was like a wing, and floated above times or darted into gulfs with decision.

" We sold your husband good land," said Mr. Willing, "but I wish he had gone farther, if he would go so far, and taken a part of our tract in Western New York."

" Yes," said Morris, " that region has cataracts to sound its praises. It ought to be the seat of empire. The climate is more energizing there than Pennsylvania, and the prospects not so narrow."

" I should think this might be the seat of empire," answered Lizzie, quietly glancing around at the infinitely repeating mirrors, Italian paintings, and luscious-pattern carpets, the painted ceilings, soft lights of candelabra, and easy, sensuous Philadelphia beauty.

" This might also be, my gentle friend, the seat of care and apprehension," said Robert Morris. " I almost envy your father, Priestley, his capacity to draw reality from bubbles, or my friend Hamilton, here, the love of the science of finance without its avarice."

He presented Hamilton, who had just come up with Mrs. Adams.

" O Mr. Morris ! " corrected Hamilton, "if the imputation of avarice can come upon your fame, vindication will be cruel rather than let it stay. You fed us when we were hungry and our little credit gone. General Washington borrowed from you when you had nothing, for your faith was like Moses', and you could smite rocks and make them flow."

" Doesn't he talk beautifully ? " cried Morris, turning Hamilton's face toward Lizzie Priestley.

Aaron Burr glanced at Mrs. Priestley's face. It was beaming as toward a lover's.

This was Colonel Burr's construction of it, and he thought he knew women, if anything.

"There is everything in the talker being honest and true," the Englishwoman declared, still looking with admiration upon Hamilton.

"Don't spoil our Secretary," Mrs. Bingham archly added. "Everybody falls in love with him, *even a Mrs. Reynolds.*"

Hamilton's face became flushed. He was looking at Mrs. Priestley as this word, mentioned for the first time in elegant society, rebuked the praise of his honesty and truth.

"Mrs. Bingham is not herself to-night," answered the Secretary with an attempt to smile, but it was more like anger.

"Ha! Hamilton," Mr. Bingham queried, with his mixture of enjoyment and deportment, "I hope our Philadelphia beauties have not been too much for your good Scotch principles?"

There was a twinkle in Mr. Bingham's eye as if he rather hoped Hamilton had been fond and weak.

It might have been mischief or pique at his reproof which caused Mrs. Bingham to perceive Hamilton's temper and press the subject:

"It is not a Philadelphia beauty, Mr. Bingham, but a New York one. So my cousin, Mary Livingston, tells me. It seems that the lady in question is of the Livingston connection distantly. Well, good blood will tell, if not in prosperity, then in beauty; and I have noticed quite a striking lady in the streets, and find that her husband was in Colonel Hamilton's department. She mentioned Colonel Hamilton as her greatest friend to Cousin Walter Livingston."

The fact that Mrs. Adams was upon his arm, a prim subject to interpret the matter in hand, made this running satire the worse for Hamilton.

He had only come to the party upon official pressure and for personal relief, and here, at the threshold of the drawing-room, the so-recent degrading scene in the attic of "His'n truly, J. Clingman," was revived and freshened.

"*Secretary Randolph and Mrs. Randolph!*" was the next announcement from the hall, repeated at the head of the stair.

The Secretary of State, in his grandee manner and

perfect recovery of spirits, appeared with the married daughter of Mr. Jefferson.

Martha Randolph looked the perfection of family loveliness, as Mrs. Bingham that of society.

As the Randolphs were disengaged Martha exclaimed: " Now, Cousin Ned, you wanted to finish that controversy with Mrs. Adams, and here she is. It is my last chance to meet Colonel Hamilton before he leaves the government. Come, Hamilton, and give me your arm."

Relieved by this kind and attractive spirit, Hamilton's troubled face came forth in roses, but he noticed that Aaron Burr had been an interested witness of the scene over Mrs. Reynolds.

" You want to know what are these rich people," said Burr to Lizzie Priestley, as they promenaded. " Well, then, Mrs. Bingham is that old merchant Willing's daughter, with the added character of a brilliant and beautiful Irish mother. At sixteen she married Bingham, the richest single man in the United States. Four generations of thrifty Quakers, commencing with a blacksmith, concentrate their property upon that happy man, and beauty yielded to his golden shower."

" But they love each other ? "

" Unquestionably. Elegant creatures like that, married before the mind wanders, in the very dew of childhood, are loyal wives. He has filled her mind with family ambition. During the war he was in the West Indies, . an alternate British and American consul, multiplying money and cultivating English society. He came home to marry in the best official life, so that the blacksmith's anvil would not be heard to ring in his family shield. His exquisite girl-wife is a Penn, a Livingston, a McCall, a Willing; the best, in connection, Bingham could get. Thus fortified by beauty, virtue, youth, and family, he carried her abroad for years till she learned the etiquette of courts and he the leading-strings of finance. Then back to this rich land to keep at the top, socially and in fortune. He means to marry their posterity to bankers and nobility abroad."

" You speak of all this, Colonel Burr, as if there was something criminal about it. Should not your beautiful Americans, the heirs of great fortunes, be equal to the

best alliances ?   You would not have them marry only in
the second and third class of foreigners ? "

" Not I," answered Colonel Burr, looking around before he spoke, and speaking low.   " My daughter shall
have a throne if I can get it for her."

The night was warm, and Hamilton felt oppressed by
the extended recognition of his acquaintance with Mrs.
Reynolds.

As he led Mrs. Randolph to a cool seat in the arborage
of the Bingham park, he sat by her, more and more unhappy, while she chatted with a free heart, for she had
not a grain of subtlety or deceit in her nature.

Wit, sparkle, warmth, joy were attributes of Jefferson's
daughter in her twenty-third year, and the source of them
was courage, the want of which had chilled her father's
manner in spite of effusiveness and protestation.

The sorrows of the shy, in this case, became the dis-
trustfulness of a nation, through Jefferson's literary skill
and intercourse. He had the ideality and panic of Rousseau, passionate sentiments, cold methods, love of man
in the abstract, unjust and silly dislikes.   But his daughter was rich with young maternal loves and friendship's
ardor.

" Dear friend," breathed Martha Randolph, " you are
not playful to-night.   I do not like it.   There never was
a man who could throw off official care like Hamilton.
You and father have met again and had a friendly talk.
What can ail you ? "

" Little Patsey," said Hamilton, "except the pang of
dying, young, I think every pang begins in a violated
commandment."

"You should not violate commandments, Phocion.
I cannot conceive you breaking any commandment, unless it might be coveting your neighbor's horse."

" Or his wife ? "

" Oh, no !  You are too precise for that.  Even as you
say it, there is a queer tone of bitterness, which is little
like gallantry, Phocion.   I think you are suffering from
the spitefulness of so many people since you criticised
the French Revolution.   Now, as an almost unfilial secret,
I commend your good sense.   Such things as I saw in
Paris—let us not think of them.   The coming of that
great bloody snake for his human meal out of the slimy,

reeking *faubourgs*, day after day, was like reading some
awful book of what could not be true."

"I wish to be liked," said Hamilton, "but I can wait
till people like me. It is like children crying and raging
at their mother ; she does not take it to heart. Are you
very happy ?"

"Oh, yes! I married for nothing but love. My husband is perfectly representative of the young gentlemen
of fortune in Virginia, honorable, impulsive, not too well
employed, noble, and unbroken. I am finding that I have
in him both my lover and my child."

"Then you could forgive him even the greatest injury ?"

"Of course. He would not be responsible like you,
for example, who seem to have been born perfect. And
yet, I sometimes think of you, Hamilton, and wish that
the beautiful government of your passions and inclinations could be general among husbands. Our slaves
supersede methodized life too much. I watch the families of the birds and the domestic animals, and they have
no servants."

"Strange," said Hamilton with a groan, "that woman
is expected to forgive man where he, with all his philosophy, is unable to forgive her."

"Not strange, sir. The compensation of the children
the husband does not have. They are mightier ties than
love itself ; they dwell with the mother like gratitude,
that speaks and loves. For him, their father, they are
pleading advocates and ceaseless sentinels of his honor.
If his love is withdrawn, they supply his love to his
wife. He may wander and forget himself, because the
offspring does not go with him. By that dear offspring
the wife is always the richer of the pair, and she can
lend forgiveness."

"Little Patsey, you are a Christian."

"Why not? You say that woman is never forgiven
for her greatest error by man. Do you not remember,
Hamilton, that exception which for nearly eighteen hundred years has comforted and lifted up thousands and
tens of thousands of our sex and made the name of Mary
twice as dear to every woman? Not the Mary who
could not sin, but the other Mary whom the First Gentleman forgave."

6

" Wonderful proof of Christianity's sway," exclaimed
Hamilton, " that to-night such an incident is remembered !
But has it ever been repeated ? "

" If never, that condescension of the highest and the
holiest is still woman's example, fresh with every generation.  Our greatest happiness is to forgive man."

" I know you will always forgive me, plenteous soul,
whose name was drawn from Mary's sister ! "

" Believe me, with my life happy as it is," said Martha
Randolph, " if I could lay it down to have you and my
father love each other and descend to fame together, I
would die."

Hamilton raised her with his hand and felt a happy
thrill go through him from her palms.

" The architects may quarrel," said he, " but our house
is built for such mothers and their children, and it will
last."

Secretary Randolph, coming by, carried his cousin off
and left Mrs. Adams with Hamilton.

" There is no time like the present to put in a thrifty
word," said Mrs. Adams.  " You and I have been friends,
and you and John Adams have the same political sentiments.  What is your objection to his succeeding General
Washington in the presidency ? "

" Have I objected ? "

" He thinks you are against him.  I suppose Jefferson,
or some of these lovers of government by detraction,
told him so.  Now, Colonel Hamilton, I have got only
one political principle——"

" And that is a certain John Adams ? "

" Just that.  He is full of ability and without an
ounce of management.  I have put my life at his service, and as he will be forever unhappy without the
presidency, therefore I come to you confidently, for I
never knew you, like some people, to put everything
down that is said, and try to lay history by the heels."

" Institutions are the true history of the Federalists,
Mrs. Adams.  That is why I hesitate to support your
husband for Washington's office.  Suppose he should
fail, after such a man !  Would he be any happier ?  And
my fear is that his self-esteem would some day become
our Constitution and laws, and the times of Washington
be confused with the eccentricities of Mr. Adams."

"Perfectly frank! But I would be there, also. So would you; so would Washington. We are not all going to die, probably, in six years. Would you rather have it Adams or Jefferson?"

"Hard question, dear madame. Understand me to appreciate your wife-like devotion. If you were John Adams, we would elect you."

"I *am* John Adams, and that is partly why you will give your consent; for I must go to Jefferson if you refuse me, and I really regard you much, in spite of your French composition and great imagination. That artist quality which makes you project governments, as Calvin projected churches, is to your injury in some minds. These think you ought to have grown with more regard to habits and precedence. But I can see, in spite of my New England principles, how here and there an extraordinary man can produce himself."

"Precedence in a brand-new republic! Fie! With whom can you have been talking, Mrs. Adams?"

"Clairvoyant! I will not tarry to let you read me. Hamilton, if you separate from my husband you will make me his partisan, and I may have to join Jefferson. Jefferson will have no friend who is yours. On that subject he is nearly a monomaniac."

"Then, not to be blamed if his reason be disturbed, if Mr. Adams can forget himself in his office, and serve his second term in his first, imitating Washington in everything but the double term, he can bequeath his office to the friends of Washington, and I shall not be in his way."

She clasped both his hands and drew him away. Toward the mansion they met Willing and Morris, the late partners, and the former became Mrs. Adams' escort, while Morris, returning to the arbored tree with Hamilton, sat down to say:

"I would like society better if my mind was not in the wilderness where my lands are."

"How much have you now in the Genesee country?"

"Over a million acres."

"How much in the Massachusetts-New York Company?"

"Quite four million acres."

"In the Pennsylvania Property Company?"

84

84 MRS. REYNOLDS AND HAMILTON.84

"Ten thousand shares."

"In the Asylum Susquehanna Company?"

"Two millions."

"And the North American Land Company?"

"There are six million acres in the whole of it."

"How many Washington City lots?"

"Six thousand are in our coalition."

Morris heaved a sigh.

"I am not yet troubled by my lands, but last year I lost one hundred and twenty thousand pounds *money* in Dublin and Bristol. I took so much real estate to get that back, but the land sells slowly. Now, Bingham, and my partner since boyhood, Willing, dissolve from me. The new bank here is trying to break my credit. Can't you help me?"

"I have got five hundred dollars. Take it all. I can send my wife to Saratoga with her father and go out against the Insurrection myself."

Robert Morris laughed:

"Colonel, your five hundred dollars would be like a rush-light to make my Aladdin's cave of obligations shockingly visible. No; I want to give you money and to make you our land-agent in Europe in place of Temple Franklin. You are on the eve of retiring and are poor, but your reputation is great. No man could magnetize the foreign money market like Alexander Hamilton. Your commission will be a fortune."

"Morris, this is not *your* proposition?"

"No; I told Bingham, Nicholson, Greenleaf, and the rest that you wouldn't hear of it. The voice of my necessity brings you the message, but I advise you not to accept it."

"O my friend! the plaintive wail of that necessity will reach through all our history, for there is no fame like a great man's sorrows."

"I have always carried a load," said Morris, reflectively. "I shall carry it to my grave—or my prison cell. I would rather have it my grave."

"My personal credit I would take the risk of, if I believed it would redeem you; for I am not Levite enough to go by on the other side and leave you wounded—you, who named me to Washington for his financial secretary when I was poor, youthful, and obscure! But it is American reputation I should lose—the honor of Washington's companion. They abroad would say we had no character, and huckstered our virtue in the very honeymoon of official credit. A little while I might make money for you, but at last I should not be esteemed enough to be your friend and shed my tears with you."

"I will not have you make that mistake. Not to make you rich ! There is Aaron Burr, who solicits the situation. He is loaded up with our lands now ; we are carrying him. Indeed, he sold us the New York lands, as one of the commissioners. But even a penny an acre is dear if you buy the globe."

" I shall go to the law at once," said Hamilton. " Nothing but the defence of the country shall take me from it. My passion is for arms ; my duty must be the law."

" By the way, what did you want with that parcel of papers you left at the shipping-house, Hamilton ? "

" The private papers I left with you so long ago ? I never sent for them."

" Yes, you did. A Mrs. Reynolds came and described them, and flirted with Bingham, and carried them off."

" Retributive Heaven ! Morris, my honor is gone already."

He sat upon the bench, and his abstracted senior was gone.

" Oh ! let me haste," thought Hamilton, "to leave this capital. But no, I will never run away."

He placed his face in his hands and tried to think. Nothing would come to his mind but the verse of Robert Burns, so lately reprinted in the States. He repeated it aloud :

> " The sacred lowe o' weel-placed love,
>    Luxuriantly indulge it ;
> But never tempt th' illicit rove,
>    Though naething should divulge it :
> I waive the quantum o' the sin,
>    The hazard of concealing ;
> But, och ! it hardens a' within,
>    And petrifies the feeling ! "

A woman heard him and stopped.   .

She looked at the graceful figure with arms raised to his eyes, and paused because she pitied.

He looked up and recognized Lizzie Priestley.

" Did you hear me, too ? "

" I did, Colonel Hamilton."

" Could you understand the poetry ? "

" I think I can when I remember a scene the Sunday after we arrived in Pennsylvania. That fine-looking woman has probably some hold upon you. I thought so at first ; your conduct, also, at the reading of the Bible lesson made me feel for you. I wish to speak to you like a woman and a friend."

" No," said Hamilton; " I cannot let a pure woman share a disgraceful secret."

" It is not a secret to me. I felt a deep sensibility and friendship for you the day we met, and to share your repentance can be no stain. Go to your wife.! Make her the sharer of this secret, too ! Then everything will be passed in ˉone hour of anguish and you will be free."

" 'St ! *Prenez garde !* " lisped Hamilton, " my wife is here. Let me present her."

Mrs. Hamilton looked disturbed, and her mettlesome little figure trembled.

" Sir," she said, " I merely paused at the gate to have you take me home. Have I disturbed a confidential talk ? "

The wife's escort to the spot was Aaron Burr.

---

## CHAPTER X.

### HAL AND MARIA.

"STRANGE, my dear," said Doctor Priestley to his wife, " that of all the English liberals who raved about the Susquehanna—Coleridge, Campbell, Lloyd, Wordsworth—I am the only one to come here. What do you think of our Northumberland ? "

" It will do, Joe. Nothing can surpass the rivers which meet at our door, nature's looking-glasses ; and the big hill across there to the west stands like a buffalo, such as, they say, roamed here since we were born. As for the Indians, I seem to see them every time an ark or raft floats on the rivers."

"They passed away, Mary, hardly ten years ago, and now the Indians have no homes in Pennsylvania."

"Thank Heaven, then, that we are out of wars and conflicts. I do hope, my dear husband, that you will let all politics and controversy alone. Beware of the eager, interfering spirit of Thomas Cooper!"

" Here he is, Mary. Now, Thomas, how have you settled yourself ? "

" I tried Sunbury, but it was too far from you and Mary. So here I am, a member of the Northumberland bar, right at your side. To-day the Jeffersonians are to raise a liberty-pole and defy Hamilton, and, no doubt, there will be fighting, and some clients for me. I am against the government; so are you."

"Against the government? Again?" called Mrs. Priestley, with a pale face. "For whom can you be?"

"For the resistants, of course."

"Do you mean *rioters?* Thomas, it was the government that paid us for our property destroyed at Birmingham. Even that government was better than none. It acknowledged a responsibility, though my husband and you had been against it."

"Oh! put on your hat, Mother Priestley, and come out and see the frontiersmen, your fellow-citizens. The town is filling up."

They left the large log house where they were stopping and descended a hilly lane to the banks of the beautiful river, upon the green, natural turf of which was the excavation for Doctor Priestley's mansion, and the framework and other building material lay copiously around. But the laborers were gone to lose their time in the political affray, and poor Doctor Priestley, who had hoped to get in his house by spring, made a loud—

"Tut ! tut ! tut ! "

Lizzie Priestley and Mrs. Reynolds were seated on the building material, looking at a large green island, over which barely peeped the hamlet of Sunbury, and the wide meadow or delta between the mountains on the other side.

Fall birds were making melody everywhere ; willows drooped greenly to the current, intermixed with crimson and lemon-colored arborage ; the large stream went onward with a full sound like ocean waves under a ship, and where it joined a greater river, just beyond, their united width seemed to be a mile.

Little Northumberland town, of which the Priestleys had heard so much, occupied the terrace between these two mighty streams, which here were still a hundred miles above a tide, and three hundred miles inland from the sea ; and yet these antlers of the Susquehanna, forming the united stream, came each from two hundred to three hundred miles farther up and rose three hundred miles apart.

The Susquehanna drained twice more land than Egypt.

The Priestleys expected that this river would be improved and carry the products of all inland America speedily past their door ; all Western New York, all between the lakes and New Orleans. Hence they had selected their home.

Alas ! Governor Mifflin was giving his eleven years of rule not to navigation but to politics, and the New-Yorkers tapped the Susquehanna at the head and took all the trade off to the Hudson. When Priestley went to the Susquehanna two thousand arks of grain a year passed his door ; soon after he died the commerce of the stream was as dead as the Indians.

"What a joy to a poor old woman," spoke Mary Priestley through her tears, "to anticipate my rest and my grave in this delightful, illimitable vale, where the spirits of so many waters shall flow past me and the kindredship of a gentle people shall respect my husband's name ! O Joe ! feel the breath of this golden air, and thank the Lord who mixed it for us in the cup of such skies and streams."

" It is a little larger, Mary, than the Vale of Llangollen, where you took me. My apprehensions are all passed since you and the children are not disappointed."

Mr. Cooper called them all away to go up into the town and see the Liberty-pole.

They ascended the slope from the water and found the humble homes of Northumberland agitated with the first real occurrence in its brief history.

Everybody was either moving toward the market space or looking from the low doors toward it, while boisterous children ran back to give the news. Much of the population was English, not long moved to the country, and these in general stood back, as did the later German villagers.

But when the Priestley party came to the widening in the market street they beheld a hundred men or more around a forest pole, dancing, drinking of free liquor, brandishing staves, and striking the pole in procession around it, meantime uttering whoops like Indians.

The pole was seen, on nearer inspection, to be driven full of nails, so that no person could climb it to cut down the flag which waved from its top and plainly showed the words :

**"LIBERTY AND NO EXCISE."**

Just as the philosopher's group drew near there appeared a singular commotion at the corner where this pole was being guarded, and all the boisterous people there faced away from the Priestleys and gave their curiosity to two strong, hale old men, who advanced down the green and brought between them a rather reluctant yet frightened citizen. To these the crowd around the pole advanced threateningly, yelling, cursing, pointing to the flag, and it was manifest, both from their countenances and actions, that they were nearly all Irish-bred people.

" Advance, you cowardly and false magistrate ! " called one of these old men to the person they had fetched along. " Order that standard of rebellion to be pulled down !."

" Gentlemen, I can't resist the people," answered the magistrate or justice of the peace. " The people is sovereigns and they put up the pole. Jedge Wilson, excuse me. Jedge MacPherson, don't scrouge the Freemen of Northumberlin ! "

" Three cheers for Dan Montgomery an' no excise ! " came from the crowd, and they formed around the two determined old men as the loud yells ceased, intent to frighten them or to do them bodily harm.

" What is that thing the man behind Judge Wilson is raising ? " exclaimed Mrs. Priestley.

" That ? " answered Mr. Cooper, looking. " Why that's an Indian tomahawk."

As they looked, the braggart or drunkard who held the

hatchet-thing aloft and wore a big fur cap, was set upon
by a stout boy in corduroy clothes, who raised both
doubled hands and by fair blows knocked the fellow
down.

At least three female screams came from the Priestley party, for all had recognized in the defender of his
country's judges young Harry, the baby of the family.

Harry Priestley was down in a moment and a savage
and intoxicated crowd was tumbling upon him. But
when his parents thought him dead he was seen to come
up and to be fighting yet, taking advantage of no weapon,
laying on with honest hands and scattering the wildly
attired assailants from him by skilful blows and cool
selection.

"Down with the dirty Buckskins! Down with the
drunkards and rebels!" came voices from the respectable
edges of the crowd, and the battle widened till it seemed
that half the population would be found murdered, at
least. The Priestleys were afraid to retire while their son
was surrounded, and were yet amazed to stay.

Many of the trespassers wore remnants of Indian or
forest dress—moccasins, fringed breeches of deer-hide,
hunting shirts, caps of skin. In the *mêlée* the naked feet,
hips, or backs of these wild runners of the woods were
often seen flashing in the air, as they leaped or rebounded,
or were thrown violently up.

A kennel of dogs fighting over a few bones would have
made no less and no more gnashing, clinching of teeth,
yelling, and somersaulting.

At last the combat seemed to end by general exhaustion
on both sides, and the two parties retired from each other
and left, in the space between, the two old judges of that
vast frontier County, which reached from the Blue Mountains to Lake Erie.

As Harry Priestley limped back to the place where his
family were grouped, the judge he had protected drew a
paper from his pocket and advanced toward the flag-pole,
supported only by the other judge, MacPherson.

Both of these men were of serious and authoritative
bearing, more military looking than judicial, and yet so
manifestly superior to the bandit crew they confronted
that some of these drew back and slunk downward,
whilst whiskey was rapidly and unlimitedly drawn from

a barrel at the base of the flag-pole to refresh the rioters and keep their refractory spirits up.

"Hear the reading of the riot act!" exclaimed the · senior judge. "There may be some of you too ignorant to understand your duty."

He read an order of his court, or the State, to suppress disorder; but active emissaries of some mysterious power —whether that of politics or alcoholic commerce was not clear—kept plying the whiskey, hallooing, sneering, and making interruptions, so that few could hear or tried to do so. ·

"Now," spoke the judge, as he took off his spectacles and put them in a leather case, "here stand two men, Judge MacPherson and myself, who were in the Revolutionary line, protecting the liberties of our country, when such as you, who would insult us if you could, were boiling whiskey in the mountains—you and your fathers— to sell it to the quartermasters for our army rations."

"Down with the old fool! Crack his skull!" came voices from around the whiskey barrel, as their breathed and re-stimulated instruments moved forward again.

"I tell you," cried the old man, "that we are still the soldiers of our old general, against whose proclamation that pole and that flag of treason have been raised. It shall come down! Your justice of the peace has played the varlet to this day's disloyalty, but there is a law, also, for him."

A musket, handed from back in the crowd to a desperate-looking fellow, was pointed directly at Judge Wilson as he marked the derelict borough squire with his finger.

"Down with him! Kill him!" cried a hundred cowardly voices.

The judge, turning his head from the local justice of the peace, looked with the greatest coolness and contempt a moment into the barrel of the flint-lock musket, though the assassin's finger was on the trigger.

Then he drew from the pocket of his large coat-skirt a mighty pistol, that seemed big as the spirit of giant courage in his eye, and cocked it and extended it without taking his glance from the tall' Celt before him.

"Put that musket down, or I'll blow your brains out," quietly said the judge.

The fellow dropped his musket in the ecstasy of fear.

For a moment there was a pause, and then voices cried :

" Jedge Wilson's broke the law. He's pulled a gun on a feller-citizen."

" Arrest Jedge Wilson ! Arrest him, Dan Montgomery !" shouted the multitude.

Again that pliable local demagogue, the justice of the peace, shrank before the crowd and smiled at them.

" Jedge Wilson," fawned he, " the law ag'in pulling a firearm on a feller-citizen is well known to you.' Sir, I take you in custody for wiolation of a law."

" I stand committed," said the judge. " I forgot myself in the presence of scoundrels like these and thought I was a soldier again."

" To jail with him ! To Sunberry jail !" howled these Jacobins of the woods, little different from the Jacobins of Paris but yesterday.

" To jail with me, Montgomery ?" replied the veteran. " I defy you !"

" I reckon I must have bail, then, Jedge Wilson. The offence, I reckon, is bailable."

" Mr. Justice," said Doctor Priestley, coming forward, "I desire to see no evil happen this day among my townspeople. Let me take Judge Wilson to my lodgings and be responsible for him."

" Oh! shorely, shorely, Doctor Priestley. You will be quite sufficient security, I reckon," cried the shuffling justice.

" Come, gentlemen, and dine with me," the doctor said to the judges. " You are not able to deal with these persons, and you have discharged your duties faithfully."

The old judge was much excited by the use the rioters had made of him, inflaming him to courage and then arresting him as a statute-breaker. He bowed his head and moved away, while, to the tune of a pair of fiddles, the disturbers danced a kind of savage *carmagnole* around the liberty-pole of Northumberland.

" Let them dance," spoke the other judge. " Mind them not, brother Wilson. The spirit of Washington and Hamilton is on the way and will soon be here."

" Now, father," cried Mrs. Priestley, when they had reached Priestley's lodging, "brew thee one of Doctor

Franklin's punches for these gentlemen and for poor Hal
here, who has barely come out with his life."

" Let me do that," interposed Mr. Cooper.

He gave them some hot water out of a strange apparatus in the room, and from another cistern in the same
thing supplied spirits.

" Judge Wilson," said Judge MacPherson, " I bethink
me that society will have a whole century before it to
control whiskey and its abuses."

" Yonder skulkers," answered Judge Wilson, " waxed
and grew fat on spirit-stilling in their secluded mountains,
recruited by our deserters in the war, and such as they
have set all taxation at defiance since the day of William
Penn.   Of late they have made a good thing by 'stilling
for our armies to the Ohio, under St. Clair and Wayne.
But this insurrection is deeper than whiskey.   Its grievances were all beyond the mountains, and why is it here
in the Forks of the Susquehanna ?   Eternal scorn be
Tom Mifflin's reward for letting this miserable smoke of
still-houses consume half of Pennsylvania !·"

" Here is the doom of the hand-still, gentlemen," cried
Cooper, with his hand upon the mysterious apparatus.
" This is the model from Count Rumford's suggestions
on distilling by steam, and you owe to Doctor Priestley
the liquor you are drinking.   Steam will allow capital to
enter the distilling business and break up these many
little excise violators."

" Ah, Doctor Priestley," Judge Wilson said, "if your
science is to extend your fame in America, it must be
practical science like that.   The politics opposed to
President Washington and the nation is nothing but re-
sistance to civilization.   In all our States is a low, illit-
erate element which considers disobedience to courts,
legislatures, and Congress to be smart.   Even in Massachusetts this element assaulted the judges and produced
a revolt, but though three thousand rebels were under
arms, General Lincoln opened on them with cannon, saved
the arsenal at Springfield, and after they were routed he
pursued them forty miles by night in the snow and broke
their conceit at one blow.   Instead of a Lincoln in Pennsylvania we have a governor who never fought a battle,
never ceased to be a politician, was dismissed from
Washington's staff for starting a panic in the army when

he was sent with an order, and who then, in revenge, formed the Gates cabal to destroy Washington. He is the shallow tool of this other skulker, Jefferson, in Virginia, whom we suspect to be at the bottom of this Whiskey insurrection.

"That is not true, sir," bluntly exclaimed Mr. Cooper.

The two Pennsylvania judges, stern official members of the Scotch-Irish race, looked at Cooper for the first time with inquiry.

"I take it for granted, young man," said Judge MacPherson, "that you would not use language like that to your senior, my associate, unless you knew positively Mr. Jefferson's relations?"

"I do," boldly answered Cooper. "Mr. Jefferson is my friend."

Judge Wilson listened, his fine profile silvery with intelligence and time.

"You are a friend of Jefferson?" said he. "You will make a witness, then, in his favor when this proceeding is punished. You will be able to testify that he never incited yourself, for example, to disobey the laws or impair the union of the States?"

The lawyer, reading witness or criminal by the light of truth, was in the old man's eye. As Mr. Cooper was about to reply violently, Mrs. Priestley commanded him to peace.

William Priestley entered with an agitated face, and said that the mob had broken into the arsenal at Northumberland and armed themselves with the State muskets.

"Ha!" exclaimed the associate judge. "Is that the use they would put the old muskets of liberty to?"

"I will return," Judge Wilson announced. "MacPherson, I summon you as my *posse*. Shake my hand, old comrade, as this may be the last action we shall fight together."

The two Revolutionary comrades, with something of the expression of man and wife parting, placed their hands silently together.

The scene touched Thomas Cooper, and he also drew near and extended his hand.

"You are two grand old fellows," he said; "take my hand, too."

Still keeping their palms clasped, the two judges turned

their eyes on Mr. Cooper and kept their countenances very sober.

" Young sir," Judge Wilson coldly remarked, " we are not the friends of Mr. Jefferson."

" No," remarked Judge MacPherson, " we are the friends of Washington. I do not think you wish to shake hands with such as we."

Raising their hats to the Priestley family, the magistrates of Northumberland passed away.

Mrs. Priestley burst into tears.

" Well, Thomas," she sobbed, " you have made our first enemies for us already."

" Pshaw ! pshaw !" exclaimed Cooper, dogmatically. " I will sit on the bench myself some day in place of one of those old Federal fools. And this is a good electioneering day."

He rushed from the house.

The little market space, or Quaker square, at the centre of the town was nearly surrounded by houses, chiefly of hewn logs or clapboards, over whose low-pitched roofs the lines of blue and russet mountains stalked through the sky like enormous pistons that were one day to draw the coal from their depths. Between the tenements the broad rivers were seen to advance in white lines, tactically, like meeting armies, to storm the great skyey ridges. The sun was warm, but airs came in from many a gap and mountain funnel to blow alternate ways the flag inscribed:

" LIBERTY AND NO EXCISE,"

which was the master of Northumberland, and, therefore, master of almost one-third of Pennsylvania.

As Cooper reached the square a volley of musketry shook the town and the smoke of guns rolled up in a cloud around the flag-pole.

Citizens closed their shutters and ran indoors.

A few persons were standing armed at the corners of their shops and dwellings, peeping at the lawless scene around the liberty-pole, where still the barrel of whiskey was running fiendishly, and many of its victims were strewn about the square like hogs at noonday, sleeping off their brutishness.

The volley of guns brought forth young Harry Priestley, whose blood was aroused at the invasion of the village
by these kern, who had dispossessed the better Indians.
He had been working all day on his land, grubbing,
ploughing, staking, with the incentive of love and domestic settlement in his mind, till summoned back to the
town by messengers who went through the responsible
communities to tell how the Buckskins had taken Northumberland. His arrival had saved at least one good
magistrate from insult, and now he was intent upon en-
rolling himself with the men of law and order and taking
a gun. Thus quickly do the necessities of a new society
transform the European to be an American !

The rude men at the flag-staff looked upon this little
struggling Northumberland, with its hundred houses or
less and hardly organized society, to be a formidable
mart of proud and oppressive capitalists.

It was to extort taxes from them and disturb their
simple methods of firing barns and expelling persons of
obnoxious pride.

A person called a "chimist" had come to Northumberland, they understood, who denied God and could
'still whiskey out of the naked air and dew.

What would be the end of existence if such infidel men
of education were to prevail and all the judges be above
the power of the people ?

Down with pride ! Down with consideration !

These were the instincts of self-esteem engendered by
isolation and supplied with grievances by political ex-
pectants.

As the obnoxious judges, whose veteran pride in the
laws and government their arms had helped to establish
reëntered the square, they were espied from the flag-pole
and greeted with hootings and whoops. Guns were fired
in the air, or low toward the earth, to tell the tale the
terrified townsmen confirmed, that the small arsenal had
been plundered of flint-locks and powder, and the trespassers were stronger than the townsmen.

Hal Priestley put himself under the orders of the judges,
and these three started separately through Northumberland to summon the law-abiding to meet under the terrace bank by Priestley's house site.

There at noon a little company was assembled, hardly

thirty strong; but the two magistrates took it in hand, assorted it, paraded it, and gave it instructions and confidence.

"MacPherson," commanded Wilson, "do you take one platoon and march to the square from the North Branch and parade your men; I will lead the other platoon under the bank of the West Branch and bring it quickly up in their rear, and occupy the corner at the flag-pole."

This plan was intelligently carried out, so that as the armed party under MacPherson emerged at the square and faced the mob, these latter made a rush upon them, leaving the flag-staff.

Judge Wilson's party silently dashed up the bank and formed at the flag-pole, after destroying the whiskey.

The two regular lines then faced each other and advanced with the steady bearing of militia, their experienced officers looking like war itself, and uttering their commands sharp and loud.

Wavering before these silent, solemn, attenuated lines, to which the judiciary gave the prestige of law, the Buckskins broke, anticipating a volley from front and rear, and ran up the square to a forest graveyard beyond it—already the last home of many an immigrant.

"Give here an axe, some of you women!" cried Wilson, "to chop down this sedition pole."

He had turned toward the environing houses.

A woman ran to her wood-pile and fetched an axe, but before she could reach the spot, her married sister, who belonged to the other faction, tripped her up, and these two women fought together with more passion than good humor, till the owner of the axe prevailed.

A practised axeman took the instrument, and by a few rapid blows felled the flag-pole.

Cheers ascended from the victors, but they omitted to put a watch upon the now deeply exasperated borderers, who repeated the tactics they had just learned, one body of them advancing down the public square in skirmishing line, armed and yelling, while another body crept along the river front, and, dashing upon the flank of the *posse*, fired their guns in a deafening volley, which was immediately replied to by a second volley from the larger party in front.

7

These loud volleys dismayed the town, and produced a panic for a moment among the judges' *posse*, but the two military men were heard to give the word :

"Form your lines ! Outward face ! Look to your priming. At the word of command, fire *ball !*"

Even official blood was up now, and the townspeople expected to see another Lexington or Concord on their public green, when there came floating upon the air, to both bands of inflamed men, the sounds of fife and drum.

Nearer and nearer the unwonted music came ; windows and doors opened as if to its persuasive power, and next there burst upon the view a military company, carrying the colors of both the State and the nation.

"Fix bayonets ! Front wheel ! Charge !"

At this command, the new arrivals to the sound of fife and drum moved upon the greater body of Buckskins, who broke and fled beyond the borders of the town, while the local *posse* also bore down upon the subsidiary column of sedition, and chased it through the outbuildings to the brush.

With loud acclaims the townspeople poured to the green, and mingled their cheers with those of the soldiery ; and water, food, and new cider were produced to reward the town's deliverers.

In the midst of this apparent conclusion of many troubles, a small body of horsemen galloped upon the square, wonderfully epauletted and slashed with colors.

"Three cheers for Governor Mifflin !" exclaimed a fat and yet stalwart lieutenant of the military company which had so opportunely marched in from Lancaster County.

As the cheers were given, Mrs. Reynolds, who had come to the scene with Harry Priestley, recognized in this military Falstaff her husband, from whom she had fled—Jacob Clingman.

"And three cheers for the right worthy Senator from the State of New York, Colonel Aaron Burr !"

Turning from Clingman's voice to the point where Clingman looked, Maria Livingston saw in the demure riding habits of a foreign traveller, and neat enough to have been the governor's staff chaplain, the man who had given her the money to come to Northumberland—the man she disliked and feared, Aaron Burr.

A hogshead was rolled up from a neighboring store-house and the governor was lifted upon it to make a speech. He was a sort of local Washington, portly, well-fed ; his hair, whitish at fifty, tied in a queue ; and he had the mingled lines of the lofty worldling and the peaceful Friend. Toward the crowd he was a father indeed, and rolled out the word Pennsyl-*vain*-yea as if the sermons of George Fox had been his tuning-master.

As Pennsylvanians he adjured them to enlist in the army to put the insurrection down. As Americans he never addressed them.

The stern vigor of Washington and the firm and prompt responses of the adjacent States had put in jeopardy Mr. Mifflin's chief political capital, his military standing. He was therefore "stumping" the State to raise the troops he had refused to raise as the magistrate who should have taken early cognizance of the outbreak.

As a speaker to the crowd he was the perfection of that cajoling art—loud, gracious, animated, pious, prac-tising the rush of the blood to the head, which was the rarest feat of the stumper—flattering the local pride, assuring all that there would be no trouble, hinting that the Fed-eral army would leave all its money in Pennsylvania, and finally pledging himself, "before his God," that the excise laws should be speedily repealed.

Before night the governor was boozy, and to the last was exercising his vocal art on imaginary audiences.

The two judges indicated the chief spirits of the day's disorders, and these were sent to Philadelphia for trial— among the first culprits seized in the insurrection.

Mr. Thomas Cooper proclaimed himself their coun-sel, and so the government men looked askant at Doctor Priestley.

As the public speaking concluded, Colonel Burr came over to Mrs. Reynolds and Mrs. Lizzie Priestley, who were looking on, and he introduced a plain, travel-worn personage with him as the Duke de Liancourt, who was going to the Genesee to look at Mr. Burr's lands.

They were taking pleasure in such a distinguished ar-rival when there broke into the circle the huge being aforesaid, whose regimentals were splashed and dusty and his countenance grimy with perspiration and dirt.

" Jehosophat of sinners ! " exclaimed Lieutenant
Clingman. " What does J. C. see but his'n truly, Mari !
O Mari ! your cruelty has busted this gizzard. Etarnally
deserted by her'n truly, Clingman has helped to raise a
company and may perish in the war."

" Jake," answered the lady, coolly, " get out of the
company of your betters ! Don't you open your mouth
to me again ! "

Her languid eyes showed a spirit. The young Englishman at her side she suppressed by retaining his hand
firmly in her own.

" Begone, fellow ! " exclaimed Aaron Burr.

" Well, I reckon I'll forage on the illicit stills, then,"
Clingman observed, after a brief and meaning study of
the social situation. " Whiskey has riz. I've got a sutlery in this army, too. Some day the amassments in
cash of J. Clingman will be juiceful, I reckon, to some
people."

---

# CHAPTER XI.

### MARIA BELEAGUERED.

HARRY PRIESTLEY had a bad night with his heart, the
excitement of the battle on the green giving him, in the
reaction, a gasping pang there like the last hour.

His mother and brother's wife wished to watch him,
but he would have none but Maria.

" Leave *her* here, sweet folk," he would say; " she do
comfort me like."

" Hal," pleaded Maria, " you are too ambitious. You
will kill yourself grubbing up those great roots. They
will be there, Hal, roots still, when we are dead."

" 'Tis for thee ! " sighed Harry, his mouth forced open
by the suffocation at his heart. " If I do not live, all is
thine."

The woman of pleasure listened to him with sincere
and almost bitter pity.

" Dear Harry, my poor friend, let me go back to the
cities and so correct your ambition, which is making
you, in a few months, like all the American race—
grudging the body sleep and the mind play. When I

am gone you will not work so hard.    Let us quarrel,
and you will be saved."
    " Quarrel ?   For what, my beautiful mistress ?   If I
work too hard for thee, I can knock off.   No, it is a castle
we shall have, and overlook the vale, and our boat shall
aye be ready on yon current to carry us from the northern cataracts and glens to the bay that is full of rivers.
Where is my axe?   You all keep me here too long.
Afield ! afield, I say ! "
    He started up, full of purpose, and the light of family
care in his eye, but a fulness of the heart seemed to
burst him, and drove forth a shriek.    Back he sank in
Maria's arms, and was bathed in her tears.    His heart
was very low, as she knew by his pulse.
    " O God ! " Maria sighed.      " This may be the ec-
stasy of love telling upon a weak heart—and such pure
love for whom ?   For me ? "
    " You surely are a part of his illness, madame," Mrs.
Priestley said, while the boy lay unconscious.   " You
have displaced his mother and his sister.   He is clay in
your hands.   And he will be clay if you leave him—
clay, I fear, for the grave.   What *are* you ? "
    " Yes," Lizzie Priestley took up her mother's question,
" we desire to know in whom our brother puts so much
confidence.   You are a wife.   I have seen your husband.
What plague are you to Colonel Hamilton ?   Something
lies there, too.   Next, this soldier on the green to-day was
strangely familiar with a lady of your condition.   Why
did you come to Northumberland, and come with that
boy ?   Was it a plot ? "
    " Hush !   Speak low, for mercy's sake !   I would not
have your son, your babe, fall dead in contention with
you over such a thing as I."
    " That might be better than that he should live and be
the dupe of some cold woman older than himself," whispered Lizzie Priestley.
    " Stop, daughter ! " Mrs. Priestley sighed.    " I shall
bless the physician who saves me my boy."
    " Dear madame"—the intruder looked upon the mother
with entreaty and sympathy—"that is my only interest
here; not to rob you of your son, but to give him back to
you free from such a bond as mine would be.   I shall
not stay one moment longer than I can be his cure.

He gave me assistance, but in the generous service lost his young heart to me. I would at the proper, the sovereign time, tell him how worthless is the heart he esteems, and the weary, purposeless life he would take into his own. Surely, this is not that opportunity ! "

Harry feebly murmured " Maria ! Are you near ? "

" Yes, Hal, right at your side. Lie still, my boy, and ease your heart."

" Dear love," the sufferer lisped, as he lay in the half-swoon of weakness and relief.

" Tell me your power over Colonel Hamilton," spoke Lizzie Priestley, low and firm. "Answer me that only, with satisfaction, and it will do."

The large, listless stranger quietly flushed, as if her languid temperature resisted passion's flood. She raised her blue eyes from their dark woodlands, and replied :

" You are a married woman, too. What can be your interest, madame, in Colonel Hamilton ? "

" Friendship," answered Lizzie Priestley, " friendship such as I dare avow before my husband's mother here. And yours? "

" It is love—love as fierce as your friendship, madame. I shall refuse to account for it to any woman but his wife. Perhaps not even to her."

Maria had expanded herself as she gave this defiance, and her hand trembled. She grew more agitated and stood up.

" I hope your friendship for Hamilton, madame," she continued, " will be more prudent than my love, which began in friendship, too."

The recognition of a rival in the control of a man was the expression of her countenance, no longer heavy and negligent, but obdurate and kindled, too.

Lizzie Priestley's face also showed the blood, but it was in the sense of recognition of the remarkable, if reckless, personal beauty before her.

" I am glad, Mrs. Reynolds, to see you really angry," she said, after a pause. " Now I can see your character ; you fear nothing."

" No, you cannot read me, madame," Maria breathed, still under the control of her quickened intellect, and cool as the English wife. " I fear to kill that boy. He is my friend, my only one. When his mother feels secure of him, I shall go."

" Then stay," Mrs. Priestley entreated. " I bless you for the unspotted, the gentle love he bears for you. It pleads to a mother's heart. It may rest thine own."

The kindness, the tones, the word, fell upon the one fresh spot in a trampled soul. Maria Livingston sank to her seat, covered her face with her hands, and echoed :

" Mother ! "

Her voice escaped confinement and awoke the drowsy youth from his laudanum dream.

" Mother ?" he muttered. " *There's* mother ! Whilst I live she will be thine. Kiss her, mother ! "

Harry's mother bent over and took the wanderer in her arms and kissed her brow.

" We are all far from home," Mrs. Priestley breathed. " Let us go not too far from God ! Sleep thee, also. The love of my boy will make thee holy and rest thy spirit."

The cutting thing to Lizzie Priestley was that her husband, Joseph, Jr., also took a very large interest in Maria Reynolds, and gave her a horse to ride to his farm, some distance out of town.

She was a stylish, rather grand horsewoman, requiring this strong sort of exercise to bring her indolence up to full animation.

Joe Priestley was a solid, uninquisitive, hearty man, giving himself concern about little more than his father and his wife, and he liked Maria's independence and looked upon her as the detached woman of Northumberland, and cared nothing about the mystery which brought her there. He probably did not care if his young brother would marry her.

To this stout, animal nature Maria was frank and free, and equally self-reliant were Mr. Cooper and his wife, except that the latter was her husband's echo in everything, and sustained his self-confidence till it was a match for the aggregate opposition of mankind.

" There, Mrs. Reynolds," said Joe Priestley the day following the riot, when he had ridden out to the farm with her, " rest thyself till I pay off the hands. I will send Colonel Burr when he comes up."

The spot was a partial or temporary lodge in the midst of a wide patch, and shaded and watered.

Maria's indolence suppressed her curiosity as she lay down where she was left, in the arbored porch of the silent dwelling.  Nothing stirred but the feet of robins coming near and piping and the long drum-roll of locusts in the lofty trees.  It was warm, though the air was stirring between the mountain ridges and cooled by the rivers.  The wild grapes upon the porch trellis swung in the zephyrs, leaf and cluster articulating the sunshine with quivering effects, and Maria fell into a doze that was hardly a doze till it was endorsed by some voices a little way off, carried to her ear on the electrically dry air of autumn.

"You will not get the letters back, Clingman," spoke the familiar, suave voice of Aaron Burr.  "They involve the family name of my great constituent.  You have no business with matters of that magnitude.  Colonel Hamilton is a member of the Cincinnati Society with me.  I won't allow him to be degraded and blackmailed by such as you."

"Damn him !  If I can get a shot at him up yer in the mountains, whar they say he's coming with the President, I'll squar accounts with his'n mortually, A. H."

"Why, what do you hate him for ?"

"I suspect he's run my gal up this way.  She has always been tractable to me.  Yisterday she cut me like a 'ristocrat.  I don't mind her rogueries ; she had 'em before I married her.  I never put a snaffle curb upon her, but let her nater run free, satisfied that she'd come back to the stall ef I left the door open.  But this trick looks like a rubber cut, clean and fine, on her'n truly, J. C."

"Take it as a blessing, Jacob.  Fine, graceless creatures, of Maria's breed and course, mature upon adventure to a point where the social ambition arises equal to their quickened wits.  Then they cast aside their lower associates, and mistake their new opportunities for the spasms of virtue.  This woman hates you already ; the power she has by those letters alone would destroy you if she exerted her present influence."

"I see.  The p'int has entered my heart," Clingman said.  "The wife of my bosom looks down on her'n bustificated, J. Clingman, late of the walley of Virgeenia.

Howsomever, I've looted all the whiskey in Buffalo walley and up the Chillisquakee. As long as business is
good, no woman can break Clingman's heart."

"Think over my proposition to come to New York and
run one of my city districts. You have got the shoulders for a ward boss and a street contractor, too, friend
Jacob."

Mrs. Reynolds, as the protean lady was also called,
closed her eyes and anticipated a presence.

A step came near, a breath and a shadow fell upon
her, and she was kissed.

"I might know *that* to be Colonel Aaron Burr," Maria
remarked, in her long, musical, nasal tones, deliberately,
without color or resentment. "He is a gallant gentleman, who is not ashamed to prevail by force over the
captive and weak. Do you respect yourself, sir?"

"Not till I have made you full amends, my lovely
creature."

"Then go drown yourself in the Susquehanna, for I
shall never forgive you, Mr. Aaron Burr."

"Why, you were abominably treated by Hamilton."

"Do you think so? I heard his fiercest reproofs with
the sorrow of a daughter hearing her father's affectionate anger. I thought of the kind words the preacher
used to say, when I was in church at Hyde Park, New
York: 'Though He slay me, yet will I trust Him.' O
Hamilton! I hear his considerate tenderness yet, saying
to me: 'I know the wilful spirit in the blood of human
nature; all cannot be evil there, and years remain for
you to recover your better nature in.' Mr. Burr, why
cannot you woo a woman like that?"

"He threatened to expose you at the very last."

"Oh! he will not. He would rather be accused and
misunderstood. Do you know why I am infatuated with
him?"

"Not I, indeed."

"Because he paid me the great compliment of breaking his constancy for me. I have been roving enough
to understand a modest man, and this was surely one. I
felt in his tones and words, when he was compelled to
confront me and Mr. Clingman, the sorrowful upbraiding
of the old lover."

"Oh! that was natural to Hamilton's station, and the

delicacy of his errand. He was not going to bully
you."

"Like Senator Aaron Burr? Of course he was not,
because his nature was not made so. I have seen him,
as a gentleman of virtue, impregnable ; I have also seen
him, as the human being, misled, the wooer, the pur-
suer, the lover. But I like him best in his last character
—the magistrate, the master! O that I had a master
like that, to whom I could look up, whose rod would
comfort me, who would stir in my passive, pleasurable
veins the work of conscience, duty, and obedience !"

"To what end, visionary Maria?"

"To the end of honor, of social influence, a true and
adequate career. What is Hamilton's wife like? I have
seen her—a little thing, a morsel, and I am sure not up
to the romantic, ardent character of Hamilton. He is
French, they say ; Scotch, too. Oh ! what imagination,
what ardor, what devotion ! And shall I never see him
again? Give me back my letters, you dishonest, unscrupulous Mr. Burr ! I heard you refuse them but now
to Mr. Clingman."

"I destroyed them, my beautiful friend, because I regarded them as dangerous to you. Their unjust use
might put you in prison. Besides, they gave you the
means of seeing Hamilton again, and I want to divide
you."

"As a lawyer?"

"Bless you, no. As a lover ! "

"Folly, sir ! You can never love any one but yourself."

"I came here particularly to see you, on an errand of
the heart."

"And now I perceive that you will presently give a
reason for that impulse, whereas all real impulses, like
my own, seek for no reasons. By kindness and sloth I
did my erring ; the way was easy. At last I found myself embarrassed by dangers and took a counsellor. He
robbed me of my documents, and now wants me to be
fond and grateful to him."

"Maria, you shall not say that I am a mercenary
lover."

"You command me already, then? Sir, I will say
that all those letters from ladies which you showed me

at your rooms—your daughter in the next chamber—
letters assorted, labelled, and tied, looked to me like
genteel villany. Men are afraid of an adventuress,
and, if she gets the reputation of dealing in their
secrets, they fly from her. But I never heard of a
man making a commercial matter of his love letters
before."

" Except one of your husbands, Mr. J. Clingman."

" Yes, poor Jake is a kind of wolf, greedy by his race
and circumstances. But he is always tender with me.
You might suppose he would murder me for the way I
am treating him now, because he is a devil in courage. I
lay here, however, and heard his talk to you without a
single anxiety. Do you know why ? "

" You control him by intelligence."

" No, sir. He loves me ! Nothing that I can do will
exasperate that savage against me, and, therefore, in my
worst situations I go back to him and leave him as I
please."

" The effect is none the less destructive to your social sense. It trains you downward like Romulus, who
was suckled by a wolf, and of course he slew his brother.
This wolf set you on Hamilton. He has you in his
power, as Hamilton has said, because you are a biga-
mist. You hardly seem to apprehend the gravity of your
offence, Maria."

" I do, sometimes, but I do not like to carry any
worry. I supposed that bigamy was made so much of to
protect people of condition, not to stir up the poor out-
laws in the hedges and heaths of the wayside of the
world."

Her voice had been gay, in spite of the serious things
she said, skirmishing with Mr. Burr; but now it became
bitter, and when he dropped the next sentence he saw her
already in tears.

" Madame Reynolds, you owe the penitentiary five
years for your offence. You live with a childish heart
over a pit that is dreadful. Let me arouse you ! "

She turned upon the bench beneath the vine where
she had been reposing, and rested on her face, and there
sobbed for a long time.

Colonel Burr sat with his buff riding gaiters crossed
upon each other, his hair waxed into its queue very

sleekly, and his clean profile and strong chin calm as an inquisitor's looking at some lovely Jewess suffering on the rack.

Nature had kept up her growth in this woman till she was like a lovely tree, luxuriant everywhere, and pleasing the eye and the taste, yet wild as the forest, or the gipsy beneath its boughs.

At last the brunette spoke, in broken accents, the gropings of her intellectual sense:

"Wretched, wretched sex of woman! We are made for the society of men. They coax and flatter us country girls till we arrive at full wisdom, to discover that we are only society's criminals. Little did I know when I married Reynolds that I was a felon. Had I stolen anything? Was my heart cruel? I made another step to extricate myself from a false one, and now, if I dare to think, I shall be reckless. Yes, I may hate men!"

"I sent you to Northumberland at your suggestion, for the purpose of coming by this way myself, Maria, to put this subject before you; to show you the real danger you are in, and to propose a remedy. You must get rid of Reynolds. He is the second husband, and having married him constitutes you a criminal."

"He is enlisted for the excise war. He is gone— gone, he says, forever."

"Ha! ha! Don't trust to that. Bad pennies and indictments are always turning up. If Hamilton would prosecute him for swindling he might run away, but that is not likely. Let me see! If I could convict Clingman as a felon, your marriage to him would be dissolved, *ipso jure.*"

"Convict poor Jake?"

"He forged pension papers, or uttered them. His decoying of you from your legal guardians was crime enough. You were then under age. The act was done in New York, and in the city where I am the head of the bar."

"I will never consent to that, Colonel Burr."

"Well, take your choice between Reynolds and Clingman. Reynolds may die in this excise campaign. The other proposition I make to you is a serious one."

She wiped her eyes of tears and resumed her careless, indolent, languishing ways.

"I want you, Maria, to take the place of the late Mrs. Burr."

Maria burst into laughter.

"Ha! ha! ha! That is the way every moral lecture ends when a Member of Congress delivers it : Be careful! be discreet! don't get exposed! Remember your youth and beauty! *And love only me!*"

She arose and pinned the ravelled ruffle in his shirt and called him the "old granny of forty." He saw that she was at least inquisitive.

"Listen," said he. "You are an astonishingly fine woman. Time only adorns you and the buffets of worldly vicissitude have made you keen. The associations you keep are contemptible in the light of your family stock and striking appearance. I would not have appreciated you as a runaway, heedless girl, but now, in the dawning of your social passions, and the refined management of your charms, I see all the possibilities in you of a companion, an adviser, and a cherished instrument."

"I am too lazy for all that, Colonel Burr."

"Did I not see, coy Maria, that wonderful performance at Clingman's rooms when Hamilton called? It was indescribable. If acting, or virtue, either was superb! You melted Hamilton down. You were a mighty artist."

"Who could not be before the only man she had won and feared? Was I adroit? I did not know it."

"I sincerely appreciate you, madame. You are my constituent; let me lead you home! The necessities of my public life require me to be more circumspect in New York. My widower condition lays me open to temptation and distracts my studies. My daughter is to find a distant home and to become my ally there. I shall be President of the United States : New York will make me so. You are the friend of Hamilton, and I shall need the Federalists, perhaps, to unite with me and defeat their great enemy Jefferson. All reasons unite to make me trust in you."

"Reasons, sir? Reasons always? Oh, that your brain could feel the spark of another happiness than your own, if it were only the happiness of folly—like Colonel Hamilton."

"I swear I love you," Burr replied. "Join me on my

return from the Genesee and I will extricate you from your dangers, shelter you, consider you in everything. Finally, I may marry you."

The proposition was at least a social enlargement for Clingman's wife and Reynolds' name-bearer. Morally there was no rise for her but repentance and to stand at some man's crucifixion.

But the dread of hunger and the ultimate need of shelter, disease's wasting apparition, the black chasm of absolute friendlessness, all which crowd upon the trifling, the gay, and the indolent at such times when they dare to anticipate, stepped across the threshold of her mind. Here was a Senator, esteemed to be rich and sure to be a successful lawyer,—and the law she had commenced to dread.

"I am asked to become your mistress, I suppose?" she slowly, reflectively said.

"My friend," corrected Aaron Burr.

"You were my friend, indeed, when you mentioned my necessities to Doctor Priestley's babe; he gave me relief, and in the giving gave me his heart. It is that which strengthens me to refuse your suit. No, I will not become your friend."

"What have you to depend upon?"

"Nothing. But if I am to make the next step into mercenary life, I shall depend upon some one who is never harsh with me, never subjects me by fear; consults my nature, knowing what it is, and makes my evil path indolently descending."

"This is ever the course of the scarlet woman, Maria; she prefers to ruin some innocent man when she can befriend a spoiled and lonesome one. I see the man your eyes are seeking out. If Colonel Hamilton would make the offer I have made you, you would not refuse."

The answer of the grand brunette was a genuine, unexcused, unstinted blush.

"Hamilton I have thought to fear me," continued Aaron Burr. "He behaves as if he wished to go past me and not offend me. But if Hamilton saw the blush I see, Miss Maria, in the association which has raised it, he ought to fear *you* most."

"Do you think I would injure him?"

"You have no control over what you may do. Ham-

ilton's enemies already hold him in their power, and
through you alone. Where every man failed, you tempted
him into a crime, and that crime is known to at least three
persons upon this earth, and to how many others the
drunken threats of James Reynolds, the blabbings of
Clingman, never can recount. It is suspected in this
Priestley family, far in the interior of the land. One protection alone is thrown around Hamilton: his secret is
confined to his fellow-soldiers of the army."

"Sir, you exaggerate a simple truantry of a great favorite of the ladies."

"But I do not exaggerate your peril. Reynolds,
Clingman, Hamilton, Aaron Burr—either of these men
could throw you into Northumberland jail to-day upon
lodging an affidavit. Conceive the effect of this knowledge upon my infatuation! Can you conceive it, lovely
Maria?"

Aaron Burr set his rich, devouring, serpent eyes upon
the woman who had lost all her defences, losing virtue.

She dreaded him. He held her already as the slave
he had set his price upon in the sales-rooms. He looked
her over leisurely, confidently, boldly, till she shrank and
seemed to have been stung by him, and to be congealing.

"Think over what I have said, Maria," Burr observed
at last. "I shall be back this way in a few weeks. You
will then need a lawyer to answer this charge of bigamy, I fear. My fee will be to train you, to give you
the protection that the splendor of your beauty deserves.
I am entitled to you; no bid you expect can be as high
as mine."

He was called away by young Joe Priestley, and Maria
lay perfectly quiet for some time, with darkening countenance, gloom, and, at last, the flashings of an interior
spirit like lightnings.

She rose and leaned upon the saplings of the trellis,
and spoke aloud:

"Revolting alternative: to love that man or herd
with murderers and robbers in a prison! For what offence of mine? Only for yielding to the suit of James
Reynolds. I married him, and he was unworthy of my
respect. What does he not deserve for bringing me to
this degradation? If I have been fugitive in my ca-
prices, I have always been free to choose. Aaron Burr

alone has imposed upon my weakness, and now would make me his slave for the remainder of my days—at least, for the residue of my charms."

She heard a man whistling, and recognized the whistle of Clingman, setting his whiskey team forward for the East.

A thought occurred to Maria which made her dark complexion grow pale.

She looked within the dwelling and drew again into the gloom of the little porch.

In a moment she was shuddering. •

" ' Ever the course of the scarlet woman ! ' " she said. " ' I have, indeed, no control over what I do.' I am a slave already ! "

She stepped into the sunlight and was revealed to her husband. By a slight motion of her head she called him up.

" Mari ? Your'n abjeckly, J. C. Nothin' else—no, never, Mari."

" I cannot speak to you here, poor Jake. It is not dislike of you but policy. You are going to the war ? "

" Fur a stake or a snake-bite, Mari. To be pizened or wictorious. We march to Carlisle at once. Do you want for anything ? "

" Have you seen Reynolds ? Colonel Hamilton said he would enlist."

" Yes, Mari, that friend of our'n is in the same brigade with your'n obejently, J. Clingman, leftenant, and —under the rose—I am backer of the sutler of the brigade."

" Jake, I hope Reynolds is killed out there in the mountains by somebody. As long as he lives I shall be in dread. Colonel Burr has threatened me with the penalty of bigamy unless I go to *him;* and God knows I loathe him. What shall I do ? "

" You have said enough," the mighty ruffian answered. " If Reynolds ever quits the mountains alive you can gaze on the suspended circumference of J. Clingman and say he missed his man."

The woman's sight grew indistinct as Clingman passed away. She heard a word ring through the tenement, and could not tell if it had been born in her brain or shouted in her ears.

That word was "*Murderess!*"
Joe Priestley found her on the grass, insensible.
" A mercurial race this ! " reflected Joe.  " It's all of
nursing brother Hal so close, I fancy. "

---

## CHAPTER XII.

### HAMILTON MARCHES.

THE troops of New Jersey and Pennsylvania were to
be concentrated at Bedford, and those of Maryland and
Virginia at Cumberland, places thirty miles apart.  The
latter was approached by the Potomac River, but the former only by advancing down the Great Valley of Cumberland or Carlisle, and then crossing successive waves
of high mountains in almost perfect wilderness.

For Carlisle set out Washington and Hamilton in the
pleasant autumn of the year, using the new turnpike
toward Lancaster and crossing the Susquehanna at Harrisburg, which was some fifty miles south of Doctor
Priestley's.

They travelled in carriages, attended by a little escort,
in which were Tobias Lear and Rob and Larry Lewis.

Those lads were in the bliss of war and love ; their
girls had seen them off.  Nelly Custis, in tears and pride,
had looked at Larry's military trappings and obeyed her
grandmother's command :

" Kiss your cousin !  Tell him that I shall not think of
his Uncle George oftener than you of Lawrence."

At the word the hearty housewife threw herself into
Washington's arms, and looking at the example of grandmother and granddaughter in love's embraces, Theodosia Burr stood in tears and kissed her hand to Robby
Lewis.

" I cannot kiss you more, Robby," she spoke.  " I have
promised my father.  Oh, that I could go with you, too,
past the mountains, and down the great river, and forever out to the sea !  But we must never meet again."

The time was to come when Theodosia was also to
make this western journey over the Alleghanies, down
the long River Ohio, and, under the guardianship of her

8

father and her husband, heaven's appointed protectors, to aim at a Southern crown.

Hamilton needed all his philosophy to set out on that journey, because his mind bore a load he had no room for, with General Washington to be entertained.

Washington was not easy to entertain in a time of responsibility, especially one like the present, when the urgency of the public order had drawn him from his capital during the session of Congress.

The morning he set out that young Parisian jackanapes, Franklin Bache, had published a diatribe, inspired by " the faction," arguing that he could not constitutionally command an army while Congress was in session. This was plain notice that the President would be attacked during his whole absence.

Hamilton had quitted Washington's staff at one time in the patriot war for impatient words spoken to him by Washington, which roused his self-respect. This was just after he had married General Schuyler's daughter, whose father was in many features Washington's Northern counterpart.

In the interval of fourteen years he had become Washington's youngest and leading counsellor, the most frequent cause of Washington's policy, greatness, and grief.

The only Northern minister to throw himself against the arrogant and unsafe politicians who were making a French Europe out of America, Hamilton's genius and wisdom prevailed with Washington's reason alone. This, and the steady rectitude of Northern society, had slowly won Washington away from the Virginia which had such fascination for its sons ; he beheld with pain the power of sinister and violent advisers in his native State, hardly one of them a soldier of the Revolution ; yet the carelessness of habits in Virginia, the want of private and public finance, had prepared the people for Job's comforters, offering them delusions of theory and insubordinate citizenship.

Hamilton sympathized with the large, worn, mastiff temperament at his side, as they rolled over the new, rough stones of the Pennsylvania turnpike—an aged servant of the public for forty years, neglecting his private interests, the pursuits of home and books and sports, to be pestered and insulted by the infants of affairs, who regarded Rousseau and Robespierre and Thomas Paine to be altogether Washington's superiors.

" General," said Hamilton, " this is probably the last occupation we shall have together, and I fear I repeat the burden of your thoughts when I say that it may have been your misfortune that we ever met."

Washington remained silent, listening as for more. The hoofs of the few dragoons upon the road stones made the hard echoes of this affectionate confidence.

" But for me," said Hamilton again, " you might be on the popular side in Virginia, unplagued by any who have the art to irritate you, lost at least in your estates, the past of fame secure to you ; your sleep, your hunt, every domestic good sound and grateful. Why did I not agree with all those who opposed me and let them manage these restless, volcanic times? I have not been sensitive to what they have said against me, but every stroke at you over my head has cut me cruelly. Surely I am guilty in some way of having brought you this un-just pain ! "

There was a pause. The older man was passing the subject up into his judgment-box. Perhaps he remem-bered that his strict clerk, Tobias Lear, whom he had created a colonel for this expedition, was also in the carriage.

Some minutes passed. The President was in deep counsel.

Finally he cast his arm almost accidentally around his minister's shoulders, and let it drop on the other side to Hamilton's hand.

" Colonel," he observed dryly, " ' surely you must be guilty in some way,' as you say ; for I never heard you make a desponding remark like that before. What are you guilty of ? "

He nudged Hamilton's side with his immense hand ; that hand had the blue veins of age now standing clear upon its almost feeble, shrunken tendons. Hamilton had seen it throw the bar in camp farther than any giant could pitch the iron. Something in the contrast made the minister's throat twitch. He was silent.

" You must have parted from Eliza in a tiff," Wash-ington remarked, seeing the emotion.

" I did, sir," faltered Hamilton.

" That is strange," the general exclaimed, cordially. " Her son had just got well ; she had nearly lost him, too. Her father took her home to a much cooler place than Philadelphia. She is lucky to be so near those wonderful springs of Saratoga. I am told there is a new one they call the *Congress* spring. *That* will be a bubbler, Colonel Lear ! That will emit continual wisdom ! "

His mood was so natural that Hamilton and Lear, both laughing—since the relapse of real dignity to jocundity is always funny—wondered if he could have disguised a comfort for Hamilton's spirit so artfully.

Hamilton wished he could tell Washington what was on his mind, but there seemed to be no way. Yet he was in great need of a friend, for what had happened was both silly and unprecedented.

His wife had either guessed something or lost her usual wifely equipoise ; for after he explained away his conference with Mrs. Lizzie Priestley and was kissed and apologized to most beautifully, Mrs. Hamilton had packed her portmanteau to go to Saratoga Falls with her father, had sent her children ahead with General Schuyler, and waited as if for the last moment with her husband.

Then, by a revulsion of feeling Hamilton could not understand, she had departed haggard, fiery, phenomenal.

Could it be that the packet Mrs. Reynolds had obtained from the bankers had already gone to his wife ?

Might she not be now effecting a separation ?

All the night when they rested on the road Hamilton turned this over.

The thought of his children was agonizing.

How could he ever commence his private life and practise law and find clients without his wife ?

To quit the Cabinet had seemed freedom and career only a few weeks before, but then he was to dwell with love, in mutual trust, his youth returned and the whole world reduced to his little brood.

Now the widower's fate, without the widower's peace and religious indwelling, might be his portion ; outcast from a high-spirited wife who never had injured his self-respect in one particle, either by a word unsaid or a word oversaid, a look that was not in partnership with his spirit, or a thought that was not as loyal to her husband as to her babes.

The infinite descent from greatness and security to contemptibility and everlasting self-accusation afflicted Hamilton with deep, unutterable humility.

He thought of his early poverty, his pressing himself upon public attention when an assisted student, his lucky picking up of Washington, and the struggle upon the staff till that straight-eyed, well-descended little soul of courage, old Schuyler's daughter, came to the camp and gave him his first social commission and all herself.

Nothing had he then but youth—no land, no family, not even birth or poor kindred in these States ; till, like a little Catharine of Russia, Eliza had responded to his admiration with her full glance and raised him from the ranks to be her consort.   She had asked him for nothing but love, and this he had been false in.

As real misery, moral timidity, and a tortured imagination, conceiving all the worst, oppressed Hamilton, he heard the language of General Washington, who might have been talking half an hour for all Hamilton could tell, saying this:

"The pride of a little woman in her husband is the most dependable thing to lean upon ; it is my support near the end of days as at the beginning.   I was not the first in my wife's affections nor the father of her children, but she has merged into my career till that is before everything ; and this I consider to be the chief compensation of the public life, Colonel Hamilton—that it teaches the women greatness of soul.   If the man is true to his career the wife will never ruin him ; but if he becomes voluptuous, indifferent to his high respect and her pride of support, the death of her pride is the knell of him.   He can find no such constituent."

The words awoke in Hamilton a feeling without self-reference.   He knew that his wife was proud to the very core.   The old general's remark made him proud of her.

"Though she slay me yet I will praise her !" he exclaimed aloud.

"Praise her always !   Find where her pride lies, and she will never slay you !" replied Washington, emphatically.

He gave Hamilton another dig with the big knuckle in the side.

" Lackadaisy !" exclaimed Tobias Lear. " The General is getting a great deal of comfort out of that kiss Mrs. Washington gave him when she despatched him off to circumvent Jefferson and Mifflin and all her enemies."

Hamilton believed—he could not tell how—that Washington knew his defection.

Whether the old chieftain had heard it or had guessed it was immaterial to the great comfort Hamilton felt.

" Sir," he said to Washington, thankfully, "those who do not appreciate you take care not to come near you in real times, like defeat and shifting councils. I take joy to myself that I have felt your strength when I had none. It is like an elephant's, I think, which can twist off a tree or pick up a needle."

" No reflections on my oft-described nose, I hope, Colonel Hamilton," said the general with some severity, that large feature slightly swelling at the nostril.

The laugh he seemed to invite came to both his companions at once, and the dragoons and the staff lads saw that there was laughing in the carriage, the President apparently very grave, and they smiled, too, and quietly winked, saying :

" The old man's blood must be up."

" Dear me !" remarked Hamilton, when he had cordially laughed, " I wondered this morning what I was to do to enliven you, Mr. President, and you have made me cheerful before I could try."

" Welcome, Colonel Hamilton, all that can try and refine you ! Welcome, sir, the detection of your errors ! Welcome the failure of your counsels ! If you can slip past your mistakes they will never correct you. The game animal always takes his flogging ; the untrainable mongrel fawns and fails to retrieve again. I was defeated at Long Island and at Brandywine ; both disasters were in the nature of providences ; but where are they who prevailed so early and met their disasters late ? Where are Gates and Arnold and Charles Lee ? Fine pride led to false pride, and what is false must destroy."

The new road was already filling up with wagoners' hotels. They saw the national flag everywhere, and at the toll-gates groups were gathered, holding up their babes to

look at Washington—blest sight! that for eighty years to
follow gave more credit than owning an estate. The exercise of law had already rekindled the fires of nationality.

Hamilton recovered every mischievous sensibility, and
Tobias Lear proved to be no dull companion, his dry
Yankee criticisms on wayside things having an old child's
face to embellish them. Thus they passed along the
Brandywine and over into the abundant Conestoga vale.
The short route to Harrisburg led through the German
settlements and by the old Dunker mills and convents.

The backbones of the great gray and blue landscapes
raised themselves in the distance, and the deep streams
seemed to flow at the bottom of the world. They climbed
another hill and saw the Susquehanna swim in its islets
like a silver baldric.

As they drew near Harris's Ferry, Washington said,
with his face turned full upon Hamilton, and something
of embarrassment in it:

"This may be the last opportunity for me to recall,
Colonel Hamilton, the only instance of our personal falling out, as we are to separate in a few weeks, you say."

"I beg your Excellency not to speak.

"Pardon me!" said Washington, gravely, "I have
long felt that it was due you. You came upon my staff
and became indispensable to me; you were both ardent
and discreet, ambitious and faithful. I felt that I was
robbing you of a great career in the field, but the exigen-
cies of the country required that I keep you at my camp,
Colonel Hamilton. 'Where shall I duplicate that man?'
said I."

Colonel Lear was probably asleep, for his eyes were
closed as the President glanced warily at him.

"You married General Schuyler's daughter," continued
Washington, in a subdued voice. "It released you, I
feared, from the dependence—perhaps I should say the
career—of a military secretary, long worked unmercifully.
I became jealous of your future movements, sir. One
day you seemed to lack promptness and on your return
my temper broke forth——"

"O General, say no more!" cried Hamilton. "This
scene is cruel. I left you!"

"I had precipitated the result I feared. You met my
accusation with a self-respect natural to your character.

You went into the lines, and I felt your mettle at York-town in the main assault. Let me say that your behavior on the first occasion I have named, has often restrained me when the ardor of your character brought momentary embarrassments to me in my present political office. I have always forborne to do you another injustice. And so there has been spared to his country its only man of universal accomplishments, and to me the affection of my equal and my son."

The old general was moved to the point of solemnity and of deep embarrassment. He seldom gave way to emotions of any kind, but now he was fluttered in all his pulses and his blue eyes were sparkling with standing tears.

Opening his arms toward his friend, Washington leaned forward, and a single sob burst from Hamilton on the President's breast.

"Colonel Lear," exclaimed Washington, after a long pause and effort, "this is Harrisburg; will you please awake and look to the baggage and to my nephews?"

---

## CHAPTER XIII.

### ARKEOLOGY.

THE whiskey insurrection stopped all work at North-umberland, and Doctor Priestley, making the best of the delay upon his house, preached a sermon to the soldiery and straightway became swallowed up in a new contro-versial work.

This seemed to be, from his description of it, "An ex-plicit statement of the errors of Methodism, with refer-ences to the prophecies of Job and Lazarus, and notices upon the composition of gunpowder as erroneously set forth by the late M. Lavoisier. Together with a defence of Phlogiston in a reply to M. Adet, the French Minister to America. By J. Priestley, with notes by Th. Cooper."

Mrs. Priestley remained with the doctor, to see that his mind was disturbed by no details while setting on this large nest of scorpion's eggs, and Mr. Cooper devised a little excursion for his chum Joe and Joe's wife and

Madame Cooper of Manchester; namely, to descend the Susquehanna on an ark to Harrisburg.

The excuse for this excursion was to enable Mr. Cooper to examine the dyes of American plants, but the probable end was to draw near the excitements of the campaign, for the soldiery were crossing the river at Harris's Ferry.

Cooper was not sure that he had not been cut out for a great commander. He was already pooh-poohing the requirement for officers in the militia to be at least five feet four high, and he thought of hurling a pamphlet at the head of President Washington, comparing him to the Duke of Brunswick, the Duke of Cumberland, and other historical reactionaries.

Joe Priestley insisted that Mrs. Reynolds be invited; his wife bit her lip but held her tongue, reflecting that the intruder might loosen her influence on young Hal by absence and perhaps depart for good.

"Wilt thou have me go, Harry?" the brunette asked.

"Indeed wull I, Lady Maria. I know 'twill be thy pleasure; but I must clear my farm and get my cabin ready; for soon thou art to be free and all my own!"

"If ill happens to thee, Harry, or to me, my own dear, shall I have thy blessing to the last?"

"Yes, yes! If yon mountains should speak to me against thee, I'll not believe them."

"Harry, the gazettes say Colonel Hamilton is coming this way. I want to see him. Colonel Burr is neglecting my interests."

"Thou dost not love Hamilton, nor fear him either, dost thou?"

"No, no! He is my friend, and yours, too, Hal."

"Adieu, then, lady. I'll work and think of thee till Heaven returns thee here."

The ark they descended the river on was a light, clean affair, built for a woman, some kind of a New England mystic who had settled in Western New York, and called herself the Universal Friend, and founded a colony. The arkmen were her converts among the Pennsylvania Dutch, returning to remove the effects of other disciples to the paradise of New York. They gave the Priestley party the Universal Friend's cabin and awning, and attended to their own duties at steering and poling the ark, and were four days dropping down the current among the shoals.

Almost alone among great rivers, the Susquehanna stands virgin to the steamboat down to the present day ; but from both its shores the railroad engines continue to solicit it, since its beauty and youth never fade.

In the years of Priestley it had neither railroads nor canals, but was the feasible road for peltrymen and emigrants from the tidewater of the lower Middle States to the new land empires toward the great lakes of Erie and Ontario ; and the rising city of Baltimore was the easiest port to make for it, being west of the unbridged Susquehanna, so that Philadelphia was hastening with its turnpikes and schemes of inland navigation to recover its own inland provinces.

Lovely valleys, almost savage yet, led up from the river where the many creeks entered it, and straight, arrowy mountain ranges enfolded successive zones of verdure, lying on the lines of latitude, while the immense stream, in lochs or pools, swam under the insteps of the hills and lapped the beaches of lovely islands in the gorgeous foliage of such an autumn as seemed to the English visitors the paint and plumage of the departed Indian host.

Already the wild fowl from the north were coming down the Susquehanna, the instinctive path of their immemorial ancestors, and wondering if its broad reaches were not their destined feeding grounds, since they only knew it by the recognition of transmission, which man is the dumbest animal to feel.

The great swans, squawking and wheeling as their leader took them on, seemed barbaric descendants of rambling angels, degenerate from the seraphim host, but lovely yet.  The geese, by night lost on the river, were calling to each other to find the way ; the wild ducks flew straight, like human hearts, pulsating through the air, silent as hearts disembodied and shot from the bowstring of fate to whither they did not know, yet beating, flickering, as they sped low to the bosom of the pool to see themselves reflected, as broken hearts fly over Lethe and see but memories of themselves.

By day the world was splashed and blood-dyed in colors, and the gorgeous butterflies were hardly as rich as the straying leaves ; by night the high-purposed and bold-striding mountains stopped and stood in abutments to let the moon spin a bridge between them and dance upon it with her fairy host.

This wilderness pathway of nature, the full-breasted river, gave forth low noises in the night, of leaping fish or grounded arks, or great paddles of rafts swung to a " Ye-ho ! "

Rapids, cascades, suck-holes, the eternal murmur of descending fluid, the cry of owls and hawks of darkness, dogs baying from the hewn cabins on the shore, and louder than all, the spacious silence of the night, the dreaming splendor of the perfect day, made the unpropelled travel of the English party seem the only proper way to go down the Susquehanna.

Mr. Cooper had plenty of time to go ashore or land on the islands and select dye-stuffs—the sumach, the black walnut's hull, vermilion-backed insects, wild indigo and litmus, rare oxides of iron for his dyeing "mordants," and madder and nutgalls.

He brought with him from Priestley's library the foreign authors on the subject, and two new American books on dyeing, by Ellis and Bemiss, and his taste for this subject was the most kindly and sincere of all his o'er-positive energies.

He was chased about everywhere by his little wife, calling him "Tommy! Tommy! Where be thee, Tommy, ducky?" And now and then they could be seen kissing each other in the copses, indifferent to the sluggish water-snakes upon the stones, which gazed at this caricature on Paradise.

Cooper was one of those men whose heart and intellect are ill assorted; when left to domestic scenes gentle, pliable, and natural, but in facing the world an excitable, obstinate, self-destroying man ; always yearning for the dangerous side, and finding the unconsonant part.

"Tom," said Joe Priestley, who was reading medicine, as the Coopers got aboard one day laden with flowers and findings, " why don't you go down to Philadelphia and be a dyer? It must be such a pleasure to you to give anything the full color you want it to have by just sousing it, and compelling it to be blue or red, maroon or black."

"And I dare say," exclaimed little Mrs. Cooper, with a broad accent, "that Tommy would make no herror in the color, Josie. Oh! he has got the taste of a French citizen! All the countries want my Tommy! What 'asn't he been?"

Mr. Cooper, with his low spine and mighty head, seemed sitting down when he stood up, and ready to bark.

"I love the dyeing art," he said. "In my shop where Lavoisier broke me, I superintended the dye and color department ; often did I think what waste all that blood was under the guillotine. Such rare coloring matter! And to think that felons and aristocrats should not contribute to the economical arts!"

"Fie! my Tommy," cried Mrs. Cooper, "thee will have to be a judge out 'ere and give these republicans some learning."

"I tell ye, Joe," exclaimed Cooper, "that ultimately we shall need no government at all except the economic or practical sort. At the birth the lad shall be considered preparation and laborer ; at the death he must contribute his chemistry to the society ; if he be executed, all of him shall belong to the law. No waste! No waste! How much we are taxed for sentiment—flags, religions, heraldry. Stuff and nonsense, say I!"

"Hear! 'Ear! 'Ear 'im! My Tommy!" from Mrs. Cooper. "O Josie! O Lady Marier! Did thee ever hear my Tommy address his club at Manchester? His Majesty George the Third could 'ave done it no better with 'is hushers at 'and in their black rods and carryin' of the mace. It was almost a hawful thing! ''Eavens!' I reflected, 'is that man my 'usband!'"

The ark had one day passed out of an expansive pool into a rapid between sundered mountains; and rocks, both barren and wooded, sprinkled the cascade, which had the wilfulness of fate as it slided onward and foamed white, like cotton into the teeth of Mr. Whitney's new gin.

The navigation required a knowledge of the river and apprenticeship at the steering gear, for the flat-bottomed ark was an American adaptation, and the rudder was a kind of sheering-oar, broad-paddled and heavy, to be moved by sleight of the wrist under precision of the eye.

"Here, my man," exclaimed Mr. Cooper, "you're

doing that all wrong! Hydraulics demands that you do
it so——"

He threw his little dwarf body upon the shank of
the paddle just as the blade was dealing with an eddy
as big as a house ; the ark swerved, the paddle blade
was sucked down, and the shaft rose in the air like a
catapult. Mr. Cooper experienced at the same time a
colic and a bath, the wind being knocked out of his
body just as he needed it all for a swim.

He sank like a bullfrog, and the ladies uttered a
scream, whilst the ark, sufficiently deflected from its
course, rose upon a rock at the bow, and swinging
around in the rapid, was forced higher up the rock by
the very hydraulics Mr. Cooper had been a professor of.

"Tam dot feller!" said the German skipper, relapsing
from grace. " He knows so much he ground my ark; now
let him drown."

"Save Tommy! Save him, heverybody!" cried Mrs.
Cooper. " 'E's the government. 'E's the crown. 'E's
everythink!"

A deck-hand seized a boat-hook, a contrivance better
than heroics for such occasions, made like a halberd,
with two iron hooking-points and a spear, on the end
of a pole, which could impale a log or turn it, from the
upper or under hold, and draw it in.

This apparatus was poked through the bagging of
Mr. Cooper's Manchester breeches so indifferently that
as he rose from the waves he squealed with pain, the
iron prong having bevelled the flesh as well.

He was hauled in like one of the ray family of fish,
chiefly head, and Mrs. Cooper rolled him on the deck,
as he had instructed her in other times to do with
drowning people, so energetically that he revived shout-
ing:

"Woman, leave off! I'm not a garden-roller noi an
accumulated Monday washing."

" Ducky!" cried Mrs. Cooper, "A must roll 'im well.
Tommy said it, and Tommy knows!"

Finally Mr. Cooper started up, holding his wound in
one hand and raving with the other, and retreating before his wife, who marvelled that he behaved so contrary
to his own *recipe*.

Joe Priestley and the two younger ladies and the boat's

company beheld the Cooper couple with mirth too great
for concealment. They laughed, and laughed again, and
finally made an end of trying to be considerate, and
wore nature out with paroxysms of the delight that is
at another's expense, yet the whole genius of comedy.

Laughing "till they could laugh no more," his friends
finally regarded Mr. Cooper's serious and accusing countenance with some remorse and solicitude.

" Never mind," observed Mr. Cooper, leaking like a
pump, and seeming to need a drop of brandy more
than wifely consolation—" never mind paying any respect to me. Don't think I expect it of you. It is the
expectation of persons like myself, who take upon themselves the public character, to become martyrs and to
incur ridicule. In spite of the apparent discomfiture I
have experienced, I shall insist that mine was the true
way to steer arks, and that all other ways of steering
arks are mere Yankeeisms, mere stuff and phlogiston.
Phlogiston, I say, Mr. Joseph Priestley, Jr. ! "

" Anything, Tom," retorted Joe, Jr., heartily, " except
too much hydrogen in your lungs."

It took all the rest of the day to roll the ark off into
the river again, and the Coopers, feeling wounded in their
dignity, went ashore and pursued the dyeing art excur-
sively.

Mrs. Reynolds had gone to sleep—her method every
afternoon. She rose late, slept in the afternoon fervor
of the sun, and was in her planetary power after supper,
glowing more wondrously as midnight approached.

Lizzie Priestley saw that her husband was up very late
with Mrs. Reynolds, but gave the subject no concern,
being absorbed with a question that was greater and
deeper than any she had been brought to deal with since
her marriage.

She had committed an act of grave and gratuitous consequence, and had not taken her husband into her confidence.

This was now giving her some remorse, yet remorse
that was more like religion than any happiness she had
ever known.

The remorse was in doing anything affecting any other
man that she did not immediately reveal to her husband.

The fear before the remorse was that she *could* not

divide the confidence of this act in counsel with her husband.

The religion of the act was to be, she hoped, in the sequel. And yet she had never come so near a great impropriety in her life.

" Joe," she said to her matter-of-fact but well devoted spouse the afternoon the ark had been foundered, " I wish I had told mother something upon my mind before I left Northumberland."

" Why didn't you, dear ? "

" Because as I could not tell you, I felt it might be putting you in the background to tell mother. It is my only secret."

" If you can keep it you are a great woman. I shall be afraid of you."

" O Joe ! afraid of me, and not afraid of Mrs. Reynolds ? "

" Is that your secret, Lizzie ? There's nothing of her to fear, I'm sure. She has merely been stranded upon the glittering shoals of official life, like many an ambitious woman before her in England."

" Heaven forbid that I should ever touch those shoals then ! " exclaimed Lizzie, devoutly.

" Indeed, I thought you brightened up to official society in Philadelphia like another Madame de Staël, especially to Secretary Hamilton."

The wife gave a little scream.

" Why, that can't be your secret, Lizzie ! " exclaimed the husband.

" O Joe ! you give me such pain. I wonder if I have not been doing wrong."

" No, I don't believe you have. It would hardly be natural for you to do anything wrong and not tell me of it. I might do so, but I think it would make you too unhappy."

" Husband, I have done something that may turn out wrong, and I do not see my way clear to tell you. If it turns out right, I may *never* be able to tell you."

" That's exceedingly funny. It sounds like a riddle of Mrs. Barbauld. But I never could guess one of those things, because the people who make them start upon the answer and make the riddle afterward."

" Joe, were you ever jealous ? "

"Not since I have been married.   Were you?"

"Never.  Before the time for jealousy love's confidence should be destroyed.  Love and married love are too sacred for jealousy to be a ward in the family.  Only false love, selfish love can be jealous.  And yet I wonder if your love for me could ever be shaken under a great provocation."

"I don't believe you could give the provocation."

"That is no answer, sir."

"Then, no."

The wife turned suddenly upon her husband and kissed him, and remained trembling in his arms.

"Tell me that I am a modest woman, a faithful wife," she demanded, with pride, her eyes still streaming.

"You?" said Joe; "of course you are."

"If you ever tell me I am not, if you ever doubt me, sir," the wife spoke under the same strong, mysterious excitement, "I will leave you forever!"

"Queer country this, to disturb old habits and heads so!" reflected Joseph when she had gone.  "It may be in the climate.  Perhaps it's Equality."

Nevertheless, a slight change had already come about, through something concealed or withheld in the marriage understanding.  The husband had been deprived of the duty and right of comforting his wife.  The wife had chosen to think that there was a duty above her great and passionate task of household confidence, though she had never exercised it before.

The ark was put on rollers and rolled from the rock by the joint application of the current towing from it and of levers behind.  To keep the Coopers in cordial relations that night, Lizzie Priestley went below with them, and early to bed, while her husband held the vigil above with Maria Livingston far toward morning, as the ark passed down through the Kittatinny Mountain.

"You were not lucky in love, Reynolds?" asked Joe, curtly, of that beauty.

"Not in marriage, Joe.  Hardly lucky in love."

"Dear me!  Was there a difference?"

She thought, with all her heightened intellect after the day's whole rest, and felt that the moment might have come to punish Lizzie Priestley.

"Yes," she said, slowly, "marriage is a failure."

"That's queer. What can be a success then, my lass?"

"Marriage is a formal arrangement; love is a success."

"Illustrate that."

"I married Mr. Reynolds; the question of duties and rights and mutual conduct came up at once. I *loved* Hamilton; it was joy and glory till another cut me out. But the ardor of this love never can be told. If I could live another life I would give it all away for that brief, wild experience. If deception, it was bliss."

"What kind of person, Mistress Maria, could have cut out graces like your own?"

"Dear Joe, I cannot tell you that. And yet I have an intuition that here, at Harrisburg, will be my rival and that we shall see her."

"Then, of course, you will point her out, for I am a dull sort of being. And you say marriage is a failure?"

He lay down and felt troubled. The large islets near the Juniata's outlet went past to flying star throngs overhead, that seemed to Joe like populous America, and himself to be a heavy flat-boat drifting past unrecognized constellations. What star up there might be his wife?

The woman talked on, and was piqued at last to find her listener asleep; not even disturbed love could unsettle the equipoise of that cheery nature.

She felt offended now at both man and wife, and wondered if she could not think of some wanton trick to punish them equally.

Her experience was full of hide-and-seek incidents—the ruses of borrowing, the freaks of coquetry, the impostures which had just escaped blackmail. To plague a husband's heart and by almost breaking it recompel affection had been her wifely prelude to other adventures beyond the family circle, and one of these came now to mind.

"Go down into the cabin," she said toward morning to a lad among the boat's people, "and ask this gentleman's wife to come on deck and see the campments around Harrisburg."

Lizzie Priestley was awakened by the voice of Mrs. Cooper.

o

"Lizzie, husband have sent for thee to go hup and see 'Arrisburg. It's comin' day, my lady."

Grateful to be remembered by her husband, the wife donned wrapper and shawl and came out under the infinite starlight, repeated in the river's broad lagoons, with the mountain lines and shadows far behind and rolling landscapes enfolding the current. Some fires were blazing along the tall banks not far to the south, where the troops were cantoned, waiting for the ferry.

"It's not like Joe to call me so early," thought the wife. "Where can he be?"

She picked her way along the broad, cargo-littered floor, and in an alcove made by coops and bales saw something move that lay upon the deck.

"Joe, did you send for me?"

A blanket-shawl was drawn aside, and Mrs. Reynolds, springing up, gave a scream and uttered the words:

"O madame, mercy!"

"You here with Joe?" asked Lizzie Priestley. "Joe, did you send for me just now?"

"Not I," answered Joe, looking up from his part of the same shawl gapingly. "It's too cold for you up here. What's the matter?"

"Nothing at all. Reynolds tried to play a trick on you; that's clear, *madame!*"

"Well, I'm too dull to see through it."

"It's not worth your while, Joe. Come, wash up and be ready to land at Harrisburg. If Hamilton is there we may miss him, for I believe soldiers move at dawn."

With ease above contempt the wife drew her husband up and away.

"Not at all jealous," Maria Reynolds reflected; "however, she must remember it, if more comes to pass."

The coolness of an adventuress quite understood is equal to virtue's own coolness, and explanation was neither asked nor extended between the two women.

Harrisburg was a little place, with an unfinished courthouse and a market square, in sight of the Paxton Hills, where a gentle congregation once set forth to kill Christian Indians at Lancaster and capture Philadelphia for its Quakerness.

Washington had found there the French flag flying over the court-house and only five Federalists in the town, which had lately possessed a United States Senator, who with his neighbors had expected to have the seat of government at Harrisburg, and accused Hamilton and Robert Morris of sending it to the Potomac. They did not equally accuse a typhoid fever which had raged in Harrisburg for two years because some curmudgeon would not dispense with his mill-dam in the middle of the place. A disappointed woman is cheerfulness compared to a disappointed town which expects to become a capital. Nevertheless, the burgesses had been prevailed on to present an address to the President, and were to get it in this day; so Harrisburg was full.

At a small hotel on a corner of the market square Hamilton and Washington were quartered, and there the Priestley company repaired. As they entered the door Mrs. Reynolds gave a real scream, and turning, Lizzie Priestley saw its cause to be the sentinel at the door.

"Reynolds? My God!" exclaimed the errant wife.

"Very well, then," spoke Mrs. Joe; "let Reynolds and wife be happy, and we, Joe, will go up to see Colonel Hamilton."

"One moment, my dear friend," pleaded Mrs. Reynolds, catching Joe Priestley's arm; "I am afraid of this man. He may attempt my life, being armed. Won't you protect me? Oh! I have no other friend here but Hamilton, and he is too great to descend to me."

"As soon as my wife finds her friend Hamilton I will return to thee, Reynolds," answered Joe, soberly.

The sentinel had already obtained a change of guard and faced his wife, or her who bore his name.

"Stopped here," thought Mrs. Reynolds, "while my rival can see Hamilton? I am the jealous one now, but it puts down my fear. James Reynolds, what dare you want with me?"

"To pardon you, Maria. And to say farewell."

## CHAPTER XIV

### RIVAL WOMEN.

In laying out his town of " Louisburg in the County of
Dauphin "—the Dauphin now an insane, tortured child
and King Louis a headless corpse—John Harris had re-
served the broad high river-bank or " bench " before his
stone house for a sort of boulevard, which was in 1794
bushy yet, with a path, and used by the Harrisburgers to
feel the river air.

To this path Reynolds led the way and Maria followed
sullenly, her outlaw nature now aroused by jealousy and
anger, though she noted that soldiers were loitering by
the walk, and what remaining fear she had of Reynolds
was benumbed by hardihood.

He took her arm and continued on beyond the farthest
loiterers, to a place where the path entered a half-circle of
trees and in front opened upon the wondrous view of the
Cumberland Valley across the Susquehanna ; the strident
North Mountain above, just cleft by the river like a tree
by an axe ; the peaceful South Mountain below, bending
as if to drink from the river like garlanded team horses ;
and in between a land that gambolled with abundance,
and from its hillocks flowed the milk of corn and wheat
in creeks like young rivers running savage free.   This
was the great valley of the Scotch-Irish, leading off to the
Potomac, the Monongahela, and the Tennessee.

" That runs like me," Maria said, looking at the shallow,
flowing current, " past green things like those large islands and green things like you, Jim.  Why don't you
get out of my treacherous bed and go down that valley
over the ferry and find some real world like a man ? "

" I am going far enough," Reynolds said ; " as far as
the Ohio, if I live to get there."

" Don't come back !   Never be a government clerk
again !   Turn Indian first ! "

" The very Indians, it seems to me, want to be government clerks, Maria.   That is the whole cause of this
war—to get the government out and fill the places.   O
heavens ! what will be the agony of them who *succeed !* "

" You're right, Jim, if they bring their fine wives to the

seat of government; some will end boarding-house keepers and some will end bigamists, like me. The rest will hang on endlessly. Dear me ! one government is just like another. The courtier of the king has to surrender his wife ; the government clerk has hard work to keep her. If a woman can ever be in more temptation than at a seat of government where the politicians control the employment, the very angels will excuse her. Haven't I been through it ?"

She gave a long sigh and patted her foot, for the world she derided was calling her.

" It seems to me," said Reynolds, " that the more that becomes understood the more of these careless women want to come to the capitals."

" Ha, ho ! And always will. Men exaggerate women above themselves, but women do not love work. Jim, in leaving me you leave a lazy, languid, selfish creature. We tried matrimony, and I could not be faithful to you if I had to stay in-doors and to work. 1 was spoiled already ; you were dissipated. You wanted my beauty, as you thought it was, and you would not give up your gambling and cups. So we were both selfish. I really thought our marriage would be happy, and tried it in good faith. You see that it was a failure. Now, let me go !"

" Stop, my wife ! That name is precious, Maria ; it is painful, too. O God !"

He threw back his tall figure and leaned against a tree.

The " assembly " was beaten in the streets of Harrisburg.

" Up, up, up and away !
Is the call of Clingman's men."

" Jim, I pity you. Indeed, I do. Go to the war ! Get habits, my poor husband ! A fine woman to possess is a poor exchange for good habits and self-respect in a man. I shall go to glory or the gutter. I feel an energy in me I have never had before. Something worse or great is going to happen."

" My company is now forming to march," the soldier breathed. " I have only a moment and my feelings will not let me speak. Maria, I loved you——"

He lost self-control again. She was crying, too, and she threw her arms around him, nearly of his own height as she was, and kissed him, saying :

" James, go and serve your country. Alter your habits. If you can do it, become a religious man. That saves some people."

" God bless you, my wife ! Men have made it hard for you. It is not your sin that you were made so attractive to us. I was cowardly and base to you. Maria, leave that bad fellow, Jake Clingman ! He it was who kept me in my cups and taught me ways of villany, and has no shame. Dear, tender, silly heart ! promise me to leave that man and I will pray for you every night I live, that the stars of heaven shall not have your brightness and you shall shine from the better world beyond. Will you promise me ?"

" I will, James Reynolds. I have resolved to go back to New York and return to Pennsylvania no more. I shall go, dear Jim, and look at my mother's grave."

She also gave way a moment to her feelings, and leaned upon the neck where she had been a bride.

The assembly was sounded from the village, loud and petulantly :

> " Up, up, up and away !
> Is the call of Clingman's men."

He gave her innocent, confiding kisses. They were given back by a redeeming impulse of repentance.

" I know you have a noble heart," he sobbed. " Good-by."

As he was about to disengage himself and take up his belt and bayonet, violent hands were laid upon him and he was thrown to the ground.

" Desertion, heigh ? " exclaimed a deep, excited voice. " Won't march, heigh ? I reckon this is the time to close him out, Mari ! "

Before Reynolds could do more than stagger to his knees and recognize his assailant with a yell of horror and pain, the stalwart ruffian was upon him again with all his giant strength, and bore him to the ground and rolled him toward the bank of the rampart and beat him there.

" Striking at a s'perior officer, heigh ? " ejaculated Jacob

Clingman, with the united desperation of the jealous husband and the hired bravo. " That's death."

He drew his sword and sought to detach himself to run Reynolds through.

The private soldier, already wounded, bleeding, and full of terror, fought to hold to Clingman's breast and save his life. They had struggled to their feet, and the grapple was frightful to see.

Maria gave a loud scream as soon as she could find breath or understanding, and cried:

" Jake, don't kill that man ! Don't kill James Reynolds ! "

" It's too late," muttered the ruffian, as he choked Reynolds' throat with both hands and by blows with his knees forced the soldier to the river bank and butted him over with Clingman's bull-like head.

The soldier fell backward down the bank, and rolled to the bottom like one dead.

" You've killed him ! Almighty God, he's dead ! " the wife exclaimed.

" Them was your orders, Mari, I reckon. To obleege you, I'll finish by cutting his throat, as thar won't be time to look for him before we march."

He flourished his sword, and glanced at her with the choler of the combat and of worse jealousy, grunting:

" A-kissin', was he ? Mari, he'll kiss you no more. That's the priwilege of statesmen and of—your'n truly, Jake Clingman."

The double wife gave a scream with all her power, which woke the very echoes like the Indian's war-whoop of other days—the scream of real horror that has no match in the universe when woman's supreme fright is come.

" Halloo! halloo there ! " answered a voice near by.

Clingman was arrested in the fell purpose of despatching his victim, and had already started down the river bank for that end when the scream detained him.

" Come quickly, and save Mr. Reynolds, my husband," Maria called. "O Mr. Priestley ! a villain has killed him."

It was indeed Joseph Priestley, Jr., coming down the river path with his wife.

" Halloo ! halloo ! " answered Joseph, running.

Clingman darted up the bank and into the bush toward the top of the cliff.

" He's down there," Mrs. Reynolds gasped, tottering into Joseph's arms. " I'm afraid Clingman has killed him."

The Priestley couple gazed down and saw the motionless figure in military buff and blue at the pebbly edge of the current, head downward in the water.

" Unwind your arms from that woman, Joe ! " Mrs. Priestley spoke in cold disdain. " Don't touch her! She's too artful to fall. I know her to be her husband's murderer."

Mrs. Reynolds unclosed her eyes and gave a little scream.

" You say a false, cruel thing, Mrs. Priestley," she exclaimed, " and not your first attempt to injure me. God knows I pitied that man and received his pardon when he was assaulted by a ruffian."

" Then the worse your crime," Mrs. Priestley continued. " I was the witness of your instigation of this murder at my husband's farm near Northumberland, when that portly common officer came there, and you said to him : ' I hope Reynolds is killed. As long as he lives I shall be in dread. I loathe him.' Is that not so, madame ? "

" No, no ; I appeal to God ! I had no part in that poor creature's fate."

" You know better, Mrs. Reynolds. It was I who then cried ' Murderess ! ' and you fell to the ground."

Mrs. Reynolds really sank to the earth now, for her sustainer, with uniform steadiness of view, had only been looking at the man at the bottom of the rampart, and now Joseph Priestley shouted, as he forgot Mrs. Reynolds altogether :

" Wife, that fellow is getting up. He's not at all dead. Merely an affray, I suspect ! "

The husband went down the gravelly bank as fast as convenient, and assisted to hold the rising soldier, who seemed stunned for a moment, till suddenly the shrill fife and drum called the assembly again at the ferry near by :

" Up, up, up and away
 Is the call of Clingman's men."

"Duty, duty," Reynolds spoke, and looked dazedly for his accoutrements upon the ground.

"Here's your bayonet! Here's your belt, my man!" exclaimed Joseph. "Are you much hurt?"

"No, I hope not. I want to march."

"But yonder's your wife. You should bring this other rascal to account, shouldn't you?"

"No, sir, no," the soldier sighed. "It would only make him cruel to Maria. It's nothing, sir, but the brutality of an officer to a private, I think. My wife had nothing to do with it."

He limped along the margin to join his company; their scows were speedily out in the current, full of blue and buff soldiery, horses, and bayonets, crossing to the western shore. The music sounded down the spacious vale as tender as if the world had no passions—not even ambition.

"Poor Jim!" Maria Reynolds sighed; "I shall never see him more, I feel."

"Lizzie," remarked Joe Priestley, "you were entirely wrong about Reynolds; her man exonerates her fully."

"I know your motive, madame," Mrs. Reynolds added aloud. "In good time it will appear."

Colonel Hamilton was now seen coming down the bank, searching for some one, as it seemed; for Mrs. Priestley called him:

"Hamilton, we are here!"

"Pardon me, Mr. Priestley, if I finish what I had to say to your wife; for I am to cross the river after the President, who has already passed."

Hamilton gave his arm to Mrs. Priestley and walked further on, relieving the suppressed female acrimony from the danger of an explosion.

The activity of the campaign, the love and encomium of Washington, had well-nigh relieved Hamilton of pre-occupation on his wife's account; but the sight of Mrs. Reynolds, to whom he did not speak, gave him the nausea of a disturbed conscience again.

Why was she here? was it to regain possession of her husband, whom Hamilton had identified in the guard at the inn? Had she been already confidential with Lizzie Priestley?

"Dare I take your hand?" asked Hamilton of the latter

as they walked together under the elms and poplars of
the river-side grove. " I feel the need to-day of a woman
friend. Do you believe there can be friendship across
the sensitive lines of sex without love ? "

" Surely. If not, marriage is an iron grate."

" It must be high friendship, though," the young secretary said, " not frivolous familiarity. In your warm
regard for me I thought I saw something like the pure
affection of my wife's sisters for me. To them ' Alexander ' is what the French gallantly call the *beau frère*,
the superfine brotherhood."

" Have you several *belles sœurs* ? "

" Yes, a most desirable family surrounding ; one sister
of my wife is the wife of the young patroon of Albany ;
they range down to delightful little girls. And Eliza and
I have five children, the last a babe. No man could be
more happily married."

He sighed.

" It is dreadful," involuntarily said Lizzie Priestley.

" Dreadful ? " Hamilton repeated. " What ? Yes, that
must be dreadful which sincere friendship has to reject
from conversation. One can be hurt anywhere, and sur-
geons, families can discuss it ; but there are self-inflicted
wounds upon one's own honor that friendship itself dare
not look upon."

" I pity your wife, Hamilton. But I pity you more."

" Oh ! do not. She is the only sufferer ; but for her I
would face this world."

" If my son were to make a great mistake I would take
him into my confidence," said the English wife. " The
mistake could not be so great that I would not do so. If
it was a transgression like——"

" Like mine," mournfully sighed Hamilton.

" If it was that mistake, it would not seem to me,—as
a mother, a woman,—the very worst."

" But as a wife, could you forgive it ? "

She felt a bitter taste in her throat as she swallowed
something hard there and replied :

" It might almost kill me ; but if I loved my husband,
no other woman should take him from me. I would recover him, if I could."

" I said ' forgive him ' ? "

" If I did not forgive him, how could I be happy again

with him ?   If I could not forgive him, it would be evidence that I had ceased to love him.   Oh! what must love not forgive ?   What is it not always forgiving, perhaps, even in its perfect trust ?   There is an allowance to be made for men.   They are not mothers."

She felt like one walking on blushes, but her interest in this man was becoming heroic.

" There, there," said Hamilton, " is man's cowardice and meanest sin : that because he foresees no penalty, probably is not detected, he can break the vows that, if his wife also broke them, it would break his heart."

" Gallantry, some of our courts and kings still called it."

" So did the French who came to our assistance—marquises, gentlemen upon the magnanimous errand of courage and liberty, and still bringing their *belles Gabriels* over.   I could speak their language and was popular with them.   Perhaps *there*—but, no.   Why plead the inclinations of one's wayward heart to be from another's example ?   I see no honorable way back but manful ruin and confession."

As Lizzie deliberated what next to say, for she was profoundly interested, and with some restless, undefined idea of helping Hamilton, her hand came in contact with a letter in her pocket.

" Oh ! Colonel Hamilton, here is a letter to you from Colonel Burr ; he gave it to me to mail at Harrisburg unless I should see you."

As Hamilton broke the sealing-wax and read, Mrs. Priestley remembered what he had said about Friendship—that it was impotent in man's only forlorn necessity.

It could watch, she reflected, and suffer and survive at the death-bed of man; but if his reputation was as much as scratched, Friendship would run away like the cowardly Levite.

He had said that the point of despair in his offence would be his wife's discovery of it.

" Strange," queried Lizzie of her ardent heart, " that a man like this is not afraid of the world, but only of his wife, who is vowed to his honor and obedience !   And yet, if my husband had Hamilton's public career, would I not smooth his way to peace and courage, if my heart had to be the step on which he would rise again ?   No, I would not let him fall."

And yet, even as she spoke, a feeling of avoidance toward Hamilton was perceptible in her mind, and she wondered if her husband would excuse her for ministering to this contagion.

The word " contagion " made her indignant at herself. " Salvation cannot be contagion," she thought, fiercely. " It is the individual redemption of a soul. God, let me find some way to rescue this man and put his enemies to confusion ! "

" It seems to surround me everywhere, Mistress Lizzie," spoke Hamilton, with a smile of resignation, handing her Colonel Burr's letter.

" Am I to read it, sir? "

" Certainly; you have become my only friend—you and one more who is far away. Two women—alas ! I must say *three*—have read me through."

The others in his mind were Mrs. Reynolds and Martha Jefferson. But not the better two could be a match for the wanton one.

Lizzie Priestley read the letter with increasing fear. It said:

" NORTHUMBERLAND, Oct. —, 1794.

" COLONEL A. HAMILTON.

" *My Great Constituent :*—There is a certain Lieutenant Jacob Clingman among Mifflin's Pennsylvania contingent whom it would be well for you to have observed when you enter the lonesome and gloomy defiles of the Alleghany Mountain country. He is a guardian, relative, or something like those, of my Protean client, Maria Livingston, or Maria Reynolds. She also is in these Susquehanna parts at present, possibly following the army, in which she may have one or more lovers.

" Clingman has twice in my presence expressed a deadly hatred of you, and the last time it was so flagrant and overt that I would have had him bound over in this place to keep the peace but that our friends, the Priestleys, who have settled here, might ascertain something of the cause of his offence; and gentle Madame Priestley the younger thinks we have nobody like Hamilton.

" A female scandal, of however ridiculous quality, affecting you, Colonel Hamilton, would be nuts for Jefferson, Randolph, Madison, and the Virginia party, and my hope continues to be that we shall unite our interests and confound them all. I told you that I would not give you up. We must be together for long politics; for continental strategy.

" Clingman intimates that if he can waylay you on the mountains he will put a ball into you; so be warned by

" Your obedient servant,

" A. BURR."

"Oh ! do not go into that wild country and incur this risk," cried Lizzie Priestley, taking Hamilton's hands in both of hers. " I have just seen this ruffian Clingman nearly murder a man, and in the very presence of his wife——"

"Clingman's wife—she who is *there?*" Hamilton pointed back.

" No, Reynolds' wife. It was Reynolds they designed to murder. I heard her instigate it at Northumberland. It would have been done here, where we were found by you at this river-side, had Joe and I not come upon the scene. Such a determined, blood-thirsty assassination never was attempted. He will certainly kill you, Hamilton."

" Fear not them who kill the body, but them who kill the soul," Hamilton replied gently, taking Lizzie's hands in his to keep her calm. " I fear Senator Aaron Burr far more than Mr. Clingman. He has my letters to Mrs. Reynolds and hers to me. He is my unscrupulous opponent in public life, and the enemy of my wife's father and family. As for Clingman, you must know, since you have penetrated so far with the noblest motives into this matter, that he is the only, the first, the legal husband of Mrs. Reynolds ; and both Reynolds and I, and perhaps Mrs. Reynolds, also—for I would not implicate too much evil to a poor woman—have been Clingman's dupes and puppets."

Mrs. Priestley gave a scream, so loud that it might have alarmed people near by.

Hamilton placed his hand upon her mouth.

" Remember, dear friend, that others may be near ! "

"O Hamilton ! I see more than you can see. It was that perception which made me scream. Aaron Burr has made this woman, Clingman, a proposition to be his creature or companion. I overheard it all ; and she resisted him, and then he threatened her. If Reynolds had been murdered by Clingman just now, as nearly happened, you would have been coming down this path alone, would have been found by the body of the dead man, and your injury to him, with his assumed wife's presence there, would have made you appear the Murderer."

He reflected with his fine blue eyes, threw away an instant's care, and said :

" My dear Lizzie—shall I dare to call you so ?—a good soldier is hardly to be charged with a murder.  But I perceive how monstrous is the yawning gap made by a single moral offence ; it is like the assassin's thrust in the leather doublet through which, said King Henry the Great, the English army invaded France.  If I could keep Mrs. Reynolds from the influence of Aaron Burr ! "

" Hamilton, do not try !  Let them unite their natures, which do more mischief dispersed than together, like all the children of Evil.  I made you my friend the day I saw you first.  That day this spot and burden upon your life were revealed to me.  God must have sent me to lift the cloud from your life and character.  Oh ! tell me, sir, what would be the greatest service any human being could render to you ? "

" To have faith in me," said Hamilton, "and be silent. Be sure one's sins will find him out."

" Do you dread the publicity of this offence ? "

" No ; it would rather be a relief to me, if my wife could stand it.  But that is impossible." .

Lizzie listened, trembled, and paused, then spoke, with a sad face, these words :

" O Magdalen among men ! O Hamilton ! Raise your hand and swear to me that you will never again forget your character and wife ; for I see a way to help you, and this promise must be the consolation of my friendship and the assurance to my conscience in the sacrifice I am to make."

He hesitated and endeavored to speak.

" It is too late," exclaimed Lizzie Priestley.  " I have made a resolution.  I have taken up a cross.  Swear to me, Hamilton, to be a spotless man for all the remainder of your days ! "

" That I can say, my gentle friend, upon my knees, in the depths of contrition, in the hope of love and heaven ! My hearth shall be swept, my heart shall be purified ; I shall strive, through a nature victorious, to see God ! "

He sank upon his knee and raised his hand, still holding in his other hand her own.

The woodland enclosure where he knelt was disturbed, and the bushes and boughs parted.

In the interstice appeared Joe Priestley and Maria Reynolds.                                    .

Lizzie Priestley heard the words from Mrs. Reynolds, languidly uttered :

"I told you, Mr. Joseph, that marriage was a failure and love a success. There stands my lover and that is the lady who has cut me out from him."

Hamilton arose, with the barest trace of embarrassment upon his countenance, and instantly rejoined :

" That is Mrs. Reynolds' misunderstanding, friend Priestley. Nobody has cut her out, as she terms it. I have been her lover and none other's. From your wife I have just accepted an extravagant offer of a nameless friendship, and I hope you will esteem me to be a gentleman."

"Joe," spoke Mrs. Priestley, still holding Hamilton's hand, " I ask you before that woman if you have any distrust of me ? Speak, sir ! "

"Well," said Joe, blankly revolving the situation, "I can't say that I have. As a citizen of this country, or, at least, one subject to its laws, I think I should take Minister Hamilton at his word. Surely there is no occasion of his doing any trespass upon me. If I thought any injury was meditated, I should not hesitate to speak out like an Englishman."

Hamilton led Mrs. Priestley to her husband and took his hand.

"Appearances, Mr. Priestley, which lie against one who would be a gentleman, are the test of sincere friendship and of the confidence of society. If you will believe me, there is no limit you cannot extend to this lady's freedom ; everywhere you will find her your wife. And with this belief, I bid you both, for a time, farewell. Mrs. Reynolds, shall I take you into Harrisburg ? "

He raised his hat to husband and wife.

A thrill of pleasure and of triumph passed through Maria Livingston. She raised her large eyes to Mrs. Priestley, and sighed :

" Hamilton, then you love me still ! "

No agitation, nor resentment, nor competition appeared upon Lizzie Priestley's countenance. Her girlish figure and silken curls and clear gray eyes expressed a mixture of weakness and strength, of desertion and resources.

" Joe," she exclaimed, with fervent pain, as the other

pair passed away, "I am going to put your confidence in me to its greatest test. I want you to go to Philadelphia with me, and not to ask me what I am going for."    .

"Lizzie, wife, I cannot go. Father is dependent on me. For him only I came to America. I am his right hand—and mother's."

"Then, Joe, I want you to put me on the stage for Philadelphia, and let me go there alone."

"Art thou to leave me, wife—to leave me in America without thee? Hast thou gone mad?"

"Oh! kiss me darling, here in the woods, where the birds are singing free, and there is no jealousy between male and female. Let me fly a little way from your sight. I have a crumb of charity I would fly with. Keep thee by father and trust in Heaven's purposes and let me go!"

He folded her in his arms, and his frame was a moment convulsed with emotion.

"I can't tell, Lizzie, lass, what has come into thee. It can't be anything religious, like Madame Jemima Wilkinson's call or Mistress Ann Lee's mission. Everybody here seems to fly off to make another church or sect, like to father's; but it can't be *that* with thee. If you would stay with me, I could live where the panthers breed and the bears make their dens. But in coming to America with me, far from native England and its olden, settled ways, thy walk was so unselfish and thy heart so brave that I ask no greater evidence of thy love and faith. Yes, go to Philadelphia! Return when thou wilt do so. And I must stay by father."

Every word had been an effort, and the concession was such a mighty sacrifice that it left him piteously tender and empty and streaming tears.

"My darling," spoke the wife, "I cannot promise thee. I leave my love right here. Nothing have I to take away——"

"Thou hast! thou hast!" from suffering Joe. "Thou hast to take away some deed of friendship, wife, I think."

"Joe, some day mother will die, and father Priestley must see her go. Thou or I will die, too, and not together. Look at me now, as if I was leaving thee, at Heaven's wish, and kiss and bless me as I tear me from my heart."

There was a cannon fired, and it made the couple tremble in each other's arms.

Hamilton was crossing the Susquehanna.

---

# CHAPTER XV.

### FINANCIER IN TEMPTATION.

HAMILTON gave no concern to Lizzie Priestley's excited proffer of some possible or impossible sacrifice. He had resolved to make a last effort to conciliate Mrs. Reynolds and take her from those who controlled her, more especially Aaron Burr, and this problem expelled from his mind romantic expectations of what any other woman might do in his behalf.

Of an eminently practical Scotch mind, Hamilton had also a French imagination, suggestive of the union of the Hamiltons and Grammonts in literature, and this French gallantry in his nature made him averse to threatening a woman whom he might convert to friendship.

He had already detached Reynolds the husband from the cabal. If he could now annex the wife of Clingman, —which it was perfectly easy to do, if he would further tamper with his conscience,—he might recover the correspondence between them. But could he trust himself?

That which had originally tempted him was in his nature still—the ardor of youth, the bequest of inflammable races, partiality for female society, the coquetry of the staff and the camp.

Already the strong October air of the Pennsylvania upland was in his pulses and his brain, and his fondness for a soldier's life was stronger than ever as he saw the army, obedient to his Treasury regulations and Cabinet control, coming to rendezvous by obedient thousands at the town of Carlisle, within musketry sound of Harrisburg.

Washington and Hamilton were the names the soldiers cheered. Determination and indignation were in the bright, onflowing multitude of youthful patriots, called from their desks, merchants' counters, mechanical trades, and farms to administer chastisement to the sneaking and insolent assassins of the new nation.

As the columns trod the bad roads and carried their unwonted burdens, they grew madder and madder that this strain and sacrifice had been imposed upon them by frontier rustics and fellows of but partial civilization; whereas the army was the flower of the best condition in the Middle States, recruited upon the stem of voluntary militia organizations in all the prosperous towns and cities, and Hamilton beheld in it such an army as the French first sent to famished America in the gorgeous clothing of Louis the Sixteenth.

The music of the bands as fragments of soldiery almost hourly arrived, the broadcloth uniforms, the superior instruments and arms, the pride of bearing and of patriotism, made Hamilton sigh to be in the ranks or lead his regiment again.

And above all times of opportunity, war is the time of love, releasing the mind from its business fetters, giving to life a holiday attire, strengthening the physical nature by spirited exercise, and bringing to the wayside and the windows of houses the delighted, the magnetized maidens and young dames to see the millinery of grenadier hats, gold buttons, epaulettes, standards, flushed, clean, manly faces, and eyes that speak admiration and acquaintance. Sad is the lot of jealous husbands 'and suitors when the soldiers come, and the soldier whose spirit was in this army and who shared its every fervid attribute, was Alexander Hamilton, the more distinguished by his civilian dress.

With those thoughts triumphing over his late depression, he turned and saw at his side the incarnation of love.

Maria was more beautiful·than ever.

Country exercise and travel, rest and gentle association, the revival of good family points, and an interesting, if neglected, nature—she was a Livingston, and there was some pride of political rivalry in having possessed her— had given Maria a splendor that made Hamilton almost faint. The words he heard had caused this faintness in him :

"O Hamilton ! to touch you is so sweet. To find you kind consoles me in a moment for all your cruelty. I love you, Hamilton."

She stopped and sighed and inhaled the golden harvest air, with its evaporation of fruitage and of the early, delicate frosts, as if the aroma of Hamilton's condescension scented the world.

Her head turned upon its fine, warm neck to this side and to that as she expanded her large frame with successive drinkings of that pippin air, the warmth and smoke of autumnal decay, and the tingle of the blood oxygenized from the ozone of rivers and of mountains. Suddenly she opened her arms and articulated the breath :

" Hamilton, won't you kiss me ? "

In the awkwardness of the instant, when duty and temptation seemed to require nothing less than a miracle to compromise their contention, a band of brass instruments in the town above brayed forth a strain that might have been the overture to the last judgment.

In another instant a battery of artillery pealed with vehement energy, shooting fifteen guns, the number of American States.

The interference was Hamilton's relief.

" You hear my commands, my friend ? Governor Mifflin is setting out. The President is far on the road to Carlisle. Let me ask you where you are to stay in this exposed time and place ? "

" What does that matter so I am near Colonel Hamilton ? Perhaps I will stay here at Harrisburg till you return."

" That will do," said Hamilton, taking the quickest pretext to make his dispositions. " I hear that Reynolds and Clingman have had an affray. Is it so ? "

" Yes; Jake used his advantage as an officer to whip Mr. Reynolds dreadfully. It was on account of Mr. Reynolds going over to you, I suppose."

" I shall observe Mr. Clingman," said Hamilton, blandly. " I suppose that you wish to be emancipated from his mastership ? "

" I ask but one master, Colonel Hamilton, and will obey him like a child. You know whom that is."

" I suppose I do," he answered gracefully. " You must completely separate yourself from Clingman, and he can then harm neither of us. It is but a step from his beating Reynolds to beating you. He will find before many days that Falstaff is without either honor or

humor in this army.   You are not going to transfer your
dependence from Clingman to Colonel Burr, Maria ? "

" Indeed, no, Hamilton."

" I thought you would not do me that injustice.   You
know that I have never harmed you, never would wish to
do so.   But you must be very careful.   While you hold
my honor in your silence and can somewhat injure me,
the instant you speak you will be destroyed.   I shall be
made to blush, but you will be entirely shunned and
friendless.   This I tell you, Maria, from every motive
of humanity.   What have you done with the letters you
extracted from Mr. Bingham's bank ? "

She had no time to invent or cajole, for his illumination
overspread her in the sentence:

" You  have  given  those  letters, Maria, to Colonel
Burr ! "

She looked upon his high Scotch forehead and rose-
and-brown complexion, now flushed with stern intelligence, and his lucid blue eyes reading her, and she fell
upon the ground and clasped his feet.

" Dear,  dreadful  Hamilton, Colonel Burr  stole them
from Mr. Clingman  at the point of the pistol that day
you came with Reynolds to confront us.   Oh! if I could
make Colonel Burr return them ! "

" It is too late," replied Hamilton.   " He would hardly
keep in · his custody letters  your  lawyer  might  replevin.
Where  would  be  the  place  of  their  ultimate  disposition ? "

Hamilton raised his fingers to his forehead, gazed a
moment upon the ground, and answered himself silently:

" Jefferson!   It is well to know the worst."

" Mercy, Hamilton! " exclaimed the woman at his feet.

" Maria, when those letters come to light I shall stand
forth and relate the truth.   It will be necessary to name
you and to  describe you.   Before that hour comes what
will be your character that is to be described ?   Go, my
poor girl, and improve it, that you may have a better
account to give of it.   I pity you with all my heart."

He was gone, and she was dismayed by the seriousness of his kindness.

In an aimless way she strolled into Harrisburg, and
saw Joe Priestley putting his wife in the Philadelphia
stage at the tavern door.

As Joseph turned away with weeping eyes he ran against Mrs. Reynolds.

"Where are you going, Reynolds ?" he asked, without motive.

There was a roll of drums at the ferry landing ; Hamilton was being received on board the barge, and was about to cross the Susquehanna.

" Joe, you're a widower ; I am a widow. Both of us are deserted. Won't you take me to Carlisle to see the army?"

" I don't care, Reynolds ; it's but sixteen miles, I hear. Yes ; come along, lass, and drown our sorrows."

Almost everything wheeled and every sort of beast of burden were engaged to carry congressmen, contractors, politicians, and belated military officers to Carlisle.

The only conveyance Joe Priestley could get for Maria was a seat in an emigrant farm-wagon bound for the West, and occupied by flying Marylanders from the Eastern shore, who had taken the universal alarm at the yellow fever's visitations to the cities, and resolved to quit their typhoid and bilious fever districts for the new land of the Maumee and the Wabash, which had just been cleared of Indians by General Wayne.

Those emigrating poor white classes were found in the subsequent march sprinkling all the way to Pittsburgh, giving amusement to the soldiery, and alternate days shaking with the chill or hectic with the fever. Moving westward before the day of public education, they were to seed much of the farther West with a poor quality of human grain, and be the demagogue's sickling for two or three generations. The soldiery were often seen with the greatest wonder and alarm by these people, who had observed nothing of the Revolutionary War in their remote peninsulas except the persecution of some sectarian or other, held to be "a Tory."

Joe Priestley manfully walked by the rickety wagon, where Maria yawned upon the best quilt of the emigrants, whose eyes never ceased to be distended as they gazed and gazed upon her from their household rubbish —bed, chairs, spinet, tin pans, and kitchen junk.

There were six children, a grown daughter, man and wife, and two doleful slave boys, four small oxen, and two forest ponies. The daughter was of a pallid, sweet expression, and Maria said to her :

"Why do you move all these poor effects so very far?"

"Lord-a-massy!" exclaimed the girl's mother, "it's tuk us a lifetime to get 'em, honey. We don't want to sleep in the pore-house out yonder, wha' we gwyn."

"I wish I was your daughter, going too," Maria spoke.

"You?" broke forth the girl, "with them rings on your fingers? I reckon you never go barefoot, du ye? I had a pair of shues one time, tu."

The old man shook the fabric of the wagon as his ague rattled his bones, and the little children cried because the "pone" bread was gone.

"O Joseph!" sighed Maria, "what a price they pay to keep virtuous. But," she added, to her own premonitory heart, "there are also poor-houses for the vicious and lonely dyings in them."

The glorious Cumberland Valley stood high between the crystal drains within the parallel mountain ridges, and the limestone outcrops had lured the German in from his adjacent settlements of York County; fields were already clean and worm-fenced; the farm settlements were changing from log to limestone; the unfolding valley, twenty miles from side to side, seemed to be the cathedral nave to some glorious chancel at the centre of the continent.

It was nearly night when they entered Carlisle, a large village of log and limestone dwellings and trading-stores, with the Penns' square in the middle and on it the established church of North Ireland—military Presbyterian. A clear limestone spring ran by the town to one of the neighboring creeks, and on the public square the military were burning the whiskey liberty pole before the court-house—having chopped this pole down and killed during the day two swaggering fools who presumed that the soldiers had orders not to fire.

These deaths, self-provoked, cast upon the situation and society that awe in which communities begin to realize the existence of war.

In the midst of that indescribable dread the governor of Pennsylvania, with a huge staff, was entering the borough at the head of three thousand men of his own line, and at passing the headquarters of Washington in the town, the respective companies broke into cheers like battle-feelings.

Their uniforms, generally blue and hardly soiled as yet by exposure, were finer than governments give their soldiery—broadcloth lined, slashed or striped with buff and gold. The number of cavalry was large, and their steeds, caparisons, and bearing magnificent—the horses frequently of the same color in whole companies, with bay predominant, and bridles, stirrups, and martingales glittering with silver. As the wide lines rode into Carlisle, every trooper raised his sabre or sword to Washington, and every nostril was seen to expand.

The foot kept step, and their officers were in many cases from the Revolutionary line—men who had inflicted death, and by the interval of peace looked back with holy joy and worship to their military service, of which the emblem was the consecrated nation. And now, amid the booming and clashing of bands, the scream of the fife, and the terrifying roll of drums, with short, repeated orders shouted down the lines to wheel, or keep time, or present, the Revolutionary veterans and their sons in arms beheld the man they held to be God's vicegerent and his humanity almost sacred, standing out in the light of torches, with Hamilton and Bradford of his Cabinet behind him, and others of mark also looking down from Montgomery's house, at dinner.

While Washington stood there—oldish, impersonal, passionless—and the daylight faded away, the courthouse broke into illumination, for Governor Mifflin was to make a speech.

A large transparency before that plain forum of justice bore the words :

" Washington is ever Triumphant."
" The Reign of the Laws."
" Woe to Anarchists."

As the soldiery were distributed for the night's bivouac —some to the old Hessian prison quarters outside of the town, some to warehouses, and some to churches—Joe Priestley ran upon Mr. Cooper and his wife, and asked where they were quartering.

" I presented Doctor Priestley's compliments to Doctor Nisbet, president of the college here," replied Cooper, "and was invited to take a room with him.    Come along and I'll make bold to ask quarters for you."

The college was a limestone house in a narrow street or alley, off the public green.    The old Scotch president, who had been imported to set up another Cambridge on the frontier of the world, greeted Joseph Priestley and said :

"I can put the two ladies in one room above, and you two men in a little room on the street.    Here, Master Roger Taney, go light these friends to their quarters ! "

Hamilton had been dining with President Washington, and quarters had been found for him at a small stone house upon a street corner by General Hand, the old adjutant-general of Washington at Yorktown.

"Hamilton, I brought you here," said Hand, "to save you from importunity for favors and rank.    The town is full of camp followers, men and women, and new whiskey may do its work to-night.    Here you will be unobserved. This is the same house where poor Major André and his friend, Lieutenant Despard, were confined in 1776, after they were captured in Canada."

Hamilton put his portmanteau down and found himself alone.

"André's first prison," he thought, looking around. "I saw him in his last prison ; I took his last wishes ; I saw him die.    These walls have echoed the voice whose last appeal I shall never cease to hear : ' Must I, then, die on the gallows ?    I am reconciled to my fate, but not to the mode.' "

Hamilton had been taking wine, for the dinner was made merry by the wit of Judge Peters and old army chords and revivals.    Hamilton had sung his song of " The Drum," and relaxed to the gayety of the camp.

As he sat in this small stone corner dwelling, with windows on two streets, he looked around the plain, clean room, with its one feather-bed and bright-burning fire, and felt that some society would be preferable to sleep.

His mind ran upon the beautiful bride of Arnold, who had been also the tender friend of André, and by her too assiduous correspondence laid the temptation for these men to communicate and then to corrupt each other. Hamilton had seen her with her first, her bridal babe, in her arms, her husband just fled and her lover taken as a spy, a frantic woman, countryless, homeless, and compromised with both armies, and he spoke aloud :

"Never did man suffer death with more justice than André and deserve it less! Even a virtuous woman may pull down history upon many men by her too diffusive charms. The law of safety is in selfishness. Poor Margaret Shippen! In his last hours André told me it was love of her which drew him past the British lines. How love makes way with honor! From being adjutant of the king's army he died upon the criminal's cord."

As he spoke, the door opened from the street, as if by the autumn wind, and sent the fire sparks from the cheery logs up the stone chimney.

Hamilton could not see from his bright interior against the opaque night.

The door opened easily, slowly, and also mysteriously.

Hamilton felt as if the spirit of Margaret Arnold might have opened it, to revisit André's prison and himself who had invoked her.

There was a something there like the evasive outline of a female.

He started forward, and at the sill a moan came out of the dark :

"Oh! shelter me ; take me out of the cold streets of Carlisle!"

He had not time to distinguish the personage by his ear or mind when a tall form in robes slipped past him and threw out its arms and clasped the bed at the farther part of his room.

"A man has pursued me all over Carlisle. Two men, I thought. And all men I have seen looked at me so boldly I was terrified. Mr. Joseph is intoxicated and has taken my bedroom. Thank God, I found you, Hamilton!"

Colonel Hamilton closed the door.

Maria Livingston, Reynolds, or Clingman was his visitor.

He felt mingled emotions sweep through him, and one was something like pleasure.

Not the serious associations he had invoked brought a visitant to him, for rectitude is seldom haunted, being without ghosts of its own. But he had almost wished for society instead of sleep, and society was here, in form not altogether unlike the wayward nature of his wish.

" Maria, how did you find this place ? "

" By fear," she answered. " I thought I was pursued. Terror took me to the nearest door, and it is the door of compassion—I hope, Hamilton, of love ! "

" Pursued *here* ? " queried Hamilton, opening the door again and walking forth.

The night had come down with a frost and merciless wind, starless and repelling. Loud laughter and contention made the human sounds of the perfect dark, broken by the call of " Halt ! " and " Pass on ! " from unseen sentinels. Finding no skulkers around the André house, Hamilton went in and shook himself between the chill without and the glow within. He lighted another candle and put dry wood and corn-cobs upon the fire.

" What am I to do with you, poor girl ? "

She arose and walked to him and seemed to suffer for a moment as she put her hand upon his shoulder and glanced down, tarrying, embarrassed.

" It is midnight," continued Hamilton; " too late for me to find quarters without much inconvenience. And you——"

She raised her eyes, looked him in the face, hesitated, and smiled, and pushing him off with her hand, stepped backward, and with her hand behind her locked the door.

" This room is good enough for me," she spoke with a twinkle between pathos and humor. And suddenly a flood of fervor, a flash of mischief, a giving way of every embarrassment to a tender boldness, raised her spirit and her stature up.

With hands lifted and arms stretched wide she impelled herself on Hamilton's neck and clung there obstinately.

" This is my room," she whispered, " because it is yours. You came to mine and asked it from me. You pleaded for that shelter, Hamilton. It is too late to turn me out ; I will not go ! "

Her head was upon his shoulder, heavily, drowsily. He had to support her weight, for she was reckless whether she fell or not.

Some demon whispered to him : " Now is the time to

annex this woman to your interests, and by love.   How
easy ! "

"Two years ago we separated, Maria," said Hamilton, "by means you invented or acceded to.   I paid the
price demanded of my weakness.   Unlock the door, or
I cannot remain in this chamber ! "

"You shall not leave it, sir.  I will scream if you wres-
tle for this key with me or break the stout lock.   Listen, my dear old ardent, violent, unappeasable lover !
It is nearly two years since you have kissed me.  Yes,
all that time, sir !  I followed you to Carlisle, because
I knew you would appreciate me here, where nothing
but men are found.   Not to be your tempter in the city
—only to be your solace in the lonely camp, I came because I understood your nature, Hamilton.   Confess you
are glad I came to you ! "

"The key !  I command you, Maria ! "

"Ah ! no.   If I draw that bolt it will break the spell
I feel I am throwing upon you, dear, hypocritical truant.
You were so good, so kind to me at Harrisburg that the
tones you spoke to me in called me like sweet bells as
far as Carlisle.   I said to myself, ' One day, or, perhaps,
some days, of happiness I shall have there with him—the
only man I can ever love.'   I called God to confirm or
punish my honesty, if I loved you, O exquisite man! who
misled me.  Shall you, who once pleaded so hard with me
for love, refuse to hear the despair you have awakened ?
No, sir; it is my turn to sue.   Are you any better than I
was when you found me, and swore you were my admirer ? "

She held his frame in her languorous yet half-resolute
hands, and looked at him like one with wrongs, willing to
forgive.

He felt the divine excellence of creation in her stately
mould and kindled life as she asked for justice between
moral offenders.   He sighed :

"I am better by chastisement, I hope, my fellow-sin-
ner.  I have paid the penalty of prodigals ; I· have
eaten husks.  I have seen my child suffer.  My pride has
been pulled down.  I could not even confess my shame,
as the good papists do.  All confession, and therefore
all sympathy, were closed to me."

"You are mine," breathed the woman, with a shaking

off of her drowsy indolence. " I can hear your groans, I can pardon your sins. No woman in this world can kiss your tears away but I."

" I cannot confess myself," said Hamilton, "but woman's affection can see to the bottom of a well where truth is. A woman has guessed my offence, and blessed me with forgiveness."

" Your wife ? "

" Do not speak that holy name ! "

" I know the woman, then," Maria said. " I am American and not to be replaced by her, the English lady who has come between us. Sir, my blood is the best in the province of New York. If I have dragged the Livingston stock through dirty places, that is still my race. No Priestley blood is better, nor Schuyler, nor Hamilton."

She stood erect, yet easily, drawing back and looking at him from a skin more pale than flushed, her expression that of pride's self-possession.

It became her better than any look she had ever worn, and raised her higher in Hamilton's regard, for he recognized that race which, in public station or personal force, disciplined or wanton, had been felt in New York since its foundation—agile but unconquerable, Scotch and Dutch, the marrying Livingstons.

Unconsciously the temptress had led her highest trump. It was now a lady before Hamilton, with the delicacy of her haughtiness among the other treasures she had to offer him, and the Livingstons were his foes.

He felt the healthy warmth and exhilaration of the fire, and the fatigue of his encounter with so various charms and resources.

As the quality of this renewed amour grew upon the enlarged experience and mentality of the Livingston " black sheep," the secretary seemed contending against fate.

" There is always an appeal, my well-derived friend," he struggled to say, "from one woman's cruelty to the court and jury of her whole sex. In the counsel of women a broken man, misled by strong temptation, is heard, confessed, and shrived. It is not one woman only who has guessed us out, Mistress Livingston."

She took his chair, there being but one chair in the

room, and stretched her feet toward the fire with wounded
sensibility upon her face, and after an effort said :

"I suppose I need not be an unwelcome vagrant seeking shelter in vain from my lover, even in Carlisle.
Major Armstrong, who is now here visiting his father, the
general, and Doctor Armstrong, his brother, is married
to my distant relative, Alida Livingston. Blood is thicker
than water, though Hamilton does not admit it. They
keep a fine large house in Carlisle. I will go and ask
*shelter* there."

If this had been artful, it deceived Hamilton. Spoken
in a chord nearly plaintive but resisting the disposition
to give way to grief, the words melted Hamilton to distress by their helpless pride.

He knelt at her feet.

"I will not drive you out," he said. "Let *me* go to
Doctor Armstrong's and tell him you are here."

She wavered, struggled, fought down a sob, and answered:

"Very well. I can trample on my self-esteem no
longer. I have asked you nothing but what you taught
me. I hope I am not as worthless everywhere as to
Hamilton."

The tears came now in a flood. Hamilton caught the
weeping Juno in his arms and cried:

"O heaven ! is there no repentance but in streams
of tears like these and hardness of the heart to women's
groans ? What can I do ?"

She neither resisted nor consented, but continued to
weep, and he implored her pardon as the moments wore
on ; angels might have separated the guilty one from the
better one, but these two could not, in the neutral light of
their past transgression. He was already reasoning her
to be a victim of circumstances.

She appreciated the demoralization that was coming
upon him, and as he once looked into her eyes, she
seemed to shiver.

"Sir," she lisped, "my feet are wet. I have walked in
the pools of water and mud where the soldiers have been.
Will you take off my shoe and let me dry my foot ?"

She stretched herself languidly back. The fire shone
along her elegant stature, warming its long proportions to
life like Pygmalion's egotism.

Hamilton hesitated.

"What!" she smiled, heightening and bending forward. "Have you forgotten your courtesy? This room is more hospitable than you. How genial feels the fire, Hamilton! And I am very drowsy. O soldier, *man!* are you made of stone? I cannot kill you with my little foot."

He looked at her, and it seemed that virtue was passing out of him as by the touch of her foot and her extended hand.

"Here," sighed Maria, with a laugh, "take this key and let me out, if you dare!"

In the interval of his irresolution she threw the key into the fire and herself into his arms.

Steps, voices at that instant drew near.

A knock of a man's knuckles fell upon the door.

"Who is there?" gasped Hamilton.

"It is I, Colonel Hamilton. If you have not retired I will have a word with you: THE PRESIDENT!"

The woman's lips turned pale. They shaped but did not speak the word:

"Washington!"

In a moment she had glided through a door at the rear of the chamber and closed it behind her.

Hamilton drew the key from the ashes, though it blistered his fingers, and he opened the street door to General Washington.

The President took the chair and the secretary stood before him:

"I had consulted all but you, Mr. Hamilton, and before General Hand issues the order, I thought it reasonable to lay before you my selection of Governors, according to military rank, in this campaign. For commander-in-chief, Henry Lee."

"He is warmly attached to you."

"Second in rank, Governor Mifflin."

"This leaves Governor Howell, of New Jersey, to be third. He is the only Federalist of the three."

"I cannot put in order the future. Howell is too good a soldier to take offence; Mifflin must now act the principal part in spite of himself. He is already much elated and will make better speeches than ever. I hope I have given him a chance to make his lasting peace with his-

tory, for I would have no man think at my death that I
had abbreviated his career. As for Lee, he is matchless
for discipline, despatch, and decision. His self-esteem is
great, but this need not be a mean quality, and gratitude
and services are cheaply bought by praise. Governor
Lee hardly expected this appointment, since Pennsylvania is the seat of war."

"Mr. President, your reasons are conclusive."

"I would like you, Colonel Hamilton, to ride with me
on my way to Cumberland as far as the Conococheague
settlements. I am told that you can cross the mountains
expeditiously thence to Bedford. I want to lay before
you the necessity of discipline in this army. The Phila-
delphians have killed one man, the Jersey troops another.
If this was unavoidable, it was also unfortunate. Among
these Scotch-Irish the killing of any man starts revengeful passions. By good treatment they will come through
this purgation the greatest race in the American family.
The proper thing to do, Mr. Hamilton, is to make an
example of the first law-breaking officer of this army. If
you can hear of one, let him not be overlooked, but punished."

"I will accompany you to your quarters," said Hamilton as the President rose and wrapped his long cloak
about him.

"It will be unnecessary, as I shall go at once to bed."

A man's form was seen in the dark alley as Hamilton
passed it. When he returned the form was still there,
and the secretary laid hold of it without roughness.

"Let me see your face, friend," he said.

Throwing open his shutter to let the light illuminate
his prisoner, Hamilton saw a bruised, swollen, fevered
face, in which he finally made out the likeness of James
Reynolds.

"A good soldier and marked like this without a battle, Mr. Reynolds?"

"That is the handiwork of Jake Clingman, sir. As
he is in Carlisle, I thought of you and that he might
kill you, sir. So I came to watch your house."

"How did you learn my location?"

"I heard Jake tell it to—to my wife, that was. He keeps
about a sutlery here, which I reckon he has an interest in.
He also keeps a gambling place near town, or supports it."

" How do you know that ? "

" I have been there, sir."

" Can you lead me there, Mr. Reynolds ? "

" I think I can, sir."

" Then sit in my room till I send for you.    What do the Clingman family want of me ? "

" The old trick, sir ; your money.    That is Jake Clingman's god.    He set Maria on you to-night."

Hamilton passed out, and paused in the dark to murmur to his horrified soul:

" Almighty God. Thou art my preserver !    Had Washington not been sent by Thee, I had been exposed to jealous Reynolds, prying upon his wife at my window shutter.    And she, who could play the injured lady to perfection, was on Clingman's errand to lay me low again ! "

He thought of Reynolds' information, and a calm decision came to his mind.

" It will never do to treat my private injuries as public offences.    Neither will it do to let public offences pass because of private delicacy.    ' Make an example of him,' said Washington.    ' Let him be punished.' "

In a few minutes a small body of cavalry was before the André house, with a saddled horse for Reynolds.

" Go show these dragoons the place where gaming is done, Mr. Reynolds," commanded Hamilton, locking his door and going to bed.


North of Carlisle, on the banks of the Conedogwinit Creek, was a cave with an arched portal of nearly perfect curve, and not far within stretched out a low chamber of limestone of considerable depth, where the army gamblers had been in secret possession all day.

A fire lighted within took away the dampness, while the cavity concealed the blaze.    Here Clingman's associates had set up their machines of hazard to get from the city soldiery the money with which they had started for the long march of two hundred miles westward from Carlisle.

Mr. Reynolds was sent in with two or three dragoons to supply evidence of the infraction of army law to the provost marshal.

Reynolds at once began to play, and such was his infatuation for gambling that when the signal was given
and the cavalry entered and made prisoners of all present, Mr. Reynolds had totally forgotten that they were
near, and had lost every cent he possessed.

Mrs. Reynolds, on leaving Hamilton, had glided off
with anger and recklessness to the man whose marriage-
tie she wore.

He was counting his money at a shop or booth down
toward the little stream called Le Tort, which ran through
Carlisle and supplied a distillery that Mr. Clingman's
combination had leased for the campaign.

Clingman threw his arms around Maria, his wife, and
found her not indisposed to his attentions.

"Ducky, did you blackmail Hamilton?" he gurgled,
with eyes darting like talons revealed by the yellow glit-
ter of a heap of money before him.

"No, Jake. I had almost conquered when Washington came and scared me away. But I will not give him
up."

She swore an oath, the first evidence of the pollution
of the soul in the false woman's progress. It made
Clingman rejoice that she was coming nearer to his
earthy foundation.

"Yes, cuss him, Mari! It will do you good. Damn
him, too, for a-refusin' charms that makes J. Clingman
pray in vain. Wifey, this is the home, the humble-bee,
the busy-bee home of J. Clingman and his Mari. Ain't
it your'n to-night?"

"You can't kneel like Hamilton, Jake. Get up! How
much am I to get of that plunder? I must have
clothes."

"All you want, Mari. The sutler store runs like a
quarter hoss. I've sent a hundred men to-day out to the
faro-bank an' snapper-wheel. Take all you want, for a
hunderd days of glory and loot is before J. C. in this
campaign."

"I'll take what I want in the morning. Leave it
there."

At early morning Mrs. Clingman softly arose, took all
Mr. Clingman's money in his bandanna handkerchief,

and fled away to the little Dickinson academy of a college in the alley.

There she saw in the downstairs room Joe Priestley fast asleep, his solitary condition and pilgrimage on foot having been the cause of many hot whiskeys the night before.

Mrs. Reynolds looked at him with dislike and mutiny.

" He may never get drunk again," she thought, " any more than Cassio, in the play. He has kept me out all night and does not know it. Why can't I get in my own bed ? "

The light was coming up in the west. The *reveille* began to sound in the town's environs.

" Hamilton may insult my advances of love," mused the parasite woman, " but I shall punish *this* dolt for his indifference. For him alone I would not take the trouble, but his wife is Hamilton's guardian angel, who 'blesses him with forgiveness' for my transgressions. Mrs. Priestley 'can see to the bottom of a well where truth is.' Now, let her try ! "

She stretched herself upon the outer edge of the bed with so little compunction that she went almost immediately to sleep.

The morning was well advanced, and the smell of many breakfasts took the chill from the frost when Joseph Priestley was awakened by Mr. Cooper putting cold water on his head.

" I say, Josie, arise ! These be odd capers for thee."

Poor Joe, with a throbbing head and hot coppers, followed Cooper's eyes to where the mould of Reynolds lay, still sleeping fast.

" I don't remember anything that took place last night," muttered Joe. " I can't remember going to bed —nothing whatever."

" If appearances will convict you, Joe," said Cooper, with a dry sneer from virtue's depths, " you are a divorced man. I wouldn't have believed it."

Mrs. Reynolds opened her eyes, gave a little nervous scream, and covered her head with whatever clothing came to hand to conceal her mischief.

" Joseph has a wife, Mr. Cooper," she vouchsafed from this retreat. " Oh ! pray bestow no misery there."

Joe Priestley looked more blank than sad.

"Well," said he, finally, "I can affirm, that I was in my cups. But nothing whatever can I deny."

At *reveille* Lieutenant Clingman awoke. He looked beside him and around him.

Wife and money were gone.

"Mari!" he cried. "She has indeed taken what she wanted, and it is my all."

"Turn out! turn out!" called the guard. "This battalion is ordered to march three miles before breakfast. The order from Colonel Hamilton is that any officer tardy, absent, or loitering is to be put in irons. Forward to your platoon, Clingman!"

"Go forward, Jake!" a co-partner whispered. "The speiling was pulled last night. Your poncess has mizzled. Reynolds was the stall."

The music of the march resounded:

"*Forward, march!*"

"Death and hell!" muttered Clingman. "I'll live to settle with them all."

---

## CHAPTER XVI.

### JAKE CLINGMAN DRUMMED OUT.

WAR cures broken hearts, and Bobby Lewis saw so many pretty girls as he rode down the valley with his fortunate brother, Larry—through Shippensburg, where the army turned off, and through Chambersburg and the Conococheague settlements—that he told Mr. Lear and his uncle Washington he meant to cross the mountains and take a wife and farm.

The President now proceeded to Cumberland, while Hamilton and a few mounted friends moved out from the Welsh settlement to pass the great Tuscarora Mountain by a trail. The mighty mass of rock and woods seemed to open as they approached like a gray cloud, and showed a cove that had a low gate cut by a brook, and beyond this opening seemed nothing but a deep, round bowl of forest and rampart, sublime and serene. Yet within the cove a little way they came to a "store" or settler's shop, of stones and logs, and found some

pack-horses loading with supplies for the Monongahela.
Within the Irish trader's cot the gentlemen took some of
the cove whiskey and a snack of venison.

"If I had my Eliza here," said Hamilton to the young
trader's wife, "I should be the happiest settler in this
cove.   What is this little fellow's name ?"

"James—James Buchanan, sir," replied the young
mother, giving her child to the secretary.

"May the United States last after Jamie is its President, madame !"

Out of the cove, like motes ascending within a blue-
bell, the travellers wound, and gaining the summit after
miles, looked over upon a small valley like a grave, posied
with new-broken farms, and pebbled by a small, new
hamlet.

Down the mountain, up the next one, down the next
and over others, the party went along in forests illimitable, till they found the army the second day, toiling
up the heights and wondering at the profusion of mountains, also marching like themselves upon converging
lines through stars and storms.   But the human army
seemed hardly a caterpillar, dwarfed by the Nature it had
entered on.   The few settlers, however, were sickly creatures compared to the soldiery, who were only worn with
unaccustomed marching.

Hamilton's soul thrilled with the soft yet sacred scenery,
which seemed to his chastened spirit the revealment of
God's mercy and majesty—stupendous as the meaning,
"I was set up from everlasting, before the mountains
were settled, * * and my delights were with the sons
of men."

The predestinarian in his Scotch type carried his
imagination no farther than the Scriptures and belief,
and out of this faith came his love of fond authority
on earth and love of raising altars of institutions instead
of playing the worshipper like Cain, razing his brother's
altar.

"God bless Pennsylvania, gentlemen !" exclaimed the
constructive soul of Hamilton as he came to the Juniata
crossings.   "Though she slay us, yet will we praise her."

He saw the Little Juniata sweep the mountain's base
and hug the mountain's ribs and the mountain promon-
tory, like that vast galley stranded on Ararat, feeling the

Deluge subside in the gentle stream that flowed about its beak.

There, in the night, Hamilton lay in a log tavern, with the witty Judge Peters and a fellow West-Indian from Jamaica, named Dallas, who had here escaped from the political contaminations of Mifflin's group.  All three were joyous natures, and in the rare, cold air blowing through the chinks they lay and laughed at repartees and listened to the passing wagons and fed their green-wood fire till nothing was heard at last but the Juniata muttering underneath as to the meaning of those camp-fires burnishing its rapids.

All was still.

The man from Jamaica saw a shadow from the fire strike upon the naked wall to which his face was turned; he did not move, but watched this mysterious shadow in the late chamber of mirth and anecdote.  It was that of one in prayer, with hands raised and head uplifted.  Not a sound was heard but the softest sigh.

The tall Scotch head, the Roman nose, the well-produced and already historic jaws and chin, described that shadow's original to be the man from Nevis, the hated opponent of his faction, Hamilton.

Both these men were Scotch West-Indians.  The *prestige* of Hamilton had already softened Dallas' prejudice when it so youthfully relaxed to fun and fellowship.

" That is my enemy," thought Dallas, still as sleep, but thrilled in all his Scottish type.  " Let me pray, too, from that example. 'God bless Mr. Hamilton ! ' "

Twenty-one years were to pass before Dallas was to become a successor of Hamilton as the Finance Minister. He found the finances, taxation, the public *morale*, everything deranged and almost destroyed by fourteen years of Jefferson's prejudices applied to the state.  The capitol, the President's house, lay in ashes, burned by the foreign enemy.

The new secretary felt it hard to tear himself away from the illusions of party, but reason pointed the only way — increased, candid taxation ; a tariff, a national bank.

" Dare I recommend these things we have rejected with their author's fame ? " Dallas thought.

Then he saw the shadow of a head long since given to the worms—a tall, Scotch head and Roman nose and martial profile, in the act of prayer.

"Back, back to Hamilton!" exclaimed Secretary Dallas, seizing his pen. "I say again my mountain prayer: 'God bless him!'"

And yet, so close together lie the godlike and the human, that Hamilton's prayer that night had been for his wife's pity and forgiveness.

They came to Bedford next day, occupying a level shelf above the Juniata, where once had stood an old Indian stockade; some stone and log houses around a court-house now, and two hundred residents, and the great army encamped upon its all-surrounding hill-sides, in lines of fleecy tents by day and golden fire by night, lighting up the great ox-backed mountains, while the rare air bore the strains of music to the stars that spread above like the field in the floating ensign at each headquarters, Jersey and Pennsylvania.

The old Jersey governor was a Revolutionary soldier who had made a song that was thought very fine, and his band played it several times a day, as follows:

To arms once more! our hero cries;
Sedition lives and order dies;
To peace and ease then bid adieu,
And dash to the mountains, Jersey Blue.

CHORUS:   Dash to the mountains, Jersey Blue,
                   Jersey Blue, Jersey Blue,
              And dash to the mountains, Jersey Blue.

Pennsylvania had no song, nor was there any national song, and Hamilton was not a poet. However, with some assistance, to gratify the Pennsylvania boys, he sang them, to an accompaniment of flute, fife, and drum, his old Revolutionary air:

### THE DRUM.

Hear the gentle sheep soft bleat,
   "Ba-a-ah, ba-a-ah,"
As they wheel like soldiers' feet,
   Ra-ta-tah, ra-ta-tah.

Like their gentle souls we come,
          Ba-a-ah, ba-a-ah,
And the sheepskin makes our drum :
          Ra-ta-tah !
          Ra-ta-tah !
          Ra-ta-tah !


Hear the lover softly sigh—
          " Ba-a-ah, ba-a-ah "—
For his love he'll march and die,
          Ra-ta-tah ! ra-ta-tah !
Helpless hands do overcome—
          Ba-a-ah, ba-a-ah—
Like the fingers on the drum :
          Ra-ta-tah !
          Ra-ta-tah !
          Ra-ta-tah !


Hear the little children weep,
          " Ba-a-ah, ba-a-ah,"
Like the tender little sheep—
          Ba-a-ah, ba-a-ah.
But their terrors rouse the dumb
          Ra-ta-tah ! ra-ta-tah !
And their sob is in the drum:
          Ra-ta-tah !
          Ra-ta-tah !
          Ra-ta-tah !


Do you see this harmless flock—
          Ba-a-ah, ba-a-ah—
Filing up the mountain rock ?
          Ra-ta-tah ! ra-ta-tah !
There is nothing quarrelsome,
          Ba-a-ah, ba-a-ah,
In the bleating of our drum :
          Ra-ta-tah !
          Ra-ta-tah !
          Ra-ta-tah !


We are only clad in wool,
          Ba-a-ah, ba-a-ah;
We are marching in from school,
          Ra-ta-tah ! ra-ta-tah !
And the lesson that we hum—
          Ba-a-ah, ba-a-ah—
You shall hear upon the drum :
          Ra-ta-tah !
          Ra-ta-tah !
          Ra-ta-tah !

If the wolf is in these hills—
    Ba-a-ah, ba-a-ah—
'Tis the fife the wolf that thrills :
    Ra-ta-tah ! ra-ta-tah !
'Tis a little drummer's thumb,
    Ba-a-ah, ba-a-ah,
Thrills the sheepskin to a drum :
    Ra-ta-tah !
    Ra-ta-tah !
    Ra-ta-tah !


Can that be Columbia's cry?
    " Ba-a-ah, ba-a-ah."
Forward, march ! For she may die :
    Ra-ta-tah ! ra-ta-tah !
Dear mother, straight we come,
    Ra-ta-tah ! ra-ta-tah !
'Tis your sons with fife and drum—
    Ra-ta-tah !
    Ra-ta-tah !
    Ra-ta-tah !

President Washington and Governor Lee arrived at Bedford from Cumberland the twentieth of October. Four dragoons were the President's only escort. Instead of the magnificence which attended the mighty Mifflin's movements, fifteen guns welcomed the President, and all the camps cheered, and straightway business began.

Philadelphia troops were despatched into the surrounding country for offenders, and brought in thirteen miserable objects, who had been locally greater than Washington. As these "leaders of the people" rode on their forest-fed ponies through the army, each preceded, flanked, and followed by a trooper of noble air and knightly uniform, the militia looked on in astonishment that these degraded beings had caused the State such expense.

Lieutenant Jake Clingman began to feel very uneasy as his sutler's operations were put to an end. Not a sutler was now allowed in the army, which was attended by seven hundred wagons, the government doing its own feeding.

So Clingman contemplated a little well-sheltered gambling, but his attention was arrested by this order, signed by General Lee :

*PROCLAMATION.*

*" To the above parental counsel of our beloved Chief Magistrate, the commander begs leave to add the flattering hopes he entertains that the conduct of the army will justify the favorable anticipation formed of it. Thus shall we establish to ourselves a character the most amiable and exhibit to posterity a model to all future armies.*

*" Lest, however, some individual may have crept into the ranks, callous to all the feelings of honor, of virtue, and consequently the fair character so justly due to the great body of the troops may be snatched from them by the licentiousness of the few, the commandants of divisions, brigades, regiments, and corps are required to examine minutely their respective troops before the army moves, and dismiss all whom they deem unworthy of participating in the honorable service in which we have embarked."*

Mr. Clingman at once undertook to desert, but it strangely happened that the Secretary of the Treasury met him, and without further notice gave him a reading look which frightened him back to his camp.

" Durn that villain ! " was Mr. Clingman's reflection. " I reckon he'll have me drummed out of camp." Then, considerately, " No, I wisht he would. But he won't. Fur I have a proclamation of my own in that ewent, signed J. Clingman, wolunteer, and his Mari."

The oath Lieutenant Clingman uttered at the name of his Mari was too extravagant to be entirely printed.

" Let wengeance fall upon that fickle roe ! " he called. "Let hell horn-swaggle her ! How tender I have been ! And how indulgent ! She's played me the shakedown, the tetch crib, the ordinary, femiliar, redickelus panel foolery, fit for infants an' collegians. Me, that's fetched her up from childhood fur a great career and downed my belchins of jealousy like a noble mind ! My genius," added Mr. Clingman, weeping, " has been insulted by this high-steppin' New York Yankee star-gazer. What kin I do ? "

As he reflected, with somewhat sincere sensibilities aroused, he saw glancing at him in the streets of Bedford, the second husband, Reynolds.

" I've got it ! " muttered Clingman ; " she wants that feller killed. I won't leave the army ; I'll go ahead, though thar's but one road back, unless I escape down the Ohier River. My gun'll go off in these yer mountains some time before we git to Pittsburgh."

The news from the West at the main seat of rebellion, a

hundred miles away, was so assuring that President Washington returned to his capital, while Hamilton accompanied the army.

The marching out of Bedford was for that period magnificent, as the small organizations composing the wing wore their own selection of uniforms, modelled upon everything contemporary and traditional—Prussian bear hats, mediæval helmets, thigh boots, French chasseur leggings, Continental uniforms.

There were twelve hundred cavalry and seven thousand of other arms; artillery plentiful, trains heretofore unequalled in American wars; and the route was an old and narrow military road cut nearly forty years before, which stretched the line out many miles.

Before went the pioneers to take off fallen trees ; the Quartermaster's men were corduroying and filling hollow places. In the solemn shades the music of cities and civilization dismayed and held spell-bound the savage beasts. Many a rattlesnake disputed the way to bite himself and die.

As they left below the sources of Eastern rivers and climbed the amazing grade of the Backbone or main mountain, many a soldier thought of Braddock's march to be massacred upon that parallel road, where now the Left wing, five thousand strong, was also moving, yet a week's distance from mutual relief with this Right wing.

The solemnity of the march soon gave way to a nearly universal exhaustion. Green muscles, tender feet, were strained and bruised by the unusual toil, and backs and hearts suffered from carrying burdens, while the rare air made the lungs pant, and disabled men were often seen at the wayside livid as death. Yet even in this ghastliness one could mark their terror of being left behind to spend the night in the tall, tawny forest, which stretched like the billows of the sea before the mariners of Columbus westward and ever westward.

Water gave out ; the dry, baked mountain, pulverized beneath hoofs, wheels, and feet, seemed to yield no springs, or those which flowed were sucked dry by this unexpected progeny of men. Some, who read the little science that was known, thought with bitter mockery upon the great Doctor Priestley's assertion that vegetable and human life exactly supported each other by exchanging

oxygen and carbon.   " Why not water here, then, in proportion to our numbers?" was the challenge.

Alas ! man's overcrowding breaks nature's providence
everywhere, in war or cities, and in that day not one, however superior in education, who clambered up the last
terrace of the Alleghany chain, knew the first principle
of geology.   To the most knowing all these rocks were
mere *menstruum*, or chaotic fluid hardened, some thought
by fire and some by water; and in proportion to their
speculative ignorance the children in science were the
more positive and intolerant.

But there was one sound among those rock ribs no solemnity of suggestion or scenery could appall—the sound
that has come down the world as long and as old as
the nations, before Babel was built or the Sphinx pro-
pounded—the hearty, the wholesome, the lurid, and individual swearing of the teamster damning his team.

At that almost innocent, unpremeditated, and perfect
concession to the fact of a Creator and the advisability of
a hell, the tired army stopped to laugh, the Titans in the
clouds appeared to hold their sides, and in the pauses of
the cursing was heard the Diogenes of a crow flying overhead and getting in his word of " Caw ! caw ! "

The monstrous shades opened at the mountain summits,
where some poet among the pioneers had ordered a clearing to be cut, and the standards of the commands as they
successively arrived were there unfurled amidst cheers
and the reverberation of cannon, which seemed to roll
over that illimitable sea of mountains without homes like
the voice of the lonely Creator on the earth before he had
made man.

While these guns were thundering, the woods were being
felled at old Presqu'ile, the future Erie City, for the first
time, and no American town existed on the Great Lakes.
Oswego was still in British hands, held till the Americans
should fulfil their treaty conditions. Pittsburgh and a few
forts down the Ohio comprised the civic world beyond
the Alleghanies.

West of the Alleghany Backbone the army entered upon
the pleasant sour lands called the Glades—mountain-top
pastures where streams without purpose wandered like
truant children till the old schoolmaster of gravity should
determine in what class to place them—whether to send

them to the Alleghany, the Monongahela, or the Potomac.

Between the Backbone and the Laurel ridges this fine,
pure land was stretched like an Indian blanket, and the
bells of cows were heard tinkling that night as the soldiery dropped down to sleep, not waiting for their mat-
tresses to be filled with straw ; but these cows were safer
than if the Gladers alone heard the advisement of their
bells, for discipline had extended across the mountains,
and these seemed to be the first timid bells of law tinkling
that government had come.

The army, since leaving Bedford, had set its pickets
with all the care of an invading minority in a hostile
land.    The little town of Bedford, behind them, was the
lawful capital of these great glades, in whose midst was
a settlement where leading malcontents harbored, and
there was an apprehension of some semi-savage surprise
of the army by night which might be magnified in the
East by the faction there and turned to the government's
ridicule.

Hamilton's highest passion was for military life.    He
had bent himself toward the sciences of finance and pro-
duction in pains and toil ; but that union of civil wisdom
and commandership provided for in the American executive had its preferential part, for him, in the command.

Public science had brought him care and enemies ; war
was the science of his heart.    He moved through the
camps, and took the disposition of the army.

That night, upon the golden glades whose poppies
seemed to flower in the perfect stars, he made the rounds,
provided with the countersign, to see that no man slept
upon his post.

It was long after midnight ; the lines facing westward,
where the enemy was expected, were stretched along a
mountain creek fresh from the water pressure of that
great trunk of primal stone which rode through the depths
of night like a stately barge.

The small-sized, sure-footed Hamilton stole his way
from man to man like a light puma for his prey, giving
the word, which was " Harry Lee," soft as a whisper.

He desired to test the soldier capacity of the young
generation and their sense of duty, for his mind was
filled with ideas of campaigns : Miranda had been im-

ploring him to break the Spanish chain which stretched across these waters from the Pennsylvania glades to the far southern citadel of New Orleans.

Hamilton came to a break in the sentries; no challenge arrested him ; no voice called " Who comes there ? "

The secretary looked round and about, and at last he saw reflected in the stream the bright sheen of a musket, to which he picked his path.

It was leaning against a tree, beneath which stretched the picket's form, so deep in sleep that Hamilton could hardly rouse him.

" Asleep upon your post, my friend ?   For shame ! The consequence is death."

" I know that," spoke the defaulter.    " I welcome it."

" Why, sir ? "

" I have no wife ; she has rejected me forever."

Hamilton heard, and his heart was disturbed like the culprit's.

" Is that your only excuse ?   Discipline can recognize no private grief, my boy.   I perceive that you are young."

" Sir, I have been worn out with this heavy march. All my spirits were gone when I left Carlisle—where I saw *her*.   I persevered and did my best, but this last big mountain broke me down."

" Give me your musket," whispered Hamilton in commiseration.   " I will mount guard for you awhile and let you sleep."

The boy dropped off, indifferent to death, so that Master Nature had his fill.

Hamilton took the musket and paced back and forth, seeing now and then the gleam of the reciprocal patrols on other sides.   This had continued till his walk became purely mechanical, and he took no note of the owl's hoot or the wolf's distant bark.   His thoughts were upon the course of empire, the providence of God, and the necessity of woman's love.

He was roused from his reverie by the muffled cry of " Halt ! " as if spoken through a sleeve or glove.

" Halt, *you !* " replied Hamilton, peering through the shades.

" Is it Jim Reynolds ? " asked the other voice.

" Yes."

The reply was a musket's discharge a few paces before,

and a ball whistled past Hamilton's head. It seemed to cut his hair.

Prompt as in old days, when he put his company through the manual, Hamilton raised his long flint-lock and drew the trigger, aiming at the sound.

A voice with no disguise uttered a groan and then an oath.

The two shots awoke the refreshed delinquent.

" Take your musket, Reynolds. That is your name ? "

" Yes. God be thanked, it's Mr. Hamilton ! "

" Some one yonder has fired at you, or at me. Take your place, your gun at ready, and see whom it is."

In a moment Reynolds returned, and whispered with a voice which revealed the hate and almost the pallor of his face :

" Colonel Hamilton, it's that Jake Clingman. He is the officer of the day, and stood me here on picket. Somebody has shot him through the arm."

" Come, let us see him," said Hamilton. " He aimed to assassinate either you or me. There is but a moment to act, for the sentinels have fired up the line and the guard will turn out."

Clingman it was indeed, found kneeling, and stanching blood from a ball through the left arm, probably received while still steadying his musket.

" You are caught at your tricks, Mr. Clingman, I find. Did you mean to kill Mr. Reynolds or me ? "

" Hamilton, ha ! " answered the ruffian. " If it had taken a ball of gold with the British crown, and I had known it to be you, by the snake rattles of old Nick you should have got it ! "

" Then you have not done me harm enough, nor Mr. Reynolds here, but you would kill us both ? "

" I'll plead to nothing. Infer your wust. If I had you both together on this mountain-top alone, and this arm was less of a pump-spout than it is, your dead carcasses should bear the teeth marks of your'n tru——"

In the sentence he swooned from rushing blood. ,

" Colonel Hamilton," spoke Reynolds, in a low voice, " let me rid the world and you of this monster by emptying my gun into his breast."

" No, Reynolds. My offence shall take its just sentence, as Heaven wills. Stand by him, and when the guard comes, let him explain how an officer of the day was guard-mount, and also alarming the camp. It was at you he fired, asking for your name. But shed not his blood."

The next day, on Reynolds' statement, a brief court-martial dismissed Lieutenant Clingman from the army as a man of unfit character to be in the service. Upon the sufficient healing of his wound he was to be walked at the tail of a supply wagon to the Susquehanna, there stripped of his uniform, his sword broken over his back, and a stave of the "Rogue's March" played for his especial delectation.

Private James Reynolds was promoted to a lieutenant's place for vigilant behavior on picket duty, *vice* Clingman, cashiered.

## CHAPTER XVII.

### HAMILTON RESIGNS.

HAMILTON continued on with the army, the dread representative in official place, if not in military command, of Washington and the state.

He now began to demonstrate those great persuasive and impressive personal powers which reënforced his perceptions and intuitions.

At the hamlet since called Somerset, and made seat of a flourishing county, two out of the three chief citizens were arrested for high treason and endeavoring to carry the flame of sedition eastward. Their relatives came to promise and to plead with Hamilton.

He saw with pain that the German population had been infected with the Virginia idea, that it was tyranny to impose taxes, the same opinions which had lain latent since Jack Cade and Jack Straw, no more original at Monticello than at Smithfield, or under Jack of Leyden at old German Münster. The child was to prescribe its own medicine, the debtor to be his own sheriff, the local bully to have priority over constable and marshal.

The army toiled up the Laurel Mountain and descended into the plateau of the River Youghiogeny, which flows out of Maryland, and it crossed the Chestnut ridge and was on the Monongahela waters flowing out of Virginia.

Beautifully, dreadfully the long line unfolded to the valley of the Mississippi, its flashing bayonets and silver instruments of music, its clouds of dust and triumphant strains, such as the little children heard with ignorant delight ; its colors of state and Nation, never separated but in minds of low degree ; its miles of white teams, significant of the public resources ; its scouts, skirmishers, artillery, engineers—miniature of all the world knew, or was to know, of war under King Frederic, Washington, or Napoleon.

Now came the old men and the good men out, to shout and praise God that the reign of Democratic societies was over, and no loyal settler need longer get drunk and curse Washington.

Intelligence and morality lifted up their heads. Congregations listened to their preachers instead of threatening to murder them for giving good advice. The army paid for everything it needed, and scattered money where none had been seen before.

There burst upon the local political economists the memorable discovery that there was another way to dispose of grain than by sending it three hundred miles in the form of whiskey, or to drink all the whiskey that was left ; namely, to have the country inhabited by men like these invaders, and sell them the original grain, and to drink as little whiskey as possible.

The news spread that there was a United States judge with that army, one of the terrible new judiciary made by Congress ; that the Attorney-General of the United States was also coming to identify the mail-robbers, the incendiaries, and the rebels ; and that every actor in the public crimes of the year was marked and a warrant ready for him.

Cowardice began to tremble ; the Ohio River was filled with rascals flying to Kentucky, Illinois, or Louisiana, and at their head that frothy orator, Bradford, who had lived in three States, commencing with Virginia, and did himself no credit in any.

The remaining subservient or demagogical lawyers and winkers at political insurrection resolved to put in the universal plea that they had only helped the rebellion on in order to be able to control it and keep it from damaging anybody.

Privately they all resolved to write books if their necks were spared, and injure Secretary Hamilton with the next generation.

These gentry sought Hamilton out with trembling and profound apology and respect.

He received them all with the courtesy of a fellow-citizen and man of sensibility, a mere servant of the laws, like themselves.

There is not one honest record that he ever bore harder upon any offender than to say at one time, in answer to a recreant and craven lawyer's statement : " That will be a subject of future inquiry."

And these men, to be elected to Congress, or to retain the law practice of law-breakers, had abdicated all the heroism of honest and faithful citizens, and were not the equals of the private soldiers of that army, each of whom offered his life for his government. A hundred thousand dollars apiece was the measure of their robbery of Hamilton's public treasury in the cost of this expedition.

Among the names of evil repute in the guidance of the excise rebellion was that of a Virginia Swiss named Gallatin, commonly called in this wilderness refuge to which he had come, *Gallantine.* The soldiery hated his name, and the young staff officers at their toasts lifted the cords of their jackets as they ominously cried : " This for the Swiss Frenchman ! "

Hamilton did not know this man except as his invariable and gratuitous assailant, specially keen and insidious in the methods of his attack.

The name of this man was sent to Colonel Hamilton as the army entered " Gallantine's " adopted county of Fayette.

The culprit wished to see the public man he had injured, for enemies were pressing him hard.

The left wing under General Morgan had come near his settlement, called New Geneva ; the right wing cut him off from the East.

As a European he knew what treason called for, and just now he was freshly married to a second wife, a young and superior woman of America, whose distress was no less than his own.

12

" Admit him," said Hamilton, instantly.

There appeared in the *marquee* a thick-set yet tallish man, in cloak and boots.

His head was of the John Adams kind, flattish and bald, but none of the narrow lines of Adams were in that dark and yearning face, which had something Jewish about its extensive nose; strength and suffering, too, in the well-bred mouth; and the plaintive brightness and fulness of his hazel eyes told Hamilton that if this man was Swiss he was an unusual one. His chin receded, and was too childish for his broad face and meaning nose.

Hat in hand, the visitor came as far as the middle of the tent, bent his brown eyes like a captive upon Hamilton, and articulated in a foreign accent :

" Sir, I am the unfortunate Gallatin."

As he spoke, there was in the type, rather than the man, some reminiscence of John André.

" Be seated, Mr. Gallatin," said Hamilton, with dignity.

" No, sir ; not till I have established an interest in your sympathy. You have had great provocation from me, because you were the only man among our opponents worth my attack. I wished to attract the notice of the *chieftain*. Beside such merit I expect to find generosity. Sir, we were both strangers in this country not many years ago. The subjects of your public attention and discussion are my student's consolations. We both have wives—and love them."

Standing, yet rigidly, hardly gracefully, the gems of tears took the focus of light from the pleader's eyes. He sighed, and it was like the sound of a viol bow across his heart.

Hamilton went up to Gallatin, slightly his senior, and took his hand.

" You have said all and said it eloquently. If you are in any danger here, I will let you sleep in my tent to-night. Of course you give your *parole*, Mr. Gallatin."

He laughed and called an orderly for a glass of wine.

" What do you meditate, Mr. Gallatin, of benefit to these people whom we have come so far to correct and improve ? "

" If I am not tried—and hanged," said Gallatin, " I will establish the glass manufacture on these headwaters of the Ohio, and every family in the great West shall have native glass—glass which educates the refined as well as pleases the savage ; glass which lights the pioneer's cabin and the rich man's mansion. If they give me life, I will leave them glass."

In seven years more, Albert Gallatin was the Secretary of the Treasury, and President Jefferson said to him :

" Make haste to expose the corruptions of Hamilton's system."

" There are no corruptions, Mr. President," answered Gallatin. " Hamilton was a builder. All his lines are plumb."

The army having waded in mud to the knees for much of the march and stood the fierce mountain rains heroically—which caused the deaths of many gallant youths and Revolutionary veterans in time—paused in front of the chief insurrectionary district and formed and lay in divisions for inspection, connected the wings, and stood arrayed under Howell, Mifflin, Daniel Morgan, and Smith of Maryland, with Henry Lee for general captain.

In another week the whole body of fully twelve thousand men advanced toward Pittsburgh, covering both rivers from the south.

The next advance enwrapped the hostile centres, and into Pittsburgh itself marched a portion of the troops.

The little town of logs and planks upon the alluvial of the hills behind it, overlooked by mighty mounds from across the rivers, had now seen the army of Wayne go to beat the savages and the army of Hamilton come to deliver civilization in the course of a single year.

The two campaigns created the great Northwest.

To this day that fair land has been true to the national love, blessed by the federal fatherhood, fortunate in its children, honest in its finances, and of clear public faith, and has become opulent and controlling.

Sitting down at Pittsburgh by General Knox, the Secretary of War, Hamilton saw the benevolent yet firm administration of law recommence. It was his only experience by the Ohio.

The weak being sifted and the guilty only marked for example, writs were issued, and in one night the government took every prisoner by the simultaneous movement of its troopers accompanying the marshals.

A portion of the army stayed in the hostile country to winter and protect those who had assisted the law. The rest was ordered eastward, but hundreds of mechanics settled down in Western Pennsylvania from the army, and from that moment the golden star of the West stood perpetual in the heavens above its harvests, workshops, national roads, and inland navigation.

Somewhere in that great West is the posterity of James Reynolds, who found in occupation and discipline the right and the zest to love and wed again.

Hamilton turned back to pass the mountains before snow.

His official life was forever ended.

---

## CHAPTER XVIII.

### ANACONDA AT HOME.

MR. JEFFERSON sat in his bedroom at Monticello, writing letters.

The room had something of a jail character, with its two small-paned windows and its deep-embrasured sky-light. At the end was a kind of hole, or alcove, between two wardrobe doors, where Mr. Jefferson's bed now stood up on hooks, and exposed, through the hole, his library.

When he designed to cultivate his peas, vetches, Jerusalem artichokes, and other green material, he took his writing materials from the library to this sinister bedroom, and the household knew that he was gardening.

Nobody was then permitted to enter but his favorite chamberwoman and slave, or his daughter, Martha Randolph.

Mr. Jefferson brought daintily out of one of the side doors his French *écritoire*, unlocked it, and looked jealously at the contents, and through into the library and out of the windows upon the immediate mountain lawn and the deep blue panorama five hundred feet beneath.

This was the first letter he wrote :

" DEAR SIR : *The information and copies your customary courtesy transmitted to me from Harris's Ferry and from Carlisle have been attentively read. Aware of the very moderate remuneration under the present administration of affairs clerical men of the educated class and of distinguished ability like yourself enjoy, I hope you will not take it amiss if I send you ten pounds in this communication, as an earnest only of my personal regard for those who esteem me worthy, in my present complete retirement, of sharing some of the secrets of the public world. My sincerest regards to General and Mrs. Washington, and to Miss Nellie Washington.*

" COL. TOBIAS LEAR."                              " TH. JEFFERSON.

As he folded the fifty-dollar note into the letter, Mr. Jefferson groaned.

"If I ever leave these bucolic joys and draw the President's salary, the faithful Mr. Lear shall be consul to the Barbary States, there to trade baked apples, or have his head served to the Dey."

Jefferson folded, creased, and waxed the letter. He was about to put his seal upon it, but refrained, and stamped the seal with a paper-knife.

The omission of the seal gave him a suggestion. He walked in his slippers through the alcove and glass door and into his library, and back again.

"I'll risk it," said Jefferson. "He is old, courteous, and unsuspecting, and he may reply."

Then sitting to his task, holding the pen in his reverse or left hand, the host of Monticello wrote a decoy letter to Washington, and signed it " John Langhorne," slowly.

The exertion fatigued Mr. Jefferson's " off " hand. He changed the quill to the right hand, re-pointed it with his knife, and wrote a cordial letter to the President upon his new manner of " cropping."

There entered a comely specimen of the "bright mulatto " blood, neither young nor old, but what was called a confidential servant, perhaps thirty years of age. She was easily at home before her master and smiled upon him and handed him his mail.

As he took the letters from her hand, feverishly, the hand seemed to linger.

Jefferson spoke :

" Pshaw ! Suke, as soon as I am dead and you are free, you will forget me."

" Not if I am free, master. When am I going to be free ? I think if I was free I could love so much better. Then if I loved anybody it would be with all my heart —my gratitude, and my free will."

" Be off ! My mail is important to-day. What is that visitor doing ? "

" He's not as drunk to-day as he was last night. He's writing something funny. I reckon it is, for he's laughing to hisself."

" Then he's writing something bitter. Keep liquor from him. Give him buttermilk. I want him in the library at three o'clock."

As the woman passed out Mr. Jefferson's hands paused upon his paper-knife.

" Free to love ! " he sighed. " Love of the free—that must be consolation. But I cannot afford it. We are all slaves—to our debts, our ancestors, to social appearances, to public purposes, to great movements upon the earth."

The first letter broke Mr. Jefferson's calm :

" DEAR COUSIN TOM :—I was ordered to publish Monroe's despatch to the general public. You will see that a few days of France have brought Monroe to denounce the Jacobin Club and its influence through auxiliary clubs upon all France. Consequently our Democratic societies are going to pieces all over the United States, especially since the clean sweep Hamilton and Lee made of the whiskey insurrection.

" Robespierre has fallen : he was executed July the 28th. In the two previous months he and his faction guillotined 1,507 people.

" ED. RANDOLPH."

Mr. Jefferson's freckled face grew white and his lip trembled. Even then he smiled an outline smile and checked his unruly respiration.

" So, so," he said, patting his heart, " not too fast ! *L'empire est pour le phlegmatique.* And Robespierre is dead—the greatest man in Europe, or the world ! Sometimes I have thought I was like him—the dispassionate, austere, and vigilant friend of liberty. There is no more reliance upon favoritism in America for France, but we have still left hatred for England. Let Mr. Jay take care ! "

He opened his large parcel of newspapers and glanced them over.

" Monroe has become a pliant office-holder," said Mr. Jefferson. " Perhaps if he was President he would turn Federalist. If Madison had courage——"
He took up another letter.

" MY DEAR SIR :—Having visited the new lands of Western New York, I returned down the Susquehanna and found the Priestleys, our friends, mysteriously disconsolate over the absence of their daughter-in-law, who is said to be somewhere in the State of New York. A Mrs. Clingman, whom I discovered at Wrightsville Ferry on my return, tells me that Mistress Joseph, Jr., is in love with Hamilton. The same charming informant states Hamilton's private satire upon you to be ' a man of malignant passions, great ambition, and profound hypocrisy.' You will acquit me of any uncivil end in repeating this when I might state his worse opinion of myself. It seems that my very correct constituent has had a mistress, whose husband is in my political service now.

" Western New York is filling up with the picked population of New England. We flatter ourselves here that by a quarter of a century we shall turn the census of Virginia down and be the first State in the Union. Your obedient servant,
" A. BURR."

The letter aged Mr. Jefferson's face.
" Familiarity ! " he observed. " Does he think the repeater of a poignant analysis to its subject is ever forgiven ? To repeat it confesses an impression made upon the common carrier, and that is an insult. Virginia will last almost as long as I will—the controlling State. God bless her ! New York may have *Vice*-Presidents. This Burr was a soldier ; so was Hamilton. *There* is an idea. Soldiers gravitate to Hamilton ; civilians to me."
The next letter was in cipher, and caused Mr. Jefferson to repair to his secret closet and bring forth a key. He spread the letter out and clamped it to his portable desk, and proceeded to copy it by aid of the cipher. The interpretation was this :

" WHEELING CREEK, *October.*
" DEAR FRIEND :—This will reach you when I am ruined. Every man besides took water: Gallatin, Marshall, Findlay, the whole crew. I promised you that I would carry out your full instructions and never flinch. Have I not done so ? My last attempt was to make a new State of West Pennsylvania and have it secede from the Union.

" Jefferson, sometimes think of me ! I did not know how I loved you till I gave my country for your regard. It is better to give than to receive. But since I had the Pittsburgh mail robbed there has been no forgiveness for me. To-night I drop down the Ohio to find shelter, I know not where. But I have kept my word.

"Considering your interests to the last, I have burned all your letters to me.  Do you the same quickly, for this Hamilton reads men,
and Monticello is not proof against a district court warrant.

"Devotedly,

"DAVID BRADFORD."

Mr. Jefferson crumpled the letter in his fist, glided
again into the masked closet, and reappeared with a great
mass of correspondence and a copying book, of which the
letters were the sequel.

He lighted a candle upon his library hearth and looked
carefully on till book and letters were consumed.

He breathed with relief and also sighed.

"What power has Hamilton—to march an army and
to burn those letters !  I hate to sacrifice correspondence,
for a dead man's letters haunt the earth and become terrible as Belshazzar's phantom hand.  Perhaps it was
temerity to quarrel with him—the petulance of my wom-
anly nature.  He was always honest. So am I.  I have a
client he cannot appreciate—ideal, severe, Spartan liberty!
I am but one, no warrior, and out of power, but I can arm
a legion with those goose-quills and pass the word that is
destroying : 'Detract ! *detract!* DETRACT !'  The Federalists have not one politician."

He raised his hands slowly to the level of his eyes,
looked upon them, and with each hand wiped an eye.
His fingers were wet with his falling tears.

"Come, tricklers !" he apostrophized, seeking to smile;
"like other springs ye are born of pressure and prove
me still possessed of the winning powers of gentleness :
I am not yet dry.  Flow, flow !" he continued, in calm
raillery, "but that is all ye can do, for I shall persevere.
My last blow at Hamilton shall be delivered now, to re-
buke these tears and acquit me—inflexible."

He retired anew into the closet and brought forth the
package of letters received from Mr. Monroe—letters
signed with the names of Maria Reynolds and James, her
husband.

"Callender shall see them," observed Mr. Jefferson,
"and charge corruption in that Hamilton paid Reynolds
money.  Let Hamilton explain for what."

Still calm, deliberate, lady-like, he went and washed
his face and set forth to find Mr. Callender, the historian
of the Republic as he had been of Britain.

Martha Randolph saw her father pass through the hall, and she smelled smoke in the damp library chimney, which could not at once draw after disuse. Taking her little son by the hand, she entered the library.

Mr. Jefferson bowed with composure to the carpenters and plasterers, who were still at work, after twenty years of tarrying, upon his elephant of a house, with its square hall all dampened by the classic portico, its lean windows and dingy saloon.

The bust of Voltaire seemed to smirk as Mr. Jefferson went by, whereupon he stopped, turned, and dispassionately regarded that plaster gentleman.

The great clock, with its cannon-ball weights, rasped like a watchman's rattle and struck two.

He passed into the grounds and looked up at his mansion with its balustered cornice, pediments, and dome. Already it grew old, the bricks dull, the pillars mouldy.

His horse was ready saddled, and a spare beast as well for Mr. Callender.

That demi-tipsy son of the saturnine classical only required hoofs and horns to look the red goat, and he was assisted to mount against his will.

" Come, Mr. Callender," called Jefferson, " a good trot will dephlogistonize you. Look down yonder at Charlottesville, where I will place my university when the monarchists are reduced, and make you and Thomas Cooper professors."

" Tha' be the place, mon, wha' Tarlton came in and ran ye to the woods ? " asked the leering barbarian, who had cultivated evil saying till he must bite his proprietors if his foes were out of sight. " Folk tell me ye made tracks that day—*hoot!* Ha ! ha ! ha !"

The host was silent yet fierce, to hear to his face the frequent imputation that he had run from the enemy while governor.

This Thersites at his side had pretensions to become an historian. He was to publish " The History of the United States in the Administration of Washington," and Mr. Jefferson had incurred the nuisance of his society and habits for the purpose of forestalling his mind and narrative.

They rode around the truncated mountain edge to look off at the fine views—the far southern cone or peak, the Blue Ridge in the west, with its characteristic gaps, the Rivanna River flowing red paint beneath.

"Ye must think ye're Jupiter to dwell on a dommed mountain," was the polite reciprocity of Mr. Callender for all this attention.

The cleft between Monticello and the next knob was the scene of that dreadful day when the British troopers terminated for years Mr. Jefferson's official life, the panic going deep to the foundations of his nature and adding to his infinite opinions a hatred of wars, and, it was to be feared, of the brave.

Threatened in the legislature with an inquiry into his public conduct on that occasion, Mr. Jefferson had fled from the empty scabbard of the office itself, while Washington and Hamilton were reaping the glory of Cornwallis' surrender upon Virginia soil. In the midst of his sense of total public failure and disgrace his wife had died— she whose fortune had made him rich in slaves, adding to his own little parcel of those bondmen the number of one hundred and thirty-five, constantly increasing by system and diminishing by sale. To his Monticello and neighboring lands of five thousand acres she brought him forty thousand other acres, redeemed him from a country lawyer's drudgery, and founded in his heart the public ambition.

They stopped at her grave on the descent of the mountain road. Through the leafless trees a peep was afforded of Charlottesville, where Jefferson had been the village lawyer and a plain surveyor's son. Hence arose his democratic radicalism, upon the graft of this Randolph aristocracy, which had been so supercilious to his talents till he espoused the child-widow and her slaves.

"Never shall I marry," remarked Mr. Jefferson to the Edinburgh Bohemian at his side.

"Nae need! nae need!" exclaimed the wretch, grinning imputatively, and deaf to this real pathos.

"I have a work bequeathed me, Mr. Callender, to destroy the monocrats and paper men, who want armies, jobs, and debts."

He led the way into the woods, which he had grubbed and threaded with secluded riding-paths.

The labor of the day was to dig another pitfall for Hamilton.

Toward five o'clock Mr. Jefferson came home alone, with a woods bouquet of fringed gentian, ferns, and brilliant leaves for his masculine-minded daughter, who kept his house. He ascended the narrow winding stairs to her room and could not find her; he went down to the library, and she was not there.

Glancing through the glass sash in the alcove, he saw her seated in his bedroom on the ground-floor, at the desk he had left open.

The blank sides of the room caused the pale light to fall from the east whitely upon her matron form and falling ringlets, which were dark as her eyes and showed the Randolph personality.

Upon Jefferson's bed slept her first child; a second was absent in a slave's custody, and missed his mother's breast, for his fitful cry was now heard. Maternity again seemed not remote, expressed chiefly in the nervous, preoccupied countenance of one who had many of Jefferson's features and the beauty of fruitfulness that became her and added to her character.

"Here," said Jefferson, "divide the posy with Maria and pay me in a kiss."

"I will, father, when you take a suspicion from my mind. Ever since you left this house I have been here, not minding my baby's cry, waiting for you to come and tell me. Do these letters accuse Secretary Hamilton?"

"They do; the villain is exposed."

"I have read them all; they are terrible. If Eliza were to see them they might kill her. Father, what are they doing here?"

"They passed through various hands to me." ·

"How fortunate, father!"

"Yes; at this time a windfall. He comes home victorious—generalissimo, drum-major, what not? Next thing he will prance to some domestic music when these things are read."

Mr. Jefferson assorted the leaves and wild flowers into two parcels and moistened them at the wash-stand. His daughter sat looking at him.

"I don't think you understood me, papa. I said you were fortunate in getting the letters."

"Yes, Matty, I understood you. They are the first, the only tangible things I have got upon him."

"I see," said Mrs. Randolph. "You will make him your friend with them; I am glad of that. I was afraid this dirty man, Callender, might snook around here and see them. He has been asking insinuating questions of the household servants. Why don't you send him to the tavern? This morning he asked sister Maria why we kept no sheep, unless we were afraid they would clip wool for Hamilton's manufacturing system."

"Did he?" mused Jefferson, measuredly, but with a flush. "Well, he is a coarse fellow, but just the brute for this necessity. What was that you said about making Hamilton my friend?"

"Of course you will send him the letters, and that will prove friendship."

"Matty! Matty! why, he would hate me ten times worse. He might fear me, but never love me after that."

"Dear me! Men are not like women. I have known sisters to send back the letters written to their brother by a lady. What can you do, then?"

"Smile, and let him explain."

"Explain what?"

"Why he gave eleven hundred dollars to this woman's husband, Reynolds, his treasury clerk."

"Why, pa, I understand that. It was extorted from him between those wicked people. O God! to think Hamilton, of all men, should so misbehave and be so demeaned! But I shall stand by him."

"You?"

"Yes, sir." She rose and stood and walked. "I shall stand by him, as I hope good women will stand by my husband if he ever grieves me like that."

"You were always partial to Hamilton," said Jefferson, restrainedly jealous.

"Partial? I loved him."

"Hush!"

"I loved him as a dear friend, my father's associate, the youngest of Washington's little family. His wife was like my sister. Poor Eliza! But, father, there has been some villany here. That minister has been taken unaware. He has fallen suddenly, and repented hard. I claim these letters, sir."

She tied them up decisively and put them in her pocket.

"Stop!" called Jefferson. "They are not mine."

"I know that. They are Colonel Hamilton's, and can be nobody's else."

"Yes, they are Colonel Burr's; he deposited them with my old law pupil, Monroe, who turned them over to me."

"Therefore, I say," exclaimed Jefferson's daughter, with brusque words and rising temper, "it was fortunate that they came here. Christian interpretation will be given to them in the house of Jefferson. In my mother's name I assume any impropriety in writing to my friend : 'Be delivered, Colonel Hamilton, from this great misfortune. Go hence, like Mary Magdalen, and sin no more.'"

She had looked like that once before, when he compelled her to leave the convent in Paris. Now, with life quickened within her and without, in the shadow and the fruitage of woman's destiny of love, she was indignant ; she was mad.

"This is sad business to mix yourself in, Patsey. Purity, purity, child!"

"Oh! there is no Pharisee in me; nothing uncandid. I can go to a broken man's relief because my hope is Christ, the Saviour of sinners. To me a strong man's social sin is nothing but his sickness. Hamilton is lying in the *Hôtel Dieu* upon the hospital cot, and here is medicine to make him well."

She drew the letters from her pocket.

"Do you think I would stay another night in Monticello, sir, if I thought you would use these letters to Mrs. Hamilton's anguish and Colonel Hamilton's shame? No; the curse of that cruelty would descend upon my little children. Oh! could you feel the burden of the unborn, the helplessness of them who have come and who cry at your breast, your heart would be hungry as a desert place for the abundant rains of love and pity. You would see the need of grace—grace perpetual!"

She crossed to her child, and waked it up.

"This is the voice of them who are born to live," spoke Mrs. Randolph, as the child raised a little wail. "This, also, is the voice of them who leave the world.

We cannot fight against the instincts of love.   It has a
thousand aberrations, and to me this man, who has stepped
aside from virtue, is but a little child.   He is unclean,
but his heart is pure.   I lament for his folly, but if the
sacrifice of my hairs could wipe his brow of degradation,
they should all be his."

Her palms stretched out her hairs.   She faced her
father like the male.

" This is extraordinary," lisped Jefferson.

" No, sir ; this is Virginian, the old, old Dominion of
hospitality.   Let Aaron Burr—whose glance to me was
impure contagion—peddle in these private letters ; and
horrible blasphemers, like Willy Giles, swear at God and
Washington in the orgies of that saloon " (she pointed
toward the banquet-chamber).   " We, who are of old
derivation in Virginia, our patron saint a virgin queen,
will wrong no stranger going through our vales, but be
the Good Samaritan and lend him our beast to take him
wounded to the inn."

" God be thanked ! " exclaimed Jefferson, carried away
by her plea.   " Your mother lives in you, Martha.   I
see my error, and feel the wholesome gust of your impulsive love."

" These letters are mine, father ? "

" Yes.   That is, if I have any title in them.   They
were a trust to me, but whose they may be on a last appeal, some judge must settle."

" Here comes one," cried Martha, " my husband !   He
is Hamilton's opponent, too, but a fair, fierce man.   Let
Mr. Randolph decide, like Solomon, whose babe is this."

She held the letters up.

A dark, rugged, Indian-like man was entering the
library with Maria Jefferson, who was the perfection of
delicate, almost consumptive beauty, and already in love.

" No," exclaimed Jefferson, hastily, " do not present
the case.   You have won."

# CHAPTER XIX.

### BLACKMAILERS.

IN the frosty days toward winter Joe Priestley was drawing near the town of Wright's Ferry, on the Susquehanna.

He had been examining the new capital city on the Potomac, where his father thought somewhat of making a " town-house." Joe had seen little of a city there but ox-teams hauling stone to the big hole of the Congress House and the President's palace, and scattered blocks of dwellings in gulfs of mud.

He was now returning in the Baltimore stage to meet his wife at Wright's Ferry, the most convenient spot on the Susquehanna to Lancaster and the eastern turnpike. Lizzie had addressed him from New York, and he was meeting her commands with obedience and remorse.

Since his oblivious night and morning at Carlisle he had been oppressed with a sense of recreancy and a fear of discovery and ruin. How would his wife meet him ? By what woman's clairvoyancy or world's whisper might his compromising situation with the beautiful Mrs. Reynolds be betrayed ?

Joe was not a subtle fellow, keen to lie out of an offence. He feared his wife the more because he deeply loved her, and knew her tempered mettle.

Nothing whatever occurred to him to say in his own behalf. If she should accuse him of taking Reynolds to Carlisle after the high words between that adventuress and his wife, and of being found there after a tipsy night in Reynolds' chamber, he could not even deny the charges.

To other men it might have occurred to turn the tables on his wife and anticipate her inquiries by a stern demand to say where she had been so mysteriously travelling. Already Mrs. Reynolds had accused her of being in love with Hamilton.

But Joe never so much as thought of this device. It never crossed his mind for a single instant that his wife's errand had been other than charitable or heroic. He was hardly inquisitive on the subject, considering that

there were many abstruse things not to be fully understood between man and woman till back into Adam's
nature the wife should be restored, and, with the missing
rib in its place whence God had taken it, confidence
should rest on love's complete unity.

"She will not destroy me," thought Joe. "It's not
like her. But how can I ever take her in my arms with the
sense of my criminal unworthiness? No; I dare not go
to Lizzie's chamber. It would be to act a lie and deceive
love."

He crossed the river in the stage, which was driven
upon two boats lashed together, a pair of wheels in each,
and ferried across the wide, shallow, rock-ribbed current
that had the span of a mile and an eighth. All that day
he had been riding through the German settlements out
of Maryland, in the midst of tidy farming; and now
"Columbia," as Wright's Ferry was re-named, began to
show under the huge rock which sheltered it from the
north winds, a slope of houses and stage taverns back of
a ferry-house, with the latest marvel of enterprise, the
"brick tavern," looming above everything.

To the "brick tavern" Joe bent his way, and was
quite alone in the tavern parlor, which was on the second
floor, when his troubled but conscientious mind was
visited by the wraith that had haunted him for the past
three weeks—Mrs. Reynolds.

She entered wringing her hands, and so much preoccupied that she did not identify him. She was dressed
in a style unseasonable, with black lace upon her noble
arms and bust and a black widow's robe. A kind of
turban of white and black lace completed the appearance
of a widow too young and strong to wear such weeds
forever.

"O God!" the woman moaned, stepping like a tragic
queen to and fro, "to be robbed of my whole independence, my provision for the long, cold winter, after what
I have endured to procure it! Not one dollar, not my
stage fare to Philadelphia is left."

Joe's unselfishness immediately betrayed him where
he sat in the shadow of the chimney-jamb near the
decaying fire.

"You say 'robbed,' Reynolds? Who has robbed
you?"

He stood up by the dull-burning chandelier of whale-oil lamps.    As he spoke he was also blushing.

"Oh! Mr. Joseph, is it you ?    How unceremoniously you left me at Carlisle, sir !    What would your wife give to know why ? "

" For mercy's sake, dear woman ! " entreated Joe, " I heard you say you had been robbed."

"Yes ; it was only last night.    I came here directly from Carlisle, and have been at this house ever since. There has been stolen from my room I fear to say how much money.    We have been quietly at work all day to recover it, but the troops returning, the emigrants going, the swarming European refugees of desperate fortunes, have so filled this town that we might arrest a hundred people and get no remedy.    What shall I do ? I thought to wait for Colonel Hamilton's return and be in easy circumstances."

" Madame, you must surely know the amount of your loss ? "

" I do.    It was more money than I ever before possessed ; almost two thousand dollars."

" You had no such money at Northumberland.    You came there with borrowed money, I understood "

She hesitated, looked boldly at him in spite of her haggardness, and exclaimed :

" My husband left it to me.    He is dead."

" Mr. Reynolds ?    God bless my soul !    You're not sorry for that ? "

" No ; I am married again.    Take care that you do not meet my husband."

She left the room like a fury, and poor Joe was plunged into a kind of stolid despair, which was not dispelled when the evening silence was broken by the horn of the Lancaster stage.

From the stage his wife fell into his arms.

" Joe, Joe ! " she cried.    " Thank God ! I am back to you.    Have you suffered for me, dear, darling, indulgent Josie ? "

Her kisses were all over his bearded face.    He was happy as the wretched ever are in their domestic compensations.

" Why don't you speak to me, Joe ?    Tell me how father and mother are, and poor, dying brother Harry.

13

Oh! I have been far and seen much, and the day will be when I can take it all out of my mind and tell you, too, Joe.   Do you believe in me ? "

" Always," said Joe.

" As I do in you, husband.".

" Stop," said Joe.   " If I have not gone to the devil, lass, I can't prove it.   I got drunk at Carlisle.   Your going away upset me.   I'll make a clean breast of it right here, and then I shall close my mouth."

For a moment the wife was silent.   His blunt, hard, helpless English expression had paralyzed her faculties. There rushed upon her mind the sickening fear that for a wilful friendship she had sacrificed a trusty love.

" Come, sir, to your chamber," Lizzie remarked when they had reached the parlor flight.

" No, I'll not go theer, wife.   My heart is not clear. Go you with this servant, and I'll wait by the fire till you are ready for supper. "

" What ?   Ashamed to enter your wife's room ? "

" I'll not lie to thee, wife.   I have been a hard case."

She looked one instant, and her heart sank down.   A great something had happened in her absence.

As the wife felt the solid floors, her feet, her head giving way under her fainting spirit, a shape went by that recovered her pride and kept her from falling.

It was Mrs. Reynolds, accompanied by Senator Aaron Burr.

" Why, why ! is this the charming, cruel Mrs. Priestley ? " exclaimed the senator.   " I heard of you, enamoured creature, being as far in my constituency as Albany.   Was Hamilton there, too ? "

Every word was an unconscious stab to the wife's hungry, desolate heart.

The household enemy pealed forth a mocking, exasperating laugh.

" Ha ! ha ! ha ! " came from Mrs. Reynolds.   " When the cat's away the mice do play.   Oh! Colonel Burr— ha ! ha ! ha ! ha ! "

The bells that toll when the dead is passing from his wife's joy and darkened household are not as cruel as the laughter of the woman who cheats woman of her living spouse.   This fiendish glee is the music of the

mighty judgment, when they who have been false to marriage vows upon the earth, hear the reverberation of their
confession strike the ears of the faithful injured who can
suffer not.

With almost lifeless powers Lizzie Priestley was guided
to her chamber. She waited till the German attendant
was gone and she bathed her head and temples in cold
water, and looked piteously at her stage-weary, aging face
in the little mirror.

All at once the sob, the flood, the deep relief came,
and she sank upon the floor and waited till the fountains
of her tears, the agony of the first pain of desertion,
should be spent.

The relief went at last and left her very weak.

She lay still and only sighs came from her. She was
a little woman and a brave one, but the exhaustion was
all the greater.

"My Father!" she breathed, at last, clinging to her
bureau and looking upward, "the only Father of the poor
in spirit, who dwellest everywhere and never is out of
the hearing of our bitter sorrow! I know thou art trying me by the injury I have excused to another, the
sorest temptation of women who love and have not de-
served *this*. Forgive them who have trespassed against
us! Let this suffering, Lord, be to my children's account when they are motherless! My heart must break,
but I shall not upbraid him."

Her sighs had been heard. Her husband appeared
before her.

"Lizzie, don't take on like that! Wait a while, lass,
and something may come to pass, I know not what; but
let us wait a bit."

She raised herself and put her arms about his neck.

"My little boy has fallen into the gutter," she said.
"Let me clean his face and tell him I shall not punish
him."

She wiped his face, also travel-aged and coarse. As
she did so there came into her mind a picture from the
homely Scriptures of the woman washing the tired Saviour's feet.

"How good, Joe, are these consolations from blessed
reading! My boy, what wicked thing have you done?
Tell me, and never fear."

Poor Joe broke away from her endearments and stood a minute, ruefully meditating.

"I'll be dommed," said he, candidly, "if I know. Whatever it was, I'll not make it worse by lying, or throwing it on another. Lass, I can swear, wherever my poor, drunken carcass has been, my heart has never flickered in its love for thee, and, by that love, I'll never cheat my soul to get out of this scrape. Whatever there was of it shall stop at the first offence."

"Come, take me to supper, Joe."

There was a long table at the tavern nearly filled with boarders and travellers, for Wright's Ferry was the base of the late military operations and the inland route to Fredericktown and Virginia from the Lehigh and New York. German and Quaker girls waited on the guests, and Dutch cheeses, apple-butter, and hog's scrapel were among the dishes.

Mrs. Reynolds had taken her place by choice beside a large, black-eyed man in the dress of a Mennonite—walnut-dyed clothing, coat collar erect, and hooks and eyes upon his garments instead of buttons.

The alert intelligence of Lizzie Priestley identified this man, with some remaining doubt, as the person who had come to Northumberland in soldier clothing.

He was talking in a low tone of voice to Mrs. Reynolds. The subject of their talk the wife believed to be her husband and herself.

They were not left long in doubt.

After the supper was over the music of returning companies from the seat of war drew away from the tavern nearly everybody, and left the public parlor to the Priestley pair.

To these entered the huge man with the greedy, hard face and the black eyes, and said :

" Do I behold a Mr. Priestley, of Northumberlin ? "

" Yes," said Joe.          .

" Exackly. Will you step this way fur a minute, my friend ? "

A sense of evil meaning possessed Mrs. Joe. She felt the occasion to be a time of war in a strange land among lawless camp followers, and the scenes of the Northumberland riot were fresh in her mind.

In a moment her husband reappeared, pale and ex-

cited, but with his honest lineaments seeking to find the
composition of courage and self-respect.

The burly Mennonite followed him fiercely.

" Not a penny will I pay you as the basis of more
pennies to pay," observed Joe to the stranger. " In such
a case the first step is half the journey."

" Then I shall call in the law."

" I prefer to settle with the law at the worst," said Joe,
" rather than compound on such a matter with you."

" I am entitled to your life," exclaimed the man, with
a menace as if he had a weapon.

" It is not worth as much as it was," answered Joe,
grimly glancing at his wife, who started for his side, " but
I doubt if it can belong to you, or if you will take it."

" Stop ! " muttered Clingman.  " I did not mean to
pester your woman."

" That's just what I mean you shall do," replied Joe,
by no means at ease, but with a brave effort.  " If I am
guilty of what you charge, my wife is equally injured with
all the rest.  If this is a case of what is called blackmail,
I shall show you that it cannot be extorted from me by
my fear of my wife. Here she is ! I am more afraid of her
than of anybody in this world, and to her I have already
confessed the whole matter.  So come on with your wit-
nesses and lawyers."

" There is no time like the present," spoke Lizzie
Priestley.

" What is it, husband ? " asked the fair-haired wife, as
the great ruffian disappeared.

" The same thing," answered Joe, gloomily, " a demand for money because I have come between this person and his wife."

" And it is not true ? "

" I can't swear that it is not."

" You were intoxicated ? "

" Perfectly drunk—oblivious.  When I awoke in the
morning Mrs. Reynolds was in my room.  She appeared
to be accusing me.  So did Tom Cooper.  I slipped out
of Carlisle and crossed the South Mountain to the Dutch
settlements and on to Baltimore.  This is the sequel of
it.  It's hard to happen the night you arrive, Lizzie, but
an honest confession is good for the soul."

" Joe, I have promised you and my heavenly Father

that I will not desert you or upbraid you. Let me meet this charge for you. I will not believe that an honest man loses his nature in alcohol."

" The case is all in the enemy's hands," moaned Joe. " I will not swear that I know the contrary of anything they say. There's an old proverb that 'drinking kindness is drunken friendship.'"

Mr. Clingman appeared with what seemed to be a notary. The latter ordered the plaintiff to make his charge.

"We appear by counsel," said Mr. Clingman. " I will call in Colonel Burr."

The Senator from New York appeared with Mrs. Reynolds upon his arm. He gave the lady a seat. She sat in indolent grace, and from time to time looked in well-bred ease at Lizzie Priestley's childish figure, silken curls, and face where spirit struggled against depression and anger.

" Friends," said Aaron Burr, carefully closing the public door, " I was on my way to Philadelphia when I heard of this misfortune. The best way out of it is concession. The last thing we want, Heaven knows, is publicity on such a charge."

" That is the first thing *we* want," exclaimed Lizzie Priestley, with clear-spoken decision. " Open those doors, Joe ! You are no criminal yet. Let everybody see and hear."

Joe started to execute the order.

" Wait, wait ! " interposed Mr. Burr ; " the charge is graver than you think. The plaintiff's wife extenuates for herself by charging Mr. Priestley with violence. He ran away from the State, and on his return has just been apprehended. In the mean time, Mrs. Reynolds has been stopping at this hotel for a period of several weeks, and has run up a board bill of considerable amount. Yesterday she was robbed of all her means. Her husband has suddenly quit the army, and he finds her here injured on all sides—in person, reputation, pocket. He has laid a claim upon Mr. Priestley, who, it appears, decoyed Mrs. Reynolds to Carlisle and quartered her conveniently to his ends. If Mr. Clingman is satisfied with a settlement, I advise Mr. Priestley to make it ; for a scandal like this will follow his father's fame across the ocean."

"Persecution is the cause of father's fame," answered Lizzie. "We are strangers in this land, and it is inhospitable that a great man like Colonel Burr should join these shameless people against us. Never mind, sir ; I understand your friendship ! Let me be sworn."

She advanced to the notary and commanded that he present the Testaments.

"Now," spoke forth the English wife, "there have been other women lawyers than Portia. To take our children or our husbands from us you need all your wits ! If that vile woman—yes, stand up, madame, for you do not frighten me !—expected to divide me from my husband, she has failed already. I forgive him the greatest offence I believe he has been guilty of—squandering a single day of his time upon her ! In what is now happening, he learns what I felt from the first,—to despise Mrs. Reynolds. Creatures of her experience become so sharp that they forget their own tricks. It is my solemn testimony that a few weeks ago, inspired by jealousy and dislike of me—husband, open those doors, I say, and let the really guilty hear the truth of themselves !—she played the very trick upon the ark as we came down the Susquehanna which is the basis of this charge. She threw herself, at my approach, beside my sleeping husband, and having sent for me, affected to confess the imprudence."

"That is not true, madame !" the wife of Clingman languidly spoke, yet with passion restrained.

"All true ; it is an old trick of yours, I suspect. The cabin-boy informed me that you sent him to awaken me. I accused you then, I accuse you now, of having created this scene at Carlisle for at least one purpose, which you shall see has failed. Joe, my pure-hearted, well-acquitted, blameless husband, come and kiss me ! "

The husband and wife embraced without bashfulness.

"This is not testimony," said Colonel Burr.

"No ; it is better than that. It is the confusion of a woman who expected to lodge in a wife's heart the doubt of her husband's marriage loyalty. It is the scarlet woman's overthrow, to see how love beats down deception. If this be a court, and that notary not an accomplice, let the past record of that woman and that man "— she pointed to the Clingmans—"be inquired into and set beside Mr. Priestley's innocent life. Whom are they? Come, now!"

The notary seemed to be uneasy. The Clingman family looked at Colonel Burr for help, but he was only interested. Mrs. Reynolds seemed quite cast down, as if she had underestimated her small, fair, active opponent.

"Indeed, madame," she rejoined, "there is nothing in your husband, I am sure, a lady would covet. Is it for him I throw contrivances around you?"

The English wife answered "No!" with rapid spirit, and stopped short.

"Let her say for whom, then, before her husband?" challenged Mrs. Reynolds with jealous deliberation.

"Oh, no!" replied Colonel Burr. "She has condoned her husband's truantry. Let him do the same if Madame Priestley has fallen in love with Colonel Hamilton."

"I have," in a burst of candor and exasperation' answered the English wife. "My love for that man none of you can conceive, who know not disinterestedness or the Christian love. It is to pour that abandoned woman's cup full of bitterness that I confess this passion for Colonel Hamilton, and its return. All things are made ready for his complete appreciation of me. I shall shine in the mirror of his affections. I shall be named beside his wife. His household altar will contain my lamp. Bright and glorious will my love appear there when you, Mrs. Reynolds, shall be a word of dishonor uttered upon the lips of any of Hamilton's name!"

The scene had changed from a battle of wits to what looked very like two jealous women defying each other.

"You hear the truth, now, Mr. Joseph?" called Mrs. Reynolds, deeply moved yet alarmed. "Has she not followed Hamilton from Philadelphia to New York, to Albany, wherever he has been? . But he is still *Maria's* friend."

"Listen, Joe Priestley," continued the wife. "I will not have that woman ever pursue me with this charge again. I tell you before her that I love Alexander Hamilton. Now let her understand it! And by that love—the perfect love which casteth out fear—I shall make Hamilton describe Mrs. Reynolds in her real character to the world."

"That he will never do, madame," replied Mrs. Rey-

nolds. " I have been waiting here for Colonel Hamilton
all this time.  He entertained me at Carlisle.  Till disturbed by President Washington there, his tenderness
to me was divine."

A light, firm step was in the hall.  Lizzie Priestley,
with a scream, the climax of her high feelings, welcomed
a stranger at the door.

With marks of mountain travel, Hamilton entered and
bowed to them all.

" Did I hear my name ? " he asked, looking around at
the contents of the room.

" Yes, Hamilton, I mentioned it," spoke Mrs. Priestley.
" We have just been accused here by that woman—Mrs.
Reynolds—of an infamous crime.  My husband is still
beneath her imputations, and she is sustained by this
person, Clingman.  You see our situation.  Now describe
them to us in the light of justice to all.  What are they? "

" They are a pair of what are called Blackmailers," replied Hamilton, quietly.  " I thought the woman might
be better than the man, but I have discovered differently.
It was I who had them both expelled from the army district.  The only night Mrs. Reynolds spent in Carlisle
she visited my room and plied her wiles upon me again.
Her putative husband, Reynolds, told me that her errand
was to rob me.  Failing in this, she robbed Clingman, her
real husband, and fled the lines to this place, where she
had accumulated, I am told, considerable money from
passing officers and purveyors of the army, by the arts of
decoy and of crime, until she was stripped of it yesterday,
probably by a confederate."

" My God ! Hamilton," moaned Mrs. Reynolds, "you
are killing me.  May I never live from this moment if I
sought you out at Carlisle from any different motive than
Love ! "

" Madame," said Hamilton, "there is no such motive
among your effects.  In injuring this lady you attack
your sex and your country's hospitality.  Come, my friends
Priestley, and sit with me an hour.  What man is that, I
pray ? "

The alleged notary, with a sudden dart, slipped past
Hamilton and ran down the stairs.

" Colonel Burr," remarked the Secretary of the Treasury, as he led the Priestleys away, " I hope you will settle

with that pair of miscreants, who are not above accusing you of complicity in their scheme against Mr. Priestley. Since you advised me so considerately of Clingman's desire to kill me, I am sure you know how to deal with him."

The Priestleys also left the place.

Aaron Burr closed the parlor door, and bolted it.

"This little scene," said he, turning to the Clingman pair, "was arranged by me to have Mr. Clingman's room searched while we kept him busy. Maria—I shall call you so hereafter—I have had the signal that all your effects are recovered."

Jake Clingman started.

Mr. Burr was playing with a pistol.

"I hear steps on the stairs, Jacob," remarked Mr. Burr, quietly. "There is no way for you to escape but by the window now. Before you go, let me say again that your Ward is ready for you in New York."

With a glance at the pistol, a menace toward his wife, Mr. Clingman cleared the window and was gone.

Colonel Burr turned to Clingman's confederate, who was weeping :

"Maria, I have come back, as I promised, to receive your answer. You know that you must be mine."

"My heart is broken," sobbed the lady. "The man I love has mocked me before my rival. Oh, what a revenge Reynolds took upon me ! I would not have harmed Mr. Hamilton at Carlisle for the wealth of Robert Morris."

"Come with me to New York, Maria, and Hamilton will be there. I shall not be an exacting guardian. Freedom is my own way and my concession to the fair."

She rose to her feet and looked down upon his cool, self-centred little presence.

"Aaron Burr, you know that I hate you. The indignity you put upon me that day when Hamilton came to Jake's I never shall forget."

"It is that repulsion which attracts me, Maria ; your last genuine feeling, fresh to-day as once were your modesty, truth, and principle. If you loved me I might have caution. Since you do not, I shall be the more your master. I possess all your winnings. You are destitute here. A widower's friendship is open to you, and winter's protection from the despair of the castaway."

He had put her situation irresistibly. She slowly answered :

"Well, then, she who hates you surrenders to you again. If I am yours, you are mine."

---

## CHAPTER XX.

### HOUSE-MAKINGS.

THE literature of a new country is house-building, and the most happy, anxious, wretched time of Priestley's life was building his house at Northumberland. He had to rely on neighborhood mechanics of that republican equipoise nobody could drive but anybody might coax, and the doctor soon learned the whole basis of Jeffersonian politics, that they who served in America ruled their masters.

"They also serve who only stand and wait,"

was the main resemblance in Pennsylvania to the Miltonian commonwealth—among the mechanics.

The doctor had about four thousand dollars hard money annual income, and a capital, besides, of quite ten thousand dollars. He, therefore, could undertake to build an unusually large and complete house for the United States, and in building it he separated himself the more from the common run of people, who beheld a "gentleman" where there were no gentlemen expected, but all were earners or traders. Many English were in the place, nearly all of them free-thinkers, and Priestley found that an English free-thinker was another sort of sectarian, without humility.

He pined for the time when he could unpack and assort his library and fall to the study of his Master ; when he could have a commodious laboratory and relieve scholarship with experiments.

The house moved on so slowly that he went down to Philadelphia the second spring and delivered his lectures on the Evidences of Revelation, in the Universalist church.

The man who had dismembered the air and proved life

and vegetation to be exact correlatives, could not get another conventicle in the city to defend the Scriptures from. No wonder that in time Revelation howled for Science to come to its support, like the priests of Baal for rain.

But it became fashionable to go and hear Priestley, and President Adams and Vice-President Jefferson attended nearly all the lectures,—invasions of the Sunday night monopoly of those who rejected information from their sermons.

The elegant Philadelphia belles were quite put to shame sometimes by the doctor's plain language in describing the pagan rites. But our English dissenter had no mock modesty, and the great judges and attorneys listened with hunger to the first manna of science dispensed in a wilderness of greed and superstition.

There sat Hamilton, too, who had come on to make his maiden speech before the Supreme Court, and Priestley went to hear him.

Worn down with study, the retired secretary spoke for three hours on the carriage tax. His old followers were affected to tears as they heard him say that a carriage was a mere article of luxury, and add :

" It so happens that I once had a carriage myself, and found it convenient to dispense with it. But my happiness is not in the least diminished."

Congress was deserted to hear Hamilton earn his daily bread, and the Supreme Court, in the extension of the old State House, was as unable to accommodate Hamilton's auditors as the church to hold Priestley's pupils.

Doctor Priestley found Mr. Adams in a great state of rage. He said that the ridiculous homage to that quite ordinary creature, little Aleck Hamilton, was as absurd as the great booing scene at Washington's Farewell Address.

" They went there to boo," shrieked the new President ; " men and women to boo, sir ! Boo, boo, boo ! "

Here President Adams stood on his tip-toes and made an imitation of people crying into their pocket-handkerchiefs. Then he shouted :

" And me, sir, *me*, ME, who had been presented to the majesty of England in the private cabinet—*me* reflected upon by all that booing, as if it was to be an affliction, sir, to have me rule this second-class realm after Mr. Washington's retirement ! "

Mr. Adams then fell to some muttered comments upon the way the battle of the Brandywine was lost, and remarked, " *That* was the time to boo."

The doctor was a poor worldly observer, but it occurred to him that Mr. Adams had already introduced the American epidemic of two terms of the presidency. Washington having been president twice, Mr. Adams was afraid he should be president only once, which some said was already once too much.

The heart, the head of the Federal party was with Hamilton. This Mr. Jefferson admitted to Doctor Priestley, saying :

" Hamilton may save that party from Adams, but Adams is quite as likely to come over to us as to permit Hamilton to be paramount. Hamilton loves the powers of government ; Adams has the Boston complaint of thinking the honors—the halberds—are the powers."

Mr. Jefferson then described to Doctor Priestley how Hamilton was " for monarchy bottomed on corruption," and Adams for sniffery bottomed on monarchy ; called God to witness that he was not like other men, even like the new run of lawyers, and added that his new peas were of the size of cantaloupes and embarrassed the livestock wandering through his pea-patch.

The engines of defamation were still running strong, however, and kept John Adams dancing with pain. Every time he was going to accuse the Vice-President of feeding those presses Mr. Jefferson flattered him with the idea that he was a remarkable improvement upon Washington and Hamilton.

The Federalists now started a navy, to Mr. Jefferson's abhorrence, who had a method of whipping England by the United States going into a shell—and closing up the shell. This he called the *escargot*, or embargo, or something the good doctor could not remember.

Senator Aaron Burr, however, had been retired from the Senate without an appealing vote, and the father-in-law of Hamilton unanimously restored.

The house at Northumberland was nearly ready when two of those who had waited to inhabit it proved the old proverb that a new house is christened by a funeral.

All the family had seen that new-world home rise carefully from the immense excavation to the great framework, forest of studding, and mighty-hipped gable.

When the purlines were carried out on the dizzy beams by the American carpenters and venturesome town boys, all lifting the timbers by props to their mortises, there were barrels of cider and of ale, and sides of beef set out upon the lawn, and the American flag streamed from one of the two tall chimneys amidst boughs of fir-trees. From Shamokin Hill and Island, from Blue Hill and Montour Ridge, and, it almost seemed, from the White Deer Mountains, people and spirits were looking on.

There stood the fair house of " the chimikil doctor " at last, with two stories, two wings, and liberal attics. At one end was the laboratory wing, twenty-one feet square; at the opposite end was a kitchen of the same size. Through the middle of the dwelling the hall was eight feet wide and nearly fifty feet long, and gave access near the street front to the airy stairway. Another wing hall, proceeding from this, divided the great pantry from the dining-room. The full side opposite was devoted to the library and living rooms, with large connecting doors. In the auxiliary hall were several closets and a companion stairs.

Upon the second floor were two bedrooms over the library, of about eighteen feet square; a hall in front wide as the great triple-mullioned window there ; a cosey bedroom closing the foot of this hall; a small bedroom between the back stair and the corner front, and Priestley's own bedroom, twenty-one by eighteen feet, in the southwest corner, with a parti-hall to separate it. All these five bedrooms, and the whole house, indeed, had large, perfect fireplaces.

The garret consisted of four immense rooms, in one of which opened the stairway.

The hand-carpentry, wainscot rails, plastering, and flooring of this house were of the best material and workmanship extant, and everything was dry, well ventilated, roomy, and high.

Externally, Doctor Priestley's mansion made the impression of a great, bright yellow frame manse or villa with a roof gallery, and about one hundred feet long, and half as wide.  In front were wooden palings, and behind was a grass lawn, sun-dial, rare trees, a young orchard, and the beautiful river, eight hundred feet wide, on each side of a large green island.

It was the noblest house the doctor ever possessed, and, like most perfect homes, it had only come when he was losing his teeth.

During the building of the house, when sons Joe and Harry were bringing up their farms, the residence of the family was temporary or fugitive.  The third son, William Priestley, took a Pennsylvania wife and emigrated to the Mississippi region.

The beautiful library, of which Priestley's works made a large case, was already being unpacked and the scientific apparatus shelved when Harry Priestley died.

He was the youngest son, his mother's last bearing, and the end of fruitfulness.

The last rose of summer may awaken a sentiment, but the last child of a good mother is hardly less precious than the first, as her last pain and joy and sight of one's own babe.

This was her final piece of authorship, wherein she was her husband's literary master, for his books were automatons, and hers had the immortal tongue which is promised to be heard among angels.

Harry was expected by his father to become his successor as priest and naturalist ; but the instincts of the heart precede all such artificial selection, and he was as candidly in love as his family were uncandidly kind to him.   They dared not tell him what Mrs. Reynolds had been and was.

The boy's heart-disease soon reduced his hours of labor, and he put his head in his mother's lap, when the doctor forbade him to chop and lift stones from the fields ; and there, like a child, he wept.

" Mother, now I can never marry Maria !  I cannot make me a home to bring that saint to."

The appellation of "saint" to a woman now well understood in the Priestley household—even if misunderstood—gave the pitying mother a signal to help her boy.

In another room Doctor Priestley, with all the British dissenter's zeal, was showing up the fallacies of " popery."

His wife, an unconsciously constructive theologian, revived to her son all the possibilities of comfort in the Virgin's name.

To the love-sick boy, stricken out of the ranks of house-makers, not even the name of Jesus was efficient, unless coupled with human love, and his mother began to realize upòn the morsels of the story of the mother of Jesus, which repeat the miracle of feeding the multitude forever upon their leanness, and ever basketfuls of fragments remain.

"Ah !" said the boy, "she was like my lady—persecuted, sent up to be taxed, made mother upon the way and in the stall. But wise men found her out, and Maria is the same. Mother, will not the Virgin come and let us all see her ?"

"Father do say so, Harry. Father thinks Christ's second coming is very near. It may be thirty years, father argues, not longer."

"Then we shall not have long to lie, mother, in the house of clay. We shall be raised early. We shall not be forgotten."

"O Harry ! our new house is all but ready. Shall I not hear thy voice in its chambers, my son ?"

"I will be dead but a little while, and Maria will not forget me. As she stands by Mary's side in the court of the King, I shall be pointed out. 'There's Hal !' will my lady say."

The August weather came, and Harry added the bilious fever to his organic complaint, so that he was soon worn, between the furnace and the chill, to a remnant of his rugged self. He drew his mother's life out, too, upon the suction of his own ; she saw the fever fire up his weakened heart and drive it beyond nature. Her lean hand was always on his pulse,·and it seemed to be her own—to make her aged heart gallop with it, like a young horse harnessed with its dam, or to flutter and be cold when her baby fainted.

Priestley himself lived very little in this world, and his wife had taken everything off his hands, so that he could engage in the ancient pagan battles with the Stoics, Pelagians, Arians, and all the different popes. He came in sometimes and looked at his dying boy and wrung his hands in helpless pity, and went out again.

" If I only had my laboratory ! " exclaimed the doctor, "and could get him some oxy——" •
" Dephlogisticated air! " remarked Mr. Cooper. " He is phlogistonized and burns. Why don't you answer the French minister, Adet, on that Lavoiserian heresy ? "

" There is no chemistry to restore life but the resurrection, Thomas. ' Blessed and holy is he that hath part in the first resurrection ; on such the second death hath no power.' "

" Stuff and phlogiston, Doctor ! " remarked Mr. Cooper. " Come and write that article against commerce for Duane's paper. Mr. Jefferson says your pen must be exerted, as they are dephlogisticating Liberty."

So the doctor, who knew no more upon the subject than college professors ever since, made his virgin appearance in the American press, saying :

" *The additional price to the carrier to indemnify him for his risque, the expence of ambassadors, and that of fitting out ships-of-war, I cannot help thinking must be much more than all the profit that can be derived from the carrying trade. By laying up our ships we are in no danger of quarrelling with our neighbours. If one nation affront another, the people would do best to take it patiently, and content themselves with making remonstrances. There is the truest dignity in this conduct. If any person will send his goods to sea, it should be at his own risque.*"

Had instigation been able to throw its shadow over such nonsense, Mr. Jefferson's shadow from Monticello would have fallen on Priestley's paper. President John Adams, who was trying to create a navy to protect the rich commerce of his country, read this article of Priestley and grew furious.

" Such aliens who preach sedition," he roared, " deserve no more mercy in America than in England."

At that time our manufactures were not great enough for Mr. Jefferson to attack them, and he was setting his incendiaries upon American shipping, as the great harpy of the land, eating the farmer up.

In time this little navy of the Federalists redeemed the honor of his land, after he had fled from the White House to Monticello at the first broadside of Mr. Canning's guns.

When next Doctor Priestley went to Philadelphia to lecture, the fashion, character, and patriotic manhood of the

14

land was not in attendance. Neither honor nor reward
was his return, but silence and neglect.

Mr. Jefferson was not done with him, however, for his
motto still was : " Let *us* cultivate Pennsylvania, and we
need not fear the universe."

Lizzie Priestley was drawn close to her mother-in-law •
by natural sympathy and by a certain bereavement of her
husband's natural confidence.

Ever since the night she had declared her affection for
Hamilton, in terms beyond their meaning, Joe had looked
preoccupied. Mrs. Reynolds had left a certain sting
behind her, vanquished though she was. She had
exasperated Lizzie Priestley to admit that she loved the
man whom she loved only with the affection of rectitude
and of service.

But that service she could not betray to her husband,
because its concealment was the continuation of her
sacrifice.

In the mean time Colonel Aaron Burr was writing to
her husband, as she well knew, and Joe did not show her
the letters.

So there were two secrets between man and wife, and
each kept one secret, like a disease or a hidden defect.
In the marriage chamber, in the perfect union of mutual
parentage, was a closet more delicate than Bluebeard's
chamber, and its forbidden key unlocked the doors of
dreams and made man and wife mutter : " The chain of
confidence is not complete."

They never quarrelled, but to pure affection a quarrel
is a clarifying thunder-gust. Alas for them whose love is
sundered and who quarrel not !

Each felt a sense of injury, and that is where the
enemy of love finds its golden mail opened—in self's
impregnability, the entertaining of a grievance instead of
confessing to be the injurer.

Joe had escaped lifelong woe by his wife's defence of
him, but was too human to stand the echo of the boast :
" I love Alexander Hamilton. I confess the passion and
its return. All things are made ready for his appreciation of me."

He knew his wife had not a gross element in her nature,
but the bestowal of such an ethereal fire as hers upon
the altar of another man, and that man fresh from a

common amour, started the latent aristocracy of Joe's nature.

The wife's aristocracy was started, too, in that the holy right of charity was impugned in her and possibly accredited to a meaner impulse.

"Mother, I hate to see Joe so silent, but I cannot speak."

"There will be a time, daughter, when his heart will break for thee. Then be thy heart all ready and take his upon it, and let your tears flow upon each other."

That time almost came when Harry Priestley died.

To the last he panted for the story of the espoused Virgin of Nazareth, who feared the angel's salutation : "Hail, thou that art highly favored ! "

"Highly favored ! " sighed the boy. "So is she."

"And Mary was troubled in her mind at such a saying and its manner, but the angel said : 'Fear not, Mary ! ' "

"Fear not, my suffering love ! " the boy repeated to his mother.

"'The Holy Ghost shall come upon thee, and the power of the Highest shall overshadow thee.' And Mary said : 'God hath regarded my low estate : He hath scattered the proud and exalted them of low degree ! ' "

"So may Maria overcome her enemies, mother. Oh! where is the farm I cleared for that dear image ? The bushes will grow over it, and she cannot find my grave."

"Son, the voice of Mary's Son can find thee out, and bring all true hearts together. There is a trump to blow, and we shall hear it and come forth."

"No," answered the boy, whose eyes were glazing as they all stood around him. "I'll not have Maria called. She and I shall lie still, and the wild roots shall grow from me to her like our hands that were always together. We want rest, and that shall be heaven."

"Harry, I will not be long after thee, my boy, if thou art to go."

"Let Maria and me stay behind when all the rest are rising, and ours shall be this gift of the earth and the life we have lived. It is all we want. You never liked. Maria, friends. Why are we all divided because a poor girl is loved by one of us ? "

"My son, love is the cause of our being. God so loved the world——"

"That is it," said the boy. "This world was beautiful as Maria. The radiant eye of God fell on it, and all the mire and mud gave way to flowers and herbage. Oh, how I loved my farm!"

His sob was so mighty now that it was echoed in all hearts, and the room was the wailing place of blood kin.

"My farm!" exclaimed the boy. "I fought for it, father, against weeds and woods and rains and washes. Oh! I knew it,—every clod. My ploughshare broke its enemies to pieces. It killed me, but it was to be my home and the castle of my love."

Father, family stood round, and felt the pathos of this earthly toil which makes one spot so dear that heaven is bare without it.

"Can't I find my farm in heaven?" wandered Harry. "Oh! heaven is all made, and *I* made my farm. There is the stall where the poor Maid lay. All the wise men peeped in. The cows and calves and plough-horses are mounching, and I see their great, calm eyes. What is it yonder, mother, streaming in my barn with light so soft and red? Praised be the evening star! 'Tis Venus. That is the wise man's lamp upon this world. It tarried on my farm and was my star of Bethlehem to me, because its beams seemed my Maria's eyes."

The pulse was almost done. The fever had burnt the poor human furnace to the ribs. His feet were cold.

"Let me rest here, forever, in the new world," the boy sighed, "by my own farm—beneath the star of Mary—which was love. Forgive her—all."

There was a pause to see if the pulse had ticked the spring of life away. Then rose the mother's cry—the same from Indian, black, or Saxon, where Rachel is weeping for her children, and will not be comforted:

"O my God! My baby's dead!"

The little quartette of grief struck all at once the strings of music in their throats, and around the pale blue form played the fountains of unavailing tears. The voice of the father, whose literary nature was tempered coldest, recovered the first, saying:

"Let us pray!"

And so, kneeling, he who had analyzed the air was impotent and ignorant as a child of the mystery of life that was here an instant ago and now is gone—and where?

Mrs. Priestley never recovered from Harry's death. She wrote Mrs. Reynolds a letter, and received a contrite reply from New York, which said:

"NEW YORK.

"DEAR MADAME:—*I heard of Hal's death with sorring tears. Indeed I loved him as a bruther. That he spoke of me to the last was butiful and strange—me, so unfortnit! Could I have loved a good man, who would have kerected my faults, I might have done some good. Mrs. Priestley, some of us is not held to the same account as others, because we are temtid more. I hope there is a Jesis for us all. That name was for the good and bad. Excuse my bad quill, and believe me,*

"PENNYTENT MARIA."

As Mary Priestley put her affairs in order to lie beside her son in the town graveyard, she omitted not one provision before she lay her down. To the last this world and not the next was the subject of her husbandry. To that unknown land she looked, with the dark hand of fate upon her, like the great poet's metaphor:

"There's husbandry in heaven,
Its candles all are out."

With life wasting, she saw that nothing was wasted else.

"These are your Joe's woollens, Lizzie, and those my Joe's," she would say nearly every day, going over the household blendings. "Daughter, my Joe will be alone. My daughter Sarah can't come over; she has marriage troubles, too. If you can't stay with father, take him back to England with you. That is my pain. I do not fear my Maker. *He* is better than his preachers, and gives us all this holy pain to increase this life's elixir. Praise him to have lived! Trust him when we die!"

"Mother, those hammers plague you, building our new house."

"Lizzie, you think they remind me of nailing my coffin up? Yes; but that is an enduring house. I always loved the ground and the grass. If it was the Lord's will, I could lie undisturbed forever, making the earth green and flowery for others. My religion was to serve, because I had been blessed to love. O my

Joe ! I have been married to him nearly thirty-four years. What a poor child he is, with all his knowledge ! "

The hammers of the new house were driving many nails.

" I shall never live there," said the dying wife. " But, Joe, I shall never haunt your house, though sometimes I hope you will haunt mine. No ; I shall never do you any harm. Live out your days, and come and lie by me. We are too old to change our habits now. Go on and finish your house ; think that my wishes hover over it, for I shall have no spirit but love."

To her son Joe she one day said :

" Son, here are some letters I request you not to open till I am buried. I could tell you, Joe, all that concerns you about Colonel Hamilton and your wife. They say women cannot keep secrets. Oh ! what severity and mistake ! How many thousands of poor mothers have been the only ones to know of a daughter's ruin, a son's disgrace, and never spoke ! I tell you that your wife is only interested in another man because she is better than most other women ! My son, I will bear testimony to women. Few of them are wicked. I shall leave you to your wife in peace."

To Mr. Cooper she one day said :

" Tommy, my sons and you were friends, and so I never quarrelled with you ; but you are of a bold and eager spirit, and my husband is a poor preacher and teacher. Do go away from him, and not embroil him with this country ! What do you know about government, ungovernable Tommy Cooper ? Must the furious rule the peaceful ? Go to Kentucky, or Virginia, or Carolina, and let Joseph Priestley alone ! "

But Mr. Cooper had now got hold of a newspaper partly his own, and was shaking up things and puffing Doctor Priestley in every number, so that his scorners confounded him with Priestley.

The doctor was to dedicate his new work, " The History of the Christian Church," to Mr. Jefferson, who now and then addressed him as his " venerated friend."

The autumn day came when Mary Priestley was to die. They saw her bright eye ranging, not for angels nor portents, but for omitted earthly trifles to make her house orderly when she was gone, and once she said, in whispers :

" Lizzie, be careful when you dust father's worktable ! These literary men are womanish, and have an order of their own which often seems to us disorder. Study their method, for everybody has some. You can lead a man if you study him. Lead, my darling, but never drive ! Horses are to be driven ; give the reins to men, and then you can persuade them where to drive."

She was very low, and made a motion with her eyelash. The family leaned over and heard her sigh :

" Have I forgotten anything ? "

There was a spasm, or a catching of breath, and the tears of them to live began to flow, when out of the wandering soul in the dark and tangled footpath toward silence came the dying words :

" No rioters—no contention—peace."

" O Lizzie ! " cried Joe, " mother is gone."

She caught him in her arms, and said :

" Joe, I will be wife and mother to you as long as I live. I will stay with father faithfully, as if mother were still here."

" I shall never hear her footstep in my house," Doctor Priestley cried. " My house will miss her till I die."

The nails were being driven gayly that day in the great new house of Joseph Priestley, for it must be closed in before the frost.

-----

## CHAPTER XXI.

### BELL AND BOOK

WHEN Hamilton had returned to Philadelphia from the Western insurrection he was distressed at the appearance of his wife.

She had a young babe, and he had supposed her to be at her father's, in the high parts of New York ; on the contrary, she came in a friend's carriage to the Schuylkill ferry, and when he embraced and kissed her she fainted in his arms.

Remorse, love, pity worked in Hamilton's thoughts, for his Eliza was not a fainting spirit. In the camp she had been a steady soldier when the British, lying in front of the Jerseys, had constantly menaced the freezing army, and alarms came almost nightly.

Reared to be a housekeeper by a good Dutch cultivator's wife, Eliza had never complained of poverty, but delighted to go into the kitchen and keep her servants cheerful, for Alexander might be expected to bring an army friend to eat almost every day. Though the Federalists were called aristocrats, their wives, almost uniformly, were housekeepers, while what were called the Republicans talked French politics and depended upon slaves. Hamilton wondered if his retirement from office and official salary had caused his wife to fear.

No ; she desired to go to New York and have him begin the practice of law.

" My darling, what ails you ? " asked Hamilton.

" Nothing."

" Yes, it is more like everything than nothing. This is not the Eliza I left. Don't you love this last little babe ? "

" As much as any, and each the same as all."

" Sweet girl, give me a little bit of confidence. What is your pain like ? "

" Loneliness."

" What can I bring to help it ? "

" Truth."

He looked at her wonderingly.

" Ask me no more," she breathed, and seemed to tremble. " You are cunning-witted and will make me proclaim a woe that is my cross and my crown."

" You are not in a religious daze, dear wife ? "

" I must go to my babe," answered Eliza, for they had reached the little house at Third Street and Walnut.

" My angel, my gift of strength and peace ! " said Hamilton, with fervor, " if I have left you lonely I will never do so again. Not even my country, not Washington, shall take me from your side. I will labor for our children, and as we sat up together in the camp and I worked half the night in your sight, I will sit with you again over my law books, and my library shall be our bed-chamber, where I can hear you breathe."

" O Alexander ! there is an echo of something I miss in your voice. You shall never miss it in mine."

He thought over her strange reference to Truth.

" Does *that* give an echo ? " Hamilton asked himself.
" There may be in the responsive heart of love a- real
echo, and when we conceal or deceive, our voices will not
wake it.   O that I could bare my bosom and tell my
one mutiny from this household perfection !   But we
have children."

When they settled in New York and Hamilton kept
his household promise, working faithfully in his house,
keeping his office there, and absent only in court, he saw
no want of interest in his wife, but sometimes too much
interest—a kind of excitability that seemed the ecstasy
of love with irrational fears to ferment it.

" Eliza, are you jealous ? "

" Sir, do you suppose I have so little self-respect as to
entertain that ? "

She was a slight little woman, with more soul than
body, and the courage of blended provincial families that
excels all peerage pride—the pride of the barons before
the crown subdues them to be mere peers.   In her was
the blood of Rensselaers, of Livingstons, also—whence
her injury had come—of the Van Cortlandts, and more.

This New York pride, kept self-conscious by the
swarming of all ranks and increasing *parvenue* riches to
New York, was in Eliza Hamilton elevated by the universal appreciation of her husband's intellect.

She had fallen in love with the unrelated, unallied
staff captain and married him, opposite to the habit of
her considering family, and he had become the public
genius of the country.   It was the State saying that
" the Clintons had offices and power, the Livingstons
lands and connections, and the Schuylers had Hamilton."

This little West India man with the wax-and-rose
skin and high head and small, perfect body, had become
the head of the Schuyler power, the preservative limb
of their family tree, her father's chief elector to the
Senate ; and he had made the nation rich and  disdained
helping himself.   Now he was measuring that talent
with other men, and laying himself at the bar beside the
adroit Colonel Burr and the money-winning lawyers.

Every child she bore, Eliza felt to be another Hamilton, the only seed of that rare and solitary exotic in the
United States.

She watched the prince who had dropped down to her heart from floral land with the love that was almost sacred, and she knew, as well, that if he ever felt " virtue go out of him," like another divine Teacher, it would be at woman's touch.  For Hamilton was ardent as husband and lover, with a warm intellect, and his nervous contents were electrical, receiving as well as giving currents of life and admiration.

" Can she doubt me ? " thought Hamilton ; " is there a second-sight in such love as hers, that perceives me and is dumb ? "

He felt this superstition the more when one day, on Wall Street, he and his wife came upon Colonel Aaron Burr, with a large lady upon his arm.

Colonel Burr looked straight at Mrs. Hamilton with all his piercing quality and ever-attuned dignity, but Mrs. Hamilton only saw his companion woman drop her eyes at the recognition of her husband and blush.

" Who—who is that lady, Alexander ? "

" Oh ! you do not want to know her, Eliza.  That is a Mrs. Clingman, who is said to be living with Colonel Burr."

" Do you know her, sir, then ? "

" Yes," replied Hamilton.  " In the past I have met her."

" I hope never to see her again," remarked Eliza.

This bright little creature, indeed, was the complete balance and remainder of Hamilton, making him at union with himself.  As she sat like the queen bee in the hive, he was a working member, composed by her presence ; when she was gone he dropped his tools and became a rover through the fields of sun.  It was in such an absence that the soldier forgot his arms and became a forager in the neutral lines.

Eliza had a spice, also, of daring like her own lover's character.  The Schuylers, no more than other people, were uniformly proof to human and individual impulses.  Though one sister was married to the patroon of Albany, and others were already, or were to be, very considerately married, now and then one took the bit between her teeth before the old general could consult and determine.  There was Angelica, who had walked around the corner with a fine merchant army contractor, Mr.

Carter, and returned Mrs. Church, her husband, for family reasons in England, having concealed his American identification.

The incentive of love is never remote in a capable family, and Eliza Schuyler, who had taken the greatest risk, was married in the chiefest honor. Four sons and a daughter were already of their brood, and little Phil, whom Washington had nursed, was now fifteen.

Suddenly a new assault was made upon Colonel Hamilton, after he had been, as he supposed, completely separated and absolved from his one truantry.

A book was one day put into his hand with the title of " The History of the United States for 1796." It was written by Callender, the Scotch slanderer, and related the commencement of Hamilton's troubles with Reynolds and wife and Clingman years before, but only in a way to mystify that intrigue and convert some private letters, now for the first time published, into evidences of Secretary Hamilton having divided money with James Reynolds.

Hamilton had paid Reynolds, through ₄ Clingman's manœuvring of Reynolds and wife, about eleven hundred dollars, nominally borrowed, but artfully exacted.

In this present publication the woman was kept well out of sight, and the bare fact of the money being paid to Reynolds was confirmed by letters from Muhlenberg, the patron of Clingman, from Monroe and another, who had joyously formed a cabal to investigate the impregnable Hamilton. All this had happened two years before Doctor Priestley arrived in America.

In that investigation Aaron Burr had also played a part, without distinctly understanding the female implication. Speaker Muhlenberg had desired to get his subaltern, Jake Clingman, out of jail, and Monroe had been the tool of Jefferson to see what was the matter.

The shameless Giles, the public insulter of Washington, a Virginia Congressman, had at that time accused Hamilton of Treasury peculations, but the secretary's honesty and address had proved triumphant.

Without flinching, Hamilton had kept both Reynolds and Clingman in prison for fraud upon his department, though the unsoldierly Monroe had sneaked to Mrs. Reynolds and sounded her, and had procured the des-

perate Clingman to make the charge that Reynolds was
Hamilton's broker, while his clerk, to speculate in the
funds.

At that commencement of his miseries Hamilton threw
himself upon the generosity of his opponents, and by the
display of the letters of Reynolds and wife to Muhlenberg and Monroe, showed those comrades that he had
been a victim of blackmail, and had paid Reynolds not
to speculate, but to spare his domestic peace.

Alas ! those letters of Reynolds and wife were now in
Jefferson's hands.  Hamilton no longer had the means
to protect himself from the public charge by proving the
private error.

As if aware of his helplessness, the Callender slander
made light of the real issue, and said that Hamilton had
invented a pretended amour with Reynolds' wife to hide
his payments of a speculator's commissions to that clerk.

By this perversion the statement and letters of Monroe
and Co., and bits of notes between Reynolds and Hamilton, were made, in the " History " of Callender, to confirm the old exploded charge of Hamilton's public specu-
lations.

He saw that a crisis had come.

His wife must be faced ; his family life would probably end or lose forever its serenity and exist in everlasting distrust and contention.

The baseness of Monroe in betraying these papers,
after giving his pledge of honor as a man of the world
and a soldier—adding to them, indeed, by other writings
of an imputative sort—gave to Hamilton's despair the
anger of battle.

He knew that Jefferson was the malign prompter of
both Callender and Monroe ; but Jefferson was a well
understood non-combatant, so advertised in the proceedings of his legislature, and an object of literary and philosophic sympathy, as one who might insinuate and stab,
but could not strike.

Monroe, however, had been an officer, if an obscure
one.  He was the only anti-Federalist in the Virginia set
of any military pretensions, and had been running for
office on his military record ever since the war.

Hamilton called Mr. Monroe to account.

"It was incumbent upon you, sir," he wrote, "as a

man of honesty and sensibility, to have come forward in a manner that would have shielded me completely from the unpleasant effects brought upon me by your agency. This' you have not done. . . . The result in my mind is that you have been and are actuated by motives toward me malignant and dishonorable ; nor can I doubt that this will be the universal opinion when the publication of the whole affair, which I am about to make, shall be seen."

Muhlenberg, a Pennsylvania Dutch preacher, in politics one of the Mifflin men, hastened to back out. Monroe's Virginia ally felt ashamed of himself and apologized.

But Monroe had just come back from the French mission in disgrace, and had been accused of selling his country's interests to the French jockeys of the " Directory " for a bribe. Not destitute of courage, though it was courage without quality, he had plunged like a country bull into Mr. Jefferson's net, who incited him to write a book and attack Washington directly.

He was not a party to this attack of Callender's. Mr. Jefferson had the whole credit of that.

Nor was Monroe a corrupt, though a very professional, politician.

His sense of injuries, his smarting under Hamilton's raking pen—probably, also, his conceit at being made so much of by the luminous man of the time—impelled him to solicit a challenge from Hamilton.

" That man is dangerous, Monroe," said Mr. Jefferson ; " who knows but he may come here some day and attack me ! "

The Vice-President was a picture of apprehension and artfulness, and clung to his revenge with a pallid face. "I tell you," he resumed, " do not fight him yourself. He will be sure to kill you, for he is standing on family ground. His wife's hand will be on the trigger. We shall all stand in history as assassins, if you kill *him*—first of his family and then of his life."

Mr. Jefferson trembled.

" Pshaw ! " exclaimed Monroe. " Have some character, Mr. Jefferson ! A challenge is a challenge, and if I have made a mistake and expose my life for it, who can take exception ? "

"Send Colonel Burr with your challenge," observed
Jefferson, after a long pause. "He is one of your cool,
deadly Yankee men. An army man, too, jealous of
Hamilton at the bar. An unscrupulous fiend! You
were his advocate for the French appointment. He
wants our Virginia countenance. So shift the quarrel to
Burr, as your second, and then——"

"What?"

"If either or both be killed, *we* gain."

Minister Monroe looked at Jefferson with a hard, rustic
stare.

"You can't understand my case," he answered, grimly.
"Old bulldog Washington could see it. There is a thing
above politics called Honor, and on that I stand. To
manœuvre Burr into my place would extend my unpopu-
larity; I could never be governor of Virginia."

Mr. Jefferson listened automatically, always cultivating
coldness in formalities and crises.

"Now, see here," concluded Monroe, "it is the easiest
thing in the world for me to satisfy Hamilton. That
book of Callender's was all printed before I came back
from France, so I could not have furnished those letters
and *mems*. Do you know why I am ready to fight Hamilton?"

"To become governor of Virginia?"

"No; to save you."

"Me?"

"Yes, Tom. Venable and Muhlenberg have disclaimed
supplying Callender with these papers. If I do the same,
Hamilton uncovers you, as the only man who could have
supplied them. He might make you fight, or if you declined, break you down in Virginia. I shall stand in the
way and take the blow, Tom, for your sake, whatever it
is. I am your only soldier."

Mr. Jefferson started very deliberately to rise and walk
to his washstand. He overdid the appearance of deliberation; for his complexion, ashy white, became deathly
as he stepped out, and he fell.

Monroe caught him in his arms and found him insensible.

"Fright, pure fright!" sighed Monroe. "Here is a
man who would have been altogether lovable, like a
woman, if he had not taken up politics. Yet to him we
are to commit our country!"

He sprinkled water on Mr. Jefferson's face, and supported him, kneeling, with his law instructor's head upon his knee.

" Wake up, my friend ! " gently called the hard Monroe, "no harm shall come to you.   When I became your follower I felt for you as for my wife : that you were made to be loved and protected.   Colonel Hamilton will obtain no explanation from me.''

Jefferson arose and tottered to the settee of his lodgings.

" Oh ! if I could restore those originals," he sighed, "and appease Hamilton !   But they are at Monticello, and he is fierce."

Colonel Burr did become Monroe's second, and had the effrontery to call at Hamilton's house in Cedar Street ; but Hamilton repaired to the law office of a friend, and there, with closed doors, received the politic invitation of Monroe to send a challenge.

Hamilton looked up and found Mr. Burr very curiously regarding him.

" Depend upon it, Colonel," said Hamilton, " I shall send Major Monroe no challenge.   I have sent him a chart of his conduct in this affair, and if he is willing to make a public test of it, on the correspondence, you will confer with Colonel Jackson."

" Hamilton, he will not stand upon his conduct.   It means nothing else than to hold you between a domestic exposure and a silence which will be your political confession.   Let me serve you."

" I cannot let you serve me in any way, Colonel Burr. I would not even accept from you the tender of the letters you took from Clingman and wife and conveyed to Mr. Monroe, and which are now, I am morally sure, in Mr. Jefferson's hands."

Colonel Burr was a little surprised, but very steady and ready, after he had wiped his nose and replaced his white handkerchief in his laced shirt bosom.

" You are too penetrating, Colonel Hamilton, to make it worth while to deceive you.   I thought it no injury to you to take those letters, so fatal to your domestic peace, out of the hands of the Clingman family.   I put them in the hands of an army comrade of ours, where your honor would be safe.   He turned them over to

Jefferson without any examination. To be frank with
you, I should have used them in good time to compel
that alliance I have always sought with you—which I
still seek."

" It can never be made, sir. Dismiss the idea."

" It can, and this is the time for generalship. Why will
you be pursued in your retirement as Jefferson is pursuing you, with his filthy foreign mercenaries ?   I am the
man you need.  You will surely need me.  This moment
is our mutual opportunity.   Let us expose Jefferson to
the spirit of the Cincinnati brotherhood ! "

" That would seem an evasion of this charge of Callender's against me.  I must answer that before I expose
the motive of my accusers."

" Do both.   Post Jefferson as your only real enemy,
the concocter of every plot against you.   Accuse him of
holding your letters from Reynolds at this moment !
Monroe and I would have to sustain you if you appealed
to us ;  the result would be that every man of honor in
the country would fly from Jefferson.  He would be defeated for the Presidency."

Hamilton looked up.   Colonel Burr seemed to have
stopped too short.

" There might be situations where I would not want to
defeat Mr. Jefferson for President."

Colonel Burr was pale, almost submissive.  A look of
eagerness, too, was frozen in his face.  He never had
looked so perfectly respectable as at this minute to Hamilton and never was to Hamilton so wholly repulsive.

The idea of this man being President of the United
States made all other pretenders to that honor and power
comparatively acceptable.  The nation was to Hamilton
like an only sister, grown up at his side in beauty and
virtue.

" To be frank," continued Hamilton, " I have a real
regard for Mr. Jefferson's daughter.  To stigmatize her
father would deeply hurt her feelings.  Public life does
not require such incivilities."

" Is that all ? "

" No ; I also pity Mr. Jefferson.  He is torn and
racked by ambition; such acts as this with Callender
encourage the vulture that feeds upon his vitals.  He
may wound me, but he poisons himself.  It is the weak-

ness of his courage which leads him to stoop so low.    In
satisfied conditions he might be a safe ruler.    Many of
his tastes are respectable.    Certainly he is at the head of
his party."

"You are complimentary."

"I did not say he was as good a politician as Colonel Burr.    On the contrary, we have easily beaten him
where he has set the policy.    You have not been a French
Jacobin, a whiskey insurrectionist, or in any way a volatile leader.    You might be able to run Jefferson hard for
the next Presidential term."

"If so——"

"I could not support you, Colonel Burr."

Hamilton had been sitting by the garden casement;
Mr. Burr was standing with his tapering-crowned beaver
in his hand.    His face was passionless yet cruel.    The
intellectual gifts of educators and theologians, prying
into the nature of God with metaphysical coolness, had
been punished by some cross or curse in this scion, who
had the small majesty of an Augustus Cæsar, and no
feelings but self-love.    He was looking at Hamilton with
steady eyes, as at a problem in mathematics.

"I cannot believe that you would carry a pique as far
as that, Hamilton.    Your wife's father and I have alter-
nately beaten each other ; in no case have I attacked
you.    Come ! I make the last concession, and give her
up."

"*Her?*    Whom ?"

"*La Belle* Livingston."

"Your mistress ?"

"Yes.    I knew that to be your pique against me.    She
is a great concession to make to you, but, like Zeid, the
freedman of the Prophet, I feel for your passion, and give
my noble Zeinab to Mahomet."

"Return Clingman's wife to me ?"

"I wonder at your skill, Hamilton.    My way seemed
the right one, but yours works the miracle.    No doubt
your intuition has told you that Reynolds still loves
you."

"Yes," said Hamilton wearily, "she loves to subsist
upon us all."

"She tells me up and down that I bear no comparison to Colonel Hamilton, and were it not for a certain

15

piquancy in her resisting me, I might have been jealous. To tell you the truth, I am the party in love with Maria; and yet, in view of your immediate need of her aid, I shall send her to you this night."

" Sir ! "

" Yes, it is your instant delivery. None but you could have seen it. Maria will confirm your statement that her husband took advantage of your amour and robbed you of the very money Callender says you paid him as your financial tool."

" Colonel Burr, your proposition is astounding ! "

" So are all Hamilton's *ruses de guerre*. By heaven ! for you Reynolds would kneel to your wife and swear that you were still the spotless pattern of a husband. I tell you she will come this night with the swiftness of a shooting-star and explode the magazine of Jefferson, Callender, and Monroe the instant she strikes it. I shall again be a lonely widower, but to have made such an unspeakable sacrifice will incline to me the heart of Colonel Hamilton at last."

He closed the door behind him and left Hamilton speechless from the misinterpretation of his mind.

Though Aaron Burr had left a loathsome influence in the place, he had also left, from the nature of his character, a moment's great temptation.

Without the Reynolds letters, what could substantiate Hamilton's defence but Mrs. Reynolds herself.

Without her he was empty-handed ; with her he could face the world and his wife.

She would swear to Mrs. Hamilton that an infatuation for her husband had lent Mrs. Reynolds to join a conspiracy which was now turned against Hamilton's public character, and which she would dissipate from the sense of penitence and honor.

As the evolution of this path of cunning permeated the upright soul of Hamilton, he folded his arms and looked off into the infinite space where the finite being conjectures the Ruler of justice to be.

"Almighty Author of good and sorrow !" exclaimed Hamilton, "stern was thy law to spare not them which taught their abominations to wandering Israel. For years I have been lost in this wilderness of deceit, and shall I now be directed by a lie, even to save my blameless family? No; there is no end to double-dealing. Jefferson and Burr shall see that I will not lie; my adopted country shall learn that I do not steal. I can leave this land if my family cast me out, and take a broken heart to my poor old father in the Isle of Nevis."

As he returned to his house two letters were put in his hand. He sat down among his family to read them. The first letter was postmarked Northumberland, and it said:

"DEAR FRIEND:—My husband has put in my hand the book which charges Hamilton with a secret speculation. It is the time for you to declare the truth and shame the fiend.

"I beseech you not to let others prevaricate now and continue you in this maze of folly. Cry aloud, Hamilton, and receive the blow! It will soon be over. Let no mistaken mercy set loose upon society the tigers which have drunk your blood. This is the supplication to her friend of                    LIZZIE PRIESTLEY."

Mrs. Hamilton had raised the enclosure from the carpet and read the postmark. Her black eyes were either quizzical or flashing.

"Northumberland," she said, "and a woman's hand? Alexander, can this be the daughter of Doctor Priestley, whose *tête-à-tête* with you I disturbed at Mrs. Bingham's garden-party?"

"It is the hand of an angel," exclaimed Hamilton, forgetful of the jealousy he might inspire.

He broke the next letter's seal.

There fell into his hand a bundle of papers and scraps.

"Charlottesville?" spoke Mrs. Hamilton, raising the 'enclosure. "Here also is a woman's handwriting. Sir, it is time you explained all this secret correspondence."

Hamilton was reading the letter with wondering eyes. It said:

"MONTICELLO.

"DEAR HAMILTON:—For a long time I have preserved the contents of this packet, though several times moved to destroy it.

"Having possessed myself of it when it was about to be used to your injury, I feared to mail it to you for two reasons. It might be opened by my dear friend Eliza. And I did not think you would be otherwise than unhappy, Hamilton, to know that I was aware of your sin.

"If I send you the packet now, it is from an instinct that you will need it. Receive with it the forgiveness of your friend, for friendship like mine is almost as much wounded by an infidelity as a wife's love.

"Hamilton, you deceive your wife by avoiding a confession.

Good women love to forgive a mortal wound. If she is proud, remember the divine nature in yourself and walk bravely to your cross and die for that.

"In consideration of my feelings for you and yours, do not insult my father!

"If we meet not here again, through earthly contentions, I believe that we shall meet in a realm without night, where we shall be washed and made white in the Lamb's blood.

"Adieu, Hamilton.

"MARTHA JEFFERSON RANDOLPH."

As Hamilton raised his eyes, with tears flowing from them, he sighed:

"'And there followed Him women which also bewailed and lamented him.' Eliza, you are welcome to read these letters. Will you do so?"

"No; my help is limited to your public correspondence, sir."

"To-night, Eliza, I shall sit by your bed and write all the night long."

"That is nothing new, husband."

"Yes, Eliza, it will be all new this night. The truth is always new."

## CHAPTER XXII.

### CONFESSION.

WITH no feeling of self-righteousness, nor yet with the confidence of an acute purpose, did Hamilton draw his table to the window in the warm summer night and screen it from the many strollers in the little street.

The Scotch Presbyterian Church, at the corner of Broadway and Cedar Street, was attracting people to its revival. New York was then a cape city, full of gardens and churches, sloping toward the side rivers and their bay, with ponds and creeks above the city park or common; and some fifty thousand souls were gathered on the tip of that extensive island like flies on a sturgeon's nose.

"What, then, is man?" sighed Hamilton, lighting his candles and taking up his pen.

The phrase recalled old John of Barnevelt, projector of this colony, as he had been brought forth to die. Other grisly phantoms came also to Hamilton's discouraged mind. He thought of Eugene Aram forty years before, executed for a murder that had been done fourteen years and forgotten, until the murderer's false wife, who had caused the crime, disinterred the body of her paramour, and accused her husband.

Hamilton took up his quill.

" Perhaps this instrument of my exaltation will now console my humility," he said, and put the point to the paper.

Instantly he began to think clearly and to see his way, as if a finger-board guided him.

As the Pointers in the Bear go round the Pole Star and take the solar system with them, so the infinite issues in Hamilton's mind took order and ran to his pen's point. He felt the whole nation to be before him and the host in the heavens looking down.

The truth, justice to his family, example to his country, proportion, sensibility, suffering, candor, manhood, drew all together, and he heard the bell of Trinity strike eight as he commenced :

" *The spirit of Jacobinism, if not entirely a new spirit, has, at least, been cloathed with a more gigantic body and armed with more powerful weapons than it ever before possessed.*

" *Incessantly busied in undermining all the props of public security and private happiness, it seems to threaten the political and moral world with a complete overthrow.*

" *A principal engine by which this spirit endeavours to accomplish its purposes is calumny.*

" *It is essential to its success that the influence of men of upright principles, disposed and able to resist its enterprises, shall be at all events destroyed. Not content with traducing their best efforts for the public good, with misrepresenting their purest motives, with inferring criminality from actions innocent or laudable, the most direct falsehoods are invented and propagated with undaunted effrontery and unrelenting perseverance.*"

The image of Mr. Jefferson was in the mind of Hamilton. He blotted the next sentence out, lest it might wound Martha Randolph.

A titter was heard very close to the window, and little whispers.

" Pa," spoke the voice of son Phil, " here's Theo Burr. I have brought her down from Richmond Hill."

" Children, you must excuse me to-night. I am deeply busy."

They were already gone.

Something dropped in the open casement behind the screen.   Hamilton stooped forward and picked up a copy of Callender's book containing the charge against him.

" It must have been intended for my wife, as this is next to her chamber, and is her sitting-room," thought Hamilton.

" Father," noted Mrs. Hamilton, coming in, " I was bowing the shutter above when I saw Colonel Burr and the fine brunette woman you call Clingman come past.   It seemed to me that Burr pushed something in your window."

" Yes, my dear, another publication of the Faction. Do you want to read it, and see how bad a public man I am ? "

" Yes, I will take it to bed.  The night is warm and the mosquitoes bite the baby.   I can look at you as you are at work, and say, ' God bless you, Alexander ! ' "

" In the  morning, Eliza, you will  know how bad I am every way."

The wife was soon in bed, and the folding doors stood open between her chamber and the writing Hamilton. As she lay with her face toward him, sometimes her black lashes looked to be her black eyes gazing out.  He wrote again:

*" Lies often detected  and  refuted are  still revived and repeated in the hope that the refutation may have been forgotten, or that the frequency and boldness of accusation may supply the place of truth and proof.  The most profligate men are encouraged, probably bribed, certainly with patronage if not with money, to become informers and accusers.  And when tales which their characters alone ought to discredit are refuted  by evidence and facts which oblige the patrons of them to abandon their support. they still continue in corroding whispers to wear away the reputations which they could not directly subvert."*

He was now pointing at the creature Callender, whom Jefferson and Burr maintained as a reporter of the congressional debates and an irresponsible pamphleteer.  It was not to reply to this man that Hamilton had been moved, but to explain the mysterious correspondences Callender had been the means of presenting to a gaping public.

That Aaron Burr had first obtained these letters, that

he was now the supporter and ruler of Maria Reynolds, and that Hamilton's domestic crisis was being watched and guided by these people, nerved him to move rapidly to the direct issue.   Hamilton resumed :

*" If, luckily for the conspirators against honest fame, any little foible or folly can be traced out in one whom they desire to persecute, it becomes at once in their hands a two-edged sword, by which to wound the public character and stab the private felicity of the person.*
*" With such men nothing is sacred.*
*" Even the peace of an unoffending and amiable wife is a welcome repast to their insatiate fury against the husband."*

His baby cried, and the echo of his feelings made him also grow blind with tears.   He knew by these tears that he was writing well, and stopped to hear his wife's lullaby, as she nursed his child :

By, by, oh ! by, my babe, forsooth,
It hurts to cut his little tooth ;
But bite it on his mamma's breast—
Her milk will give the baby rest.

"O God ! " thought Hamilton, "what a tooth will be drawn through that precious breast to-morrow, which is the sustenance of my soul !''
The child's fretfulness yielded to Eliza's bounty, and the man pleading for his honor continued to write :

*" Even the great and multiplied services, the tried and rarely equalled virtues of a Washington can secure no exemption.*
*" How, then, can I, with pretensions every way inferior, expect to escape ?*
*" And truly, if this be, as every appearance indicates, a conspiracy of vice against virtue, ought I not rather to be flattered that I have been so long and so peculiarly an object of persecution ?   Ought I to regret if there be anything about me so formidable to the Faction as to have made me worthy to be distinguished by the plenitude of its rancour and venom ?*
*" It is certain that I have had a pretty copious experience of its malignity.*
*" For the honour of human nature, it is to be hoped that the examples are not numerous of men so greatly calumniated and persecuted as I have been, with so little cause."*

Here the retrospect of gratuitous toil in the public fields, draining life of its nerve and blood, denying sleep its entreaty, soliciting heavy tasks which yielded not profit, straightening out the deformity of the finances and taking upon his shoulders the literary defence of the whole government, touched Hamilton with a mighty disappointment.

He thought of to-morrow's work in the public court, with his case unprepared and the public expectation great, and his fee imperatively needed to pay the expense of printing this present defence and supporting his brood. All the agony of the author shuffling between immortality and hunger arose to his eyes, and shut out the hideous picture of democratic ingratitude.

The little streets were now pealing with laughter and animated talk. The Tontine Assembly, around the corner on Broadway, was dismissing after a ball and supper. His nature prone to sociality, Hamilton bent again to his expiation. Still the dire confession would *not* be made, and he continued to write around the matter of his transgression.

He appealed to all men for the " unblemished pecuniary reputation " with which he undertook the office of Secretary of the Treasury, and showed that the assaults upon him were based upon his firm opinion " that the public debt ought to be provided for on the basis of the contract by which it was created," and upon perversions of those congressmen who " did not understand accounts."

He reviewed a double investigation of his office by Congress, and his complete exoneration, especially when assailed by " a worthless man of the name of Fraunces," and added in a foot-note : " Would it be believed, after all this, that Mr. Jefferson, Vice-President of the United States, would write to this Fraunces friendly letters ? "

At last the declaration of his weakness had to be written.

He penned it with a dry heart but also with dry eyes, and looked to see how it would read.

Very, very naked it seemed to him, as follows :

" *Of all the vile attempts which have been made to injure my character, that which has been lately revived is the most vile.*

" *The charge against me is a connection with one James Reynolds for purposes of improper pecuniary speculation.*

" *My real crime is an amorous connection with his wife, for a considerable time with his privity and connivance, if not originally brought on by a combination between the husband and wife with the design to extort money from me.*"

" That little door which admitted me five years ago," thought Hamilton, " when the shades of night embowered it, I now perceive to have been wide enough for four millions of Americans to enter in and view my weakness !"

He rushed on and presently was in the deep morass of this sentence, which seemed to swallow him to the eyes :

> *" This confession is not made without a blush. I cannot be the apologist of any vice because the ardour of passion may have made it mine.*
>
> *" I can never cease to condemn myself for the pang which it may inflict in a bosom eminently intitled to all my gratitude, fidelity, and love.*
>
> *" But that bosom will approve that even at so great an expence I should effectually wipe away a more serious stain from a name which it cherishes with no less elevation than tenderness."*

As this appeared under Hamilton's hand he suddenly experienced a wonderful change of feeling.

Until he had written it there was an obdurate something upon his heart like cowardice mixed with rebellion.

The moment he had admitted to the paper his unadorned confession there came a rush of penitence, followed by love, such as the subdued child feels after chastisement, when its affection is again turned to its parent.

The compliment to his wife he had not meditated. It swept in upon his feelings, after confession, like a stroke of inspiration or of genius.

The more he looked at these unstrained and flowing lines of kindness the more beautiful they seemed.

He rose, all suffused with eager happiness, and walked back to Eliza's chamber and leaned over her.

She seemed to be lying with wide-open eyes.

He bent to kiss her, and her eyes were closed.

His tears fell upon her face and caused her to waken. She raised her arms and put them around him and sighed :

" I was almost dreaming that you trusted Mrs. Priestley more than me. Do you ? "

" Yes," said Hamilton, to whom all truth now seemed easy ; " I did trust her, first. A friend is sometimes love's alternative."

" Make me your friend ! " breathed the wife.

" To-morrow, Eliza, you shall be my friend or my enemy."

" Can it not be to-night ? What ails you ? I hate to see you crying. Fear not but you will put all your enemies under your feet ! "

" My only enemy I have this night dislodged, dear wife—a stubborn heart."

" Go back," Eliza said, " and finish your work. You look so happy though you are so haggard, Alexander."

As Hamilton reached his candelabra table near the low-stooped house front, he thought to inhale from the street a breath from the sea breeze, and placed his head through the unswung casement.

As he did so a woman on the narrow pave whispered to him :

" I am Maria. Do you want my help to make your defence, Hamilton ? "

" Never your help, madame, again. Let me rely only upon your hostility. I have worn your yoke for six long years, and now you come to turn me back from expiation as the fallen angel of that fiend——"

" Yes; the emissary of Aaron Burr. But I would rather have your curses, Hamilton, than Mr. Burr's caresses. Do *not* fear to treat me fearlessly in your public defence ! I can stand it for the love I bear you. This is my real errand to-night—to tell you that I never can be used again to injure you ; to say that your defence shall not provoke me to any denial or reply. Take any advantage of Maria's love ! "

A movement of whiteness like a spirit was at Hamilton's side.

The being in the street seemed to disappear in the ground.

" Have I been your friend to-night—myself and this cherub ? " asked Mrs. Hamilton, standing in her gown with her arms around her babe.

" You have, indeed. Oh ! why did you ever leave me, my wife, even for a summer ? "

" I thought I heard you talking to yourself just now. Or was it with that man in the shade of the tree lurking opposite ? "

At the word a large body was seen to glide away under the shadows of the Dutch-gabled shops.

" Tigress ! " muttered Hamilton.

He had recognized the form and movement of Mr. Jake Clingman, Aaron Burr's new man of all work in Ward politics.

The morning came with ringing bells. From the Old Dutch church cupola in Nassau Street to the new chapel in Ann Street the steeples were vocal, and the printer's boys were crying special gazettes :

" Capture of Wenice by Bonyparty ! Capture of Rome and the Pope by Bonyparty ! Capture of Paris and the French Congress by Bonyparty ! Capture of Wienny . by Bonyparty ! "

Mrs. Hamilton saw upon the writing-table a great sealed package of manuscript to be sent to the printers at Philadelphia ; and the candles were burnt out in their sockets.

Hamilton had thrown himself upon the bed, like one worn out, and in the attitude of supplication, with hands outstretched and buried face.

"Awake, darling ! Your coffee is ready, and it is time for you to go to court."

He aroused himself and was as cheerful as exhaustion could be after hardly an hour of stolen rest.

At ten o'clock he stood in court, before all the bar of the city and an exacting audience, to deliver his argument.

For a moment he seemed overcome, and covered his face with his hands.

Before the general sympathy for him could find expression he was ready and had commenced.

What was his client ?

It was the public press and its "*right* to publish with impunity, truth, with good motives, for justifiable ends, though reflecting on government, magistracy, or individuals."

---

## CHAPTER XXIII.

### ECHO.

THE laboratory at Northumberland was finished, and Doctor Priestley was so proud of it that he would not let a servant even light the fires, but was his own janitor.

He found apt mechanics among the Pennsylvanians and Wyoming Yankees to make his apparatus, much of which he invented himself, but they often improved his plans in a single experiment.

To the delight of a few visitors and neighbors, he performed original tricks with flame and gas ; and, like all schoolmasters, classified that which classified itself. He had his alkaline airs, acid airs, nitrous airs, fixed and common airs ; and, it must be added, his highly phlogisticated airs, especially when Mr. William Cobbett sent in a shot like the following :

> *" Cooper having burnt the velverets and calicoes which he proposed to bleach on novel phlogistic principles, having become a bankrupt, retires to America to philosophize, and, with Priestley, to enlighten Europe thence. All that now remains of poor Cooper would be a Lenten entertainment even for the crows. Despised, neglected, as Priestley and Cooper are, I would not be surprised if they were to make some desperate attempt on their own lives."*

All this was *apropos* of Mr. Cooper's failure, with two of Doctor Priestley's sons, to establish a great barony on the Loyalsock, in a new county to the north, where Mr. Cooper hoped to be at least a congressman or a judge.

Priestley's political enemies in Europe were greedy for every rumor to his detriment, and Mr. Cooper was writing articles at Northumberland, which perished there, to incite Mr. Cobbett, who published in Philadelphia and was read everywhere.

"Now, surely," exclaimed Lizzie Priestley, "this is no freedom of the press—to hope that poor father will commit suicide, and then to anger him to do so."

"Never mind that chap," exclaimed Cooper ; "old Judge Tommy McKean has got his poll-parrot nose and vitreous eyes turned on Sergeant Cobbett, and Doctor Sangrado Rush has commenced a libel suit which will sell the slanderer out."

"Thomas," repeated Lizzie, "you laugh at that as if it were something right. Of course, if you are ever punished for the same kind of printing, you will not complain ? "

"There is no use for a press which is not for liberty. A free press means only a democratic press. Cobbett's press is for monarchy."

"It seems to be the only press in favor of Washington. The American press has become precociously drunken," exclaimed Joe Priestley. "Yet the country is doing well and is alone spared from war. What does the Opposition want ? "

Mr. Cooper was living with and upon Joe Priestley, and had desired the doctor to get a Federal office for him by intercession with Adams and Jefferson, whilst he had already destroyed Doctor Priestley's influence with Mr. Adams and was also seeking to bring the doctor to aid the Jeffersonian revolution of Pennsylvania.

Controversy eternally separated oxygen and its discoverer. Priestley was like the princess of Egypt finding Moses in the bulrushes—toothsome little Jew—and seeking to controvert him into a priest of Isis.

Mr. Cooper was the interloper, the false adjutant of Priestley's mistake.

Doctor Priestley advertised his folly of phlogiston periodically to the world, and so became the sport of science, and spent the chief remainder of his days in speculative theology, or theo-chemistry.

But the poor old man was on his last score of appointed life, and his dead recalled him to the contemplations of the aged who have been happy.

He felt that the frictions of men, which heat the soul to daring thoughts, would be for him no more—self-banished here to a river without a human movement.

Already the genius of Rumford, who had been banished from America to Europe, had supplanted the experiments of both Priestley and Lavoisier.

He ruled Bavaria ; he was sent Minister of the Elector to England ; he was to become husband to Lavoisier's wife. The unfinished work of Franklin was this Tory courtier's legacy. In warming the houses of the million he was to touch the highest mystery in creation : heat to be a mechanical force ; phlogiston to be an impostor.

The mail from Philadelphia came in the day of our chapter, and brought Joseph Priestley, Jr., a sealed pamphlet under the frank of Timothy Pickering, Secretary of State.

Lizzie Priestley called her husband away from Mr. Cooper, and they went into the doctor's library and opened the pamphlet. It bore the title of Hamilton's " Observations," as already described.

" Oh, thank God, Joe ! " the wife exclaimed, with her silken curls trembling and her large, gray eyes filled with

English dew. " The very worst has come, and that is
next to the best.  He has plunged into the cold river and
has come out to the celestial shore !"

" Hamilton ?   Gracious !  how you cling to him !   Do
you know I would have been jealous of you—or, rather,
of Hamilton—if you hadn't been so open and bold,
Lizzie ? "

" And were you not jealous, Josie ? "

" Not exactly.   But I saw that you considered him a
much greater man than father, or me.   But so he was.
People are right to stick by men of authority."

" Joe, you are the bravest, truest man that lives.   If
Hamilton had been like you, this pamphlet need never
have been written.   You are true to father and true to
wife and child.   I knew, Joe, that I could trust you even
with Mrs. Reynolds, and that you were brave enough to
trust me, and so I made the journey that is, and ever will
be, the greatest event of my life."

" That was a rum kind of a journey, wife," observed
Joe, reflectively, running his hand through his beard
and lighting his pipe.   " I thought some day, when it
was quite agreeable, you would tell me where you went."

" Dear, noble Joe !   It has been breaking my heart
these three years to have that mysterious absence lying
between us, like an open grave."

"O pshaw !  now.   Didn't you stand by me when there
was a terrible case made out against me ?   I got to be a
pretty old man that day, Lizzie.   You brought me out
innocent when I thought I was guilty.   Ha, ha, ha, ha !
Of course, after that, it didn't become me to inquire where
my attorney had been roving to.   I was glad to cry quits."

" Now, Joe, that proves that you consider me to have
balanced your account with another wrong.   This day,
dear, may let me tell my tale and take your sentence
upon me.   But now I am dying to hear the Hamilton
paper read.   Joe, perhaps I was one of the authors of it !"

As they started the reading, Doctor Priestley came in
and sat down to write an article for the *Medical Repository*.

" Don't stop for me, children." said the doctor; " I
have not the nervous irritability of authors, because I
trained myself to compose in the midst of conversation,
at dear old Warrington School."

So Joseph, Jr., lighted his pipe and opened a bottle

of American porter, and heard his wife pass through the general introduction of Colonel Hamilton's pamphlet, till her voice became lower and trembled upon the unevading story of Hamilton's seduction, as follows :

"*All the documents show, and it is otherwise a matter of notoriety, that Reynolds was an obscure, unimportant, and profligate man.*

"*Clingman, Reynolds, and his wife were manifestly in very close confidence with each other.*

"*As to Mrs. Reynolds, if she was not an accomplice, as it is too probable she was, her situation would naturally subject her to the will of her husband.*

"*Frail indeed will be the tenure by which the most blameless man will hold his reputation if the assertions of three of the most abandoned characters in the community are sufficient to blast it.*"

"Halloo ! halloo !" exclaimed Joe Priestley, "isn't that rather too retributive on the fine Reynolds?"

"The shameless being!" rejoined Lizzie, "what did she not try to fasten upon you, Joe, in the presence of your wife? And did she ever feel for *Mrs.* Hamilton?"

"Oh ! children," absently remarked Doctor Priestley, "the boys will go off and behave in a way to wound their parents' hearts, but, after all, they're *our* boys!"

"That doctrine's oxygenated Christianity," softly mused younger Joe to his wife, who attempted to read the next sentence from Hamilton's publication, and had become, in a manner, too hysterical to do it. Joe took the little book and read :

"*Some time in the summer of the year* 1791 *a woman called at my house in the city of Philadelphia and asked to speak with me in private.*

"*I attended her into a room apart from the family.*

"*With a seeming air of affliction she informed me that she was a daughter of a Mr. Lewis, sister to a Mr. G. Livingston, of the State of New York, and wife to a Mr. Reynolds, whose father was in the Commissary Department during the war with Great Britain ; that her husband, who for a long time had treated her very cruelly, had lately left her, to live with another woman, and in so destitute a condition that, though desirous of returning to her friends, she had not the means ; that, knowing I was a citizen of New York, she had taken the liberty to apply to my humanity for assistance.*

"*I replied that her situation was a very interesting one, that I was disposed to afford her assistance to convey her to her friends, but this at the moment not being convenient to me (which was the fact) I must request the place of her residence, to which I should bring or send a small supply of money.*

"*She told me the street and the number of the house where she lodged.*

*" In the evening I put a bank bill in my pocket and went to the house.*

*" I inquired for Mrs. Reynolds, and was shewn up-stairs, at the head of which she met me and conducted me into a bed-room.*

*" I took the bill out of my pocket and gave it to her.*

*" Some conversation ensued, from which it was quickly apparent——"*

A loud scream interrupted the reading.

" He's told it like a lion !" exclaimed Joe's wife. " Hurrah ! hur——"

She was spinning around as she cried, with her head turned by the excitement of the Confession, and seeking in her blindness to grasp something, she caught upon a pile of books and notes, which had been arranged by Joe's father for a great knock-down argument of some kind, and fell amidst their ruins.

" There goes all my work of comparison of the institutions of Moses with those of the Hindoos ! " cried the chemical doctor.

" Get up, love ! " pleaded Joe, going to his wife. " It *was* a little stunning, wasn't it ?   There, there !   Take a sip of father's sherry.   Why, Lizzie, Colonel Hamilton was merely going to say that Madame Reynolds made love to him, and after that pushed into his house in his wife's absence, at Albany, and so became a kind of Delilah, or Jezebel, or Mary, Queen of Scots, to him."

" Went to his house, of course ! " sighed the wife, coming quickly to herself.   " Hasn't she been to this house uninvited ?   To good Doctor Nesbit's, too ?   And now she's in Colonel Burr's house, familiar as his daughter, cocked up in silks at Richmond Hill ! "

" Whom in the world are you talking about ? " cried Doctor Priestley.   " Mrs. Jordan ?   Pope Joan ?   The Red Dragon of Revelations ? "

" No, father ; about that Mrs. Reynolds who visited here when first we came and made the accusation against Josie."

" Hush, my child ! " said Doctor Priestley.   " All that I remember of that poor sinner was that my Harry loved her."

He went out to take his rowing on the river and a long walk on the cliffs, and left husband and wife to study with intentness the subsequent revelations of Hamilton.   Joe read the story of the second inevitable step in the art of blackmail—the husband's incidental cunning :

*" In the course of a short time," wrote Hamilton, " she mentioned to me that her husband had solicited a reconciliation, and affected to consult me about it.*

*" I advised to it, and was soon after informed by her that it had taken place.*

*" She told me, besides, that her husband had been engaged in speculation, and, she believed, could give information respecting the conduct of some persons in the department which could be useful."*

So Reynolds came, and the next thing was his wife's intimation to appoint him a clerk in the department, which Hamilton would not do, as Reynolds had previously been an unworthy government clerk.

The motive spirit in all this management had been the astute Clingman, and Reynolds, no less than Hamilton, a dupe.

What now did Hamilton conceive Mrs. Reynolds' part to have been ?   His disclosure told the tale.

*" Though various reflections induced me to wish a cessation of this intercourse, yet her conduct made it extremely difficult to disentangle myself.*

*" All the appearances of violent attachment, and of agonizing distress at the idea of a relinquishment, were played with a most imposing art.*

*" This, though it did not make me entirely the dupe of the plot, yet kept me in a state of irresolution.*

*" My sensibility, perhaps my vanity, admitted the possibility of a real fondness, and led me to adopt the plan of a gradual discontinuance, rather than of a sudden interruption, as least calculated to give pain if a real partiality existed.*

*" Mrs. Reynolds, on the other hand, employed every effort to keep up my attention and visits. Her pen was freely employed, and her letters were filled with those tender and pathetic effusions which would have been natural to a woman truly fond and neglected.*

*" One day I received a letter from her intimating a discovery by her husband.*

*" It was a matter of doubt with me whether there had been really a discovery by accident, or whether the time for the catastrophe of the plot was arrived.*

*" The same day I received from Mr. Reynolds a letter by which he informs me of the detection of his wife in the act of writing a letter to me, and that he had obtained from her a discovery of her connection with me, suggesting that it was the consequence of an undue advantage taken of her distress.*

*" In answer to this I sent him a note or message desiring him to call upon me at my office, which I think he did the same day.*

*" He said he was resolved to have satisfaction."*

16

" How many men of shining mark are made to pay such
a penalty all their days! " exclaimed Lizzie. " O Joe ! I
saw that something was preying on Hamilton from the
day he called upon us at Philadelphia, and that it started
with Mrs. Reynolds' presence there. I took so deep an
interest in him as a man, a fellow-Englishman by birth,
a person of genius and gentleness, that I was carried
away."

" Dear me ! " replied Joe, " you were as weak as
Hamilton."

" Now, sir, don't quiz me !—I feel it cruelly. I never
was a truer-hearted wife to you than when I went to the
redemption of that man and of the other sex, against
what I have felt to be the persecution of a bad woman.
Men always take any woman's part against any man.
Women often know better. A loving man is in the
greatest danger, if his conduct be genial and generous."

" Now, I differ," said Joe. " Women are everywhere
better than men."

" And ought to be. They were not born to be pursuers,
as men were. The lower animals respect this law ; but
here was a woman who had no pity for another wife, who
could steal to her rival's habitation and look at the baby's
cradle there without remorse. No ; I do not ask men to
take Hamilton's part," spoke the curling-haired lady with
rising fire, " but as the mother of your boy—of my own
little Joe—I defend the man though I cannot exonerate
him, and against this woman I defend him against all the
world."

" You are pugnacious, surely, wife. But wasn't Reynolds rather a lazy, good-natured being ? "

" Such are often the chief animals, Joe. Their first
sin is idleness, letting a mother or a sister work for them
while they lie abed or stand languid before the toilet,
appreciating their own beauty. The deep, deep self-love
commencing there, goes on in time to a hideous capi-
talization of its superior charms. The brave, daring men
marry early, and God blesses them with power and dignity.
The indolent thief of such a gentleman's loyalty and
principle is she who finds about him nothing to worship,
but seeks beneath his nature to break his paradise up and
feed her miserable folly with his golden time."

" By Jove, Lizzie, you're a heroine ! "

" Thank you. I almost believe I am. But let us finish Hamilton's clean-breasting of this monstrous horror. Of course he was next taxed of his family's support ? "

" Yes. It says that after backing and filling, Reynolds wrote that ' he was willing to take a thousand dollars as a plaister for his wounded honor.

" ' I determined,' says Hamilton, ' to give it to him and did so in two payments as per receipt.

" ' I received letter No. 5, by which Reynolds writes me to renew my visits to his wife.' "

" That is not possible," said Lizzie. " I saw Mr. Reynolds and he was a weak man. It may have been that Clingman."

" It was, for Hamilton says : ' There can be no doubt of the sufficiency of Clingman's influence, when it is understood that Mrs. Reynolds and he afterward lived together as man and wife.' "

" How much, Joe, did they get out of Secretary Hamilton ? "

" Here are eleven hundred dollars accounted for. They even nagged him for money for Mr. Reynolds to subscribe to the Lancaster turnpike stock. It was borrow, borrow, borrow—must have this to-day, must have that to-morrow noon. And, finally, Reynolds and Clingman got into jail and sent to Hamilton to bail them out. That was the time, it appears, when Clingman, *not* Reynolds, dropped the remark to Monroe and Muhlenberg,—the first of ' smelling committees,'—that Secretary Hamilton had used Mr. Reynolds to job in the public stocks for him."

" Was there ever such a villain ? And this Monroe, to get even with General Washington for recalling him from France, forces all this scandal out. Some day, if the Lord is just, *he* will know what it is to need money and honor, too."

" Well, Hamilton is going to suffer with the cowardly element of the world, which considers the greatest sin ' to be found out; ' but he will be a caution to future blackmailers. See how he draws the distinctions, finely as in a novel. Hear this, Lizzie :

" ' *It was a persevering scheme to spare no pains to levy contributions upon my passions on the one hand and upon my apprehensions of discovery on the other; and it was contrived, notwithstanding all the caution on my part to avoid it, that Clingman should occasionally see me.*' "

" Does he defend Mr. Reynolds in any way ? "

" Yes; he says that 'in the workings of human inconsistency it was very possible that the same man might be corrupt enough to compound for his wife's chastity and yet have sensibility enough to be restless in the situation, and to hate the cause of it.' "

" And of Mrs. Reynolds ? "

" Of her he remarks that 'the variety of shapes which this woman could assume was endless.' You see, Hamilton publishes her letters in an appendix to tell for themselves, and does not clog his statement with them. And look here, wife, Mr. Hamilton says that two of her letters are signed 'Maria Clingman,' and that in them she mentions the 'circumstance of her being married to Clingman.' "

" All marriages, I fear, Joe, are circumstances to that woman. How she has crossed Hamilton's career, and spotted his fountain that had run so clear ! "

" He denies Callender's charge, I see, that he withdrew his name for President of the United States under the menace of these people."

" And what says Hamilton for himself ? "

" Only this, wife. He says, in a really fine, touching way : 'For this amour I bow to the just censure which it merits. I have paid pretty severely for the folly, and can never recollect it without disgust and self-condemnation. It might seem affectation to say more.' "

" Just like Hamilton. Now, husband, let the world comment as it will, Colonel Hamilton has proved that 'if the truth shall set you free, you shall be free indeed.' He is free. He is true."

" But I tremble for his wife's reception of this confession."

" I do *not*," fervently remarked Lizzie. " Now, when father returns, I will tell you both—and keep my solemn word to dying mother—where I was gone in the three weeks after I left you, Joe, at Harrisburg."

# CHAPTER XXIV

## THE PREPARER.

In the large Northumberland frame house the three Priestleys sat with closed doors, and the first child of Joe and Lizzie was in a crib asleep.

Word had been given not to admit Mr. Cooper or Mr. Antis, the English mathematician, or anybody.

Father Priestley had been indulged with his two games of backgammon and three of whist, and the lights were put out to let the moonlight enter the library and not encourage gnats or observations on human conditions present there.

The flow of broad waters could be heard, and the whippoorwill's rapid challenge. Forms of island and mountains filled the window frames. It was real life in the very far West, and yet with one's dead in the village graveyard, and one's husband or wife at one's elbow, and other posterity to be, this West was like the older world, and made Doctor Priestley think of the riddle whether any sounds could be unless ears were there to receive them.

"Father," was raised the sweet, ardent voice of Lizzie Priestley, "I was almost made to be an American, and the opportunity your reputation gave Joe and me to see the principal Americans was my complete compensation for coming to the United States. You, father, as a discoverer and Royal Society man, had seen public leaders everywhere ; but this advantage did not extend to your family. Joe, here, was a bleacher in Manchester, and I was of the Mill Owners' Society at Birmingham. But when we came with you to this republic we all were considered immediately as part of your greatness, and taken up by the statesmen and financiers, and their families, also ; so I felt a great, grateful interest in a land which respected services above class."

"Public men are about the same everywhere," said Priestley. "Here are no professional churchmen in the high places of the government, and the result is a more natural society. I came out here a stickler for King, Lords, and Commons, but these woods have made me a republican."

"And I have found, father," said Lizzie, "that equal advantages and liberty do not change ambition into honesty, or corruption into honor. The strife of parties here is just as fierce as in England. A vile, shrewd politician, a coarse, vituperative editor, in America, seem to have enlarged opportunities to do cruelty and evil, because the multitude is so scattered and new. It will take them a long time to acquire the experience which appreciates public character, and holds up its hands, instead of mixing that public talent with private scandals upon it, and finally judging the man by the smallest instead of the greatest measure. They may never have another Hamilton; and yet see this measure they are applying to him. Mr. Jefferson, Mr. Monroe, Colonel Burr, and Speaker Muhlenberg, of Congress, are the persons who have stooped so low. They have only injured a wife's and children's feelings, at last, for Hamilton has burst through these withes of both Delilah and such Philistines, like the Samson he is."

"Oh!" said the doctor, "they will get over that, I suspect. My seven years at Lord Shelburne's informed me that the governing class, since the Norman barons, has been licentious. Political popularity and temperament, like the stage, overturn discretion. My children, the state of mere morals may surprise anybody but a preacher!"

"Before we came to America, and on the packet coming over, I read and questioned about their public men. All authorities said that Colonel Hamilton had organized the country. Congress had come to him for reports, and to suggest measures; and he seemed to me like Alfred the Great to England. My surprise was to see him—a mere lad, nothing like forty—unaffected, unspoiled, and almost unpaid, without a patron, pecuniary independence, care, or envy. He was not like Mr. Jefferson, always decrying somebody; nor like Colonel Burr, a thick flatterer, esteeming a woman to be a dunce. He walked with us that Sunday to Franklin's grave, and entered into our family life like an English friend. My husband was favorable to his views. We all were delighted that he gave us so much of his valuable time. But I, with probably a bit of idealism in me,—which I miss among the Priestleys, I must say,—took a vast interest in that Hamilton from the moment I found he was in distress. It was the Reynolds woman who awoke my distrust and opened my eyes."

"Set a woman to catch a woman!" exclaimed Joe.

"You remember the way we met her,—a disconnected boarder in a house, who made free in our society. Next she was cornering Colonel Hamilton in the sitting-room as we left it. When we returned from our walk she was about being turned out of the boarding-house for arrears, and Colonel Hamilton was insolently beset by her husband. I fell to wondering why a needy pair like that should take a lodging-house expensive enough for us and for people above financial suspicion. Poverty is no crime, but to keep up false appearances in poverty looks uncandid, not to say designing. I suspected her, I will say frankly, to be a very subtle and well-equipped specimen of the adventuress, and of this I find confirmation in the appendix to Colonel Hamilton's confession, where he says she wanted to set up a boarding-house for congressmen, and that Reynolds demanded the money of Hamilton to oblige her, and that otherwise non-payment of board was a regular subject of their mutual importunity of Mr. Hamilton."

"Oh! it's a fine opening for a showy widow," Joe observed, between smoke blasts of his pipe. "Some of the richest Southern planters in Congress have married their landladies. There was nobody more sightly than Reynolds."

"She was the finest woman I have ever seen, and the best disguised. Her mind was apparently amiable, equal, and languid. No passions, or high activities, seemed to inhabit that brunette head, and she hardly required breeding, as Nature had cast her calm, elegant, and imperturbable. Dress became her and she had good taste, which I see is natural to the Americans. They dress for the street more than the English. With her stature, which was commanding anywhere ; with her laziness, which made it easy to address her; with her fine, long fingers and feet and rich mould of arms and bust, her even hue of complexion, and something dreamy and oriental about her luxuriance, like the Sultana, she knew every fine point she possessed with the calculation of a purely cold-blooded, if indulgently wilful, being."

" How do you know this, Liz ? "

" She told me so. That is, she would make such remarks when passing a blonde lady as : 'I can't see where they can expect to cope with us brunettes.' She used cosmetics, French washes for her skin, belladonna for her eyes to give them a brightness supernatural, and I have seen her, here in Northumberland, spend hours matching a color with her hair, or wrists, or neck, as Lady Montagu describes the beauties of the harem doing all day long. I wondered if a woman like that, without the means of gratifying her tastes, could be virtuous without industry. The next thing was the kindling of our poor Hal with her mingled charms and tears."

" That is not remembered against Harry in heaven," exclaimed the doctor. " God expects men to be weak ; men, only, expect other men to be strong. The very sons of God, says Genesis, took them wives of the fair among the daughters of men."

" I expect you to be against me, father and Joe, for all men go against a man in a conflict with a woman. I am greatly in need of your encouragement, too, for I am in great oppression and fear to-night. Bear with me till I have explained my eccentric behavior, and then judge me as a woman, also ! "

Her husband went to her and kissed her and asked her forgiveness, and dropped into her lap, unperceived by her, the parcel of letters his dying mother had given him.

With a broken, struggling voice the little lady resumed. Her one sob in that room seemed to be a ripple of the wave of sympathy, or evil, which every moral offence sets undulating, till the innocent, afar, are submerged by the rockings of the great.

" My brother's love for any woman was a tender subject to me ; for I entered this family not as some wives are said to do—to do the best for themselves and put their husbands against the other sons ; here I was of father's meeting-house, ourselves sufferers when he was burned out by the mob. I saw my husband indifferent to whether this woman entered this family or not. He, also, was taken with the handsome Reynolds, while I grew firm in the belief that it was this same woman who was the unhealing wound in Hamilton's conscience."

" Did he tell you so ? "

" I saw him, the day we ended with Reynolds in Philadelphia, refuse to read the Bible that mother tendered
him. He was full of a marvellous sensibility. Why,
thought I, should a man of temperament and genius like
that, have an overflowed heart ? The sob of Hamilton
haunted me as mother read the Bible. You, Joe, had
invited him to our family friendship ; the suggestion was
most agreeable to me. I thought that such a friendship
would bear fruit in some public ambition, and, perhaps,
employment, for you, which I knew would be very con-
soling to father and help his fame in England."

A low groan was heard from Doctor Priestley in the
darkness of his arm-chair.

He had fled from dearly appreciated reputation and
had found none in America to replace it. Career is heav-
en's chariot let down, and, when its wheels go out of
hearing, dust gathers on the heart.

" The evening I went to the garden-party at Mr.—now
Senator—Bingham's, my mind was ever returning to the
unfortunate Hamilton, in spite of the subtle flattery and
vivacious information of Senator Burr, and I could not
go away without speaking to Hamilton again. When I
found him he was in a state of woe, which his lips expressed in a monologue from one of the poets, and the
words I overheard gave me a hint to speak right openly.
I told Hamilton to go and confess to his wife and make
his peace there first, and then he would have a fortress
to defy the sinister part of all the world. Before he
could reply Mrs. Hamilton entered the grounds, and, no
doubt, the very animated, indeed, excited, appearance of
her husband and myself thus privately discoursing, gave
her a suspicion that we might be coquetting. We were
obliged to separate without explanation, and I felt that
instead of helping Hamilton I had put another annoy-
ance in his path."

" Why, wife, how much can happen to a little witch
like thee ! We dull Priestley folk never see what thy
imagination finds to be wonderful in everything. It's a
good story, father ? "

" Yes," said Doctor Priestley. " This kindling part of
Lizzie's nature is called Imagination. It appropriates all
causes to be its own, feels far toward God, and assembles

mankind for rich purposes. I feel, as daughter speaks, a great new wonder in my mind—that Man is always interesting, especially to youth."

"Now, dear friends," the little wife went on, hurrying like one pursued, or timed, in her narrative, "all this, I expected, had forever ended as an episode in my life when, to my astonishment, Mrs. Reynolds appeared here in Northumberland. Then the idea began to take root in me that, somehow, I had a purpose of Providence to serve through this woman. Her control of Harry made me burst out. We quarrelled, and I felt clearer than ever her resources to be beautiful and even touching. I saw that a supreme opportunity might make Mrs. Reynolds the most dangerous woman of the age."

"Can you analyze that power, my daughter?" asked the doctor.

"Perhaps I can't explain it, father, but I think I understand it. The sources of Mrs. Reynolds' childhood seem to have been genuine. There is a remembrance of piety and of her mother's love about her. She has never become a strong person till sin has made her so. Languor and self-love took her along like a sleeping snake upon a summer's day floating down the Susquehanna upon a swimming log. Suddenly she came to a place where pride, ambition, and crime aroused her, reënergized her, and made her an active, calculating, hissing, deadly serpent. The rattlesnakes we have studied in these hills rattle and coil and strike, as I saw that woman turn on me when she suspected that I loved Hamilton."

"This *love*," said Joe, "be the mainspring, I think, of women. If it snap—whir-r-r goes the watch, and her time is anything."

"She misunderstood me. My heart being my husband's and our child's, I could stand on the high-ground of truth and see her in the incitements of her predatory love. She was playing with Hamilton like the serpent charming the bird, and I disturbed her. She thought I wanted him. If she had not loved him so fiercely, I would not have felt him to be in danger. This, I suspect, my friends, to be the turning-point, the tragedy of that woman's life."

"To be frank, wife, I thought she was a bit daft on me."

"Vain Joe! She rose to her woman's height and courage when she captured Hamilton. It made her wise, but it was the wisdom of corruption barely moistened by a little hyssop of childishness, like her tenderness to our Harry."

"How came Colonel Burr to follow her here?"

"It seems to me that Colonel Burr had also possessed this woman by some unfair means, for she hated him as sincerely as she affected Hamilton. He felt under some incentive to compensate her for whatever injury he had done her, and he also wished her to keep me in her supervision, I believe. Joe, before we left Philadelphia Colonel Burr had commenced to write me letters. I turned them over to your mother. She advised me to let the incident rest with her, as it might unsettle you."

"Wife, his letters are all in thy lap."

"Did you read them, Joe?"

"Only one, dear. I knew that he was trying a forlorn hope in laying siege to thee."

"There is nothing profound about Colonel Burr," spoke the tired wife. "His self-esteem was always ridiculous to me. After he came here I addressed a single sentence to him one day, as we were going out to your farm. I told him that the friendship of Colonel Hamilton was as grateful to me as his own seductions were ridiculous and cowardly. Ever since that time he has hated me, and you, and all this family."

"Has he?" observed Joe, pulling on his pipe till it held red fire. "He must be short of clients to give us so much valuable consideration. I think, wife, that we will just burn all those letters on the hearth here, and they will be out of our minds."

As the fire consuming the letters of Aaron Burr shone upon Doctor Priestley's goodly library and prints and plaster busts of other philosophers, throwing the room into bright relief, a bat darted in the open window, was singed by the fire like its spirit, and vanished up the chimney.

"Indeed," remarked Joe, "that was like the casting out of a devil that one could see. Father, you must not refute *that* miracle."

"Dear children," spoke the doctor, as the shadows resumed their sway, when the girlish little woman at the centre of the room had left a pathetic picture upon his mind, "your mutual confidence and Christian freedom make me very happy. Joseph, when the time comes to fold thy Lizzie's eyes in the last sleep of mortality, what a comfort will this scene be to you, son ! "

The clear, anxious voice of the wife started on :

"That day we went to the farm. I had a place secluded, though not intending to be a spy upon any one. I hid myself because I had become excited and nervous by the *emeute* with Colonel Burr. When he revealed his degraded instincts and unfolded to Mrs. Reynolds her criminal attitude, I was paralyzed with fear. All that he said I could not comprehend, but it was plain that she was guilty of some felony and was in his power. The proof of this was in the instigation she gave to the burly soldier-man, Clingman, to kill her husband and lift this felony away from her, so that she need not be subject to lawyer Burr's lust. When I could master my speech I screamed the one word ' Murderess ! ' and she fell to the earth as if it had been the voice of an accusing spirit to her soul."

" O wife ! how thou must have feared her when going down that dark river upon the ark ! "

" No. I was growing, Joe, in the worldly experience which chiefly makes men our superiors. I felt that we were again to cross our currents with Hamilton's life. Deeper than ever upon my being lay the sense of a divine appointment, or beneficent fate, to pull up by the roots a widely filtrated plot or secret, which would have but one result—to destroy Secretary Hamilton. At Harrisburg I believed that we should see him and advance another step toward implicating the guilty and redeeming the repentant one. This sublimity of feeling made me overlook, or scorn, the cheap devices of Madame Reynolds to make me jealous."

" She overacted it, father, thee can see," observed Joe, "for wife remembered a trick of that kind upon the ark which the vixen repeated at Carlisle, and so betrayed herself. "

" Now, Joe," the wife continued, " I had done but one indiscreet thing, and that was to write Colonel Hamilton a letter and take nobody at home into my confidence."

" Ah ! dear, was it that which made thee threaten me

upon the ark—to leave me forever if I said thou wert not ever a modest woman ? "

" Yes, husband ; I wrote to Hamilton the narrative of these proceedings, as they have been at last related to you and father.   I could not tell them to mother, since her nervous excitability, ever since the Birmingham riots, was such that this dark story would perhaps frighten her from Northumberland."

" Right, my child," from the doctor.    " In the little limit of the rebellious heart lies a greater riot than Birmingham's.    It was kind to let mother rest, and she is resting sweetly now in our last garden of paradise—yon restful country graveyard."

" Dear Joe, I did not tell you, because I thought it might destroy your confidence in Mr. Hamilton, and my good ends would all have been disappointed if I had not retained my husband's interest in my only American friend."

" Splendid, splendid ! " was Joe's response.    " What made thee feel such remorse for a kind deed like that ? "

The wife's ardor was checked.    There was a long pause.

" My fear," she answered, finally, " was that Colonel Hamilton might misconstrue my confidence and think the boldness of my friendship was a woman's infatuation for him.    If that had been his misinterpretation, it would have cut me to the ground.    It would have been worse than an insult ; it would have been a stab at Mercy."

" How delicate are honest sensibilities ! " remarked Joe. " Now, some would think that Hamilton, just out of one intrigue, might catch at another ; but I think not.    One bite of the apple was enough for Adam.   Ho ! ho !  I'm glad Reynolds didn't love me.   She was a very fetching sort of Juno.   Did Hamilton appreciate your sacrifice ? "

" Oh, yes !   He made me religious.   He was pursued, if you remember, by Mrs. Reynolds, and found in the appearance of tendering me his love.   At that moment, Joe, he was saying, in all the nobility of repentance : ' My hearth shall be swept, my heart shall be purified ; I shall strive through a nature victorious to see God.' "

" Press on, brave heart ! " from Doctor Priestley, his voice in broken waves of buoyant piety.

" O father—Joe, there is indeed more joy in heaven

over one sinner that repenteth than over ninety and nine
that have gone not astray ! Hamilton called my proffered help by the name of 'high friendship,' and compared it to the proud and pure affection of his wife's
virgin sisters for him. I was lifted above all self-consid-
erations. My nature seemed to rise on eagle's wings.
You, Joe, refused to accept Mrs. Reynolds' slander of my
motives, or to quarrel with Mr. Hamilton. I was seized
with an ecstasy to end the whole intrigue, and declared
to you my resolution to go to Philadelphia."

" For what, my darling ? "

" To see Colonel Hamilton's wife."

" Why, you were taking the pastoral office, child,"
exclaimed the doctor. " Many is the family dispute I
have had to settle in my congregations, and more especially between man and wife. Churches are merely
microcosms seeded by Adam and Eve. If people would
remember that, they would cease to expect that a merely
defensive institution, like a church—a confession of weakness in itself, an association for virtue where individual-
ism was too frail—could be free from scandals. In some
cases I have thought that certain kinds of paroxysmal
piety were rank physiology."

" This case of wife's was heroic friendship, pa," articulated Joe, whose face came out periodically as his pipe-
bowl glowed. " I am curious to see what she could do
with Mrs. Hamilton. Didst thee know her, Liz ? "

" No. If I had, probably some presumption of her
character, some commonplace particular, or antagonism,
might have taken down the pure idealism of my intent.
I did not see the wife of Hamilton at all ; it was woman
—man's friend, created for his solace and family relief—
that appeared to me. I felt such zeal under the accumu-
lation of incidents and my raw experience that I started
without a plan, upon an instinct such as might cause a
dark star to shine on a dangerous place by the benevo-
lence of the light committed to it."

" *Bethlehem !* " in a trembling voice, like a vocal glim-
mer, from Pastor Priestley.

The wife's voice seemed to catch in the draught which
blew into it from the lungs.

" Oh, Joe ! " it quavered at length, " I am frightened
to-night. Come put your arms around me, love."

" What scares thee, darling ? " Joe pleaded to know, as he kissed her ruggedly.

" I feel again the fear I felt that day you put me in the stage at Harrisburg. The wheels had not turned three times when my soul became full of gloom and accusation. I had left you—left you in that dreadful female's hands, my conduct open to any interpretation, and my reasons, all of a sudden, fell away and left me without any meaning to myself. The time of trial I learned that day, God knows ! Everything would have been chaos to me but for a little passage of Scripture that went round with the wheels day and night, and ever repeated itself to my ears and brain busily. Father, dost thou know it ? "

" Is it this, child ? ' Provide neither gold, nor silver, nor brass in your purses, nor scrip for your journey ; neither two coats, neither shoes, nor yet staves.' "

" That's it, that's it, father ! 'And when ye come into an house salute it, and if the house be worthy, let your peace come upon it.' "

" ' But if it be not worthy,' " from Doctor Priestley, " ' let your peace return to you.' "

" Oh ! friends," from the wife, " if they would banish God, as some want to do, and leave us only that old, tender book, we might still get along ! If I slept at all going to Philadelphia I do not know it. I went to our former lodgings and sent to Mrs. Hamilton's house. She had gone to New York, perhaps to Saratoga, her father's plantation."

" Did thy heart sink then, wife ? "

" No ; it had a great, selfish rejoicing. The excuse had come to lay down my mission and return to you, husband, and ask your forgiveness."

" I'm glad you did not do that. We should not then have had thy pretty tale of travel, though, wife, I did miss thee doleful-like. Thou didst go to New York, I think ? "

" Joe, the day after I reached Philadelphia was Saturday, and I was bruised by staging and went all day to my bed. The next day was Sabbath, and I desired to hear music, I know not why. Not speech, nor counsel, nor even prayer was my nature's request, but soothing sounds. They told me there was a little Roman Catholic church

near Hamilton's house, kept up by the sufferance of Quakers toward Catholics, since they were both oppressed
in England. There I slipped in and sat upon a bench.
An organ rolled across my spirit, and little choristers,
with voices not yet changed, and foreign women trained
in music, piped to the organ's swell. I seemed to lie on
the floor of the great ocean and hear its vibrations, and
it was a bath of rest. By music came calm thinking and
a more religious and humble mind. The feeling of the
crusader was gone, and in its place had come to me the
feeling of Martha, the sister of Lazarus, that only the
Lord could make my friend arise again if I entreated
it."

"And now I know," said Doctor Priestley, "that
Lizzie persevered. That was the feeling that should wear
out ecstasy and also depression."

"I now took the stage for New York. It was dusty,
but the country was pretty by Bristol and Trent's town,
and the stony places and the red clay in New Jersey
were softened by the mutual courtesy of travellers. The
Americans are careful of women as they journey, and I
had no cause of complaint till, finding in New York that
Mrs. Hamilton was at Albany, I obtained a seat in the
Albany stage. As I had booked it, a gentleman came in
and booked beside me. It was Colonel Burr."

"That fellow is a leech!" exclaimed Joe. "Ask him
to sit on the door-step and he'll come and live with you.
You didn't go with him?"

"Yes, Joe. I reflected that Colonel Hamilton was far
in the West, and that my only perfect opportunity to see
his wife alone was at that time. Repulsive as Mr. Burr
was to me, I knew that he could not harm me, and that
to release my seat—for the stage was to be quite full—
might give him the conceit that I feared him. So I had
that smooth wretch's company all the way to Albany. I
suppressed my anger and treated him as became us all.
He was a great man in the stage and on the way, and
pointed out all the Revolutionary places—Richmond Hill,
near the city, where Washington had taken him on the
staff, and he seemed to triumph that it was now his. He
showed us where André was captured, and, as we crossed
the Highlands, also where Arnold sold his country. The
road was the old Dutch and English highway, some dis-

tance back from the Hudson, and sprinkled with Dutch villages, at which we slept all night in one called Peekskill. The third day we passed over the noble Livingston's manor, having slept at Rhinebeck, and we threaded Dutch Claverack and Kinderhook and came to Albany that night."

" What did thee think of New York, wife, as compared to Pennsylvania ? "

" It is a more aristocratic State. Here are no controlling families through the inland ; there the Dutch,—Hollanders, of the burgher love of marriage alliances,—settled the river levels and grew rich, expelled the rich English office-holding class after the war and annexed their manors. But the influence of New England bears more directly upon New York than on Pennsylvania, and is coming to control it. That and the deep natural canal of the Hudson, which breaks into the West, as Colonel Burr explained, and which is filling with Yankee towns, are the chief influences of New York, together with the city at the Hudson's foot, which he said was the new Constantinople. O Joe ! such mountains ! The Highlands are sublime, but the Catskills are so serene. My soul was lifted up. Even my errand, amidst such sceneries, seemed not unnatural."

" And Colonel Burr ? "

" He reminded me of the devil on the mountain-top, tempting and foiled. All day I gave him free discourse. At night I turned upon him with frigid contempt and went to the women of the hotels, who were all kind people, to lodge me in their protection. I believe he knew something of my purpose. His very appearance there was unaccountable to me, but he explained that politics and law had suddenly summoned him back through the Lehigh settlements to New York City, and professed still to be going to Western New York. The evening of the first day, as we approached the night's stop, he said insidiously : ' Your hero, Colonel Hamilton, has taken up with Mrs. Reynolds again. She is occupying his rooms at Carlisle.' I said to him : ' Sir, this is information for the stablemen. A woman has no part in it.' He was angry, and added : ' I could tell you of your husband's frailty, too. He took Madame Reynolds from Harrisburg to Carlisle, and got boozily drunk there.'

17

I answered : 'See that you do not.follow his example to-night, Colonel. But good wine is an innocent mistress.' But, Joe, my pillow was wet with my tears that night."

" For me ? "

" No. I never could think you treacherous to me; you had trusted me so far away, Joe. But if Hamilton had fallen when I was upon the errand of his salvation, I had taken up a cross in vain. That night my dreams were so painless that they gave me confidence for the next day. When we reached Albany, when we came within its influence, yet afar, I made no reply whatever to Colonel Burr, and he lost his moral courage to pursue me when we came to the hotel, and sought the company of his politicians. I merely told him that I had come north for my health."

" How did you communicate with Mrs. Hamilton ? "

" It seems that the smart Mr. Burr had barely reached Albany when he called at General Schuyler's and told the family that I, a great favorite of Hamilton, was on my way north to the Springs, in pursuit of the waters and health, and suggested that they take me along. So General Schuyler came to see me, would hear no refusal, and said I must, the very next day, start for his plantation up the Hudson. Mrs. Hamilton called and added her most cordial entreaty. They had been packing to go when I arrived, and no time was afforded me for an explanation in Albany of any other business which had brought me there. I was in great mortification, but so it was. So I rested one day at Albany, and next day made the journey to Fish Creek."

The narrator's peace-bringing voice became low, and at last it stopped.

" What ails thee, wife? You have talked too long, my darling."

" Yes, dear, I need thee, Joe. Send father to bed ! Come back, Joe, very soon ! "

When Doctor Priestley arose next morning there was found among his books and manuscripts a new work, that will be ever new, when philosophies and religions and governments have succeeded each other, till tradition is a rope of sand—a new babe lay there, and, like its mother's Jason spirit, it was a girl.

" God be thanked ! " exclaimed Doctor Priestley, marvelling at the child, " that in one little woman there can
be place for all this love and manly friendship, too ! "

---

## CHAPTER XXV.

### MOULDING BULLETS.

THE necessity of correcting his proofs and confirming
his evidence took Hamilton to Philadelphia ; but that
master of small arts, Colonel Burr, bribed an advance
copy of the pamphlet from the printer and showed it to
Jefferson and Monroe.   The latter, whose wife was from
New York, felt sheepish enough and ever after abandoned authorship ; but Jefferson, whose jealousy of written history was anticipatory, and the more torturing from
his sense of crookedness, had a fit of the blues for a
month.

" He has spoiled," reflected that subtle one, " my most
convincing *Ana*.   But my daughter's return of those
letters omits me from his vengeance."

It was soon after this time that Mr. Jefferson gave a
leading idea to Colonel Burr, whom he distrusted, with
all the New York politicians.

"Colonel Burr," said Jefferson, " I often wonder there
is not some good man in New York to play the Mac-
Intosh with this alien game-cock, Mr. Hamilton ? "

" MacIntosh ? "

" Certainly you recall Button Gwinnett, who signed
the Declaration of Independence on the part of Georgia.
He was much like Mr. Hamilton, a planter from the
islands, a British fellow, and he came to America about the
time Hamilton did.   Like Hamilton, he was forward,
pugnacious, hoggish of all the honors, civil and military,
inclined toward English precedents, and slow to break
for independence."

" And MacIntosh was obliged to kill him, I believe?"
observed Colonel Burr, pale but intent.

" General MacIntosh was like you, a purely military
man, of an established Georgia family, but Gwinnett had
made the most of a persuasive and graceful address, and

of the favor of the Council.   In one year Gwinnett rose
from obscurity to be President of Georgia.   Not content
with that, he wanted the Brigadier-Generalship of the
forces, which belonged to MacIntosh.   When Hamilton
has brought on a war with the French, see if he does not
deprive you of a commission in like manner ! ''

" Well ? '' attentively from Colonel Burr.

" There was a duel," continued Jefferson, after a pause.
" MacIntosh was the better shot.   He had the distance
measured close—to twelve feet—and received a slight
wound himself ; but he gave General Gwinnett a wound
of which he died in twelve days."

Mr. Jefferson looked behind him as he spoke.

Colonel Burr went away with a new idea.   He perceived that Mr. Jefferson's fertile suggestiveness was a
very positive influence, even over those he distrusted.

" Any monkey," observed Washington, " can commit
Hamilton's offence ; but it took a man of  the highest
moral and personal courage to publish it ; and, in my
opinion, his understanding was equal  to his courage, for
they will never dare to assault his public character again.
A devilish good  friend, too," added Washington, with a
rifle eye on Mr. Lear, " for if he had slunk from this
confession it would have seemed that he used the funds,
and so I would have been declared a fool for not finding
it out.   Of course," the general remarked, in a sentence
which became inarticulate in one of his very occasional
spasms of laughter, " I couldn't be up of nights looking
into his eccentricities ! ''

The effect of Hamilton's pamphlet on the general public was most gratifying to his public sensibilities.

The Federal party, with the exception of John Adams,
regarded him as a truer hero than ever.   He had wiped
their shield clean with his heart, and cleared their last
fears away, which the late circumstantial documentary
*exuviæ* of Monroe, had alarmed.

Only the few great-minded men could see the height
of this act of sacrifice, leaving mere moralities in their
flatness and setting Suffering high by Truth in the holy
pleiades of the Forgiven.

But Mr. Adams was skipping about like a Pharisee
grasshopper, asking everybody if such immorality was
ever heard of.

"Well," said the stiffish Secretary Pickering, when Mr. Adams was picking at Hamilton for the third time in one day, "I take it that you sing the psalms of David. How do you like 'em, considering who made 'em—David, the friend of Joab and ruler over Uriah?" The secretary sang:

> " ' Keep me from snares and wicked gins,
>     They lay for me withal,
>   And net the tempters in their sins,
>     While I but half way fall!' "

"Do you mean me, sir?" exclaimed the President, hotly.

"You? Great God, no! It takes human nature to fall—Adam and Eve and such."

"Dear me, Mr. Adams," remarked the President's wife, when he came to her for the ninth time with the great story of Hamilton's folly, "what can you have on your conscience that Mrs. Reynolds' afflictions trouble you so?"

The error of Hamilton admitted him into the sympathies of thousands of anti-Federal men who had regarded him as a precise and morally insured being. No similar attack upon a public man of distinction was made for more than thirty years after, when the office-holders of Monroe attacked the marriage purity of the hero of New Orleans.

Mrs. Hamilton was looking for a site for a country home whilst Hamilton was sacrificing his pride to his honor; and therefore, as she rode among the rocks eight to ten miles north of the city, her husband still had to brood upon her reception of the Confession.

He was in more cheerful spirits than before he had so abased himself, but the disclosure he had been obliged to make left a deep sense of injury upon his nature.

The identity of Mrs. Clingman, as she was now called, with the Mrs. Reynolds of Hamilton's amour, was hardly known at all in New York.

The publication of Hamilton's arraignment of Maria Reynolds seemed not to disturb that lady.

When Hamilton next met her on the street, instead of indignation in her eyes, she looked at him with benignity and a never-failing dignity also, which had first attracted him.

In this creature the stock was thoroughbred if the

flower was wanton.  Hamilton felt that she liked him and disliked Burr.

His wife being away on a visit in Westchester County, Hamilton was one day driving a hired chaise to a suburban property in litigation, when he met Mrs. Reynolds on horseback coming out of Richmond Hill with Theodosia Burr and young Alston, her lover.

It was in keeping with Mr. Burr's philosophic contempt of fitness that he let his daughter and his mistress become friendly.          .

Mrs. Reynolds spoke to the young people, and they rode on.  She raised her hand to Hamilton, and the horse stopped.

"Hamilton," said the lady, "I was compelled to hear all your cruel pamphlet written upon me.  Your enemy up there"—pointing to Richmond Hill—"made me hear it."

"I gave you fair warning, madame.  You persecuted me more.  I had either to say that I stripped my country or that you and your confederates stripped me.  I lament the necessity, but you are now, as you have described, the puppet of my oldest enemy, and I hold you, also, to be such."

"Do not, Hamilton !  I only heard in that defence of you the omissions of severe things you might have said against me.  How much more you could have said !  Between the lines I thought I felt you pitied me—that, perhaps, you loved me still."

"Maria, I must go on.  You can attract me no more. I did feel for you when I made that statement, so cruel to my own.  But you feel for none."

"Always for you.  I was the covetous one and led you from your duty.  My wretched circumstances made me consent to levy subsistence from you.  I regard you as my victim, but you have nobly escaped me, and I am glad you printed the truth.  Yet, Hamilton, the short amour I began with you was the golden page of my life, while the time I spend with the wretch who now indulges me in plenty is chains and slavery."

"Why don't you leave him ? "

"Because I want to destroy him.  I said to him when for the second time he took a forced advantage of me : ' If I am yours, you are mine.' "

"You are drawing heavily on Colonel Burr's resources,

I hear," said Hamilton, catching a sight of a diamond clasp at the lady's throat.

" Yes; while he has one dollar left, I want it. This is my horse. I have got something in bank. Did you ever think poor Maria could be so revengeful ? "

" Tell me, before you go, why you hate Colonel Burr. Is he indifferent to you ? "

" No, he has become enamoured of me. I tell him that I love Hamilton, and he loses his appetite. I hate Burr because he wooed me like a highway robber. It was that day you called at Mr. Clingman's garret. At your approach we retired and hid ourselves. The unscrupulous villain insulted me, and afterward robbed me of the letters which have compelled you to publish this statement. I hope your wife appreciates you, for, indeed, I desire you, Hamilton, to be happy."

He felt a sickness at his heart, but rejoined :

" I desire you also, Maria, to be happy, but it must be through humility and repentance."

" I will repent," the fine woman spoke with languid decision, " when you do me the favor to kill Aaron Burr."

She rode away and Hamilton pursued his journey.

The idea Mrs. Reynolds had broached seemed to have possession of her mind, for that night she said to her husband as the surly Clingman finished his evening meal:

" Jake, do you like Aaron Burr ? "

" You ask me that ? " Clingman retorted. " Did you ever know me to like the outside man ? J. C. could sit on A. B.'s grave and carve a picter of hell on his tombstone. Damn him ! "

" Jake, I have seen Burr practising a good deal of late with pistols. It is almost a daily thing at Richmond Hill. Sometimes he sails a skiff to Weehawken, and has had me over there to see him practise. I notice that he makes the target every time about the height of Colonel Hamilton. When he lands a ball in the body he says, ' MacIntosh.' "

" Sence this French politics has got so hot," says Jake, " they're duellin' over yer at Weehawken 'most every day."

" Burr has Southerners around him constantly. I hear them talk of having killed their man with a zest for murder that is barbarous. Jake, do you think Hamilton could kill Burr ? "

"Ef he could git a ball into him, I reckon so, Mari, onless A. B. is a chile of the Ole Nick, which he do seem to be sometimes to your'n truly. But Ham's the best soldier. He fired at me up yer in Pennsylwany in the dark and shot me through the arm. Ef he could do that in the dark, he ought to be a pizen shot in the day-light."

"Jake," said the woman, quickly, "I want him to kill Burr. I'll see that Burr don't forget the idea of a duel."

When Mrs. Reynolds passed away, Mr. Clingman gave a shrug.

"Do it, missy," mused Clingman. "Ham couldn't afford to fire at Burr. I don't believe he would try to kill him. But Burr is a cool shot and has a deadly heart. I hate them both, but I've got a stake in Burr, and as for Hamilton, durn him! my wife loves him. To the bone-yard with his'n truly, A. Hamilton!"

---

## CHAPTER XXVI.

### REST.

LIZZIE PRIESTLEY resumed her story, when she came forth again, in the emblazoned autumn.

They were going to the town of Sunbury, right op-posite Northumberland, where Mr. Cooper was in great expectations of getting an office ; and there, in a coun-try editor's bower, Mr. Cooper, like a large pug dog, sat wistfully while Doctor Priestley wrote this singular recommendation to President Adams :

"*The office of Agent for American Claims has been declined by Mr. Hall, of Sunbury. I shall be very happy to serve Mr. Cooper by recommending him. Both he and myself fall under the description of Democrats, who are studiously represented as enemies to what is called government. . . . Were the accusations true, the appointment would be truly such a mark of superiority to popular prejudices as I should expect from you,*" etc., etc.

Upon which Mr. Cooper endorsed :

"*I see no impropriety in the present application to be appointed Agent of American Claims. If I am nominated, etc., I shall en-deavor to merit the character the Doctor has given me, and your esteem.*"

Doctor Priestley was in a sweat. Mr. Cooper was in a pleasing trance or daze. Both were as flutteringly sure of the appointment as lottery ticket holders are of, at least, the second-class prize.

" When Tummas gets the office," observed Mrs. Cooper, " I suppose I shall keep my carriage at last like my Lord Mayor's lady."

Mr. Jefferson was the real author of this application, various delusive promises he had made to Mr. Cooper of giving him the presidency of some Southern revolutionary college being unfulfilled, and Cooper's circumstances had become too desperate to be further put off ; so Jefferson had devised this trap to antagonize his friends and the Federalists yet the more. Inevitably Mr. Cooper would resent a non-appointment, and, perhaps, Doctor Priestley would do the same and write a political " screamer."

" I had come to my arrival at Saratoga," said Lizzie Priestley, whose babe was folded upon her lap in sleep. " At Albany I perceived the standing of this Schuyler family in their ancient finical city house, with Dutch smithery in its gables, and their later mansion below the town, with dormers and roof balusters and a park. In the times of the Stuarts they were mayors of Albany and viceroys over those Indians near by, who ruled everything south of Canada to Louisiana. O Joe ! such legends as the girls told ! There was Mrs. Van Rensselaer, wife of the noble young patroon, who had actually fought the Indians in her father's house. From what I could hear, they all married lands except Mrs. Hamilton, and she married character. I felt that it was this character I came gratuitously to traduce, while they were all so kind to me. ' How shall I ever broach the subject ? ' I said to myself."

" What is this Saratoga ? " asked Doctor Priestley. " They tell me that it is fountains full of fixed air—that little part of air, a thousandth of the atmosphere, which yet makes the stalks of all the harvests and the forests. Doctor Black found it before I did, on the breath, in the brew, and in fire."

" We went first, father, to General Schuyler's plantation by a roaring creek and the flowing Hudson. It was a frame house with a long piazza, at the centre of a wild forest, and all the neighborhood was full of graves of the dead in the battles where Burgoyne was surrounded and surrendered. After resting there, we proceeded on horseback through the pine forests to a solitary lake of large extent, and near its marshes, at the termination of some hard foot-hills, a swampy ravine contained these healing springs. Nothing was there but a few squatters' huts for entertainment, and Schuyler's rude bowery. Yet there, in the heart of the natural woods, where the deer still ventured to lick the salt waters, and the fir-trees moaned upon the sand-cliffs above the spas, like old Indian spirits, we passed a week of physic and pleasure that was like paradise. The young men and beaux went into the woods for game ; we women fished the creeks and drew trout, salmon, and bass. Our appetites were made raging by the salt alkaline waters ; we drank neither beer nor wine. The days were warmish but exhilarating, and the sleep at night was like that of the just."

"Thy hosts were not put out by thy coming?" from Joe.

"Indeed, no. Society like that I never knew or read of—so superior, so natural, also. The mother was a perfect housewife, stoutish, short, with the sweetest manners, and such a union of gentleness and energy as kept up an agreeable surprise. The old general is called an aristocrat, but I could plainly see why—it was his unconscious honesty, the source of his power over the Indians. With dishonesty he had no patience, but he could forgive his family for anything that was candidly disobedient. There was Madame Angelica, who had run away ; and her sister Cornelia was beset by two young men,—the irregular young Washington Morton and a French engineer named Mark Brunel. Since Hamilton entered the family General Schuyler has been enamoured of ability, and he considered young Brunel a man of genius who would connect all the waters of New York by canals ; so he informed Cornelia that she should not marry Morton, but should have Brunel. The girl sat at her father's gouty feet and told him flatly that she should disobey him. 'An American is good enough for me,' she said. And it was not long afterward, at Albany, that Morton threw a rope-ladder to her window, which she climbed down upon, and they stepped off and were married and came boldly home. The general was terribly angry. 'Disobedient girl!' he cried, 'I forgive you because you did not tell me a lie!'

"There I learned to know the Federalists; they are the people of great business ideas, to expand America in every noble way and raise up a mighty loyalty here to the State."

"Well, well, Lizzie, lass!" remarked Mr. Cooper, "as we are to be an office-holder under the victorious Federalists, I suppose we will not dispute thee. Does General Schuyler regard Mr. Hamilton as his child, also?"

"But your errand, your mission, wife?" spoke Joe.

"O husband! how little the life of woman qualifies her for affairs! Many a time there I had resolved to come back and never tell my real errand. Indeed, the last day but one had come before I was to leave, by my own announcement, when I mustered the courage to say to Mrs. Hamilton: 'Dear, cannot you and I go all alone to-morrow and have some fishing?' She had a little babe, but said that she would steal away. 'That is to be the time, or never,' I reflected.

"Then, friends, I thought over every device to open the awful subject of my coming. The more I planned the more nervous I grew. At last I thought of old General Schuyler's honest, blunt way of doing everything, and it flashed upon me that to be honest was better than to be adroit. From that moment cool English courage regained possession of me. I heard a voice saying: 'Your motive, your friend, are too high for any artifice; if you become too subtle she may suspect you; if you are not frank enough she may not understand your statement.'

"We came to the creek and took a skiff there which barely held us both and floated safely. As we descended the stream, the outlet of the lake, the fish bit so fast we could not talk. At last we came to a place where we tied the boat to a tree, and under its branches took the shade of midday; Mrs. Hamilton was in that end which stretched out into the water, and I was between her and the shore.

"A sudden energy seized me and a feeling of seniority, though I was much the younger.

"'Elizabeth,' said I, 'your kindness makes me call you so, I am going to say something very surprising to

you. Will you promise me to receive it without moving
or exclaiming? This little boat might upset and drown
us both.'

" ' You call me Elizabeth,' replied she, 'and it is so
affectionate that I know you mean to be kind.'

" As she spoke the sweetness of her face was touching.
Her beauty was of that kind which grows by contact
with it, till the little body seems to enlarge by the acute-
ness and vigor of the spirit. I thought as I looked at
her that the unison of their spirits had made Elizabeth
resemble her husband. Her nose had become like his,
the strongest of her features, as if expanded at his nostrils. She had dark eyebrows, and the eyes, which really
were gray, took the dark tint of their lashes till they
seemed gleaming black, and as these eyes turned upon
me expectantly, their humor and free spirit suddenly
enlarged to a brightness like the frightened fawn. Underneath her pride of descent, fruitfulness, and station, came
the great apprehension, too soon, of imperilled love. It
was her heart that made her character.

" Slowly the clear paleness of her skin became very
white. The waves of her dark brown hair seemed to
deepen in color as the blood was arrested in the forehead. The lips of her small rosy mouth, generally com-
pressed with an excess of will, seemed to tremble. Her
hat of straw oppressed her and she pushed it off with a
motion of her delicate, thin arm.

" I felt my own vigor coming up, and yet it was the
courage of a solemn fear. I knew it to be my own face
which had frightened hers.

" ' Is Alexander dead?' she asked, and sank back in
the prow of the skiff, which just contained her, leaning
upon her long-mittened hand.

" ' No, my dear Elizabeth, but he is in danger, and of
only one person in this world. It is yourself!'

" Indignation replaced her fear, but the two emotions
played wonders in her rare, natural pallor of skin.

" ' In danger of me? You think I exact too much
from him,—that all his time and his whole heart belong
to the public? Perhaps that is so, but was it friendly to
tell me?'

" ' No,' said I, with my face set, I suppose, and my
voice as unnaturally raised in the trying moment, 'you

have not understood me ! I will tell the whole danger in another sentence. Your husband is beset by another woman, and she is a wicked one, and you, who could forgive him in one moment, will not do so, and deliver him, unless God cries into your heart, "*as we forgive them that trespass against us !* " '

" As I spoke I saw her arm yield, her head fall, and I knew that she had swooned.

" I turned to the side of the boat to draw it in to the bank, when I found my head swimming, too.

" The long journey, the sudden relief, the whole scene so vital to that wife, so irrelevant to me ; the ardor of my mind too quickly discharged, the yielding of my nerves from their tension, the disappointment to myself at the moment, in the propriety and importance of the revelation, had overcome me. My blood did not know its course in the variety of emotions it was called to supply, and stopping at my heart, left all my head sick and blank.

" When I came around and could see, the boat was hauled in shore, and Mrs. Hamilton was pouring water upon my forehead. The next thing I was crying and saying, again and again : 'I have been very wrong to cross your happiness. It was an illusion of being able to do some good.'

" She was silent, kind, yet constrained. I did not venture to study her face again until we were seated in the cart and going toward Schuylerville. Then I saw her foot tapping the floor, and, looking up, I found her expression to be anger.

" ' God be praised !' said I. ' You are only womanmad.'

" ' I am going straight back to Philadelphia with you,' she uttered, 'and inquire into this business.' Then turning to me, in a revulsion of noble feeling, she exclaimed : ' Did you really come all this way to tell me this tale ? I know your meaning was kind. Can you explain it exactly ?'

" ' Yes,' I replied ; ' it was friendship—nothing else.'

" ' Friendship generally conceals a man's domestic sins.'

" ' Yes, an ordinary man's ; but this man became my public idol. I was allowed by the Almighty, it seemed to me, to look in upon the collusions and conspiracy of his enemies, and I found that his greatest wound was to be at home. He told me so. I left my husband and my child to anticipate those enemies and have you know that, as when he first loved you, and your heart and soul could bless him by consenting, so again you can bring him perfect calm and happiness by your complete forgiveness. Let him face his real enemies bravely, with his wife on his side!'

"She was moved, and after a time she said : 'Why could Alexander overlook such a pure regard as yours for the ignoble invitations of a leman?'

"'O madame!' said I, 'do you suspect me of loving him?'

"'Indeed, I do not. The time you have spent here convinced me of your conscientious nature. As we go along I shall know the particulars of this sad, sad story. Let me tell you, as a dear, dear secret, that some other person warned me, before I parted with my husband, of his intimacy with a certain Mrs. Reynolds.'

"When we reached Schuyler's plantation, to which her child and my effects had been forwarded, she showed me this other communication.

"It was a silhouette of Mrs. Reynolds. Beneath it was written the words : '*Alexander's Roxana : Maria Reynolds.*'

"'That is the woman,' said I ; 'and I know the writing, too.'

"'Will you tell me whose you think it is?'

"'Colonel Burr's.'

"'Are you so familiar with his writing?'

"'I am. Ever since the night he took me to Bingham's party he has written me insidious letters, which have been turned over to my husband's mother.'

"'Why not to your husband?'

"'Because Colonel Hamilton told me that Mr. Burr was one of the most selfish and dangerous men in the country, and I feared for my Joe's safety.'

"From that moment Mrs. Hamilton became under a different influence. The name of Aaron Burr awoke her public and family nature—Burr, the opponent of her father and her husband. She began to see the greater conspiracy than woman's, that environed the public life.

She turned to me as we reached her room at Schuyler-ville and kissed me and said :

" ' Lizzie—our parents named us the same—I received that anonymous and cruel stab the night I confronted you and Alexander at the garden-party in Philadelphia. It awoke my jealousy, and I left my home with a woman's but not a lady's impulse, to see what my husband was about. I found him in close and interesting talk with a woman.'

" ' Myself, dear Eliza ! '

" ' After that a communication was received by me,' said Mrs. Hamilton, ' saying that my husband was to have his mistress with him following the Western army. I be-came exasperated and parted from him in anger. It was in the same handwriting you have identified.'

" ' O my friend ! that jealousy you expressed was the cause of your husband's confidence with me, the same which brought me here so far. It frightened him. Will you now assure him ? '

" ' Yes,' she said, ' the instant I see him. Colonel Burr shall mine and tunnel for naught in the Schuyler's house-hold.'

" She was full of dainty fire, like Sappho's lamp, but I blew it out. ' Elizabeth,' said I, ' the hardest is to come. You cannot forgive your husband till the time arrives when his enemies surround him. This day you have his heart better than ever before. Your sacrifice shall equal mine—to postpone the years of forgiveness, and let truth find its way from the deep well to the holy light of your reconciliation.'

" She took up her babe and kissed it and burst into tears.

" My work had been blessed.

" And so, friends, we came together to Philadelphia, and I rehearsed every point of that deep, devilish plot, which commenced the day Hamilton met Mrs. Reynolds at our lodgings. We did not know whether Burr did not start Mrs. Reynolds in pursuit of Hamilton originally ; that view Mrs. Hamilton took, perhaps in a wife's self-esteem, Joe, that it required very great combinations to seduce her husband."

" But, wife," speaks Joe, " did it appear that there was a real necessity for your intervention ? "

"Yes. Elizabeth said to me : 'Dear friend, you have given me an illness, but if this revelation had first been made to me by Alexander, it would have been my death. By your nursing I am convalescent. I shall go to my husband to be his friend as well as his wife.' 'But you will not tell him his fault?' 'No,' she answered, 'it would hurt his pride. It would also hurt mine. Let time do its work. Yet, Lizzie, do men know that their infidelity is as dreadful, as dishonorable, to us, as if they found their own hearth-stones shattered?' 'No,' said I, 'that they cannot know, not being like ourselves.'

"Joe, I came toward you with this victory on my heart, and you met me with the contrition of a castaway. I turned to God—to the Spirit which allows injustice awhile to prevail that it may die of its disappointment—and from that unseen Source, like father's oxygen, which exhilarates poor mice and rabbits, I inhaled the faith in love and the worldly courage to overthrow Mrs. Reynolds a second time, and with her Colonel Burr. It was necessary to the selfishness of my victory that I should tell that woman before my husband's face, in the fearlessness of a faithful wife, that I loved Colonel Hamilton. Do you know what I meant?"

"I do, my children," interposed old Doctor Priestley, rising, with his imperfect dental accentuation and hands outstretched. "God bless you both in your renewed and ennobled happiness ! She meant that all the promises of God are good, to women as to men. Our dear daughter meant that 'greater *love* hath no woman, also, than this : that she lay down her life for her friend.' He also said, 'Ye are my friends if ye keep my commandments.'"

"Ye do, ducky, do ye not?" cried little Mrs. Cooper, embracing her pugnacious husband. "Ye do keep to your dear wife, I know, that one hawful commandment the men do break !"

Hamilton had at last to face his wife.

He braced himself up for a cheerful martyrdom; for he knew his wife's exacting spirit and aristocratic pride.

Nothing less than a separation for an indefinite period he expected, but he dreaded the parting scene.

And yet in the immediate years of hard study and

application at the law for his children's sake, how price-
less, he felt, would this woman's society be!

" If it would please God," thought Hamilton, "to
stand me before my worst enemy and let him fire into my
breast, I would take it in exchange for this meeting with
my injured wife."

He had come from Philadelphia, and he entered her
room. There lay the book he had written beside her bed.

He stood without speaking.

" Come, husband, to your bed ! "

" Not till you come and fetch me there."

She arose swiftly and put her arms around him and
kissed him hard.

" You are still ignorant, alas ! " said Hamilton, all in
tears.

" Oh, no ! I have known everything for these three
years, and did I ever refuse your chamber to you in all
that time ? The words you speak I have waited for till
this moment. There is no condonation so avowed and so
long as mine."

" Known this and been silent, Eliza ? Who could have
told you ? Was it Martha Jefferson ? "

" No, no; it was Mrs. Priestley, our dearest friend on
earth. Three years ago and more she came to Albany
and prepared me for all this. I never was as happy in my
life as now—no, not when we were married."

Hamilton remembered.

The scene on the river bank at Harrisburg, the return
of young Priestley's wife to the same river from a long
absence, and her recent letter adjuring him to make a
public declaration, connected themselves like steps of a
golden ladder reaching from the earth to heaven.

" I thought I had many enemies," spoke Hamilton
tremulously, standing in a daze of contrition and joy. " I
was mistaken all the time. Everybody in the world has
been my friend." .

# APPENDIX.

THE scale upon which this romance was first executed allowed the author to follow all his personages to their respective fates. Publishers and public, however, now exclaim against long novels—such as are all the English classics—and the author with sorrow releases his personages, who had been two years his nearest friends, and tells the sequel of their story to the reader in a few paragraphs.

Alexander Hamilton became the ranking general of the United States Army by Washington's demand, who also rejected Burr. The latter, oppressed by debt and licentiousness, stopped his career at the Vice-Presidency, and, instead of being revenged upon Jefferson, who cruelly pursued him, he challenged and killed Hamilton.

The story represents Mrs. Reynolds as a portion of Burr's *Nemesis*, and she, his mistress, aids to bring on the duel, believing that Hamilton will kill Burr ; her husband, Clingman, rows Burr to the duelling ground. Hamilton and the Priestleys, to redeem Mrs. Reynolds, have made over to her Hal Priestley's farm. In her horror at Hamilton's fate she has Clingman row her to the duelling place, and, losing her mind there, drowns herself and drags Clingman down.

Theodosia Burr marries as her father directs, becomes involved in his ruin, and perishes with her child by an unknown fate at sea.

Nelly Custis marries Larry Lewis, and lives a long, happy, Christian life.

Jefferson lives to be President, survives to become poor, like Monroe, sacrifices the liberty of all his slaves, and sees Hamilton's star reascend in the younger Adams' administration. To be spiteful, Jefferson leaves his so-called "Anas" to be printed after his death, one of the results of which is the present composition.

Doctor Priestley died a few months before Hamilton, in the same year, 1804, and his son and daughter in-law returned to England, where Lizzie Priestley passed away young.

Through the agency of Jefferson upon Priestley's younger shadow, Thomas Cooper, the doctor wrote a pamphlet against John Adams, which may have assisted to turn Pennsylvania against the Federalists and determine the party revolution. The Alien and Sedition Bills were passed, it is thought, with reference to Priestley and Cooper, as well as Callender and other foreigners ; and, in return, Jefferson, by the aid of Henry Toulmin, who had become Secretary of State for Kentucky, forced through the legislature of that State the " Resolutions of '98," which he drafted while Vice-President. These contained the term and the injunction to " nullify " a Federal law.

Tobias Lear, as the custodian of Washington's papers and correspondence, was given office by the Jeffersonians. He cut his throat for mysterious reasons.

Mr. Thomas Cooper, the stormy petrel of that day, was rewarded with a judgeship, like Toulmin, but was removed by the legislature of Pennsylvania for browbeating and tyranny. He drifted to South Carolina, and brought that State into the Nullification war of 1830, after which the legislature there turned him down at a great old age. While in prison for a libel on an Adams, his good wife died.

To obtain two presidential terms and antagonize Hamilton, John Adams perverted and destroyed the Federal party. He was probably the last of Jefferson's dupes and gossips of record ; but he appointed John Marshall Chief-Justice, who long continued to interpret the laws in the spirit of Jay, Hamilton, and Washington.

Doctor Priestley, Hal, and Mrs. Priestley are buried at Northumberland, Pennsylvania. The great-grandson of the Priestleys, Richardson, became a noble architect, and made the court-house of Pittsburgh and the capitol at Albany.

The Reynolds affair became the uncontemplated staple of this romance while the author was devising some way to portray Doctor Priestley in America—the banished Duke of Oxygen.